the COMMONER'S DESTINY

D1601242

ALSO BY FRED YU

The Legend of Snow Wolf

Haute Tea Cuisine

Yin Yang Blades

The Red Crest Prequel

The Red Crest - Book 1: The Orchid Farmer's Sacrifice

The Commoner's Destiny
The Red Crest Series – Book 2

Published in the United States of America by

China Books Inc.
Sinomedia Group
San Francisco, CA

ISBN 978-0-8351-0307-7

Cover and book design by Damonza.

Printed in the USA

the COMMONER'S DESTINY

THE RED CREST SERIES – BOOK 2

FRED YU

CHAPTER 1

SOMEONE HAD TO die today.

Chen Han trudged along the road, pulling an oversized wheelbarrow behind him with one hand, a large urn filled with hard liquor in another. On the wheelbarrow was a long, wooden coffin with none of the handles or embellishments normally used to honor the dead. It was a coffin made for the common man. A coffin he purchased for himself.

It was late spring. The wide streets were barren except for a few beggars sitting with heads bowed, palms extended. Distant gongs indicated that night had fallen upon the town.

Han stepped onto a narrow path leading up to a banquet hall and stopped in front of a red door with bronze lion doorknobs, pondering the moment when he would pull open the door and a gush of fresh air would force its way inside. Behind the doors were hundreds of people, all warriors of the Martial Society, men and women who had spent their entire lives training in the martial arts and attaining physical abilities that ordinary people could not fathom. They were his friends, people whose lives he had once saved, people he called "brothers."

They've gathered inside to decide how to kill him.

This day, preparing to face hundreds of powerful warriors eager for him to die, he could not help but wonder why it was so difficult to be a commoner.

With a long, weary sigh, Han pushed the doors open. Inside was a magnificent banquet hall, illuminated by over a hundred lanterns, where large round tables seating ten at a time dotted the space. At the far end of the room was an open balcony overlooking a rushing waterfall.

At the front of the room hung a red tapestry embroidered with a gold phoenix, and beneath it stood the man speaking to the gathering. He froze when Han entered and swallowed hard. Han ignored him and strolled in, dragging the coffin. There was complete silence in the banquet hall. All eyes were on him.

"My friends," Han said, his powerful voice carrying across the room. "I'm saving you the trouble of having to find me."

No one responded. Everyone stared, some already with their hands on their weapons, others inching away from him, as if the extra distance between them would increase their chances of survival.

"I've brought my coffin so you won't have to worry about where to dump my body," Han said. "I also brought good liquor so I can toast those of you I still consider my friends. We'll have one last drink together."

Still no one said anything. The person speaking in the front of the hall had already disappeared. Han observed the familiar faces and the hostile expressions around him. "Tell me. What did I do wrong?"

Han shoved the coffin against a nearby table. He sat down, motioned for the server, and pointed to the plates in front of him. "Clear these and bring me some empty bowls. I'm drinking with many old friends tonight."

The server hustled to gather the plates. Han turned to the warriors around him.

"How can we talk like friends if you're all afraid of me?" Han asked.

No one approached. Han waited, scanning each face.

"Don't think anyone here is afraid of you because you're the Commoner," someone said at last. "You can't fight all of us at the same time."

"That's right!" someone else shouted from the back of the room. "You're not getting out of here alive."

Han gestured toward the coffin. "I never planned to. But before I die, I want to know why. Why all my friends have turned against me? Why even the people whose lives I've saved are in this room?"

"You know full well what your crimes are," an old man with a long white beard stood up to say.

"I don't know, Master Kwan," Han said, addressing the old man. "I've heard different accusations from different people. That's why today is the perfect day. Everyone is here."

"Oh, there is a story," a tall, lanky man said. The pugilists in the room have become bolder all of a sudden. "Let me invite someone to tell you. You know who she is."

He extended his hand to escort a young woman to the front of the room, her thin, willowy figure dressed completely in black, her face covered by a dark veil. Han did not recognize her but he could only guess.

"For anyone who doesn't know," Master Kwan said, "this is Lady Li. She is Magistrate Li's wife, but she lost her husband far too soon." Kwan turned to glare at Han. "Because of him."

Han gazed through the veil and studied the expression on her face. It was blank, absent of any fear or hate. "I'm sorry for your loss, Lady Li," Han said. "Maybe if you tell us how he died, I can one day find the real culprit for you."

"Stop the hypocrisy," another warrior said. "There's more evidence against you than we'll ever need. Justice will be delivered today."

"Let the lady speak," someone from the left side of the room shouted. Others voiced their approval. Han noticed the server had left a stack of empty bowls next to him. He picked the top one off the pile, poured himself a drink, and leaned forward to listen.

For a moment, Lady Li couldn't begin. She stood with her hands folded in front of her, face lowered. Eventually, she took a deep, shuddering breath and began to speak in a low voice barely audible across the room.

"My husband was the magistrate of this city and the twenty-two villages around it. He was loved by everyone."

"That's true," someone murmured in the back.

"He was," she said. "How many magistrates can you name who never accepted a bribe? He was one of them." Her voice was tight and hoarse. "And that night… I will never forget that night. It was late, well past my husband's bedtime. He received a mysterious man in his study, someone I had never seen before. I was curious, so I stood outside the doors and tried to hear what they were saying. They were speaking in low voices, but I heard the man mention something about a secret letter they intercepted at the border and something about the Commoner. There was another name that they mentioned more than once. I didn't know either of the names, but I remember them."

A pugilist with a long sword, wearing Taoist garbs, pointed to Han. "That's the Commoner. What was the other name?"

"The Silencer."

A wave of murmurs swept across the room. The grumbles escalated. A few hotheaded warriors stood up to shout.

"What are we waiting for? Let's kill him!"

"Kill this traitor!"

Han leaned back in his chair, raised the bowl to his lips and gulped the remaining liquor. The angry faces, the droning voices that spewed unbelievable hatred left him wondering what else she would say.

Someone shouted over the crowd. "Let her finish! Let the lady finish!"

With a long, dying murmur, the pugilists stopped talking. They turned back to Lady Li.

"I didn't know what any of this meant at the time. That night, my husband looked worried. He didn't speak much, and the next day, he gathered his officials for a very long meeting. For the rest of the day, my husband paced back and forth in his study. Sometimes he would stare at the floor and sigh over and over again.

"He never came to bed that night. I thought he was in another meeting, so I fell asleep and didn't think of looking for him. At the third watch, I woke up and he wasn't next to me. I went to his study and found books and shelves overturned. And there was a man inside. His face was covered, but I saw his eyes. I can never forget them."

Han poured himself more liquor and lifted the bowl so it would cover most of his face, leaving his eyes. She did not meet his gaze. "It's him," she said, pointing to Han. "I recognize those eyes."

Han lowered the bowl. "So, what was missing from the magistrate's study?"

Lady Li bit her lip. "Nothing was missing. You didn't find whatever you came for." She turned back to the hundreds of angry men. "And then last week… Last week…" Her voice broke and she turned away, covering her mouth.

"Last week," an old man in a coarse brown robe said. "They found Magistrate Li. I was the coroner. I examined the body."

"What did you find?" someone asked.

"All twelve ribs intact, without a single bruise," the coroner said. "But the lungs and liver were destroyed. He was killed by the Infinity Palm with such speed that all his organs were shattered at the same time. There's only one person with that kind of speed."

Again, a ripple of angry murmurs swept across the banquet hall. The coroner had a controlled rage on his face. He was telling the truth.

Then someone else out there knew how to use the Infinity Palm, Han thought. Someone who could use it with enough skill to damage the internal organs without breaking the ribs.

"Quiet!" Master Kwan said. He turned to the man in Taoist Garbs. "Master Zhou, do you have the letter?"

"Of course I do," Master Zhou said, pushing his long sword aside to reach his inner pockets.

"Lady Li found this letter under her pillow last night," Master Kwan said.

"My husband hid it there," she said in a low voice. "It's the secret letter intercepted at the border."

Another murmur passed through the room. Master Zhou handed a rolled piece of sheepskin to Lady Li. "Your husband's letter, Lady Li."

Every warrior held his breath. Lady Li wiped the tears from her cheeks and took the sheepskin, unrolled it, then covered her face again.

"I can't," she said, her voice trembling. "This letter killed my husband. I can't look at it again."

Master Zhou took the letter from her. "If the heroes in this room would allow me to read on the lady's behalf, I would be more than honored to incriminate the traitor with this piece of evidence."

The room blazed into an uproar of voices demanding that he read it. Han continued to sip his liquor, leaning back in his chair.

Master Zhou held up his hand and the room muted. "This letter is from the Silencer!"

"How do you know it's from the Silencer?" Han asked.

"His stamp is on it. It was intercepted at the border and taken from a Mongolian messenger."

"Where's the Mongolian messenger?" Han asked.

"They killed him of course," someone said. "The Silencer can't know that his secret letter was taken. Don't try these rhetorical tricks, Commoner. We all know what's going on."

Han turned back to Master Zhou. "Please. Read the letter."

Zhou glared at him once. Everyone was leaning forward, eager to hear the contents of the sheepskin. "To the great hero known as the Commoner. I am happy that you've expressed interest in working together. I accept your counteroffer of fifty thousand pieces of gold in exchange for opening the gates to the City of Eternal Peace. Your money is available right away. Once you confirm that you accept this arrangement, my messengers will be in touch regarding when and where you will receive payment."

Master Kwan slammed a table with his fist, sending the dishes leaping into the air. He stood up and pointed his finger at Han, his red face twisted into a snarl. "You! You were a true hero of your time. What you did in Ding Yi is the stuff we tell our grandchildren. How could you turn like that? For money?"

Every warrior in the room was enraged. Would reasoning with them work? Most Mongols were illiterate, and the few who could write did not know the Chinese language. Wasn't this too well written for a Mongol? Yet, the Silencer single-handedly conquered most of the steppe without ever losing a battle. He certainly would have capable men.

"I'm sorry I haven't earned your trust," Han said. "I'm sorry that, after all these years, my word means nothing to any of you. But I've lived my life with honor and I have no regret."

"With all this evidence, are you still saying you've been framed?" someone asked.

Han turned to Lady Li. "Are you sure it was me that day in the magistrate's study?"

Lady Li was trembling.

"I promise you," Han said. "I will find your husband's real murderer."

"Who would frame you?" Master Kwan asked. "Did you do something horrible and someone is out there seeking revenge? Or do you have something others want?"

"I have nothing," Han said. "I'm just a common wanderer."

"We have a witness," Master Zhou said. "The magistrate's widow saw you. We have evidence that the magistrate died from the Infinity Palm. It's your signature move. We also have a letter from the Silencer explaining your motive. In return, you couldn't name a single reason why someone would frame you." He turned to the crowd, lifting his hands to address them. "My friends, isn't that enough?"

"It's more than enough!" someone shouted. Others followed suit. "Kill the criminal!"

"Kill the traitor!"

Within a moment, the room was roaring with angry shouts, each one more damning than the last. Many of them jumped to their feet, rattling the tables, shoving chairs aside, lifting their fists and screaming at the top of their lungs. Some drew their weapons.

Han released a deep, longing sigh. He reached for an empty bowl on the table, tipped the urn and filled the bowl to the brim. "Who will drink with me first?" he asked. "One last drink together."

The room fell silent then. Some clutched their weapons, while others fell back to their seats. No one moved.

Han turned to a well-dressed, middle-aged man carrying a pair of short sabers. "Brother Lin. We've been friends for a long time. How about a toast? It would be an honor for me."

Lin frowned and slammed his palm into the arm of his chair. "Fine!" he said, jumping to his feet. He walked to Han, grabbed the bowl and swallowed the liquor with one gulp. He threw the bowl back onto the table. "I've drunk your toast. We're no longer friends," he said before he spun around and walked away.

Han pulled another bowl closer to himself and poured out the liquor. He turned to Master Kwan. "Do you remember the time when we were trapped by robbers from Emei? There were six of us and almost eighty of them."

Master Kwan lowered his face. "I remember," he said in a whisper. "They weren't real robbers."

"I know," Han said. "They came for revenge."

Master Kwan looked up. "You saved my life that day, plus the lives of four of my best students, and I'm forever grateful for that. But today is different. You're a threat to the entire country. I can't watch the world burn just because I owe you my life."

"I'm not asking you to," Han said. "I'm just asking you to have a drink and remember the good times." He pushed the bowl toward Kwan, then poured another. Master Kwan flung his sleeve with a sigh, stepped forward and grabbed the bowl. Forming a knot between his brows, he swallowed the liquor, then threw aside the bowl and walked back to his seat.

Master Zhou stepped forward. "I'll toast you next. We were never close friends, but I had respect for you. I know what you did in Ding Yi."

Han poured liquor into his own bowl. "The respect is mutual. If I don't die here, maybe we can become friends one day."

Master Zhou scowled. "Why the Silencer? The most brutal Mongol King the world has ever seen in centuries. He forced his captives to watch while his men raped their wives and daughters. How can you let someone like that invade our country?"

Han lifted the bowl to drink, and a warm tingle coursed through his body. Master Zhou drank and turned away.

"Master Yue," Han said to a tall, bony man. "Shall we have a toast?"

"I will not drink with an arrogant criminal," Yue said.

"Why do you believe I'm arrogant?"

Yue stood up. "Last year, I was at the town near Mount Oleander, and I heard that the great Commoner was in the area. I stopped by your inn three times, and all three times you refused to meet me. I may not be famous or powerful like you, but I don't deserve to be slighted."

"I remember," Han said, rising to his feet. "I remember the innkeeper knocking on my door several times that day. He told me someone wanted to see me. But I had just found out who poisoned my mother and I was going to Mount Oleander for revenge. I was still grieving then. Drink with me. Let me apologize."

"I don't want your apology," Master Yue said, his voice cold. "I think the world should be rid of people like you." He shot forward and struck Han in the chest.

Han took a step back and choked out a cough, grimacing in pain. He dropped back into his seat.

The banquet hall fell silent. Master Yue took a step back. "You didn't block."

"I slighted you," Han said. "I deserved it."

Lin grunted. "Are you going to accept punishment for your mistakes? If every one of us struck you once for the crimes you've committed, you'd be dead in minutes."

"If I did something wrong, I would accept my punishment," Han said. "But for something I did not do..."

"You still dare to deny..."

"None of you bothered to investigate the facts before blaming me for this so you can't take my life without a good fight. But first, come have a drink."

"Do you really think we're afraid of you?" someone shouted from the back of the room. The banquet hall broke into another uproar. Han tilted his head back to swallow his liquor, and then turned to them with a calm smile.

"Of course not," Han said. "So why shout from the back of the room? Why not come forward?"

There was silence. The entire banquet hall was so quiet that the hundreds of seasoned warriors could hear each other breathing. Han threw his head back to laugh. "If you don't want to fight, then let's finish our drink and go home."

"There are hundreds of us here," Zhou said. "Even the Commoner can't beat so many."

"Of course I can't," Han said. "Who wants to go first? One at a time or all at once?"

The pugilists eyed each other. No one moved. A tall man with bulging muscles stepped to the forefront, a big hammer in his hands. "Come, my brothers," he said in a coarse voice. "We can't let this scum open the gates for the Silencer. We have to stop him today!"

With a roar, he lifted the hammer above his head and charged. Several other warriors responded to his call, drew their swords and leaped in.

Han lifted the bowl to his lips and tilted his head back to drink. A tear emerged that he made no effort to wipe.

Then, in a flash, he fled from the swinging hammer and appeared in front of a warrior who barely drew his weapon. Han swept by him, taking his sword, and shot straight into the middle of the banquet hall.

The entire room broke into a mad clamor. Very few had time to even draw their weapons before Han managed to stab over fifteen men in their wrists, rendering their sword arms useless.

Utter chaos ensued. The warriors collected themselves while Han tore through them again and again, slashing and jabbing, never striking hard enough to sever their tendons but causing enough damage that weapons struck the floor like raindrops.

More than forty members of the martial society lost their weapons, retreating to the back of the room before organizing themselves to fight back. Han recognized their formations, which they had clearly rehearsed. He grimaced at the thought. His friends wanted him dead and wanted it enough to train for it.

Han shot left and right, his body a shimmer and his sword a blur. The sheer force behind each stroke caused the pugilists to stumble back in alarm. Yet, they were better organized. They advanced and retreated as one, their weapons jabbing forward like a wall of spikes.

Han snatched someone else's sword and withdrew to the outside balcony, standing motionless to break their rhythm, enticing them to advance.

With a roar, the pugilists rushed him. Han slipped away as the big warrior with the hammer swung for the top of his head, and instead, the man's weapon pounded into the floorboards. Wood pieces exploded around him.

Han lurched forward to engage his assailants, leaving the balcony behind him, pushing into the center of the room. There were hundreds of them and they had reorganized, moving forward like military, their lines four layers deep and fanning out to the far ends of the room, folding in to surround a single man. However, the Commoner was destroying their lines, pressing deep into their positions and stabbing their knees to break through. In a moment, he re-emerged behind them. Some of them turned around in time but he was already out of their enclosure.

Han knew then that if he didn't start killing some of them, there was no way he could survive this. But they were duped into believing he committed those crimes. He could not kill them for being fools.

The Commoner rushed behind a cluster of men and slammed into them into the balcony, where they collapsed against the damaged banisters. Another beam of wood broke apart and Master Zhou flipped over. Han dropped his left-hand sword, shot forward and grabbed Zhou by the belt, enduring a cut to his shoulder before pulling Zhou back.

A fish net appeared to encircle him, with one man running toward him from either side of it. Han leaped into the right end of the fishnet, struck his assailant on the shoulder, passed them and charged into another line of attackers.

Han spun around at the sound of a scream. Both men holding the fishnet had lost their balance and fallen over the balcony. Han darted toward them and grabbed the middle of the fishnet just in time. He planted himself and held on. Both men, still screaming, were dangling over the waterfall, clutching their end of the fishnet with both hands.

"Hold on!" Han shouted.

Someone charged him from the side. Both his hands were occupied. Both feet were planted against the floor of the balcony or he would not have the strength to hold their weight. He turned to glare at his attacker, and with a scream, absorbed a sword wound in his side. The pugilist shuddered, extracting his sword from Han's body. The wound was not deep but the blood flowed in earnest.

Han ignored him and yanked the two men dangling over the waterfalls to safety. The big warrior with the hammer appeared and swung at Han's head. Han glared before slipping away as the hammer slammed into the floor.

All around him, the men continued to charge the balcony. What had he ever done to these people if not save their lives and treat them like brothers?

Han threw his head back to laugh, a resounding, haunting roar of a laugh, his thundering voice sending a wave of shock to his attackers.

Then, out of desperation for survival and fury for what was happening to him, Han slammed into the oncoming crowd, his Infinity Palm pounding every pugilist indiscriminately. He may have maimed someone, but it no longer mattered. The attackers fell like crumbling stacks of mud. He never knew he had it in him, numbed by disappointment in the men he called brothers, stunned by the blindness of injustice. In a moment, he had crossed the entire banquet hall and was standing by the entrance. Behind him, the devastation was falling into place, the floor littered with injured men, some still struggling to stand, others coughing blood.

What have I done?

The tapestry on the front wall had collapsed, perhaps shredded by someone's sword. Tables were overturned, chairs smashed, plates and bowls crushed and scattered across the floor. Some of his victims were no longer moving. Maybe he had killed them.

There was blood everywhere. He had struck so many upper torsos that many were vomiting blood.

Han shook his head and continued to walk.

One man spat at him from behind. Han sensed it coming but made no effort to evade it. A glob of thick blood struck his back with the resonance of a dull hammer.

"I hope you rot in hell, Commoner," the man croaked.

Someone else climbed to his feet. "The day you open the doors for the Silencer, millions of innocent civilians will face rape and torture and humiliation." It was Master Kwan. He coughed once, then spat at Han's back. But he was too weak, and the stream of fresh blood trickled onto the floor.

Han frowned. More insults were hurled at him but he could no longer hear them. He passed by the coffin that he arrived with, intent on dying to clear his name, only to become ensnared in a melee that ended with many of his friends heavily injured.

Lady Li stood by herself in the corner of the room, her head lowered. Perhaps, she also had doubts about her own words after all. Maybe, if she told him who delivered the letter to her husband, he could help her find the assassin.

Han drew open the doors and stepped outside. The sun had set and the air was cooler than before. He headed down the stone road leading away from the banquet hall.

CHAPTER 2

CHEN HAN, OFTEN referred to as the greatest warrior in the world, had spent his wandering years defending the innocent, hunting the crooks, righting the wrongs. There was never a moment when he was not sought after to protect those who could not protect themselves. He was tireless, driven, so certain he had to be the hero the world needed that he never thought twice before answering a call to arms for justice.

And then Han wasn't the hero that he wanted to be. Something didn't make sense to him anymore. He disappeared from civilization, hiding in seclusion by West Sea for months. He was building a boat, one big enough for him to live in for the rest of his life, and he would be hidden away on West Sea's calm waters, fishing and drinking alone.

A week ago he learned that he was being accused of murdering a magistrate. Rumors were everywhere, so widespread that even he couldn't ignore them. They were hunting him. Calling him a traitor. Thousands, maybe tens of thousands wanted him dead. He had to clear his name. He could no longer remain in hiding.

Han lowered his head and stepped through the empty streets. Did he hurt his friends in the banquet hall? Did he injure too many?

I had to.

An inn with a large dining room extending out into a first-level balcony loomed ahead. Han fondled the few coins left in his pocket. He didn't need to save these coins for food. His friends would kill him sooner or later. The taste of food was a very foreign idea all of a sudden. Some strong liquor was what he needed.

Han stepped up to the porch and seated himself by the wooden banisters overlooking the main road. There were three other customers at this time of night: an old man drinking by himself with a straw hat shadowing his face, and two younger men eating in the back.

The server approached, a greasy towel in one hand and a bamboo cup full of chopsticks in the other. He wiped the table with his cloth and slapped down a pair of chopsticks.

"Just alcohol," Han said.

The server ignored him. "We have great roast pork tonight, hand-cut noodles, dried bamboo shoots in garlic…"

"Just alcohol," Han repeated, throwing all his coins on the table.

The server shrugged. "Whatever you want," he said before picking up the coins and heading toward the back of the inn.

In a moment, three large gourds filled with hard liquor covered the table. The server glanced once at the other customers and disappeared.

Han unplugged the wooden cork on one gourd and took a sip of the hard liquor. The heat reached his stomach at once and he sat back with a grimace. Perhaps tonight would be the last good night in his life. At least he had a stiff drink at a time like this.

He noticed the sword wound on his hip and drew two acupuncture needles from his pocket to seal his meridian points and stop the bleeding. After closing his wound, he wrapped a strip of cloth around his waist and pressed against the injury. He was hurt but it was not serious.

The full moon ascended through the heavens. Han tilted his head back and drank the entire gourd of hard liquor with one deep gulp after another.

A porcelain urn was placed on his table, already uncorked, and the brilliant scent of dry flowers in a misty rain filled the air around him.

The old man with the straw hat sat down across from Han, an extra cup in hand. He took off his hat, revealing a thin face with a gray topknot and a small beard, his sparkling eyes curved in a cheery way as if always amused.

"How about a drink together?" he asked. He poured Han a cup without waiting for a response and pushed it across the table.

Han forced a smile. He always drank alone. He enjoyed being alone. This old man would talk about his grandchildren, or his nagging old wife, or maybe the small business he ran. Nothing interesting. But this liquor encompassed the character of dried lilacs, deep florals and spices, a fragrance that was as exciting as it was calming, powerful without being obnoxious.

"It's not poisoned," the old man said. "I would never kill with poison."

So this old man was not just another fool in a tavern.

"Why not?" Han asked.

"Because when you poison someone," the old man said, "you are merely a spectator. Watching a man die of poison is like watching someone eat chicken without getting to eat any yourself. Killing has to be about ripping flesh with bare steel, and being close enough to watch the horror on his face, and smell the fear of death in his sweat."

Han grabbed the cup and poured the contents into his mouth, allowing it to swirl and transform on his tongue, letting it take on a life of its own before urging it down his throat. The vivid tastes of bitterness melded with the fragrance. This would be a good way to die.

"Who am I drinking with?" Han asked in a calm voice. His stomach felt warm, soothing, mellow, and complacent, yet excited enough to demand more.

"My name is Sha Wu," the old man said, leaning against the table and folding his hands together. Han sat back and waited for movement or a sound that would give away the old man's concealed weapon. He sensed nothing.

"You know who I am," Han said, lifting the liquor to his nose for a deep inhale. "I didn't even hear you approach so you must be highly trained. I assume you're here to kill me?"

"Absolutely."

"Why?"

"So you can't disappear into West Sea."

Han lowered his cup. "You know a lot about me."

"Anyone out to kill you should."

"And you know about West Sea," Han said.

"It's a lake, not a sea," Sha Wu said, his words slow and deliberate. "But it's so big that you might as well sail into a sea."

"Have you been there?"

Sha Wu shook his head. "I wonder if it's as beautiful as they say."

"It is," Han said, studying the aging face, noting the mindfulness in his gaze. "Especially at night, when the moon is floating into the heavens, and the silver light approaches you on the waters in a long, repeating echo. There is fresh water and there is fish. All you need is liquor like this."

"I heard you are building a boat there," Sha Wu said, rubbing his thin hands together. "So you can shun us mortals and be free. I envy you."

Han drank his cup of liquor and reached for the jug in the middle of the table. "You even know about my boat. Do you want to tell me your real name?"

"Sha Wu."

"I've never heard of you."

"Then maybe you should call me uncle. We are related, you know."

Han laughed, a hardy, deep bellow. "Your drink is not poisoned. You're not carrying heavy weapons. You just threatened to kill me and you're very calm about it, like you're confident that you won't die here tonight."

"Very insightful, my nephew," Sha Wu said. "But how do you know I can't kill you with my empty hands?"

"If you have that kind of ability, shouldn't you be world famous by now?"

"Maybe I am," Sha Wu said. "You didn't notice me in the banquet hall watching you fight hundreds of the best, and almost outmatch them."

"Almost?"

"They're a bunch of self-righteous fools with no idea why they should kill you. Recreational warriors thrown together with no conviction. If they understood the reason to kill anyone, you would not have gotten out alive."

"Is there a single reason to kill someone?" Han asked.

"The reason to kill a man," Sha Wu said, leaning closer, "is to kill a man. Killing out of vengeance, or anger, or hate, or jealousy, would taint the art with lust and desire. The goal then is to satisfy an emotion, and that is the wrong reason to kill. The goal has to be to kill, and nothing else. Only then will your sword strokes be crisp and efficient. Only then will your intent be concentrated behind your weapon and not distracted by impurities." Sha Wu leaned back with a smile. "This is my lesson to you, my nephew."

Han smiled back. "Then allow me to return the lesson. The reason to save a person, is to save a person. Man, woman, child, criminal, saint, it doesn't matter. If you pass judgment on a person's character, or his status in society, then you taint the art with your own interpretations. The goal is to value life, and treasure each and every person regardless of who they are, and nothing else. Only then will your sacrifices be worthy. Only then will your actions be meaningful, and not distracted by the convoluted concept of right or wrong."

"You are a true hero," Sha Wu said. "Or are you?"

The uniform footsteps of two people carrying a shoulder carriage echoed down the stone-paved road.

Sha Wu laughed. "It's too early in the night to kill the world's greatest warrior. We should wait for dawn, when more people have tried and failed. Then the cloud of hate and greed will have run its course, and it will be a more interesting fight for you and I."

Han set down the jug of liquor and leaned against the banister for a better view. Through the silk draped over the window of the oncoming carriage, there was an outline of a woman, elegant, motionless, someone used to being carried through the streets.

Lady Li, the woman who turned the entire Martial Society against Han, was in that carriage. And he wanted answers.

Yet, if he intercepted her carriage, the world would never doubt his guilt. There would be a better time to confront the magistrate's wife.

Behind her, the pugilists from the banquet hall had collected themselves and were dispersing into the side roads, most of them walking with their heads down. The two men carrying the shoulder carriage passed below Han's balcony, heading for the magistrate's mansion.

Han reached for Sha Wu's jug of liquor and poured the rest of it down his throat. He wiped his mouth with his sleeve. "That's a good drink. Thank you."

"I'm glad you liked it," Sha Wu said. "I came to see who I am up against and I have to say I am impressed." He stood up and clasped his hands together to bid farewell. "You're a true hero of our time," he said. "I look forward to killing you."

"Thank you for the drink," Han said. "I look forward to not letting you."

Sha Wu disappeared as silently as he came. Han watched his retreating figure from behind, pondering his words.

The two men carrying Lady Li's carriage picked up pace further down the road, but they halted when an old woman, hunched over a small basket, stepped in front of them.

"Candy sticks!" the old woman shouted. She hobbled closer to the carriage with a big, toothy smile.

The carriage bearers hesitated. "Hold," Lady Li said from inside.

"Misses," the old woman continued, her smile so wide that her eyes became mere slits. "How about a candy stick? They're so good."

"Go away," one of the men said. "We don't want any."

"It brings good luck to buy from an old cripple," the street vendor said with a low bow, exaggerating her hunched back. "The misses shouldn't pass up on good luck."

"In that case," Lady Li said, opening the veil to her carriage. "We'll each have one. For good luck."

"Oh yes," the old woman said, beaming with joy. "Three candy sticks for good luck."

Han corked his bottle of liquor and tucked it into his robes. He stood, arms folded, training his focus on the figures on the road.

The old woman handed the candy to Lady Li, her pinky finger stiff and straight. She collected her coins, the same pinky still rigid even when her other fingers closed around the money, and limped aside.

Lady Li closed the veil to her carriage. The men sucked on the hard candy, lifted the carriage and proceeded.

Something was wrong. The old woman remained where she was, her head bowed, a frozen smile on her face.

Then he saw it, well before the carriage disappeared around a bend in the distance. The old woman stood up straight and backed away. Han sucked in his breath with alarm. He leaped over the balcony, landing like a cat on the stone pavement, and charged down the road. He ran straight for the hunchback. He didn't have a weapon on him, but she should be easy enough to capture.

Han closed in on the old woman and clawed at her. She slipped away, much faster than when she first moved. She flashed a crooked smile and pointed another stiff finger down the road. "Do you have time for me?" she asked.

Han stopped. She was stepping away from him, her steps light and rapid. If he so much as glanced away he would lose her.

Then Lady Li would be gone forever. He glared at the hunchback, spun around and rushed for the carriage, praying that Lady Li did not touch the candy yet.

The old woman had already vanished when he turned the corner on the road.

Han halted in his tracks. He was too late. The carriage was disabled on the ground, and the two men carrying it were already dead, blood spewing from their nostrils. Han whipped the veil open.

Lady Li was leaning against the seat, her face pale, her breath short and strained.

Han drew an acupuncture needle and reached for the back of her neck, but her eyes were already rolling back, her breath short and shallow. He could not save her.

"Lady Li," he said. "Tell me how I can help you? What are your last words?"

Blood began to flow from Lady Li's nostrils. "The map. They killed my husband for the map."

"What map?" Han asked. "Map to where?"

"Willow Island," she said. Her breath was fading.

"Wait. Don't go!" Han shouted. "Where is Willow Island? Who's doing this? What do they want?"

"The Red Crest," she whispered. With a short gasp, she released her last breath.

Han shook Lady Li again, his steeled fingers gripping her shoulders with bone-crushing power, hoping to inflict pain and awaken her. She didn't respond. He checked her pulse and eased her back into the seat. She was already dead.

Han lowered his hands. He had never heard of Willow Island, nor the Red Crest.

The old woman who sold the candy sticks—how would he ever find her again? He trudged back to the street where Lady Li bought the candy, his head down, again defeated.

He had been wandering the world for four years now and he had seen it all, the wealthy, the poor, the treacherous, the honorable, the assassins who killed in the dark and the warriors who killed in the light. Warriors of the martial society lived by their own code, their own system of reward and punishment, executing their own brand of justice upon each other. The government never intervened. The murder of a magistrate, however, should have stirred up an army by now.

Lady Li sought retribution through the martial society instead of the government. Someone out there killed her to silence her forever.

Han reached a narrower street where he came across a couple of beggars tucked away in a dark corner that few would notice. They were sitting on the uneven stones on the side of the road, their heads held between their knees, leaning against cement houses that served as storefronts during the day.

Han approached an old beggar whose long hair hung over the two hands holding his face. He must have seen where the hunchback woman ran off.

Han had nothing to offer the filthy old man in exchange for information, except for his much-needed drink. With a reluctant sigh, he pulled the porcelain bottle from his pocket, uncorked it, and crouched face to face with the old beggar.

The beggar smiled, revealing a mouth without teeth. His ragged beard was even filthier than his hair. He reached for the bottle, his fingers closing around the mouth of the jug, his pinky straight and rigid. Han jerked the bottle back.

"Who are you? Why did you kill her?"

The beggar froze. Then he laughed. "What do you want from me, Commoner?" It was the hunchback woman's voice.

A knife appeared in her hand. Han grabbed her wrist and twisted the knife away. Another appeared in her other hand. Han smacked it away like he would swipe a fly.

"Why did you kill Lady Li?" He tore off her fake beard and flung it to the pavement.

The old woman laughed. "There is no why. Someone pays the money, someone gets killed. No questions asked."

"You're a professional," Han said. "But your job was done. Why did you stay behind?"

"To wait for you of course."

"To kill me?"

"Everyone wants to."

"Who is paying you?"

"You are big money," the woman said. "Big money. Every thug and whore out there is looking for you." She rubbed her wrist with a grimace. "Wouldn't hurt to try for a reward that size before heading to Zuo Mansions."

"Zuo Mansions?" Han asked. Those words triggered memories that even alcohol could not suppress. A tall mountain with a green cliff, a pagoda that he used to drink tea under, white walls surrounding the massive training halls where he learned his martial arts. The place he grew up in, and was banished from. He had been waiting for years to go home. "Did you say Zuo Mansions?"

"Somewhere up north. Big job up there tomorrow morning. Many of us are going. A lot of people to kill up there."

Han sensed movement and jerked away. Two arrows whipped by and buried themselves into a wooden door beside him.

A single archer stood at the end of the street, holding a metal crossbow with a wooden casing attached to the top. The old woman drew a third knife and slashed toward Han's throat, but Han spun around instinctively and struck her in the chest with his palm. A gush of blood flew out of her mouth, and she fell back, her limbs rigid. Without a grimace, the old woman stopped breathing, her head tilting to the side, limp against the cement wall.

Her eyes never closed. They were dull, lifeless in death. She had lived in a world where people were murdered without warning, where people died without knowing why, or for what. Perhaps there was no other way for her to go.

The archer was waiting. Han climbed to his feet and lumbered down the street, tired and weary of another fight, the sword wound in his body still stinging.

Standing in the middle of the road was a tall girl dressed in light purple. She stood facing him, her almond-shaped eyes lowered as if in deep meditation, her long black hair dancing with the light wind, her feet rooted against the ground. Her face was beautiful, distinct, her presence and aura soft and formidable, feminine and intimidating at the same time. Han recognized a powerful martial artist in front of him.

Perhaps she was there to prevent the old woman from talking.

Perhaps she was another warrior enlisted by the Martial Society to kill him.

Han approached her. "Why did you fire at me?"

There was a mischievous twinkle in her eye. He paused.

Was she having fun?

She giggled, lifted her crossbow and fired. Han slipped to the side and then charged her from an angle. Two more bolts whipped past him. She was using a rapid-fire crossbow, sixteen shots in the chamber, two strings that alternated with each pull of the lever. Han had seen these before. These weapons were known as the Zhuge Nu.

Han moved at lightning speed but the girl retreated equally fast, firing again and again. Han dodged each shot, charging while shimmering side to side. She ran up a wheelbarrow on the side of the street and leaped onto the roof of a cement house, firing in midair. Han avoided the arrow and chased her to the roof. She jumped over a small alley onto another roof, spun around and unloaded two more bolts.

Han leaned away and the missiles passed by his face. He followed her to the next roof but she had already descended, dropping onto an open square. She stood her ground and pumped the lever on her weapon, firing one shot after another in quick succession. Han ran sideways to avoid them, closing the distance. The girl leaped backwards, unhooked the wooden cartridge on her crossbow and replaced it with a new one. She pointed her weapon at Han, and he stopped.

She lowered her crossbow. "It's true what they say. You're really hard to kill."

"Who are you?" Han asked.

She smiled, that heart-stopping smile that could bring a man to his knees. "That was so much fun. Let's do it again at Zuo Mansions."

"What?" Han shuddered. Was she an assassin sent to kill the man who raised him? Yet, this girl in purple waited until he was ready before firing at him. She came to fight fair and she wasn't out to kill him for a reward.

"Wait," Han called. "Why are you going to Zuo Mansions? To kill Master Zuo?"

"Just to watch," she said, turning around to leave. "If you're so hard to kill, who could they send to kill your Shifu?"

She didn't stop walking and Han didn't follow. He stood dazed, his head lowered. He had not seen his martial arts master, his Shifu, for four years now. Nor had he seen Shifu's daughter Lan. Master Zuo was the greatest martial artist Han had ever known. Alongside his wife, a warrior of equal skill, he raised Han and taught him everything he knew.

Shifu had been in seclusion for many years. Sending a team of assassins to murder him would be unthinkable. Who even could defeat Master Zuo?

Han headed back in the direction of the old woman's body, the stinging heat from the alcohol still filling his gut. He had to go home this time, even if uninvited.

He left the empty square, winded through narrow streets paved in uneven stone, and emerged onto the main road. The other beggars had already disappeared.

He didn't realize how far he had chased the archer in a single burst of energy, and how she always evaded him. How had he never heard of such a person? She was as fast as the Commoner. She should be world famous.

Like Sha Wu should be world famous.

Han reached the old woman, crouched down and squeezed her pockets for clues. There was a pouch of money in her coat, a small fortune, perhaps payment for killing Lady Li. He hesitated, unsure whether he should rob a corpse. But he didn't have a single coin on him and he needed to rent horses if he were to reach the Zuo mansions before the assassins arrived. He would need money for more liquor as well.

If he hadn't killed the old woman, she would have disappeared again. She would be one more assassin heading up to Zuo Mansions.

Perhaps to kill Lan.

With a sigh, Han pocketed her money. She was wearing a necklace with a blue pendant, a painted piece of thin copper with two close-set eyes. Han had seen it before but he was unsure where. He pulled the necklace off her neck and stuffed it into his pocket.

Han did not know this town well, but he did remember someone telling him this morning that there were stables in the northwest corner where he could buy a horse. He lowered his head and trudged through the empty alleyways.

The old woman had waited for a chance to kill him because the payout was high. The martial society hated him enough to train together so they could guarantee his death. He thought about Sha Wu, the girl in purple, every single person appearing before him for the same reason.

Han found the stable, traded some of the old woman's money, and departed with a fresh horse. He lowered his face into the stallion's mane and took off.

Han wondered about all that had happened today. Whoever was framing him had hatched a complex, sophisticated plot, almost flawless and believable to the Martial Society. There was nothing to gain from killing the Commoner. Perhaps, someone was seeking vengeance for what he did in Ding Yi?

The horse slowed well before sunrise. Han brought it to a nearby brook to drink and rest. Zuo Mansion was not far anymore. Even if his mount walked for the rest of the night, he would reach his destination on time.

Han slung the jug of hard liquor off his shoulder and unplugged it for a deep inhale. It was not as rare or fragrant as Sha Wu's, but it was good enough. He took a sip, glanced at a small sign next to the water that read "Hibiscus Creek," and leaned back against a tree to rest. His horse drank for a long time, then grazed on the patch of grass next to him.

Han patted his horse's head and thought about home, the Shifu that he never dared to call father, his Shifu's wife that he never dared to call mother. She was a great warrior, equal to Master Zuo, who was already without peer. Yet, Han was the one person in the world who learned both their martial arts.

"I'm going home," Han said to the horse. The tall stallion stopped what he was doing and lifted his head, as if to listen, as if he understood. After a moment he returned to grazing.

"Every night, I think about this," Han told his horse. It wasn't even a horse he knew well. "The night that my mother was poisoned. She didn't want me calling her my mother by the way. I thought she wanted me to marry Lan one day. That's what I wanted to believe. But when she died, everyone thought I killed her."

The horse snorted. Han tensed. "I did no such thing you stupid horse. I would never hurt her. She and Shifu raised me. They are the only home I've ever known."

The horse cocked his ears to listen, then shook his head as if he understood.

"The other students. They chased me away," Han said in a whisper. "I think they just wanted to kill me. Lan stood between us and told me to leave. Maybe she was trying to protect me, but I didn't need protection. None of them were my match."

Han took another sip of the liquor in his hands. His horse was still watching him with perked ears. "My Shifu's daughter is named Lan. I love her smile. I love her innocence and her beauty. But that night, Lan accused me of watching her while she bathed. I did no such thing! Why did she do that?"

Han paused for another sip. The horse would never repeat his words. Maybe this animal was the one creature he could tell anything to.

"My mother thrashed me in front of everyone," Han said. "She told me that if I ever did something so disgraceful again, she would kill me. That night, I brought her the ginseng soup like any other night. She never said she would forgive me. She just drank the soup. Then, her mouth foamed, and I knew something was wrong. But I couldn't move. I was so scared. I didn't know what to do. Before the poison killed her, she pointed a shaky finger at me. She died believing I was the one who poisoned her.

"I was sixteen then. Everyone came in. All the senior students surrounded me and accused me of poisoning her. They knew they could not beat me, even if all of them attacked at once. But they tried anyway, and I did not fight back. I wanted to die. It would be easier if they just killed me."

His horse wandered back to the brook to drink more water. The animal wasn't listening. Han didn't care.

"Someone grabbed a sword and was about to run me through," Han said, his voice raised. "His name was Niu. But I fought back. I struck the back of his hand and shattered his fingers. My injuries were heavy, but the rest of them still had no chance if I fought back. They knew it. I could have killed all of them that night.

"Then Lan stood in front of me and shielded me with her body. Did she feel remorse for accusing me earlier? Or was she afraid that I would kill everyone? It didn't matter. The girl I loved stood in front of me and held off the attackers so I could escape.

"She offered a simple, 'I'm sorry,' and then she was gone. I haven't seen her since."

What was she sorry for?

Han climbed to his feet, brushed the dirt from his hands, and reached for the horse's reins. There was still a long stretch of road in front of him leading to the foot of Zuo Mansions.

Han tucked the flask in the saddle and mounted. The horse was steady, obedient, his ears turned back. Han rubbed his neck. "Good boy. At least you're listening." He led the stallion back to the main road.

"It took me so many years to trace the source of the poison," Han began again, his voice a bit louder than the steady tap of the horse hooves below him. "Venom Sect. The dried ginseng that we purchased at the market was poisoned. Someone was brutal enough to poison an entire shipment of ginseng just to kill one woman. I don't know how many more innocents died, but I hunted down the culprit. He was the leader of the Venom Sect. I killed him and dumped his body into a waterfall." Han sucked in his breath. "I did it in front of his daughters. I couldn't avoid it.

"But now I am going home. My Shifu may be in danger. And maybe Lan too."

The thought of Lan brought a nagging anguish. He had hoped to forget her, but her smile, her innocence, her vulnerability all came to him at once. If she loved him, why did she accuse him of spying on her while she bathed? Even if someone else did do it, did she really think it was him? Perhaps, she never really loved him.

Han sighed, aware that the approaching sunrise would take away the luxury of remaining in darkness. The moon was hiding behind a thin streak of clouds such that he could barely see. He refocused on the dark path ahead.

Over the years, he had thought of the same question over and over again and arrived at the same conclusion. The idea that she didn't love him brought relief and comfort, that perhaps it was just a misunderstanding. Maybe someone convinced her that he peeked at her while she bathed.

Han shook his head. It was six years ago. She no longer remembered him for all he knew.

His horse snorted, slowed to a walk for a couple of steps, and then stopped altogether. Han flapped the reins and squeezed the horse's belly, but the animal stepped back, stumbling in retreat.

Han drew a small torch from the saddle and ignited the tip. He then leaned over the side of his mount and lowered the flame closer to the ground.

The hard soil was covered with wooden spikes the length of his forearm embedded into the ground. There were so many of them that it resembled a sea of hard weeds.

Han dropped from his saddle, kicking away a cluster of spikes before landing on a flat surface. He swept his torch lower.

Arrows, just like the ones the girl in purple had pumped out of her rapid-fire crossbow, covered the land. Han crouched lower and pulled one from the ground. These were longer than normal crossbow bolts. There was a strange cylinder attached to the head, a little thicker than the bolt itself, a quarter of the way back from the tip.

Could these be fired from a Zhuge Nu as well?

The arrows were fired from somewhere, rained from above and planted almost vertically in the soil. It was not a close-range ambush.

Was there war inside the empire?

His fingers fidgeted with the torch handle, pointing it like he would a sword. Not far away, in the middle of the road, were the targets. At least twenty people, lying where they fell, were covered in enough arrows to puncture every organ at least twice. Han stepped closer, swept his feet like he would slide on an icy road, clearing the protruding arrows from his path. The dead weren't armored—they weren't in uniform even, and there was not a single weapon in sight. These were civilians.

Han slowed, a deep frown clouding over his eyebrows. A dead child lay next to his mother, both killed so quickly they never even reached for each other. A baby was in another woman's arms when they fell. The slaughter was indiscriminate, a blanket assault to ensure everyone died.

Some of the arrows had already been kicked aside, leaving cleared paths toward the bodies. The first corpse was shot by over twenty arrows, the blood on his back already dried and caked into a dark brown. He was killed before nightfall.

It was an older man with a graying topknot. His face was pressed into the ground, and his trousers were drawn back halfway, exposing his buttocks.

Han turned to a different area on the barren soil, followed the broken arrows to another body, also a man laying face down. His trousers were pulled back as well to expose the buttocks. Yet, arrows had struck the front of his body in multiple areas, and when he was turned over, many of the bolts were pressed deeper into his torso, or remained lodged in his ribcage, elevating his body off the ground.

Perhaps these civilians had something the regiment of archers wanted. After all, the thought of the military attacking civilians was unthinkable.

Han gasped. *Could it be a foreign army? Did the Silencer cross through the Great Wall and no one knew?*

It couldn't be, he almost whispered out loud, shaking his head. They were searching for something. The corpses around him all had the same thing in common. If the Silencer invaded, he would head straight for the capital. He would not stop to kill civilians, much less search their bodies.

The first rays of dawn were already upon him. Han rushed back to his horse. There was no point speculating. He would hear more in the morning.

Han pulled his horse away from the road and onto a small meadow to circumvent the area densely covered by protruding arrows. No one could have evaded such a focused onslaught.

The sun was ascending. He could see the road without his torch. Han flung it into the dirt road, extinguishing it, and sent his horse into a rapid trot.

The images of the bodies were burnt into his mind, convoluted by a whirlwind of other visuals from the evening before, and the sounds of the hunchbacked woman's cackle, the giggle of the girl in purple, the calm, almost seductive words of Sha Wu.

The road narrowed and winded into a village. At the mouth of the village, on a wooden board next to the entrance, he saw a new poster. Han stopped his horse. His face was on it, painted in ink, and underneath the portrait was a short description of his crimes. The Commoner was wanted for the murder of a magistrate and for colluding with the Silencer, an act of treason punishable by decapitation. It was an official document issued by the local government.

So now even ordinary people wanted him dead. This would make it so much harder to protect them.

Han pushed his horse into a fast trot and breezed through the village. He thought about the civilians, perhaps entire families, killed on the road and left for dead. For this many arrows to fly through the air to kill unarmed citizens, something horrible had to be brewing.

Once outside the village, he brought his horse to a comfortable walk. The golden rays of sunrise streaked across the land.

Suddenly, Han was already at the foot of the mountain, where the Zuo Mansions were built halfway to the peak.

He dismounted, sent his horse to graze, and ascended on foot. The small path was neither steep nor wide, void of distinct characteristics or charm. For all his early life, this was the way home.

The lush mountain was difficult to navigate, but Han knew the shortcuts. The overgrown bushes were easy to cut through. Most travelers visiting Master Zuo lost their way in this mountain, but Han rushed past every rock, every protruding root without pause.

He neared mid-mountain. His heart was pounding. He thought about what he would say to Lan. He pondered what he would say to Master Zuo, who exiled him from home six years ago.

If not for these six years where he endured countless battles and faced numerous opponents, he would never have become the greatest warrior in the world. From his travels and endeavors, Han became battle-tested and ready. The Commoner was no longer a fighter in theory. He had seen it all.

The Zuo mansions loomed before him faster than he was ready for. The simple structures, built on a small plateau at mid-mountain, were huddled together and fenced off by a short, cement wall. Each building was large enough to include training halls for the forty students that studied the Zuo system of martial arts. In front of the main structures, closer to the edge of the plateau, was the small pagoda where Master Zuo drank tea every morning. It was early, and Han expected to find him there.

Master Zuo was not old, but his long beard had already begun to gray. He was seated with his back to the edge of the cliff, a position he normally avoided.

Han slowed to a walk, then stopped altogether. His mentor's head was bowed with his eyes closed. Seated across from him was a young woman, dressed in white, her long hair trussed behind her. Han's heart pounded at the sight of Lan. She was as beautiful as ever. This morning, her hair, her makeup, her robe were perfect. She spent the time to look elegant before joining her father for tea.

Han's heart raced in anticipation. What would he say to them? Han was a few steps away from the pagoda when Master Zuo turned to him with a smile. Lan motioned for him to come forward. Han paused, the longing, the frustration, the self-pity all coursing through him at once.

Master Zuo lifted his face as if to taste the morning scent. His calm smile returned. "I knew you would come," he said.

Han dropped to his knees and tapped his forehead against the ground once. His mentor's face was pale. "Are you ill, Shifu?" he asked.

Zuo smiled again and motioned for him to come forward. He reached inside his robes and produced a small scroll, wrapped and sealed in an old piece of wax paper.

"There is a team of assassins coming here," Han said. "We need to prepare right away."

"Take the scroll," Zuo said, his voice weak and monotonous. "Leave now."

Han hesitated, stiffening for a moment before accepting the scroll. "I didn't kill Lady Zuo. She was the mother I knew. I didn't…"

"I know," Master Zuo said again. "Leave now."

Lan lowered her eyes.

"I didn't do anything disgraceful," Han said to her.

"I know," she said, turning away from him. "You have to go. It's too late for us."

"Too late?"

A gush of blood streamed down her nose. Her skin turned ashen white and more blood dripped out of her trembling lips. Lan collapsed from her seat. Han grabbed her arms and lowered her to the ground.

A burst of blood flew out of Master Zuo's mouth. He shuddered once and leaned onto the stone table of the pagoda, crushing the small porcelain cups in front of him. His arms dangled to his sides, and with a weary sigh, he faded away.

"Shifu!" Han shouted. He reached for Master Zuo, but his Shifu was already dead. A persistent trickle of dark blood oozed out of his nose. There was a rancid, metallic smell to the blood.

"Han…" Lan whispered.

He rushed back to her, picked up her frail body and cradled her in his arms. The beautiful face was tortured with pain and sadness, regret that she could not express with her few remaining breaths. She tried to speak but the agony was unbearable. She managed a few shudders.

There were so many things he wanted to tell her. Now there was nothing left to say. Nothing was important anymore.

"Han… I'm sorry." It was a fading whisper.

"Lan. What can I do for you? Anything you want. What can I do?"

"I'm sorry," she said, her voice fading. "I… I was the one who watched you bathe. Niu saw me and forced me to accuse you. I'm sorry. Now I've ruined you too."

"Don't say those things. Tell me what I can do."

"He… He promised to marry me. I fell for it. I fell for a handsome face and flattering words… I deserve this."

"Who? Who is this to you?"

"Fu Nandong," she whispered. She raised a shaking hand and pointed to her pocket. Han pulled out the one item inside, a copper pass with the insignia of a government official. "He gave this to me so I could go see him," she said.

Han touched the surface of the pass with the tip of his thumb. "A category three general?"

Lan choked and a mouthful of blood gushed out. Her fists clenched in pain, and her face contorted into a horrible grimace. Convulsing, her breaths short and quick, she forced herself to speak. "My mother died for a secret. Her secret… her secret… is you. You are… the Red Crest…"

She coughed once, and her cold body became limp.

"Lan," Han whispered, thoughts of their childhood together flashing through his mind. It wasn't supposed to happen this way. "I will get to the bottom of this," Han said, his quivering lips sucking air through clenched teeth. "I will find Fu Nandong, and I will make it right for you. I will do whatever it takes."

He lowered her body into a light sleeping position, folded her hands across her chest, and straightened her feet. For a second, kneeling in front of her lifeless body, he could not recognize where he was. How could Lan be dead?

He thought he was going to marry her. Years had passed but deep inside, he always thought that he still would, one day, somehow. He dreamed of returning to the mundane world when Master Zuo would accept him as an innocent man.

Han turned to his Shifu, kneeled before his body and bowed, touching his head to the ground over and over again. After a long time, Han lifted his face, tears flowing down his cheeks. He gazed into Master Zuo's peaceful expression. His Shifu had accepted his fate and went with dignity.

There was a tattoo on Master Zuo's arm, one Han had never noticed before. He leaned forward and pushed back his Shifu's wide sleeve to expose the symbol. Two eyes, linked together, colored in blue. Han drew out the necklace that he had taken from the old woman and held it next to Shifu's arm. The symbols were identical.

Han pondered the situation for a moment, then shoved the necklace back into his pocket and jumped to his feet.

The Zuo Mansion was quiet. Han didn't hold any hopes that the forty students living here, along with servants and cooks, could have survived this.

He rushed into the mansion, through the large wooden doors, and into the main hall. Multiple bodies, each dressed as students of the Zuo clan, lay dead on the tiled floor. There was no blood around them, no signs of fallen weapons or broken furniture. Han recognized them. He had trained with them, laughed, ate, and bickered with them. These were the ones he called brothers, who tried to kill him when they thought he poisoned Lady Zuo.

Han stepped closer. They were all lying where they once stood, killed internally, just like Master Zuo. He recognized Niu, a man he thought was his true brother once upon a time, his face twisted in horror at the moment of death. Han thought about what Lan had said about Niu and the bathing incident. *What did that mean?*

The same metallic smell reeked from the dark blood oozing from their nostrils and seeping into their white training uniforms.

They all wore white uniforms!

Han grabbed a sword hanging from the wall and rushed out of the main hall. This was their routine, to come in full white uniform and drink tea before training. To die all at once before the weapons were taken off the walls meant that the morning tea was poisoned.

Han bolted into the kitchen, his hand on the handle of his sword. Water in an iron pot was still boiling, the firewood in the stove remained intact. Littered across the cement floor were the bodies of the servants, blood trickling from their mouths and noses with the same rancid, metallic smell.

Han glanced at a plate of half-eaten dumplings, perhaps the murder weapon, and stepped through the door to the backyard where the livestock was kept. A couple of chickens hopped away and a pig squealed in a distant pen. Han circled the cement kitchen from the outside, his footsteps silent, until he appeared in front of a man with a pigeon in his hand.

The man gasped in alarm and tossed away the pigeon. The bird flew in a straight line, away from the mountain and over the valley. The man stumbled back, holding up both hands.

"Uncle Huang," Han whispered, his hand reaching for his sword. Old Huang was a thin, frail man, with deep wrinkles and spotted grey hair. He had a bulging knapsack strapped to his shoulder, perhaps with all his belongings. He stabilized himself and lowered his hands.

"Don't bother," Old Huang said. "You can kill me with your pinky finger. I am just an old cook."

Han drew his sword and shot forward, faster than Old Huang could see, and stabbed him in the thigh. Old Huang arched his back and silently crumbled to the ground.

"You poisoned them?" Han asked. "All these people? You poisoned them!"

"I had to," Old Huang said. "They were too powerful. I had to."

"And Master Zuo? He treated you like family."

"If you're going to kill me, Commoner, let's get it over with. I know what I did. I don't need a lecture from you before I die."

Han slammed the sword back into its sheath. "Why would you betray him? For money? Who is behind this?"

Old Huang lifted himself on one elbow, the corners of his mouth curved downwards in defiance.

"Master Zuo took you in and gave you a chance at life," Han said. "Why did you poison him? His daughter. His students."

Old Huang lifted his face to show Han his nostrils.

Han was ready to kill him with one strike, the Infinity Palm that Master Zuo taught him at age twelve.

Yet, vivid images of the old cook played over and over in his mind. He was like family, always saving a nice treat in the kitchen for him as a child, always a big smile when he saw the orphan boy.

Han took a step back with a grimace. "You were family to me too, Uncle Huang. Why did you kill Master Zuo?"

"I don't know, Little Han. Would you believe me when I say that?"

Han shook his head. "If I believe you, then it means someone else wanted him dead, and you were following orders."

Old Huang turned his face to avoid the Commoner's piercing gaze.

"If you tell me the truth," Han said. "I won't kill you. If you tell me who wanted Shifu dead, I will let you go."

Old Huang hesitated. "Can I trust the Commoner? You were accused of conspiring with the Silencer."

"You know me better than that Uncle Huang."

"I don't know you anymore," Huang said. "You left—"

"I was chased out!"

"It doesn't matter. Who are you, Han?"

"Who am I?" Han jerked forward, inches from Huang's face. "Who am I? I know as much as you do!"

Old Huang froze, an ant against the towering Commoner. He released a deep sigh. "They call him The Judge."

"The Judge?" Han asked. "Who is he?"

"I don't know."

"Then who gave you direct orders to kill Master Zuo?"

"A category three general."

"Do you have a name?"

"Fu Nandong."

Han felt his heart skip a beat.

"It was about a letter," Old Huang said. "A letter that Master Zuo received from a mysterious messenger."

"What's his name?"

Old Huang shook his head. "He came and left, not even stopping for a cup of tea. He said he had one more letter to deliver."

"What did he look like?"

"Like a ghost," Old Huang said. "Very ugly, very strange. His nose had been cut off. His hair was all white."

"And do you know what was in the letter?"

"Not really," Old Huang said, shaking his head again. "Master Zuo burned it right away in my kitchen. I glanced over his shoulder. It came from someone named Little Sparrow."

Han took a step forward. "What did the letter say?"

"I didn't get to read it," Old Huang said. "Something about the Red Crest. I have no idea what that is or what it means but I reported it to Fu Nandong. A day later, I received the order to eliminate Master Zuo and everyone he came into contact with."

Han's fists clenched and unclenched. His bulging eyes couldn't relax.

There it is," Old Huang said. "I've told you everything. I swear to you Little Han. I don't know anything else."

Han stood frozen. So many questions passed through his mind, and yet, he could not form them into words.

"And this Fu Nandong employed a team of assassins? To kill my Shifu?"

Huang managed a subdued laugh. "There are no assassins! There never were. I got the job done. If you heard of any assassins, it was to get you to come here."

"Why?"

"To kill you of course," Old Huang said. "I was told to send the messenger bird as soon as you arrived. Many people want you dead, Little Han. I don't know what you did or whether you deserve it but listen to Uncle Huang. The Judge is as powerful as the emperor. There is no safe place in China for you. If you can survive long enough to get to the Silk Road, the land of the blue-eyed strangers would be the safest place for you. At least no one knows you there."

"And why is everyone out to kill me?"

"There's a big reward for your head, Little Han."

"Is it this Judge?" Han asked. "Why is he paying so much to have me killed?"

Old Huang looked away.

"You've murdered the entire Zuo Clan," Han said, his voice low and menacing. "My Shifu, Lan, all the innocent students inside these walls. If you want to live, you better speak up!"

"I've told you everything," Old Huang said. "If I try to give you more answers, they won't be the truth."

Han took short, shallow breaths, unsure of what to do. Could he release Shifu's murderer just like that? Master Zuo was the one father he knew. The man who killed him had to die.

Yet, he gave his word. Master Zuo had always taught him that when a man had lost everything, his house, his family, his money, even his life, he would still have one thing that no one could take from him. His honor.

"Go," Han said. "You get to live with what you did today. If I ever see you again, I will kill you before you can recognize my face."

"Thank you," Old Huang said, struggling to climb to his feet. "Take care, Little Han." The sword wound in the old cook's thigh was deep, and with his head low, he stumbled away, dragging the injured leg behind him.

"Who else knows the Infinity Palm?" Han asked as the man walked away. "Did Master Zuo teach anyone else?"

Old Huang paused, thought for a moment, and shook his head. "After what you did to the other students, Master Zuo never taught something so destructive again."

A single arrow ripped through the air and struck Old Huang in the ankle. He screamed as he crumbled to the ground, cradling his wound and cursing Han for breaking his word.

Han waited. Moments later, the archer appeared with the metal Zhuge Nu in one hand, her purple robes dancing around her. "You can't leave yet," she said.

"Who are you?" Old Huang screamed.

"So that's who they sent to kill the great Master Zuo," she said. "The man closest to him. But who authorized you to kill so many innocents?"

"Who do you think?" the old cook shouted. "The Judge authorized it. Now you know. We answer to the same person. Why did you shoot me?"

"I answer to the emperor," the girl said, lifting her crossbow. "Not to some Judge."

"Wait!" Han shouted, bolting forward. The girl turned her weapon toward him. She yanked the lever on her rapid-fire crossbow, her hand a blur, the arrows flying in rapid succession. Han struggled to dodge them. He drew his sword and swept the arrows away, still advancing. The girl retreated.

Han charged her, gripping his sword in front of himself. The girl timed her retreat, waiting for the last second so he could not change direction. She fired at him at close range, so close that he almost couldn't strike the arrow before reaching her. His sword connected with her weapon, just once, before she fired again at close range, inches from his face, forcing him to leap away, and then she slipped back.

"Who are you?" Han asked, stepping forward. "Why haven't I heard of someone like you?"

She retreated another three steps in quick succession, dumped the cartridge on her crossbow and reloaded. "Should I be world famous like the Commoner?"

"You should," he said. "Warriors across the land should be talking about you."

She smiled, the cute smile of a happy girl about to enjoy the sunrise. "That's nice. But I don't want to be famous. Then everyone would be afraid of me and no one would fight me."

"Is that why you are out to kill me?" Han asked. "For a good fight? Or for the reward?"

"Reward?"

"For my head."

She paused. "I didn't know your head is worth money. How much?"

She lifted her weapon and fired, her hand rocking the lever, sending a swarm of arrows at her assailant while she retreated. Han rushed in to strike the arrows, some of them at very close range. He could never reach her. The endless barrage of arrows always kept him at bay, her persistent retreat always giving her a firing distance.

In a moment, she took a huge step back, dumped the cartridge on her crossbow and reloaded. She stood waiting for him, a smile on her face. "You really are hard to kill."

Han could not overpower her, and his speed was not enough to catch her. He lowered his sword. He had fought cowards and heroes, masters and imitators, armies in the light and assassins in the dark. None of them fazed him. But today, he felt like he was fighting himself.

The girl also lowered her weapon, taking her left hand off the lever of the Zhuge Nu, and they stood face to face, motionless except for the gentle breeze that swayed her long hair and caused the purple sash around her waist to flutter.

Han felt the soft air caressing his cheek, the sounds of birds chirping in the distance, the scent of fresh grass on the plateau below. The man who raised him was dead. The girl he grew up with was dead. His friends wanted to kill him and the world called him a criminal. Why was he fighting this archer to begin with?

"Your face is stunning," he said. "One day I will paint a portrait of you with your crossbow in hand, and generations later, poets and scholars will write about who you must have been." With a smile, he turned to walk away. "And no one will ever know. Just as I will never know."

The girl froze, her rapid-fire crossbow dangling in her hand, her lips parted.

Then, the shriek of a thousand cats being butchered, of animals being chased and slaughtered, approached with alarming speed. The darkened skies were filled with flying bolts, and the incoming missiles had blackened the heavens. Han stared. He had never seen anything like this.

The girl in purple leaped at Han, who then drew his sword and whipped the blade in front of himself in a frenzy. She threw aside her crossbow and reached out to grab him. He withdrew too late, and the blade cut her shoulder. She didn't react but tackled him to the ground behind a boulder. Dropping his sword, Han allowed himself to collapse into the soft soil. They hid behind the boulder while the darkened skies screamed above them, then past them.

The incoming bolts pounded the earth, striking the soil with such force that the sounds of impact resembled one continuous drone. Han pulled the girl closer, huddled behind the boulder, waiting until the shower passed.

Han pressed his back against the boulder, struggling for breath, his hands clawing the rough surface behind him. So, this was what happened to the civilians on the road. A single volley of arrows that came in the thousands, covered the sky and killed everything in its path. These came from rapid-fire arrows, sixteen bolts in a top-loading cartridge, and all of them seemed to have been fired together.

"What was that?" Han whispered. "How could arrows fly that far?"

Then, from the distant valley, the inevitable second round of the Zhuge Nu was upon them.

The girl crouched lower behind the boulder and motioned for him to do the same.

Han listened. The arrows were fast approaching but still a distance away. He stuck his head out. The incoming swarm didn't dance in the air, didn't carry any finesse or beauty to it. It was cold, direct, decisive. Han ducked and the bolts screeched past him, destroying every sign of life that had not found shelter from the onslaught.

"Are they firing at me or you?" Han asked.

"I should stop trying to kill you so I can find out."

The second round stopped. She turned to him, inches away from his face, and said, "I heard you have a deal with the Silencer to invade our country."

"Do you know that?" Han asked. "Or did you hear it from a rumor?"

"You don't look like you know how to find the Silencer." She jumped to her feet, picked up her crossbow, spun around and walked away.

"Wait," Han called from behind. "Why did you save me? Didn't you come here to kill me?"

After a few steps she turned, just once. "Exactly," she answered. "I have to do the killing, not the Zhuge Nu." She turned again and started to walk away.

Han took a step toward her. "My name is…"

"Chen Han," she said without looking back. "Everyone knows who you are."

"And you are…"

"Yi Yi."

Han watched Yi Yi until she disappeared, until the bushes she walked around ceased to sway and the sound of light footsteps faded. For a moment, he forgot where he was and why he was there.

He jolted back to reality, as if awakened from a pleasant dream. The world around him was full of arrows. He turned toward the valley. It was too far away to see anything, his view obstructed by bushes and elevation.

Han spun around and rushed back to the front of the kitchen where Old Huang had been immobilized by Yi Yi's arrow. The old cook was now dead, with multiple Zhuge Nu bolts protruding from his body. The chickens, the pigs in the open pens, perhaps the household dogs were all dead too.

Han turned away and headed for the front of the mansion walls, past the pagoda where Master Zuo and Lan's bodies laid, and walked to the edge of the plateau. The sky was clear and the air was crisp. The cool wind that ruffled his hair was nipped his face. So many questions he could not digest, so many memories he could not shake. He needed to focus, but for what?

The army of Zhuge Nu archers were mobilizing, perhaps a thousand men. They were on another mountain, separated from Zuo Mansions by a deep, vast forest. It was impossible. They were so far away and still struck the plateau. Arrows from crossbows could not fly that far.

Why did the incoming arrows make such hideous sounds?

Han bolted down the trail from which he came. He would get his answers from the Zhuge Nu archers themselves, he decided. They knew he was coming to the Zuo Mansions and they had been waiting for him, responding to the messenger bird that Old Huang sent.

Maybe someone in the battalion of Zhuge Nu could explain why everyone was trying to kill him, why a thousand rapid-fire archers were assigned to eliminate one man, and why a single archer was as fast as the Commoner. Since the night before, he had been hunted by everyone in the world. Someone out there had to have answers.

Han charged down the mountain, his mind a blur. He thought about Lan, how she was killed because she trusted her new lover. Her final words haunted him. Her mother was killed because of the secret of the Red Crest, and that secret was him. Old Huang poisoned everyone because there was a chance Master Zuo shared this secret with the family.

The base of the mountain loomed. Han forgot how hard he was sprinting, as limitless energy coursed through his body. His power and vigor emerged when called upon. He felt as invincible as ever.

Han scorched the terrain with his speed, plowing through tall grass and bushes like they didn't exist. In a moment, he was at the foot of the mountain, at the edge of the light forest that separated the Zuo mountain from the Zhuge Nu. The archers were no longer positioned at mid-mountain. Mobilizing so many rapid-fire archers didn't take long. He needed to hurry.

His horse was still there. Han flew onto the saddle, grabbed the reins and squeezed the horse's belly. The horse fumbled once, then collected itself and jolted into a full gallop. A thousand archers could not be hard to find, even in this lush landscape, and once he spotted them, he would follow them on foot.

Han pulled the jug of liquor from the saddle and uncorked it for a sip. It was empty. He threw it aside and leaned forward on the horse's mane, riding hard.

Moments later, he spotted a trail of men marching in single file as they descended the western side of the mountain, carrying their weapons next to their ears like they would hold a flag. They were in black uniforms, no armor, their headpieces a simple black cloth that held the hair together. In the shadows, or at night, these men would be impossible to detect from afar.

Han stayed behind a tree to watch. These were the men who murdered women and children, striking from tremendous distances like little cowards, never having to face the people they killed.

They were also soldiers, following orders without question, firing on command because discipline in the military depended on it.

Han held his fingers together, watching, waiting for them to pass. An assault from a blanket of Zhuge Nu arrows would devastate an army, but up close, Han could see these archers weren't armed. They would be vulnerable to a small group of swordsmen. Perhaps, to ensure speed and stealth, none of these archers carried a real combat weapon.

Han dropped off his horse and proceeded on foot. As long as he remained close, he should have no trouble capturing any of them.

The Zhuge Nu battalion moved in perfect order, silent, focused, steady. As the army trickled past, four tall horses with riders in normal military uniform followed behind. They too marched in perfect alignment, but they did not carry crossbows.

Han fought the urge to attack them all by himself. They weren't equipped for close combat. The civilian bodies still lying on the road, decaying in the heat, needed to be avenged.

But there was a thousand of them. Han would never be able to kill them all. Most would run away, and a much larger army would return. Then more than a few civilians would get mowed down as they hunted him.

A dense forest loomed ahead and the road narrowed, forcing the archers to squeeze together into a single file. That was where he would strike. Han tied a large handkerchief over his face, only revealing his eyes. He crept low in the bushes, waiting to pounce on his prey. As the men passed his hidden figure, the greatest warrior in the world inched ever closer. Soon the four riders at the tail merged behind one another.

Han leaped out and grabbed the last rider by the throat with a steeled grip that choked off his airway, muffling any resistance, and dragged him into the dense bushes on the other side of the trail unnoticed. Han struck him on the side of the neck to render him unconscious, threw him onto his own shoulders and ran off.

Moments later, he was almost back at the foot of the mountain. Han lowered his captive behind a tree, drew an acupuncture needle and used it to awaken him. The soldier coughed once and woke with a start.

"Who are you?" the soldier asked. "How did I get here?"

"I took you off your horse and carried you here," Han said, his voice calm and monotonous, muffled by the handkerchief covering his face.

"You? Alone?"

Han nodded. The soldier panicked. "With... without the rest of my battalion knowing?"

Han nodded again. "What is your name?"

"Lai," he said, drawing back. He tried to inch away from Han but his back was fixed against the tree trunk. "Who… who are you?"

Han pointed to the mountain above them. "When you were up there firing across the valley…"

"I was down here with the horses. The rest of the battalion went up there to reach their target."

"Who was the target?"

"I don't know," Lai replied. "Someone important. They sent an entire brigade to take down one man. Someone dangerous."

Han crouched down in front of him, placing a hand on his shoulder. "I am that one man. Answer all my questions and I will let you live."

Lai's jaw dropped, his hands trembling.

"Tell me Lai, why were you and three others on horses while everyone else was on foot? Are you scouts?"

Lai bit his lips, still shaking. "We… we are scouts and smoke operators."

"What are smoke operators?"

"We approach the target on horses and we send a smoke signal into the air above the target. Our men see it and they fire."

"Zhuge Nu arrows?"

Lai nodded. "That's how the Zhuge Nu can strike from any distance without seeing the target."

"Do they always fire when they see the smoke?" Han asked. "Even if they don't know if there is a real target or not?"

Lai nodded.

"How did you send a smoke signal all the way up to Zuo Mansions?"

"We didn't need to," Lai said. "We've waited for two days for you and we knew where the target was. The men fired when they received the messenger bird."

"Old Huang's bird," Han said under his breath. "And who wants me killed?"

"I don't know, sir," Lai said. "We are soldiers. We just follow orders."

"If you have been up there waiting for two days, then who shot the civilian travelers just north of Hibiscus Creek?" Han asked.

"It would be a different battalion, sir," Lai said. "There are many out there. They were probably assigned to take down Target One."

"Who is Target One?"

"We don't know any names, sir."

"Where is your next mission?"

"We don't know, sir."

"Are your battalions always on a mission, or do they wander the land waiting to kill civilians," Han asked.

"Both, sir," Lai replied. "Some units are sent far away to take down a target while some stay near camp and wait for orders."

"A single target far away?" Han asked. "Where? Who?"

"One of our units marched to the City of Stones three nights ago, sir," Lai replied. "They were sent to eliminate one man as well."

"One man?" Han asked. "You need that many advanced weapons to kill one man? Who is he?"

"We just know him as Target Two, sir."

Han sensed movement. Something was dropping in, fired from an incredible distance. But it was silent, and slowing as it approached. Han reached up and caught it mid-air.

It was a crossbow bolt with a note wrapped around it. Han peeled it off and uncurled it with his thumb, careful not to rub off a single line of wet ink.

Meet me at noon at the foot of the stone
bridge in Hua Du village.

There was no signature, but Han knew who fired this with such perfect precision. Without a second thought, he reached for Lai's throat with his large hands and clutched the blood vessels on both sides of the soldier's neck with his thumb and middle finger. Lai fainted. His breathing was calm and steady when Han released him.

Inside Lai's pockets were two bamboo tubes, about the length of his arm and a little thicker than a flute. One end was sealed and the other end wrapped in paper twisted to resemble a string. This must be the smoke signal. Han tucked them into his robes and stepped away. The sun was high in the sky and Hua Du village was still a short walk away.

CHAPTER 3

THE STONE BRIDGE built in the middle of Hua Du village had a name, but Han could not remember it anymore. The village was close to the Zuo mansions. He and Lan used to go there to fish under the bridge whenever Lady Zuo was away. They believed catching fish was a matter of luck and they would prove that they were lucky children. They only caught fish once. Meanwhile, the villagers stepped up to the small river to wash their vegetables and like magic, they caught fish any time they wanted. Han was baffled. He didn't realize that knowing the river was more important than being lucky. Still, they were convinced that they were lucky and invincible, and if not freshwater fish, then maybe world dominance one day. Those were better times.

Han approached the bridge with slow, deliberate footsteps. Why did Yi Yi ask to meet here? Lan died in his arms that same morning and this bridge was the last place he wanted to be.

It was not yet noon. A few villagers were passing by but none of them noticed him. Only an old woman selling rice cakes stood hunched over on the other side of the bridge. Yi Yi was nowhere in sight.

Han drew his sword and planted it into the ground, and he saw that there was still a sizable shadow until noon. He could wait under the bridge where he and Lan used to sit. It felt so long ago. It was easier to remember that she hated him.

Han lowered his tired body next to the river under the stone bridge, the sparkling reflection from the late morning sun burning his eyes. He covered them with his hand, rested his arm against his knees and buried his face in the crook of his elbow. It was quiet outside, exactly how it used to be, except something was different, missing from this world.

Lan's laughter was missing. She used to laugh at everything he said. They would sit for hours next to the river and talk about trivial things. Her beautiful voice was always next to him, and it didn't matter that she never talked about anything he enjoyed, like art or poetry, or the way of the sword. It only mattered that she was there.

The magnitude of what he had just endured struck him then. She was gone. Even Shifu was gone. He never thought this could happen.

The sun must have moved into the middle of the sky by the time he controlled himself. He breathed in short bursts to calm down. It was almost noon but he didn't want to meet with Yi Yi yet.

He started thinking about the scroll in his pocket. There was no time to stop and read when he needed answers from Old Huang, then Yi Yi, then the Zhuge Nu scout. Han leaned against the uneven rocks under the shade of the bridge and rolled out the scroll that Master Zuo gave him.

My child, you are now the greatest warrior alive. Neither Lady Zuo nor I can learn each other's martial arts, because they are so different. Yet not only have you mastered both, you have created a peculiar character in your movement and a distorted distance measurement unique to yourself. You don't have a name for it, but I will call it the Common Rhythm for you. It is distinct, and it is yours. Please don't lose sight of it.

I did not find you on my front door, abandoned by a peasant. It is normal for a coward to tell the truth before his death, and I am no better. For this, I hope to have done well for you, that I have held you to a higher standard than my own behavior, and that you will continue life and continue your legacy in this world as an honorable man, always transparent to your friends as well as your enemies, always keeping your word even in pain, suffering, and death. I confess that I did not live up to those standards. I am not asking for forgiveness; I am asking that you still believe in what I taught you and never ever stoop to my level.

Fifteen years ago, I was sent on an assassination assignment. I approached my target with four henchmen thinking I would kill a ruthless criminal that Li Yan wanted dead. I swept through the battle with ease. None of them were my match, and I killed everyone to reach my target.

When I found him, I realized that it was a small boy no older than seven years old. He stood with arms spread, shielding an older woman. I asked him his name. I did not want to kill a little boy, especially not the wrong one. He refused to talk, despite numerous verbal threats, even with sharp blades held against his throat. He said he would answer only if we let the woman go. I thought the woman was his mother, and I sympathized. I agreed to release the woman.

A few exchanges later, the boy revealed that she was but a servant woman who took care of him. I ordered my men to follow her and kill her.

The boy had the making of a true hero, and I could not kill him. He told me his name was Chen Han, which did not match the name of the target. The other four assassins wanted to kill him just in case. In a sudden move that made my wife proud, I killed the other four assassins to seal this secret forever. I reported back that the boy was dead and burned, and that I executed the other assassins because they defied orders. From there, I would forever leave the shadowy group of elite assassins to live as a hermit and teach a new generation of students.

Han clenched the letter in his fist and felt his head throbbing in dull streaks of pain. It was coming back to him. He remembered that day, a very long time ago, when he faced the masked men with big swords, and everyone around him was dead. There was blood everywhere, but a woman's voice whispered behind him, very close to his ear.

"Tell them your name is Chen Han," she said, her voice growing stronger in his mind. "Please, please tell them your name is Chen Han and never tell the truth…"

Han clawed at his own face, grimacing, willing the memories to surge forward. *What was his name before that? Where did he live before that?*

Han sat back, shuddering, gasping for air. He could not remember.

The sun was high in the sky. Han remembered his appointment with Yi Yi and climbed to his feet. The stone bridge was still empty, and the small village was quiet while its inhabitants worked the fields. The old woman selling rice cakes was still there.

Han strolled to the middle of the bridge and glanced at the clear water flowing underneath him. This was the spot where he and Lan caught their only fish, a small one that had little life in it when they pulled it from the river.

Yi Yi was nowhere in sight. Han drew the scroll from his pocket and reread the letter a second time. His hands trembled as the distant memories long banished resurfaced all at once. All he could remember about his early childhood was training in the back of the Zuo mansions, and Lan bringing him water and keeping him company. He had no memory of living elsewhere, of having parents before growing up under Master Zuo.

He noticed something when he read the letter a third time. Master Zuo was sent to kill someone that Li Yan wanted dead. *Wasn't Li Yan the younger brother of the current emperor?* He died from a fever many years ago.

"Would you like some rice cakes?" It was the old woman.

Han rolled the letter back into its original form, having memorized it by now. Should he burn it or not? He tucked it away and turned to the old woman with a polite smile. Her words reminded him that he hadn't eaten in a while, but he didn't feel any hunger. All he wanted was another flask of liquor.

Han fished for a coin in his pocket. He should be polite and buy something from her.

The old woman handed him a rice cake and said, "It's free if you answer a question for me."

"Ask me the question," Han said, taking the rice cake and handing her the coin. "The coin is for your grandchildren."

"I don't have grandchildren," she said with a cackle. "So, tell me, even if the world-famous Commoner is impossible to kill, why would anyone position a thousand Zhuge Nu archers to kill one man?"

Han froze. He noticed the resemblance, the beautiful face hidden behind a layer of fake skin, the long white hair an obvious wig.

"Why the rice cake?" he asked. "Poison?"

She laughed with her own voice this time. "I don't know how to use poison. Besides, if I can't put an arrow in your throat then I'm not qualified to kill you."

"Thank you for saving me from the Zhuge Nu earlier," Han said.

She wrinkled her nose and made a face.

"I'm glad you're having fun, Yi Yi. But why disguise yourself?"

Yi Yi remained hunched over. "People are always watching you, Commoner. Everyone wants you dead."

"Why?"

"I'm just as curious as you are," she said. "Do you want to find out?"

"More than anything."

"You will have to trust me then."

"Trust you how?"

"Trust that I won't kill you unless you're alert and armed and ready."

Han smiled. "You're not my match, Yi Yi. But I am not able to kill you either. Since it can't be done, let's stop trying."

Yi Yi released the light giggle of a child about to reveal that she stole candy. "Do you know what I did this morning?"

Han shook his head.

"I beat up a soldier to find out who would pay me if I captured you."

"I see," Han said. "You want to capture me and bring me in for a big reward."

"That's why you need to trust me," she said. She motioned for him to lean closer, and she whispered into his ear. "I found out the amount. You are worth a lot of money."

"That's flattering."

"I don't need the money," she said. "My employer has all the money in the world and he gives me whatever I want. But this will be fun. I tie you up and put a bag over your head and deliver you to the enemy for a reward. How can you resist such a plan?"

"Of course I can't."

"The person who will pay the reward is the same category three general who ordered Master Zuo's assassination," Yi Yi said. "Fu Nandong."

Han's eyes burned.

He vowed to avenge her. He gave his word that she wouldn't die for nothing. Han reached into his pocket and felt the pass that Lan gave him before she died.

"Why does he want me dead?" Han asked. "I don't even know him."

"The Judge wants you dead."

"I don't know who he is either."

"The Judge is the emperor's nephew," Yi Yi said. "No one knows where he is, only that he sends his orders through a long chain of command. His people are everywhere. Around here, the running dog is Fu Nandong. He's stationed not far from here."

"I see."

"Let's do this together, Commoner. It will be fun to capture a general and make him piss his pants before telling us anything."

"What is more fun to you, Yi Yi? Getting him to talk or making him piss his pants?"

She laughed, this time in the voice of the old woman, a deep cackle that taunted more than expressed amusement. "Half the fun is when he tells us a rehearsed set of lies, and I press the crossbow against his throat, and then he has a lot to say."

"And the other half?"

"When I press the crossbow between his legs and tell him the palace eunuchs are hiring."

Han broke a smile. He drew from his pocket the military pass that Lan gave him before taking her last breath. "This pass will get you through his military defenses."

Still hunched over, Yi Yi inspected the pass and buried it deep into her pockets. "I want this pass for the rice cakes. You can keep your coin for someone else's grandchild." She threw the coin at him, so hard that he felt every bit of her skill when he caught it.

She giggled and said, "Your rice cake is stuffed with all kinds of precious meat. Chew carefully!"

Yi Yi turned and hobbled away.

"Wait," Han called after her. "Does your shoulder still hurt?"

"It just stopped!" she said.

Han watched her from behind with a light smile and shook his head before biting into the rice cake that she gave him. There was something hard and cold inside. Then he remembered what she had just said.

She came disguised because she didn't want to be seen talking to him. That meant someone was always watching. Or did she do it for fun? Han spun around and walked away from the bridge, past the small road he came from and into a forest.

He was deep inside the woods before he pulled apart the rice cake and extracted a rectangular object wrapped in a piece of paper. Han stuffed what was left of the cake inside his mouth, chewed for a second and almost choked. It was coarse as bark, with lumps of uncooked rice flour and too much salt. At first he thought she stole it from a local woman, but no one in the village would make something so disgusting. He spat the cake onto the forest floor.

Han detected insects and birds nearby, nothing else, so he stood behind a tree and pulled apart the paper. Inside was a milky white stone, about the size of his thumb, translucent in some areas and cold to the touch. Strands of red veins flowed along the surface of the stone.

A rare blood jade. Han had never seen or even heard of one with so many blood veins on it, making it all the more precious. He could buy a city with this jade.

On the piece of paper in his other hand, a single sentence read, "This is how much your head is worth."

He rubbed the smooth surface of the jade. She didn't need the money after all. She told Old Huang that she didn't answer to the Judge. She saved his life from the Zhuge Nu.

Who was she? Why was she there?

The thought of making Fu Nandong answer for what he did continued to gnaw at him. Han flipped over the note and on the other side, written with a fine brush in very small words, were detailed instructions on how her plan would work. Han smiled. She wrote this, waited for the ink to dry, and shoved it into a rice cake. She was confident that he would cooperate with her outrageous plan. He could run away with her jade and live wealthy for the rest of his life.

No, he couldn't and she knew it. Every thug and whore was hunting him. His Shifu was murdered, and this Fu Nandong was the culprit. He had to work with her.

What would he do with himself if he didn't avenge Shifu's murder? And Lan's.

Yi Yi must have known that too. The world was large, but there was nowhere for him to go.

Han pocketed the jade and headed back to the bridge. There were many ways to die. This wouldn't be the worst of them.

CHAPTER 4

THE MOMENT BEFORE she pulled the canvas bag over his head, Han gazed into her smile, the beaming grin of a little girl, the giggles of someone who was planning a prank and could not hold back her excitement. His hands were tied in front of him and his arms were strapped with a thick rope that she had wrapped around his body again and again. Through the thin brown canvas, he could still see shadows and figures.

"Let's make a bet," she said. "I can get Fu Nandong to tell you who killed Magistrate Li."

"Magistrate Li?"

"The murder you're being blamed for. He was killed by the Infinity Palm."

"How do you know this?"

"I know everything."

"Why do you think he knows?"

"Make the bet and you'll find out."

"What do you want for the bet?"

"If I win, you don't take his life."

"Why would you keep this scumbag alive?" Han asked, his words so firm that the bag didn't muffle his voice at all.

"Because you want to kill him," Yi Yi said. "And you don't get what you want if you lose a bet."

She took his hand and led him to a horse, patted the saddle so he could hear where to mount. Han leaped onto the mount and took the stirrups. She seated herself behind him and grabbed the reins.

"The great Commoner's hands are tied and he can't see," Yi Yi said. "Willingly. Aren't you worried that this is my best chance to kill you?"

Han released a deep, heartfelt sigh. "Why do you want to kill me, Yi Yi?"

"I don't want to."

"Everyone else does."

"I don't think you deserve to die."

Han laughed, a dull chuckle with little energy behind it. "We don't have to agree on everything."

Yi Yi fell silent. "Can I dump your sword?" she asked out of nowhere.

"Why?"

"It's a training sword. It's garbage." Yi Yi tossed the sword onto the ground and kicked the horse to send it lurching forward. "Besides, the handle is just plain wood. Not a single precious stone on it."

"Why is your family so wealthy?" Han asked.

"I don't have a family. My employer…"

"Has all the money in the world," Han finished for her.

"Exactly."

The horse steadied to a rapid trot. The terrain was even and dry. There were no sounds of birds or animals nearby. The forest was behind them.

"Don't forget our bet," she said. "You don't get to kill him."

It was late afternoon and the sun was beaming through the little holes in the sack over his face.

"Do you want to hear me sing?" Yi Yi asked, breaking the silence. "You can't see and you must be bored anyway."

She began her song without waiting for his response. Her voice was haunting and distant, so different from her normal persona. She sang about a princess who was married off to a barbarian land to appease an enemy king. She never saw her home again.

Han was mesmerized, lost in a voice that was empty and dismal, and realized that behind the cheery smile and giggling jokes, the girl behind him was lonely and yearning for someone to love her.

The song ended. Han exhaled as if he had held his breath all along.

The remainder of the trip was silent, each traveler lost in their own thoughts. At some point, the horse slowed to a walk, then to a complete stop.

"What is your business here?" someone shouted from afar.

The sound of fabric and metal shuffling was followed by Yi Yi's voice, who said… "Here is my pass," she said. "I am here to claim my bounty from General Fu."

She urged the horse forward and stopped. A shadowy figure approached and asked, "Who is the bounty?"

"I will only show General Fu," Yi Yi said, pushing her horse past the figure, presumably a guard. "The prisoner is very high profile and his capture must be kept top secret."

"Wait," the guard said.

"You saw my pass," Yi Yi said, shifting her body as she drove the horse forward. "I want to put an arrow in your head, but then I'll have to explain to General Fu why I didn't order someone seven ranks below me to step aside. Could I tell him it would be fun to watch you roll back your eyes because a bolt is stuck in your brain?"

The guard gulped and stumbled away. "You're right. You have the pass. You are free to go in whenever you like."

Yi Yi rode through the entrance. A few steps later, when the guard was out of earshot, she whispered to Han. "I wish I could take the bag off your head. You should have seen his face."

"Why would I want to see a man disgraced like that?" Han asked.

"So you can make a painting of his face and sell it to some rich people."

They rode past two layers of wooden barricades, diagonal spikes protruding from the ground with the sharp end facing approaching cavalry, and into a standard military camp. Han could not see what was around him but he knew what they looked like—tents, cooking fires, archery practice, men chopping wood all day, a wide area for drills and training, a large wooden house for the general. The house would be surrounded by smaller structures for his commanders, all simple units made with materials that came with the supply wagons.

"Can I ask you something, Han?"

"Of course."

"Why haven't you asked me anything about myself?"

"I was going to ask if you ever knew your parents." Han lowered his head and hunched over. "I never knew mine."

Yi Yi was silent for a moment.

"You don't have to tell me anything," Han said.

"My employer took me in as a baby," she said. "He had me trained by the best masters. He raised me, so he is the only parent I know."

Two soldiers approached them as they passed the first row of tents, but after a brief pause Yi Yi continued forward. A few steps later, Han heard one of the soldiers whisper, "So the general has a new girl in bed tonight. That's three so far this week. This one is really pretty."

"I don't think so," the other said. "You see her crossbow? She is delivering a prisoner."

Han's face heated up. Lan fell for this General Fu. He had money and power and a different woman every night. He used her, and Han wanted to know what he used her for.

Yi Yi brought the horse to a halt, and rapid footsteps approached. "I am here to see General Fu," she said. "I have the bounty."

"You?" asked a high-pitched voice. "And who are you? Who did you capture?"

"Tell General Fu that I have the Commoner and I need to see him right away."

"You…" the soldier stalled. "That is the Commoner?" He reached for the canvas sack covering Han's head.

Han heard Yi Yi prepare her crossbow. "General Fu is paying the reward so only General Fu can see him. Go tell him I want my money."

The soldier backed away. Yi Yi pulled on Han's ropes and he dropped off the horse, pretending to struggle for a moment before she pressed the crossbow against the back of his head, pushing him forward. He heard the door of the wooden house open, the two soldiers running in, and he was ushered into a much darker space. There were shadows of at least six people in there.

Yi Yi closed the door behind them. Someone in the front of the room approached.

"I will only speak to General Fu," Yi Yi said.

"You will speak to me then," a deep male voice said. "So, what do we have here? Is that the Commoner?"

"Check for yourself," Yi Yi said.

"Pull off the sack."

Yi Yi stepped away and a soldier pulled the canvas bag off of Han's head. A gasp filled the room.

Standing in front of Han was Fu Nandong in casual military attire. The category three general was a tall man with a well-trimmed mustache, a high nose bridge and deep-set eyes. He looked foreign. There were many foreigners in China, especially in the capital, people with pale faces and strange blue eyes. Han had seen beautiful foreign women from the other end of the silk road serving expensive wine to poets and scholars in the city. But a general from outside of China was unheard of.

There were eight men in the room, including Fu Nandong. Yi Yi continued to inch away while they gathered around Han.

"Pull down his pants," Fu Nandong ordered.

Yi Yi was behind Fu Nandong then, and she clasped a white cloth over his mouth. She dragged him back without a sound, then dropped him to the floor with a thud. The soldiers turned to her. She fired, pumping the lever of her rapid-fire crossbow with incredible speed. All seven men collapsed silently with an arrow planted in each throat.

Yi Yi slashed the ropes restraining Han's wrists. "So that is Fu Nandong," he said.

"He's a pervert," she said with a pout. "He wanted to pull your pants down."

"This is the scumbag Lan fell for…" he whispered to himself.

"I have never seen a man so handsome and so unattractive," Yi Yi said. Then, with an impish smile, she held up a hand. "Let's make a bet. If you lose, I get my jade back."

Han pulled his gaze away from Fu Nandong's face. "I was going to give it back to you anyway. What are we betting this time?"

"I think he pissed his pants," she said. "If he didn't, then you keep the jade."

Han laughed. "Then I will have both my head and the jade. That's a lot of money."

He undressed while Yi Yi turned around to guard the door. He changed into one of the dead soldier's uniforms, careful to transfer everything, especially Yi Yi's milky white jade from his old pockets.

There was no urine under Fu Nandong. Han dressed the handsome general in his own cheap clothing, picked up the old rope and tied him.

"Ready," he said, lifting Fu Nandong.

Yi Yi turned around and broke into a laugh. "You don't know how to tie someone up! The rice cakes I tie with bamboo leaves look better."

Han paused, then broke into a laugh. It seemed like days had passed since he last laughed.

Han had never tied anyone up before. She was right. Most of the rope was wrapped around Fu's upper torso, pushing his clothing to a bulge under his neck that almost covered half his face. The thighs were strapped in so many layers that there was no way Fu Nandong could walk or ride on a saddle.

Yi Yi handed him her crossbow and rearranged the rope.

"How long before he wakes up?" Han asked.

"He should before sunset," she said. "We have time."

Yi Yi sent the loose rope into a flurry before strapping him like she did with Han. In a moment, Fu Nandong was restrained. Han covered his head with the same bag.

"Let's go," she said.

"Yi Yi." Han pulled the white jade from his pocket. "You won the bet."

Disappointment passed briefly over her face, then a cheery smile. She took her jade back. "You're such a bad liar."

"What do you mean?"

"Let's go," she said, lifting Fu Nandong to an upright position. The general was able to stand.

"He's not really unconscious?" Han asked.

"Just dizzy and confused," she said. "We need him to walk."

Han picked up a standard saber carried by foot soldiers and opened the door. They hustled Fu Nandong out into the late afternoon sun, their horse a few steps away. Han threw him onto the saddle, slipped the general's boots into the stirrups and leaned him against the mane. Yi Yi sat behind him to control the reins. Han walked next to her saddle and they pushed toward the exit.

The entire size and breadth of the camp was a daunting image of power and abundance. It was situated in a deep canyon surrounded by distant cliffs, built on barren, rocky terrain.

Men were everywhere. Some were next to their cooking fires. Some were polishing their armor and sharpening their sabers, while others were lying around doing nothing. Han could not count how many tents and campfires surrounded him but they extended all the way to the edge of the canyon. Twenty thousand men could be stationed here.

The Judge was hiding one of his armies in a valley, surrounded by vertical mountains that few would ever scale. Why would he keep so many men so close to the northern borders guarded by Tiger Generals?

"Who is this Judge?" Han asked. "Why does he have a massive army stationed in the middle of nowhere?"

"I heard he has two hundred thousand men," Yi Yi said. "And no one even knows where they are."

"Is that possible?"

Two guards, dressed in the same uniform as Han, approached. "Why is the prisoner leaving?"

"Under General Fu's orders," Yi Yi said, showing her pass again. "This is not the right man, so he must return alive. We are escorting him back to where he came from."

"This way to the exit," one of them said.

In a moment, the wooden gates were behind them and Han breathed a sigh of relief. He had been peerless in battle for many years, but facing an army that size was unthinkable.

As soon as they turned a bend in the road, circling a rocky hill that reached the height of many men, Han bolted for a side road while Yi Yi kicked the horse into a full gallop. There was another horse tied to a boulder, waiting impatiently for him. Han leaped onto the horse from behind, drew his weapon and slashed the restraining rope. He smacked the horse's butt with the flat of his saber and the horse lurched forward. Han hurried to catch up to Yi Yi.

Neck to neck they rode, passing the rocky terrain the camp was built on, leaving the mouth of the valley far behind them before heading into dry, grassy meadows. The horses ran across a small river and entered an area of lush greens and sweeping hills dotted with tall trees and heavy bushes.

The horses slowed. "The scouts should be right behind us," Han said. "They must have realized by now that his men are dead and he is missing."

"It's up that hill," Yi Yi said, pointing to a tiny structure sitting alone on a patch of well-trimmed grass.

Han urged his horse forward. "They can pick up our tracks after the river."

"We'll lose the horses here," Yi Yi said. "They'll follow the tracks and that'll buy us some time."

Yi Yi grabbed Fu Nandong's belt and tossed him behind a bush at the foot of the hill. She smacked her horse and leaped off, sending it forward without a rider. Han did the same, and they both landed behind the tall bush where Fu Nandong was squirming. He was awake and groaning.

Han threw Fu Nandong over his shoulder and charged up the slope. His baggage was heavy but his energy was deep. In a moment, he was at the mouth of the little structure. Yi Yi was right behind him.

"What is this place?" he asked as he lay Fu Nandong on the ground. The hill was barren, and almost at the top, sitting on a stretch of soft soil and sweeping grass, was a little cement house with no windows and a porcelain roof painted in a delicate red. The heavy door in the middle of the structure's frontal wall was partially closed. There was no light inside.

Yi Yi drew open the door to reveal a small room that couldn't fit eight people lying down. At the end of the room was a little statue on the floor.

"It's a temple for the Earth Deity," Yi Yi said, dragging Fu Nandong's squirming body inside. She placed him against a side wall, lit a small candle in front of the statue, and pulled the doors closed. The room was dark except for the flame.

Yi Yi yanked the canvas bag from Fu Nandong's head and smacked him. "Wake up. It's time for breakfast."

The small flame danced on the candle and cast uneven shadows around the room. Fu Nandong tried to open his eyes, but after a weak attempt, he closed them and leaned back against the wall.

Yi Yi smacked him again. "Wake up! You're about to die!"

Fu Nandong jolted. He squinted, turning first to Yi Yi, then to Han. He lifted a crooked finger and pointed. "Aren't you… Aren't you the Commoner?"

"So you are Fu Nandong," Han said, with deep contempt in his voice. "And you must know Zuo Lan."

"Who?" Fu Nandong thought for a moment, then flung his wrist as if a mosquito had just flown by. "Oh, Lan! I stopped sleeping with her a long time ago. She wasn't even that good."

Han tensed, his energy coursing through his veins and into his palm. Yi Yi touched his arm. Han exhaled.

"And who are you, pretty lady?" Fu Nandong asked Yi Yi. "Why are you standing next to this criminal? Do you know how much money I can offer you for his head?"

"It's a decent-looking head but it's not worth that much," Yi Yi said.

"Why did you order Master Zuo's death?" Han asked.

"Who?" Fu Nandong shook his head. "Where am I? Take me back now before I have you executed in public."

Han kicked him in the face. His head snapped back and slammed against the wall, but his hands flew to his mouth. Blood trickled between his fingers onto his lap. Two of his teeth dropped through his cupped hands.

"What did you do to me? How dare you!"

Yi Yi elbowed Han with a cheeky grin. "It's pretty hard to attract women if you have no front teeth."

Fu Nandong howled and screamed. Han jabbed his throat with a finger and Fu Nandong doubled over, choking and gurgling and spitting out the blood he lost with his teeth.

"No one can hear you from here," Han said in a hoarse whisper. "Answer our questions and you might make it home alive."

Fu Nandong's screams reduced to a whimper. Yi Yi lifted her crossbow and pressed it into his groin. "You don't need this. You have no teeth. The pretty ladies won't be coming to you anymore."

Fu Nandong was sobbing, shaking. He still held a hand over his bleeding mouth. "What do you want from me? What do you want to know?"

"Why did you order Master Zuo's death?" Yi Yi echoed.

"I don't know," Fu Nandong said. "He found out what the Red Crest meant so he had to go."

"How?" Han asked.

"He received some letter from a freak. It told him what the Red Crest is."

"And what does the Red Crest mean?" Han asked.

"Who knows? He read the letter and burned it. I didn't read it."

"You murdered your lover's father for that?"

Fu Nandong leaned back laughing, the gaping hole in his mouth still dripping blood. "What lover? You mean Lan? I only slept with her to find out whether you really had the Red Crest or not."

"The Red Crest?" Han lurched forward, then checked himself.

"Hey, who is the pervert?" Fu Nandong said, jeering. "She was the one who watched you bathe."

"What…" Han could not find his words.

"What does that have to do with anything?" Yi Yi finished his question for him.

"The symbol," Fu Nandong said. "The symbol on your butt. You didn't know that's the Red Crest? Why do you think everyone wants you dead?"

Han's eyes were bloodshot, his lips quivering. He had this birthmark all his life and he had never thought about what it was. He thought of how Lan died. Her final words expressed remorse for seeing the symbol on him, and telling Fu Nandong.

If what this scumbag said was true, then the birthmark on his body led to the deaths of Master Zuo, Lan, and the entire Zuo clan. It brought endless threats to his own life.

Even Yi Yi was speechless. She stepped back, her crossbow now hanging at her side, and she leaned against the opposite wall.

"How did you know to seduce her?" Han asked, calmer now. "How did you know that I might have this birthmark?"

Fu Nandong shrugged his shoulders. "The Judge gave the order. I don't know how he knew. All he said was that someone in the Zuo Clan has the Red Crest, and he ordered us to find out who. Turns out she watched you bathe some years ago and she saw it."

"The person with the Red Crest has to die?" Han asked.

Yi Yi placed a hand on Han's arm and whispered into his ear. "Master Zuo found out what the symbol meant right before he died. We need to find that messenger."

"She wasn't very good in bed," Fu Nandong continued. "But I made her a lot of promises and she believed every word of it, just like the rest of them."

"The rest of them?" Han asked. "Someone else you held in your arms? Another woman who trusted you? Maybe they need to see you castrated without your front teeth. Who else did you do this to?"

Fu Nandong laughed and brushed the comment away. "Who else? I don't keep track of who they are. Some live, some don't. Like the cute one with the old husband. I was assigned to sleep with her and I heard they killed her too. So what?"

There was a shout outside. Both Han and Yi Yi failed to detect the men on the hill, so bewildered by what Fu Nandong was saying that neither paid attention to the scouts approaching their location. Han reached out in alarm, but it was too late. Fu Nandong lifted his face and screamed, "Help!"

Yi Yi kicked through the doors and fired at the oncoming men as they swarmed in. Han drew his saber and pinned Fu Nandong to his position against the wall. Yi Yi leaped all the way back to the statue of the earth deity, firing again and again. Two men entered the temple but fell to her arrows. At least six others died outside. None of them had time to scream. All of them were killed by a single bolt to the throat.

Han lowered the saber. "Are you hurt?"

"Of course not. Who do you think I am?" Yi Yi asked, her expression dark and cold. Han stepped back.

She stuck her tongue out and made a silly face, giggling.

Han laughed. He sensed light movement behind him, but when he spun around, Fu Nandong had already retrieved a bamboo whistle from one of the dead bodies. He blew it loudly once before Han smacked it away from him. Fu Nandong sat back laughing.

"At least a thousand men are coming for me now," Fu Nandong said. "See how you survive this, Commoner." He turned to Yi Yi. "But I won't kill this one. I haven't had one this pretty in a long time."

Yi Yi pointed her crossbow at him.

"Wait," Han said.

"We need to leave," she said. "We can't fight a thousand men."

"I'm not done questioning him," Han said. "Let me chase the enemy away, and then we will resume."

"You're going to chase off an army?" she scoffed. "The Commoner can fight a thousand men?"

Han grabbed the candle from the incense holder with a smile, spun around and walked out of the temple.

Fu Nandong broke into a laugh. "If you give up now, I won't sleep with your beautiful archer. Otherwise, I will have my fun for a full month before she gets to die with you. Last chance for a deal!"

Yi Yi stepped forward and crouched down next to Fu Nandong, whispering into his ear.

Han waited outside. He heard Fu Nandong moaning and grunting. He wasn't sure what Yi Yi was doing to him, but he trusted her. After today, it felt good to trust someone again.

A swarm of soldiers, all dressed like him with heavy sabers in hand, assumed their formations at the bottom of the hill. There were at least a thousand men, if not more. He waited for them to gather, watching for archers and javelin throwers, even though no one could throw a spear that far up the hill.

Han waited. They were watching him as well, a single man standing outside a tiny temple, staring down an army.

Someone shouted an order. The men charged.

Han ignited one of the smoke signals he took from Lai and pointed it above the advancing troops. A stream of black smoke, as pure as it was dark, shot into the air with a burst. Then another, and another, until the bamboo tube was depleted. The black smoke expanded high in the sky, hovering over the army below the hill.

Then, shouts, screams, cries for help all swarmed the hill at once. There was little time to run. The thousand soldiers found themselves retreating in panic, stepping over each other and rolling off the hill.

Once Han returned to the temple, Yi Yi pulled the door shut

while Fu Nandong curled in his original spot, his head held between his hands.

"Why do you have our smoke signal?" Fu Nandong asked. "How do you know about it?"

Yi Yi stood with arms crossed, a mischievous smile on her face. "You lost the bet!"

"Which bet?" Han asked. "We have so many."

"He slept with Magistrate Li's wife to steal the map to Willow Island," Yi Yi said. "Someone named the Teacher killed the magistrate so you would take the blame."

"Willow Island," Han said. He could still hear the thousands of footsteps retreating. "What do you know about Willow Island?"

Outside, the sharp whistle of incoming arrows screeched through the air. Han waited. The arrows pounded the hill, the cement walls, the heavy wooden door of the little temple. The structure didn't have windows and the thick cement was impenetrable, but the sound of arrows striking the door felt like the rapid beating of twenty war drums. In a moment, the rain was over.

"No one's coming to save you," Han said. "The Zhuge Nu fired at this hill and your men won't be back to try again. Tell me why Willow Island is important and I will let you out alive."

Yi Yi giggled. Han lost the bet, so he could not kill Fu Nandong anyway.

Fu Nandong looked ready to cry. The fresh blood dripping from his lower mouth made his face ghastly against the flickering candlelight.

"Tell me about Willow Island," Han said. He crouched down in front of his prisoner. "One day, many years from now, you will be drinking with your friends under the moon, when all these wars are over and everyone is busy writing poetry and painting silk scrolls, and you will think back at this moment and laugh. You will laugh at how easy it was to get out of this alive. You just have to answer a few questions. No one will ever know what you told us."

Fu Nandong hesitated, the rapid-fire crossbow still pointed at him. "What do you want to know?"

"You said you slept with someone for a map to Willow Island," Han began.

"That's right, some young wife of a magistrate. He was guarding the map with his life. I heard the previous emperor gave it to him for safekeeping. I promised to marry that little whore if she got the map for me and she did."

"Why did you want the map?" Han asked.

"The Judge wanted it."

"Why?" Han asked again.

"I don't know. I've never even met the Judge. No one knows where he is."

"Then who did you give the map to if you've never met the Judge?" Yi Yi asked.

"The Teacher," Fu Nandong said. "The Teacher handles everything for the Judge. There. I don't know anymore."

Han grabbed his wrist and twisted it. Fu Nandong screamed. Ligaments in his arm started to crack.

"I don't know anymore," he shouted, howling and gasping. "I told you everything. Why did you do that?"

"Then tell me how to find this Teacher," Han said through short hisses of air. "Tell me so I can break his wrists just like this."

Fu Nandong froze, his large eyes frozen in a blank, incredulous look. Then he doubled over bawling.

"What's funny?" Han asked.

"Break the Teacher's wrists?" Fu Nandong said through choked howls. "You are insane. Completely out of your mind. Do you know how powerful the Teacher is? He's impossible to kill! And his student Cut Foot is the fastest man in the world. You think you're the greatest warrior to ever live? The Teacher will mop the floor with your balls."

Yi Yi crouched down next to him. "Excellent idea." She planted the mouth of the crossbow against his groin.

"Wait!" Fu Nandong screamed. "Wait! Why?" He pointed at Han. "He said I could go if I answered his questions."

Yi Yi reached for the lever on her weapon.

"The Teacher killed that magistrate and I forced his wife to blame the Commoner for it," he said, his voice reaching a higher pitch. "We didn't have enough people to hunt the Red Crest. We needed the Martial Society involved. Fake letter from the Silencer and they almost caught him."

"I know about that," Han said. "The last words Lady Li said to me before she died were Willow Island. Her husband guarded the map to this place. Why is it so important to the Judge?"

"I don't know. There's a big secret there, maybe." Fu Nandong was still glaring at Yi Yi, inching away from her crossbow. She pressed it harder and he screamed. "No! No! I don't know what it is. All I know is the Judge went there with a few men, and he came back empty-handed. No riches or anything. But once he came back, he had full authority to command the Zhuge Nu and the spy network in the country, and he seemed to have all the money in the world. Even the emperor did everything the Judge wanted."

"The emperor did everything the Judge wanted?" Yi Yi asked, her words slow and deliberate.

Fu Nandong was trembling and spat words rapidly. "Yes. He came back. Within a few days, he took charge and now he is going to attack the Tiger Generals."

"Why the Tiger Generals?" Han whispered.

"I don't know. I really, really don't know!" He was sobbing, the tears, blood, sweat trickling down his face all at once.

Yi Yi withdrew the crossbow. "Now that the Martial Society and the Zhuge Nu have failed, what is the plan to kill the Commoner?"

"Send in the emperor's personal bodyguard," Fu Nandong said in a raspy voice, between gasps for air. "Now there's someone good enough to kill the Commoner."

"Really?" Yi Yi asked, raising her voice. "You will simply summon the emperor's bodyguard and he will come do your bidding?"

"No. The Teacher has an imperial decree. The emperor gave the order himself."

Yi Yi pressed the crossbow deeper and reached for the lever. Fu Nandong held up both hands. "Wait! He said I can go if I answered his questions."

"He may release you but I won't," Yi Yi said. "Where is the map?" She pushed the butt of her weapon against Fu Nandong's groin. He screamed.

"I don't know where it is," Fu Nandong whimpered. "I gave it to the Teacher and that's it."

"Where is it?" she asked, her voice raised, almost shouting in his face. "Where is this Teacher?"

"I don't know," he said, panting for air. "Honest! I don't know."

"Then I will castrate you now," she said.

"No! No!" Fu Nandong screeched.

"Wait," Han whispered.

"I have it!" Fu Nandong said. "I have it on me!"

Yi Yi pulled the lever on her crossbow.

Nothing happened. Yi Yi stood back, dumped the cartridge on the top of her weapon and reloaded. A pool of urine oozed onto the floor.

"You're not supposed to piss in front of the Earth Deity," Yi Yi said. "Now you are cursed and you will never have children again."

Fu Nandong curled against the floor, sobbing, trembling.

Han held out his hand. "The map."

Fu Nandong reached deep inside his inner clothing and pulled out a coarse piece of canvas, grayed with age and tattered. He held it with an outstretched hand, his face turned, still sobbing.

Han ripped the cloth from his hand and shook it open. It was a map drawn in fine detail with black ink, the names of every road and nearby village carefully labeled.

The lower-left corner of the map read, "Willow Lake," and just above those words was a small circle drawn in light ink: "Willow Island."

The map resembled an ancient painting, where rivers, mountains, and lakes were painted in detail and labeled. On the back of the map was a single line of text:

Endowed by Emperor Li Wen.

The previous emperor's stamp glared underneath it. Han folded the map, first in a symmetrical half, then another. For the previous emperor to entrust a local magistrate, one so far from the capital, to guard this map meant that something very important, or something terrible was on Willow Lake. The Judge knew what it was. He most likely took possession of it.

"Let's go," Yi Yi said, taking the map from him. "His men will be back anytime." She drew open the door. The beaming rays of the approaching sunset flooded the little space. Outside, the ground was littered with Zhuge Nu bolts planted into hard soil.

Yi Yi picked up a bolt from the ground. "These are different from mine," she said. "There's a separate attachment on the front. I wonder what it is."

Han stepped outside, then turned around once to Fu Nandong. "You are not Chinese. Where are you from?"

"Turkic Khaganate," he said, his voice shaking.

"Turks from the other end of the Silk Road?" Han asked.

Fu Nandong nodded.

"Aren't you pale-faced foreigners supposed to have blue eyes?"

"That's… that's much farther West," Fu Nandong said.

Yi Yi took Han's hand and pulled him away. "Let's go."

CHAPTER 5

THE SUN WAS setting. Golden rays flooded the lush hills, and the swaying tree branches brought a sense of calm to a land covered with Zhuge Nu bolts.

Han descended the hill with Yi Yi beside him, lost in thought. The Judge had a massive army inside the nation's borders and no one knew who he wanted war with. He was after the four Tiger Generals guarding the northern border.

Han was not a military man, but he did befriend one of the Tiger Generals. General Yang guarded the border against Mongolia. Han visited his fortress once. They wrote poetry, painted silk scrolls and talked about martial arts for weeks.

General Yang was a powerful martial artist and a seasoned general in command of fifty thousand men. The training and coordination among his men were seamless. For this Judge to attack such a capable general would require an unthinkable plot. Han worried. Maybe he should go and help Yang defend his city.

The immediate questions surrounding Willow Island and the person who sent the letter, Little Sparrow, swarmed Han's head. But he didn't want to know anymore. Nothing seemed to matter that much after Lan and Master Zuo were killed.

It was official. Chen Han the wandering poet no longer had a home.

"You are such a statue," Yi Yi said with a giggle.

Han broke from his train of thoughts. "A statue?"

"That's you," Yi Yi said. "But some statues aren't as boring."

They were walking through a lush forest. The sun was almost gone, and the heavens were darkening.

Yi Yi reached into her pocket and pulled out the map, opened it with one hand and studied every inch before turning it over for the late emperor's stamp. She touched her finger to the stamp and caressed it. "We need to know what the Judge found there if we have any chance of stopping him."

"Why?"

"Why stop the Judge?" she asked.

"Why not live like fairies on a boat instead?"

"Do you have one?"

"I'm building one."

"Really? Where?"

"West Sea."

"I've heard of it," Yi Yi said. "A lake so big it became a sea."

"Not a real sea," Han said with a laugh. "It's still fresh water."

"I wonder if I will ever get to see your boat," she said.

Han was silent then. This girl meant many things to him, despite having met her just a day ago. Somehow, he felt a closeness he could not explain. She wanted him to invite her to West Sea. For a moment, he didn't know how to respond.

"Your boat is not ready," she said, breaking the awkward silence.

Han was elated and frightened at the same time. She wanted to be on his boat when it was ready. So much more would happen before his boat could be built.

"The Judge is plotting to take over the country," Yi Yi said. "Why does he have a secret army of two hundred thousand men, and who does he plan on going to war with? To kill the Tiger Generals so no one can stop him?"

"I came to find out why I was blamed for the magistrate's murder," Han said. "And why everyone is hunting me. Now I know. And it's not that interesting. It's time to go home and finish my boat. No one wants me here anyway, and I don't care who sits on the throne."

"You should," she said. Her voice, losing its strength, fell into a whisper. "Han, when you traveled north to the Zuo Mansions, did you see bodies on the road, mowed down by thousands of arrows?"

"I did."

"Innocent civilians?" she asked. "Someone reported that Target One was among them and they were all killed. But it didn't matter whether Target One was there. It didn't matter to the Judge if hundreds or thousands of innocents died, as long as he killed the one he wanted."

"Who is Target One?" Han asked. The image of dead women and children, their fronts, backs, arms and legs covered with arrows, little boys with bolts jutting from their lifeless cheeks, infants pinned to their mother's bosoms, men with their trousers pulled back, played over and over in his mind.

Han sucked in his breath, his heart pounding so hard it threatened to bruise his ribcage. When Fu Nandong thought he had captured Han, he also ordered his men to pull down his pants.

"Who is Target One?" he whispered.

"They were looking for the man with the Red Crest, Han. Target One is you." Yi Yi took his hand and pulled him closer. "While you hide on a boat in West Sea, the Zhuge Nu will continue to scour the land for you. They will shoot civilians at every rumor that you are among them. If we don't stop the Judge, this will never end."

Shaking his head, Han wrenched his hand from her grip and took a step back. "Why?" he whispered. "Why me?"

"Han, you cannot hide," Yi Yi said. "Too many people will die if you do."

Han backed into a giant tree, planted himself and stiffened. "I'm a wandering poet," he said. "I drink, I fall asleep under the stars, I wake up trying to remember the poem I came up with. I am…"

"The world-famous Commoner," Yi Yi finished for him, stepping forward to take his hand again. "The greatest warrior in the world with a map to Willow Island. The Judge's secret is there. We have to do this together. We hold a responsibility larger than our lives, larger than the throne. It's a responsibility to the people."

Han could not meet her gaze. He turned to the forest floor. Nothing seemed real anymore. He had caused all this pain and suffering. Yet he did not. If he gave himself up to the Judge, would that change anything?

No one takes the Commoner's head without a good fight.

"Willow Island," he said. "The Teacher may be right behind us when Fu Nandong reports that we took his map."

Yi Yi exhaled in relief. "It's not far from here," she said, folding the map. "He won't be faster than us. We can be there by dawn if we rent a carriage with four horses and a driver."

"I don't think so."

"Do you want to make a bet?"

Han shook his head. This woman was always trying to win something, even though she seemed to have everything. A wager for the smallest bragging rights to a jade worth the price of a city, she didn't seem to care.

But then, neither did he.

"Sure," he said. "What do you want to bet?"

"If we get to Willow Lake by dawn, you have to tell me another story about yourself," she said.

"Sure."

"You're not going to ask what you get if you win?"

"You decide."

Yi Yi giggled, then threw her head back to laugh, so hard she held her belly and doubled over. "You get to hear me sing again!"

"Then I must, must win."

Yi Yi stopped laughing then, looking almost embarrassed. She drew her crossbow closer to her side. "You haven't been very good with bets. You lost the last bet a little late, but you still lost. I got him to piss his pants."

"I lost that one," Han agreed.

She passed him a stealing glance, then turned her attention back to the forest path. "You are such a bad liar. He didn't piss his pants the first time. Everyone knows, he couldn't have pissed after being drugged."

"Then why did you bet me?"

She cleared her throat and said with her eyes cast down, "I gave the jade to you. I wanted you to keep it." Then with a giggle she turned back to Han and brushed her finger across the tip of his nose. "And you lied because you wanted me to have it."

Han smiled. "It's worth too much."

"Not too much. Only as much as your head."

CHAPTER 6

THE COACH THEY chartered was an old carriage on the last years of its life, but there was nothing else available in the middle of the night. The driver, a short man with a bald head and beady eyes, cursed and spat at them for knocking on his door at that hour, despite the military saber on Han's belt and the rapid-fire crossbow in Yi Yi's hand. Yi Yi showed him a gold coin and he swallowed his words.

The horses were as old as the carriage. Yi Yi paid another coin for all four to pull the carriage together. They managed a brisk walk.

Han sat in the cabin, half leaning against the wall, facing Yi Yi from across the floor. There were no seats built into the simple carriage, but it was a luxury for him to be driven at all.

"I need to see that map again!" the driver shouted from the front of the carriage. It was an enclosed coach, with a little square window on either side and one rectangular gap facing the horses that was big enough for the driver to crawl through.

Yi Yi handed him the map. "Make sure you give it right back."

"Why?" he hollered. "What's so special about this lake?" He held his oil lantern closer, muttering to himself, before throwing the map back into the cabin. "Here's your map you crazy bitch."

"Why did you call her that?" Han asked.

"She's going to Willow Lake that's why. Who the hell goes there? They don't even have fish in that lake."

Yi Yi stuffed the map into her pocket. "He's angry because his wife left him and his only lover is the mare he is whipping."

"Go to hell!" the driver shouted. "My wife is home sleeping like I should be. If I didn't need the money, I would tell you to walk."

Yi Yi giggled and grabbed a flask hanging from her belt. "Can you drink more than me?"

Han wanted to shrug his shoulder and ask her why it mattered. But there was something about the twinkle in her eyes, the mischievous smile, the haughty body language, as if she dared him to say that he could, even though the answer was very clear. She wanted another bet.

"You are not my match this time, Yi Yi," he said. "When it comes to drinking, don't even try."

She stuck out her tongue and unplugged the cork, inhaled the scent with a deep, lingering smile, and tilted her head back to drink. After several gulps, she exhaled. "I always win."

Han was in disbelief. She was so certain of herself, so driven to stop the Judge, but yet she was having fun. He knew nothing about her, yet he felt drawn to her beyond his control. He trusted her with his life because he was certain that she wanted neither his life nor a profit.

Han took the flask from her and sipped on the heavenly drink. "We're on another adventure together, and I still don't know anything about you."

"Now there's an arrogant statement," she said.

"I don't understand."

"I'm on an adventure with you," Yi Yi said. "But I know everything about you because you are world famous. That's why you get to complain. I am not famous enough for you to know anything."

"That's not what I meant."

"Prove it," Yi Yi said. "Tell me something I don't know about you."

Han laughed. This woman always found ways to make him talk. And he thought he never held secrets.

But there was always something a man would not talk about, even when he was drunk.

"My first poem was a love poem," he said. "I never sold it. The rich people in the capital thought it was the worst poem they ever read."

"Do you remember it?" she asked. "Maybe I will buy it if it's silly enough."

"I will never forget it," Han said. He recited from memory:

I have cringed at your deformed nose,
And flinched from your bulging eyes,
I have winced from your disfigured smile,
And quivered from your eerie whisper.

Yet I sought comfort in that twisted nose,
And found life from the piercing eyes,
I've drawn hope from the crooked smile,
And held desire in that hellish voice.

The world taunts me for loving you,
You are the most beautiful woman to me.

Yi Yi stared at the floor. It was the driver who broke the silence.

"You people are so uneducated," he barked. "Who the hell writes poems that bad?"

Han laughed and picked up her flask again. "The real reason poetry exists is to have something to say while getting drunk."

Yi Yi grabbed her flask, tilted her head back and poured the liquor into her mouth, finishing it in one long gulp. She swayed a little when she threw the empty vessel aside.

Then, she handed something to Han. "I can't forget your poem. Now I have to buy it from you."

She gave him something cold and smooth, a snuff bottle made of clear jade with an intricate bamboo forest painted on the inside, easily worth as much as his head. Where did she acquire so many fine things? Maybe she stole them.

"I'll lose it back to you in a bet, tomorrow at the latest."

She giggled. "You shouldn't bet me anymore."

The carriage halted.

"What is it?" Yi Yi asked.

"Another forked road!" the driver shouted. "What do you, expect me to remember every detail on that little map of yours? Just give it to me. It's not like I will keep it. There are no treasures in Willow Lake, just ghosts."

Yi Yi reached through the opening in front and handed him the map again. "Don't lose it."

"You're joking, right?"

The carriage shortly veered into a sharp left turn, straightened and picked up pace again. Yi Yi returned to her original position, her long legs folded in front of her to support her arms.

"Your turn to tell me your story," Han said.

"Me? I… I don't have a story. I have a boring life. I just carry a crossbow and stand around protecting my employer every day, but I never get to shoot anyone. Why would you be interested in my story?"

Han gazed into her lovely face, mesmerized by the power hidden behind the innocence, the intelligence obscured by silly giggles, the woman behind the warrior. "I will make a painting of you after all this is over, and it will be so beautiful that the emperor will take notice and hang it in his palace."

"Really?" she asked, her lips parted in amazement. "Do you think I am beautiful?"

"Of course you are," Han whispered. "All these years and no one told you?"

The carriage slowed, but Han and Yi Yi didn't notice. The old horses were becoming tired, and the driver was hunched over, not controlling the reins or urging them to move faster. He was bored as well.

"I didn't come out here to kill you," Yi Yi said. "You're impossible to kill anyway."

"I wish that were true."

"I came to find out what the Judge is doing here."

"Why?"

"He was bullying my employer," she said with a pout. "And now I know he is killing civilians and framing you to get you killed too. What does he want? What is he trying to do?"

"Let's hope the answer is on Willow Island."

"The answer is in the Red Crest," she said. "There's something special about you, so special the Judge wants you dead at all costs. Don't you want to know what it is?"

Han shook his head. "I don't."

"How can you not?"

"What would it matter?" Han asked. "Maybe my real parents were criminals or traitors, or maybe they were warlords from some faraway land who threatened the empire. I would still live the same way. I would wander the world or live on my boat far away from mankind's politics." Han turned away with a sigh. "If thousands of people attend my funeral, my life will have been a failure. If I pass without anyone knowing where I've gone, I will have lived a good life."

"Would I be allowed to know where you've wandered off to?" Yi Yi asked.

"If you want," he said, lowering his head, afraid but excited at the same time. It was time to tell her that he was interested too. "You can wander with me. If you want."

Yi Yi, beaming with joy, made a face at him. "That's the only way my life won't be boring. Because you're such a statue it makes me bouncy."

The carriage slowed almost to a stop.

Han and Yi Yi laughed, both shaking their heads.

"I think the horses are older than you," Yi Yi shouted to the front of the carriage.

"You shut up!" the driver said. "You try walking all night without resting. They're supposed to be asleep right now, just like I should be sleeping."

"The animals need water and rest," Han said. "We have time."

"The Teacher may get there before us."

"Then we will have to beat him up," Han said with a smile.

"Says the world's greatest warrior."

Han peered through the little window on the side of the cabin and pointed. "There's light up there."

"I know that place," the driver said. "It's a noodle shop. I can get water for my horses up there."

At the mention of noodles, Han realized he had been drinking on an empty stomach. Something about being with Yi Yi made him yearn for food again.

Yi Yi read his mind. "Let's go eat."

The driver pushed his tired old horses to take another step, then another. They drew close to the outdoor noodle shop.

"We can walk faster," Yi Yi said. "Let's go." She pushed the rear door open, picked up her crossbow, and leaped out of the cabin. Han followed.

The noodle shop stood on a hill, lit by multiple lanterns hanging from the beams that supported the tent covering the kitchen. The wooden tables sat under the sky, but it was the middle of a dry season, so the benches were clean and dry. There were no other customers at this time of night.

Yi Yi hopped onto a bench. "I want hand-cut noodles with roast quail and bamboo shoots, no scallions," she said to Han.

Han sat down in front of her. He unhooked the saber from his belt and placed it on the table.

The server came forward with a greasy cloth on his shoulder. He wiped the table, set two porcelain cups in front of them, and ladled some water into each cup from a bucket. He pointed to a sign hanging from the tent. "We have dried pork and pickled vegetables. No one makes roast quail at noodle stands except in the capital," he said before walking away.

Yi Yi made a face at him and cleared her throat to shout something, but he had already returned with a bowl of noodles in each hand.

"Cold noodles," Han said, rubbing his hands together.

The server propped the bowls on the table and dropped two pairs of chopsticks between them. "Pay before you leave," he said.

The carriage arrived just below the hill and the driver pulled the reins to stop the exhausted horses. He hopped off to retrieve the wooden pails hanging under the carriage.

Two boys trudged up the hill behind Yi Yi. They were dressed in tatters, their shoes ripped, and each carried a worn cloth bag.

"Get away, you bunch of little maggots!" the server shouted from inside the tent, his voice hoarse at the very sight of them. He waved his fist in a threatening posture.

The two boys ignored him and approached the table. They were fifteen or sixteen years old, with clean hands and hair well tied, despite their poverty. They stopped and stood next to the two bowls of noodles.

"Do you need to eat?" Han asked.

"Noodles!" one boy shouted. He was the taller one, and he held his hands together in a deep bow.

Yi Yi waved at the server. "Two more bowls of noodles, please!"

Han laughed. "You haven't seen a beggar eat, have you?" He turned to the server and shouted, "Make that four."

"Wow!" the smaller boy shouted. They started to jump up and down, screaming. "Thank you! Thank you!" the taller one said. They shouted their thanks in unison with exaggerated body language. One tried to hug Han while the other pushed close to Yi Yi and bowed over and over again, shouting, "Thank you heroes! Thank you!"

Their simultaneous shouts drowned out the other sounds around them.

Han leaped to his feet in alarm. He shoved aside the taller boy, sending him reeling back, and charged down the hill. Yi Yi grabbed her crossbow and followed. The boys continued screaming from behind, scampering after them on the soft soil, not at all interested in the food anymore. Han felt disgusted with himself. How could he be so careless?

It was too late. The driver lay dead next to the horses, his throat slit from ear to ear, a pool of blood expanding on the ground underneath his drenched collar.

"Why would…" Han began.

"The map!" Yi Yi said. She tore open the driver's pocket, shredding the thin cloth around the dead man's robe. The map was not there. Han swept the driver's seat and searched underneath the carriage. There was nothing.

"Who could have passed by and killed him without us noticing?" Yi Yi asked.

"Cut Foot," Han said.

One of the four old horses snorted, uttered a low cry, and collapsed. Some lay still, a couple kicked and struggled, but one by one the horses all fell.

"What's happening?" Han whispered.

Yi Yi stood next to him. "Someone did something to them."

The horses were not foaming at the mouth out of fatigue, they were vomiting blood.

"They weren't slowing down because they were old and tired," Yi Yi said. "Someone was poisoning them along the way. Someone was following us and we didn't even know."

There was a light rustle on the hill across from them, so small that it could've been a rodent running out of a bush. But Han knew what he heard. He shot forward to pursue the fleeing human figure.

Just over the hill was a sharp descent, followed by an open plain with wheat fields and flowing water. Beyond that lay a small village. There was a single visible light coming from the small clusters of houses, a hidden, flickering light brighter than the moon.

A campfire! An open flame at this time of night, in the middle of a peaceful village, could not be innocent. It could only mean one thing. Cut Foot came prepared to destroy what he just stole.

Han tore through the wheat fields in front of the village. Cut Foot was even faster than Han, and he would reach the flames with ample time to burn the map. Yi Yi was chasing from behind with one of the boys caught in her clutches and screaming all kinds of profanity while she dragged him through the fields. Her long-range weapon would make up for the distance.

Han surged forward, cutting through thick reeds and tumbling onto the wet roads that led into the village. He dashed through a courtyard between two rows of cement houses until he stood face to face with a lanky man about the same age as himself, who wore a short mustache and was dressed in black.

"Cut Foot," Han said.

The man smiled. Behind him was the campfire, and something was crackling on the pile of wood, in the center of the licking yellow flames. Han was too late.

Han had no choice but to attack. He needed to save the map; he needed answers. He struck Cut Foot with the Infinity Palm, a complex, harrowing set of palm strikes that collapsed on his opponent all at once. Cut Foot sucked in his breath and retreated as fast as he could. Han pressed him so he wouldn't have time to think. Cut Foot fought harder, slipping back left and right in bursts of withdrawal, changing angles and coping with the full force of the Commoner. Finally, Han shoved him into a narrow road leading out of the village.

Han pulled back and returned to the campfire. The map was burnt. He kicked the wood, the flames, sending charred cinders streaking into the air, freeing the edges of the map that were still intact.

Cut Foot approached but Han ignored him. He knew what would happen next.

Three arrows hissed past him, as silent as arrows could fly, but so loud that the space could not contain Yi Yi's presence. Cut Foot pivoted and shifted away from the onslaught.

Yi Yi was upon him, firing as rapidly as her metal crossbow would permit. Her target was retreating in multiple angles, changing direction at will and avoiding her onslaught. He wasn't her match, but like Han, she could not close the distance with him either.

Han grabbed what was left of the map from the ground. There

was hardly any ink on it. The center of the map was gone, burnt to ash, and the remaining corners were meaningless.

Yi Yi dumped her cartridge and reloaded, firing at Cut Foot in strange alternating rhythms, hoping to catch him in an unplanned retreat. But the master of stealth moved with equal irregularity, shimmering left and right, running backwards at incredible speeds. Before long he fled the village and faded into the forest. Yi Yi chased.

They disappeared, and the village remained as quiet as before. Not a stir arose from outside the wheat fields.

The map was gone. Even if Yi Yi captured Cut Foot, they would never be able to coerce him into leading them to Willow Island. They were far into the western territories, where few people lived, and finding someone who could guide them in such a short time would be impossible.

The taller boy who distracted them by the noodle stand was face down on the ground. Yi Yi had dragged him across the wheat fields and left him sprawled on the dirt, bruised and in tatters.

The boy was thin and lanky. He climbed to his feet, holding his head high, unyielding. He had a short chin and a rugged face full of pimples.

"Who told you to distract us?" Han asked, stepping forward.

"I have no idea," the boy said with a smirk. "You don't ask questions when enough coin is involved."

"I see," Han said. "What is your name?"

"They call me Scrawny Fox. And you?"

"They call me Chen Han. I need to know—"

"Why should I tell you anything, you piece of—"

Han shot forward, grabbed the boy by his wrist and twisted. The boy shrieked and swiped at the steeled fingers crushing his arm, but to no avail.

"This is why," Han whispered.

"Let me go! You go eat shit!" Scrawny Fox shouted. "I will shove shit down your mother's throat!"

Han shoved him back and allowed him to nurse his sore wrist.

"What were you paid to do tonight?" Han asked. "Tell me or I will have to hurt you again."

Scrawny Fox fumbled with his injured wrist. "I was supposed to pick your pocket for some map. But since you didn't have it, they told us to distract you and that archer."

"I see," Han said. "You are professional thieves. And if you did get the map, who were you supposed to give it to?"

"I don't know, some guy who moves really fast. He's faster than you."

"Cut Foot," Han whispered.

"What is that map for anyway?" Scrawny Fox asked. "You seemed to want it more than I want your mother."

"Willow Island," Han said, ignoring the boy's insults.

Scrawny Fox waited for the words to sink in, then inched away with a gasp. "W-Willow Island? The... The place in the middle of Willow Lake? Why would you want to go there?"

"What is in that lake?" Han asked, almost under his breath.

"G-Ghosts. Demons."

"There is no such thing," Han said. "It's okay. Tell me what you know."

"I don't know anything you ugly pile of shit. I've never seen that lake and I don't know anything about it."

Scrawny Fox spun around but didn't walk away. He stood there, hunched over, as if waiting for someone to rescue him.

Han noticed that he denied, without being asked, whether he had ever been to Willow Lake or not. Scrawny Fox knew about this place or he wouldn't have said it so many times.

"You work for money," Han said. "Let's make a deal. Name a price for taking us to Willow Island."

"No way am I going there," Scrawny Fox said, shaking his head. He stepped away and added, "Not for any amount of money. No way!"

"Why not?"

"No way!"

"That means you know how to get there," Han said. "Willow Island. You know what ghosts live there, don't you?"

Scrawny Fox pulled back even more, his feet unsteady, his foul mouth at a loss of words. "I don't," he said. "No one ever goes to Willow Island. People get to the edge of the lake and they turn back."

"Take us to the edge of the lake then," Han said, "as far as you can go. I promise you won't be harmed by any ghost."

"Your promise is shit," Scrawny Fox shouted. "Shit and worthless. Everyone who goes there gets possessed. Some never even make it back."

"Is that the rumor?"

"It's not a rumor," the boy said, his voice shaking. "I saw it. I didn't get close to Demon Face but—"

"Demon Face?" It was Yi Yi's voice. She emerged from behind Scrawny Fox. Her crossbow was hoisted over her shoulder. Her face was troubled.

"We lost the map," Han said. "But Scrawny Fox knows how to get to Willow Lake."

Yi Yi turned to Scrawny Fox. "Who is Demon Face?"

"Demon Face has no nose and he is just... Just plain ugly," Scrawny Fox said. "His hair is all white and..."

"Where is this man?" Han interrupted, raising his voice. Scrawny Fox startled, took a step back and bumped into the tip of Yi Yi's crossbow pointed at the back of his head.

"What... What do you want from me you ugly pile of horseshit?" His voice was shaking.

"Where is this man?" Han asked again. A man with no nose and white hair matched the description of the messenger who delivered the letter to Master Zuo. The letter that led to the annihilation of the Zuo clan.

"I don't know!" the boy said, his arms tense beside his body, his fingers taut. "Everyone knows Demon Face comes from Willow Lake. We see him walk by here at least twice a year but no one talks to him."

"When's the last time you saw this man?" Han asked.

Yi Yi stepped closer, drew a gold coin out of her pocket and held it in front of the boy.

Scrawny Fox muttered to himself with his head down, still shifting back and forth. When he calmed, he snatched the coin from her hand. "It was a few days ago," he said. "Demon Face was here again. He usually comes around this main road twice a year. We always watch him from a distance."

"Why?" Han asked.

"Because no one else that ugly comes around here," Scrawny Fox said. "He can't be human—he doesn't even have a nose. But this time he stopped at the noodle shop over there." Scrawny Fox gestured toward the hill at the noodle stand where the cold noodles were still sitting on the long table. "It's the first time anyone ever heard him speak. He was asking for directions but the owner didn't know what he was talking about. So my brother and his friend went to help him."

"Help him?" Han asked. "Or steal from him?"

"We can't stitch his nose back on, might as well get what we can," Scrawny Fox said.

"Let me guess," Yi Yi said in a monotone whisper. "He didn't have any money on him."

"Not enough to buy a mask to cover his ugly face."

"What did your brother do?" Han asked.

"I wasn't there," the little thief said. "But my brother stole the one thing Demon Face had on him. Some letter."

"What did the letter say?" Han asked.

Scrawny Fox shrugged his shoulders, backing away from the village and toward the wheat fields. Han and Yi Yi followed.

"Demon Face found out and took his letter back," Scrawny Fox said. "And that's it. Why do you want to know? Who cares?"

"What was in the letter?" Han asked.

"I... We, we don't all know how to read," Scrawny Fox stammered. "My brother could only read a few words."

Han glanced behind him to make sure that Yi Yi was still there. She had been silent for a long time. It was unlike her.

"My brother couldn't recognize most of the words," the boy continued. "Something about a Red Crest … I don't know."

"Red Crest?" Yi Yi asked. "What about the Red Crest?"

"I just told you my brother didn't know those words, you crazy bitch!"

Han held up a hand to silence the boy. "Where did Demon Face need directions to? Was it Zuo Mansions?"

Scrawny Fox gasped. He stopped in the middle of the trail with his mouth dropped. "How did you know that?"

"That's all I know," Han said. He placed a hand on Scrawny Fox's shoulder. "What else was on that letter?"

"There were two more words," the boy said. "'General Wu.' They were at the top of the letter so it must have been addressed to General Wu."

"The Tiger General?" Han asked. "I thought Demon Face was going to Zuo Mansions." Then he remembered what Old Huang told him outside the Zuo Mansions, that the messenger with no nose did not stop for tea. He was in a hurry to deliver a second letter. It must have been for General Wu.

This letter might hold answers about the Red Crest, much like the letter that Master Zuo burned right away. Should he continue to Willow Island and figure out how the Judge became as powerful as the emperor? Or should he chase down the letter first and find out why the Judge was out to kill him?

Han glanced at Yi Yi. She remained in the background, her face concealed under a shadow, her figure motionless.

He turned back to the boy. The map was gone. His only lead was this thief. If he didn't try to find Willow Island now, he may never have the chance again.

Han drew the jade snuff bottle from his pockets. It was worth more than Scrawny Fox would ever acquire in his lifetime. "Take us to the edge of the Willow Lake and this is yours."

Scrawny Fox stepped closer and stared, his mouth gaping open. "Fine!" he shouted. "I'll make the deal, you pile of dogshit. You just want someone to take you to this Willow Lake. And when you come back insane and butt naked, you don't blame me."

Han smiled and extended his hand to motion for him to start walking. "Let's go."

Scrawny Fox stomped his foot on the soft soil. "I hate this arrangement. After I take you there, how do I know you will keep your word?"

"I will," Han said. "Because when a man loses everything, he still has his honor. But when a man who has everything loses his honor, he has nothing left."

Scrawny Fox stomped his foot again, unhappy with the deal.

Han turned to Yi Yi, but she remained in the same place as before, expressionless, uninterested.

"Once we get to Willow Lake, I get paid and I leave," Scrawny Fox said. "I am not going into the lake. And I am definitely not going to the island."

"What is on Willow Island?" Han asked.

"I don't know and I don't care," Scrawny Fox said. "The idiots who wanted to know came back butt naked and insane. The demons scared them so bad they never recovered. I am not going in there."

"Let me deal with the demons," Han said. "We need to go. We are running out of time."

Scrawny Fox pointed across the wheat fields, where, under the silver moonlight, a wide trail was visible. "We can take the road up there," he said. "Let's get this over with." He leaped over a section of tall wheat, almost ready for harvest, and trotted off.

Han turned to Yi Yi. "I've heard of this messenger," he whispered. "This Demon Face sent the letter to Master Zuo. He was delivering another letter, and I thought it was going to General Mu. About the Red Crest."

He took Yi Yi's hand and felt an icy cold presence, her hand stiff and unresponsive. Han's hand faded away.

"I thought it no longer mattered to you what the Red Crest meant," Yi Yi said, her voice monotonous. Her face was blank, void of any emotion or intent, the cheerful smile and childish giggles long gone.

"It doesn't," Han said, unsure how to react. "But it matters to you."

"This way!" Scrawny Fox shouted, a good distance away. He was already past the wheat fields. Han followed.

Suddenly he didn't know her anymore.

The village was behind them and the little brook that circled the wheat fields veered away, merging into a larger stream. They climbed a hill overcrowded by tall vegetation that extended into a narrow trail.

The footsteps behind him disappeared. Han turned. Yi Yi was no longer there.

Scrawny Fox walked ahead with his head down, trampling the grass that stuck out of the road, and disappeared around a bend.

Han stood by himself. The hill was motionless, and beyond the chirps and trills of insects, it lacked any signs of life. In the distance, a lone figure trudged away, head lowered, crossbow dangling by her side.

Han watched Yi Yi leave him, fading into the darkness, her figure swallowed by the tall weeds. It felt like time stood still when the final stalk of grass stopped moving, and the repetitive notes from crickets and beetles sent him into a dreamlike state.

Scrawny Fox slowed down in the distance, pausing every few steps to wait for them. Han wanted to see if Yi Yi would return. They had planned on traveling together to West Sea just moments ago. She had even hinted that she wished to be with him on the boat, floating around like fairies, fishing and drinking into the night. Then she was gone. He could try to follow her and see if she was in trouble, but he would never be able to keep up if she didn't want him there.

With a lingering sigh, more painful than anything he had experienced before, Han turned back to the road. He had to reach Willow Island before the Teacher.

Not without Yi Yi. Nothing he was doing made sense anymore.

If Cut Foot had been following them all along, and he had memorized the map, then the Teacher and perhaps an army would not be far behind. They may even send the Zhuge Nu.

The thought of Zhuge Nu archers brought his lagging footsteps to a complete halt. His boots weighed him down, unwilling to move another inch until the thoughts streaking through his mind found an audience. *She saved him when he encountered the Zhuge Nu the very first time.* The same questions played over and over in his head, and any attempt to suppress them drove him mad. *Why did she leave without explaining herself? Who was she?*

Her bright smile, her little giggles, like a child who stole candy and dared him to catch her, refused to fade. She appeared out of nowhere, first to shoot him down, then to help him find answers and win his trust.

Now, she was gone.

Somehow Han willed himself to walk forward again. He would never understand. Maybe she was never genuine all along. Maybe she achieved what she came for and there was no need for her to talk to him anymore.

Han couldn't stop himself from watching the hills around him. Was she still nearby or did she return to her employer? Why would she travel in the same direction and not walk beside him?

Then he noticed it, a glimpse of a figure, perhaps a figment of his imagination, flitting behind the trees in the distant forest. He saw the purple robes.

"Yi Yi," Han called, certain she would hear him. The forest was still. No one responded.

She was there. Han felt a glow of joy and tried hard not to smile. She was watching.

Sometimes it was a rustle a short distance ahead, sometimes a hint of movement, but she was close by. She was silent, but so was the rest of the world. Han kept his senses on full alert, always watching and listening for any sign of her.

He could not understand why she was watching from a distance and not coming forward to speak to him, to assure him that everything was well. Perhaps, not everything was.

There was a light rustle in the distance, quiet enough to be a wild boar, but too loud and heavy to be Cut Foot. Scrawny Fox was nearby. He stopped to wait for Han.

The boy was sitting on a fallen tree trunk that blocked their trail, his body facing the road ahead. He sat hunched over with his elbows on his knees, and as he wrenched the cloth on his sleeve, he stared straight into the dark night, anxious, fidgeting.

Han stepped over the tree and sat next to him. He unhooked the bulging leather flask on his belt, took a long sip and then offered it to the boy. He still remembered when he was Scrawny Fox's age, carefree, naïve, without a burden in life except to excel in his training and attract Lan's attention. Although, he at least grew up with role models and authority figures, feeling safe each day because Master Zuo and his wife always knew what to do.

Scrawny Fox grabbed the flask without a second thought and tilted his head back to drink. A tear rolled down his cheek.

"Do you have parents?" Han asked.

Scrawny Fox shook his head. "I think so. I don't remember them much."

"Have they... Have they passed on?" Han asked.

"Maybe they did," Scrawny Fox said. "I don't care. I can only remember them leaving."

"They left you?"

"They didn't say goodbye. I watched from my window as they left before dawn."

Without saying anything more, Scrawny Fox wiped a tear, turned and spat into the foliage.

Han thought of whether his own parents also abandoned him, sending him away with many armed men and a servant woman. Where was he supposed to go? Everyone with him was killed by the man who would raise him, who would teach him everything. He touched the scroll in his pocket that his Shifu gave him. What was his name before Chen Han? Perhaps it would be best not to remember.

Scrawny Fox broke the silence. "For a long time, my brother and I were alone, but I always found bamboo shoots in the forest so we had food to eat. Somehow, we joined this man with a big beard, and he taught us how to steal and how to move quietly and swiftly. Then one day, a bunch of people came and killed him."

"That's how you became thieves?" Han asked.

"Ever since."

Han took the flask from Scrawny Fox and poured hard liquor down his own throat, before thrusting it back into the boy's hand. "Another sip of strong liquor and you will forget as well."

The moon was deep in its descent and the silver light brought a new sense of calm to the looming forest. The foliage was dense in front of them, stretching out forever, possibly.

"After these woods we will reach Willow Lake," Scrawny Fox said. "Let's keep moving. We can be there before dawn."

Han picked himself up and headed down the road, the boy walking next to him. Again, Han thought about Yi Yi. Didn't she make a bet with him that they would arrive before dawn? Maybe she was there to claim her victory now.

"Where is your woman?" Scrawny Fox asked, reading his mind. Han didn't respond right away.

"The crazy one with the crossbow," Scrawny Fox pressed again.

"I don't know," Han said.

Scrawny Fox laughed. "You don't even know where your woman went?"

"Maybe she is not my woman after all. Maybe she never was."

There was silence between them until suddenly Scrawny Fox said, "I understand. I have the same problem."

"You do?" Han asked with a smile. "Who is she?"

"She always does laundry by the river where we live so she can see if I am around," Scrawny Fox said.

"What is her name?"

"I don't know."

"You don't know?"

"Hey, I never spoke to her. I just saw her watching me across the river."

Han sighed. "Can you make it across the river?"

"Sure I can." Scrawny Fox's voice carried into the night. "I swim across that river all the time."

"Then why don't you swim up to her and ask her what her name is?"

"Well," Scrawny Fox paused, searching for his words. "What if she runs away? Then they would all laugh at me."

"You mean other boys?"

"Yes, them. They'll be shouting and jeering from our side of the river."

The moon had all but disappeared but the first streaks of dawn illuminated the heavens. Han tried to detect where Yi Yi was, but he could not see or hear her. He wondered if she was still watching from a distance.

They reached the end of the forest, which opened into a rocky area with no vegetation. A short distance away was a lake.

Scrawny Fox was silent, planting his steps against the rocky surface one foot in front of the other, almost unaware that they were approaching the dreaded Willow Lake.

There was not a single willow tree on the bank. Standing on a barren rock, one step away from a small rowboat banked by the water, was a lone figure with her heavy crossbow slung over her shoulder. Her back was turned, but her wide stance and tense demeanor were almost combative. She stared motionlessly into the murky lake.

Han stopped a short distance away. She had helped him forget that the people he once called friends were hunting him. Her little pranks helped numb the despair of losing Lan and Master Zuo. He never knew who she was, but he trusted her, enjoyed her presence, and like a whiff of smoke in strong wind, all but her menacing silhouette had disappeared.

Yi Yi pointed the butt of her weapon at the rowboat in front of her. "I found a boat. We need to move."

Without glancing back, Yi Yi leaped onto the boat, dropped her weapon in front of her and sat down with both oars in hand.

Scrawny Fox pulled back, shaking his head. "I am not going with you and that crazy woman," he shouted. "That was the deal. I took you to the lake." He rubbed his hands together and stomped his feet. "I am not going!"

"I understand," Han said, turning to him. He planted the snuff bottle into the boy's palm and closed his fingers around it. "Thank you for taking us."

Scrawny Fox opened his hand to look at the treasure. He lifted his face. "You... You are going in there?"

"I have to," Han said. He wanted to say something to calm Scrawny Fox and assure him that it would not be the last time they would see each other. But Yi Yi was silent, and she was about to row away.

"I'll see you again," Han said.

Scrawny Fox's lips were trembling. He held up his shaking hands. "Please. Don't go. Don't go into that lake. There's a woman ghost on that island. She has long white hair and people hear her laughing by herself at night. Please. Everyone comes back insane. Don't go."

Han placed both hands on Scrawny Fox's shoulders. "Promise me something."

"Yes?" The boy's voice was waning.

"Swim across that river and ask for her name. Tell me what she says when we meet again."

Han departed with an assuring smile.

He continued to the boat, leaving Scrawny Fox frozen with his mouth wide open.

The boat was larger than Han thought. He sat down on a narrow, built-in bench at the rear, facing Yi Yi's back. Without a word, Yi Yi rowed away, her oars plunging deep into the waters. The boat lurched forward, gliding on the surface of the calm waters with such vigor that it pushed waves against the rocky shore.

Scrawny Fox was still there, standing and watching. Han waved to him with a smile and motioned for him to leave. The boy remained where he was.

Willow Lake was massive, cold, and silent, with distant hills shrouded in fog. The sun was emerging, the glistening streaks of morning light reflecting sparkles of silver against the calm waters. Han did not know how to find the island. There were no signs of life anywhere, no waterfowl on the lake or birds in the air.

Much time passed while Yi Yi rowed in silence. Han had so much to say to her, so much anguish in his heart that he hoped she could relieve with a single explanation, but words could not find their way onto his tongue.

"Yi Yi," he whispered. She did not respond. The sun was peeking over the hilltop in front of them. It was morning, and they were deep in Willow Lake.

Han wanted to ask her so many questions, but he knew she would ignore him. Why did she wait for him to go to Willow Island? He couldn't wrap his head around what she was doing and why, and yet he could do nothing but follow her. He didn't even consider going back to West Sea this time. He wanted to be with her, and if that meant rowing to Willow Island in silence to help her find what she wanted, then so be it.

"I lost my bet to you," Han said. "So I should tell you another story, if you still want to hear it."

Yi Yi ignored him.

"Some years ago," Han began, "right after I killed the leader of the Venom Sect, I was wandering the world searching for something to do. I often ended up in the taverns in the capital to drink with other poets and artists. It was a good way to spend time."

Yi Yi never turned her back, nor changed speed on the oars. It was as if Han's words meant nothing to her. He shook it off, reminding himself that he needed to talk to her, and nothing else.

"One night, a beggar came up to me and asked if I would buy him a drink," Han continued. "I thought he needed one, and so I did. He drank the entire flask with a single breath and asked me for more. I bought him another one, and then another. The beggar just could not get drunk. Finally, I found someone who could outdrink me." Han smiled to himself, immersed in his memories, unbothered by Yi Yi's silent silhouette in front of him.

"The beggar then said that if I could get him drunk, he would tell me an interesting story," Han said. "I wanted to see how much it would take, so I continued buying the drinks.

"We drank late into the night. Finally, his eyes started to glaze. I counted the empty flasks on the table and I could not believe it. He drank twice as much as I did.

"The beggar began to tell me the story. He spoke in an animated voice. 'There once was a boy making a millet porridge by himself when an old man appeared out of nowhere and asked him if he could have some of it. The boy agreed but said that the millet would take a while to cook, so he asked the old man to sit down and wait. The old man then produced a pillow and suggested the boy take a nap since the porridge would take some time. The boy agreed, and he fell asleep right away.

"'He had a dream. He dreamed of how he passed the government exams and became a wealthy official, and fame and fortune were his to take. He married a beautiful woman and had two sons. Life was good. Then he was betrayed. He lost his position, his children died, his wife married someone else, and he was left with nothing. He would die on the street with nothing.

"'The boy woke up frightened by the dream, and his millet wasn't even cooked yet. The old man, of course, knew what the boy dreamed and convinced him to study the Tao. The boy became his student. As the years went by, the boy rose to fame and fortune and then lost everything, just as the dream foretold. He became a wandering sage with nothing, but he enjoyed every moment of his life from beginning to end.'"

Han took a deep breath after finishing the beggar's story. "I thanked him, even though I was familiar with the story—the legend of Lu Dong Bin, one of the eight Taoist Immortals. Even though it was an old story, I was happy to have drunk with him that night. Once the liquor was finished, I stood up to bow and bade him farewell.

"The beggar laughed and said he would offer me a drunken dream without the pillow. He told me that I would become the world's greatest warrior, and then one day, I will open the gates for a foreign threat. The world will hate me, will hunt me down like an animal. Despite that, I will become emperor, and then I will lose everything and become a commoner."

I laughed and laughed when I heard that, and he laughed with me. We were both pretty drunk. I told him I was glad that, in the end, I would become a commoner. Maybe I would call myself the Commoner. I bowed and headed to my room. I was almost out of the inn when he asked me whether I would follow my destiny with a smile on my face, or with worry at every turn? And then he was already gone. I never saw him again. The name Commoner stuck with me and that is what everyone has called me ever since."

The boat swayed against the placid waters. Ripples scattered on the lake surface, reflecting a light hue of green and purple as the force of Yi Yi's relentless oars summoned and forced them away. There was an eerie tension about the calmness on Willow Lake, a boiling point within the silence.

Han could not watch her silhouette anymore. He stared into the light fog forming on the surface of the lake, subtle, unmistakable, as if it was rising from the water itself.

Nothing made sense, he realized in this surreal moment as they glided into a translucent cloud hovering over the calm waters, him and this silent woman that he couldn't let go of.

There was sudden movement, and Han slipped away and shot his arms out to cover his face. He was on a boat, with nowhere to run, and when Yi Yi's oars shattered against his arms, he knew he was trapped. She had flung her oars at him.

She was upon him then, her left knee planted into his abdomen, the tip of her crossbow pushed against his throat. She pinned him against the floor of the boat and clutched his hair with her other hand, securing his head so he could not move.

"Yi Yi," Han said.

"You have to die, Commoner!" The voice was not her own.

"I thought you didn't want to kill me anymore."

Yi Yi's eyes were bulging, her lips trembling, her breathing shallow and irregular. With a shout she pushed her crossbow deeper into his throat until he choked.

"Why?" he asked again.

"I have my orders," Yi Yi said under her breath. "The emperor wants you dead. I have to kill you."

Han's brows knit together. "The emperor? Why would he care about some wandering poet? Does he think I have a pact with the Silencer too?"

Yi Yi shook her head, her face twisted and tormented. "I have the imperial edict. Those are my orders. I have to kill you."

"I see," Han said. A calm smile formed on his lips. "Your employer, the one who has all the money in the world. He is the emperor. And you are the emperor's personal soldier."

Deep sobs wracked her body, spasms of anguish and worry riveted through her. She leaned into Han, her elbow against his solar plexus, her weapon pushing his chin so far back that he was staring at the rear wall of the boat.

"I have to, Han! I have to!" she screamed over and over again.

Han sighed. "Do what you have to do. If this is your duty to your country, don't hesitate."

"I'm going to kill you, Han!" she screamed. "I'm going to kill you!"

The fog on the lake was thicker, higher, almost brushing against the edge of the boat, threatening to infiltrate.

"My life is worth nothing," Han said. He could no longer watch her tortured face. "I would rather die so you won't have to disobey the emperor. This would be the best way for me to go."

Her voice broke. "I have to kill you," she said one more time, trembling, choking between sobs.

Han waited. Her breathing was shorter, scattered between light sobs and gasps for air. Then, he heard a firm, rhythmic tapping against the floor of the boat. Yi Yi was hunched over to the side, away from his body. The taps against the wooden floor were her teardrops, flowing in long streams down her cheeks and falling in large, steady drops.

Han sighed. "I'm fine with it, Yi Yi. Don't make it too hard on yourself."

Yi Yi released the haunting wail of a dying animal, her frozen arms locked in a posture both murderous and nurturing. Her trembling face wobbled without control, the streaks of tears unrelenting. For a long time, she wavered between killing him and destroying herself, as direct defiance from the emperor's orders would inevitably lead to her death anyway, and the steady hand that always clutched the crossbow with an iron fist became weaker and weaker with each drop of tears.

Yi Yi inched away and withdrew to the front of the boat, and as she did, she loosened her grip on her heavy weapon and allowed it to slide off Han's shoulder. She sat against the front hull, her back striking the hard wood with a thump, and she lifted her face to the morning sky.

Between strained gasps for breath, she whispered, "I can't do it. You showed me that there are good men in this world. I can't do it."

Han sat up. "No Yi Yi. You can't defy the emperor. You'll be hunted down and executed."

"I will go home," she said. "Today, I've betrayed his trust. I'll go home to face the consequences."

"We can run together, Yi Yi," Han said. "We'll hide in West Sea. The emperor can't send his navy into a lake."

Yi Yi shook her head. "He raised me like a daughter and gave me everything. I have to go back to face him."

The fog was thick, almost encircling them. The morning sun failed to penetrate the opaque white cloud that had risen to chest level. It was not a normal mist that dispersed on the surface of the waters, but something that became thicker and taller as the boat pushed forward. Something else was creating this cloud.

Han leaped to his feet in alarm.

"Hold your breath!" Sucking in a final gasp of air, he shredded a piece of cloth from his robe, drew his flask and saturated it with alcohol before rushing across the boat. He clasped the wet cloth over her mouth and nose and motioned for her not to breathe.

The boat continued to float into the fog and they could no longer see their surroundings. Suddenly they were deaf, too, having lost even the sounds of their own breathing to remind them they were alive. The boat lilted in a haze of eerie white, and as the fog rose above their faces, their eyes welled with an acidic sting.

Yi Yi's shallow breath, already fractured by the torture she just endured, lost its clench. She exhaled with a short burst. Then, with another gasp, she drew a breath through the wet cloth. Right away her eyes rolled back and she began to sway, rocking left and right.

Han wanted to shout something to awaken her, but he could not risk losing hold of his own breath.

Yi Yi leaned back, away from the cloth over her mouth, lifted her face to the heavens and laughed. It was a strange laugh, not her usual happy giggle, but the high pitched shriek of someone possessed.

She kicked at Han's face, but he slipped back to avoid it. Then, she clawed at her own clothing, tearing it apart, and with another violent jerk that shredded her robes to tatters, she threw her clothing into the water. She stood naked in front of him, taunting him with a disturbing smile marked by mischief and perversion before turning her back.

Han choked. He took a step forward, struggling through the stinging tears, no longer certain whether he was delusional as well. Above her right shoulder blade was the light blue tattoo with the two eyes.

Without a word, Yi Yi leaped off the front of the boat but there was no splash. The bottom of the boat was scraping against wet sand, and soon it ground to a halt. The fog was thinner in front of Han, and he was able to see the rocky surface. Still holding his breath, his lungs ready to burst, Han leaped off the boat and ran for higher ground.

A few steps onto a small hill and the low fog over Willow Lake was behind him. Han doubled over, coughing and wheezing for air. Yi Yi was nowhere in sight.

This must be Willow Island. This was the one island on the map. He should be able to find her.

Han pushed himself to higher elevation, still struggling to catch his breath, hoping to memorize the terrain and establish a sense of direction. He reached the top of the little hill and stood there to take it all in. The island was wet and luscious, large enough that he couldn't see water on the opposite side, dense with tall grass and short bushes without a tree in sight. Han heard no wild animals nearby, nor birds in the sky or movement in the bushes. He could hear crickets and the rattling of other insects, but at first glance, Willow Island appeared uninhabited.

Behind him was the shoreline where he had landed, where the wooden boat hid in a fog as tall as any man. Somehow, the fog enveloped the area where there was water but dissipated on dry land. This must be why those who ventured to this island returned insane. There were poison fumes surrounding it, air that affected a person's mind the moment they inhaled.

Han turned back to the center of the island below him. He came here for clues to what made the Judge all-powerful and the answers must be here. But most importantly, he needed to find Yi Yi.

CHAPTER 7

THE FORMER EMPEROR had hidden a map to Willow Island with a local official far from the capital. This magistrate was betrayed by his own wife and murdered for the map, in a well-planned scheme that would blame the Commoner so no one would investigate the real reason behind his death. The secret in Willow Island must somehow be related to the former emperor.

Han gazed across every corner of the small island. If he were to hide something here, where would it be? The island was already well isolated, with the poisonous fog protecting its shores and enough legend and mystery guarding it from travelers. Yet, a secret big enough to turn the Judge into the most powerful man on earth must be concealed even deeper.

There were no houses or man-made structures on the island. The middle comprised of flat land with thick bushes too short to hide anything. All along the shoreline of Willow Island was a border of coarse sand leading into the waters, also barren and exposed. Nothing could be hidden there. The one area that could house a cave or an underground opening was the hill where he stood.

For a long time, Han paced on the hill, searching for a gap between rocks or tunnels leading away from the surface, all the while waiting for movement in case Yi Yi reemerged. She was nowhere to be seen.

If he were to hide a great secret on this flat, empty piece of land, where would it be?

No one dared venture into the fog.

The toxic mist hovered over the surface of the lake. There must be something in the water, something emitting the fumes to keep the island dangerous. The secret must be underwater.

Han trudged back toward the boat, unwinding his waist strap and shedding his outer robes. He thought about Yi Yi's bright smile, her little pranks, and felt strong again. She wanted to find the Judge's secret. If Han had the courage to do this, it would only be for her.

Han threw his robes onto the boat, drew a deep breath, and charged head-on into the toxic fog. His feet touched water, and they struck a slippery rock slanting into the lake. Han dove in. It was much deeper than he thought, but this was what he hoped for, that instead of coarse sand leading into the bed of the lake, he would find rocks, perhaps caverns.

Then he saw it. The morning sun pierced into the fresh water, despite the fog above, and not far to his left, the light revealed an opening. Underwater tunnels like these could stretch on well after he ran out of breath, he realized. Han swam toward the cave entrance.

The opening was large but quickly narrowed, leading into a fully submerged tunnel wide enough for one person to swim through. It was a crooked, windy passageway with murky waters and slippery moss on either side. Han pushed forward, certain there would be light ahead.

His hand reached out of the water and he pulled himself to the surface. He was inside a small, dark cavern. Streaks of light penetrated a few small gaps high above.

Han climbed out of the cold water onto a wet, rocky surface. He waited for his eyes to adjust before using his hands to navigate against the coarse cavern wall. After a few steps, his hand found a bend in the wall, another tunnel leading deeper under the island, this one so narrow that he had to walk sideways. He held his guiding hand behind him, pressed against his back with the palm always touching the wall. He inched his way inside, listening for movement with every step.

The passage was cold and the air was thin. Han emerged into a room that was pitch black. Without light he would never find anything, even if it stood directly in front of him. He coughed and listened to the echo. He was inside a small space and the ceiling above him could not be high. Perhaps there was nothing in here.

"What did I come here to find?" Han whispered to himself. He didn't know. Something was hidden here that the previous emperor had guarded, something the Judge found to become all-powerful.

Han inched his way forward until his hand touched something rough and cold. He felt around it, pressed his finger into its crumbling surface and brought his hand closer to smell. It was an iron ring, rusty, full of dust and decay, embedded into the wall. Someone had been here, chained to this iron ring and imprisoned in darkness for years, as many years as it took for this solid piece of metal to rust to its core. Han left the ring and groped his way around the room, feeling for other man-made structures.

His hands followed the cold rocks on the cavern wall, and eventually, he encountered a thick chain, also crumbling with rust, and further down he found a pile of coarse fabric sitting in a heap. Han crouched and placed his hand on the woven canvas stuffed with hay, perhaps a blanket meant to cover the prisoner.

Han knelt into the canvas blanket and groped around the bed area. There was nothing, just some hay scattered on cold stone and the broken chain at the foot of the bed. Han sat down in the darkness. The prisoner was probably restrained at the ankle. His hands would have been free.

He touched the cavern wall behind him and released a gasp. Something was there. Unmistakable grooves, chipped into the hard stone, covered the entire wall with words. The prisoner carved column after column of words into the wall next to his bed.

Han's heart was pounding. His hand groped to the upper right corner of the cavern wall behind the bed, reaching as far up as he could from his knees, and touched the carvings of the very first word.

His finger traced each line, each scratch and crease while the words formed on his tongue.

"Every night I hear them," Han read aloud in a whisper. "They come to me in the darkness, their faces and bodies shredded by arrows, dried blood falling off their wounds. My wife was the first to fall she said, shielding my baby from the rain of arrows."

Han sucked in his breath. He caressed the words one by one, careful not to miss a single engraving. "They almost made it to the boats, I heard. At the shore of Black Lake, all sixty of them were exterminated by a single blanket of arrows. But five more rounds were fired after that. My brother made sure that no one in my family survived.

"Every night they came to me, my slain wife and children, my entire household of nieces and nephews and servants. Every night they came down to hell to visit, to see if I was suffering like they had suffered. The metal pin was drilled into my foot and attached to a chain, and I will never walk again. Lying here for eternity, with neither day or night has crippled my back and I will never sit upright again. But I have not suffered compared to them. There is still vengeance in my breast and hatred in my heart. I will continue to live and one day, reclaim the throne that was mine."

Han froze. He could not think of any time in recent history that someone else ruled the Middle Kingdom other than the current emperor Li Gao, and before Li Gao, his father Li Wen. There were few words left on the wall and Han continued to trace them.

"I heard that my brother's babies may have survived. How did my men fail? But I know where they are. One day I will be free, and I will make sure they die the horrible deaths that my children faced. I will claim what is rightfully mine and destroy those responsible for my family's massacre."

Against the left edge of the wall, on a separate line, was his signature. Han tensed and touched the words a second time. "Emperor Li Yan." Han sat back with a deep exhale. Li Yan was the emperor's younger brother who died of a fever many years ago.

Han brushed his hand across the engravings again, trying to make sense of it all. Since there were no remains in the room, Li Yan's body must have been removed. How could this be the secret that gave the Judge sudden, unlimited power? Even if everything written on this wall were true, it would be something the current emperor already knew about, if not something he ordered. It could not have led to wealth or power for anyone discovering it.

Laughter echoed in the distance. For a second Han thought he was imagining Yi Yi nearby. Then he heard it again, and he knew it was not her voice. It was the laughter of someone older, the tone and pitch more sinister. There was someone else on the island and she was close.

Han leaped toward the side wall, and once he reached the rusted ring, he pressed his hand against his back to guide him through the tunnel that led out the room. He moved in silence, listening to every sound outside. The laughter could not travel through the underwater tunnels. There must have been another opening in the first cavern.

He heard the laughter again, this time from above. It was a deep, heartfelt bellow. Han reached the end of the tunnels and emerged back in the original cavern. He waited for the sound, motionless, almost holding his breath in deep focus.

She laughed again, almost amused with herself, her high-pitched voice scratchy and strained. It came from somewhere behind Han's left shoulder, high above, perhaps even close to the surface. He turned to face the wall and groped his way in the darkness, touching the wet rocks with both hands, straining to see with the few strands of narrow light streaking in.

Then he felt it, a subtle breeze of cold air descending upon him from above, caressing his face. Han leaped against the wall without a second thought, his hands gliding up against the smooth rocks and landing in an empty space, a tunnel of some sort, his fingers clutching the mouth of the opening before he pulled himself up. The opening was wide enough for three people to enter but barely tall enough to crawl. It was steep, slippery, a difficult climb in complete darkness.

Han was more excited than ever. There was more to these caverns than the prisoner who called himself an emperor. The haunting giggles were growing louder than ever. This woman may even know how to find Yi Yi.

The tunnel turned a sharp corner and a flicker of light shone through a further bend in the passageway. Han slowed and pulled himself up the shaft one overhand after another, watching the light and listening for people. The giggling woman was there, walking around, her footsteps clumsy but even. She was not a martial artist.

"Now dear," the woman said. Han was already close enough to hear her. "If you don't drink this you can still get poisoned when you go back out there. Come now, be a good girl. Drink it all at once."

There was a light cough. Yi Yi's cough. Han could not contain himself. He rushed forward, clawing the hard stone and scrambling up the tunnel.

"Wake up, dear," the older woman said. "Come, drink this."

Han shot through an opening and stopped in a room with two torches on either side. It was a large, cold cavern with chairs, a bed, a mud stove, and a number of vessels for grain storage. An older woman with long white hair stood next to the bed, holding a wooden bowl filled with a steaming brown liquid. Yi Yi was on the bed, wrapped in covers, her eyes closed and her breath short.

In a flash, Han's fingers reached the old woman's throat. "What are you making her drink?"

The old woman, shocked and straining for air, didn't respond. Under the flickering torchlight, Yi Yi's complexion was both sickly and spirited. She was dressed in white robes, the same robes as the old woman, with a straw pillow under her head and another pillow below her knees. The old woman had tried to make Yi Yi comfortable.

Han loosened his hold on her throat. Her long white hair made her appear older than her voice sounded, and then, with a closer look, she was not old at all. There were few wrinkles on her face, still bright with youth and energy, though her movements and demeanor resembled someone weathered and beaten. Scrawny Fox had told him, right before they parted at the shore, that the ghost on Willow Island was a woman with long hair who laughed to herself.

"Who are you?" Han asked, taking the bowl from the old woman and smelling it. It carried the fishy scent of the waters of Willow Lake, a noxious, rancid odor that he noticed before the fog thickened around the island.

"It's made from lake scum," the old woman said, laughing to herself again. "I scooped it right off the surface of the lake."

"The moss on the surface?" Han asked. "This is the moss that poisoned the fog?"

"Exactly," the old woman said, chuckling. "But eating the moss neutralizes the vapors. Try it! Once you drink it the fog won't affect you again for the rest of the day."

"What are you doing to Yi Yi?" Han asked. "Why is she unconscious?"

"Ha! The question should be, why aren't you unconscious? How did you get on the island without breathing the fog?"

"I held my breath."

"No one can hold their breath that long," the old woman said. "You're lying!"

"Is that why everyone becomes insane?" Han asked. "They breathe in the poison fumes and it affects their mind?"

"Unless you know what to eat," she said, releasing a long, hollow laugh. She pointed to Yi Yi. "She didn't. But she drank the scum. Don't worry Han, she will be fine."

Han froze. "How do you know who I am?"

"Ha!" she cackled. "She was calling your name the whole time. I tried to explain to her that men are not reliable. Men!" She turned and spat on the ground. "When they want to leave you, they leave."

Han lowered the bowl onto a stone ledge nearby. The rise and fall of Yi Yi's breathing was short but steady. She was in a deep sleep. It reminded him that he had not stopped to rest for three days now. The fatigue, the relief of finding her when he thought he might have lost her for good, released a flood of tension from his worn body.

"Thank you," Han said. He had so many questions, more than

he could remember, but he only thought of one thing. "Thank you for taking care of her."

"Oh. No need to thank me, Han," the old woman said. "I used to do this every day for my prince."

"Your prince?" he asked, turning to her.

"He is a prince, you know."

"Li Yan!" Han whispered under his breath. Then in a louder voice he asked, "The prisoner down in the cavern below?"

"Yes! You know my prince?"

"Who is he?"

"He is my love!" she said, lifting her eyes and opening her palms as if to address the heavens. A deep smile settled on her face as she relished the moment, the memory of the man she called her prince. "Since I was a little girl, I knew I was going to marry my prince. I knew it! I would be his love in good times and bad. And during good times, he came to me every few nights. Even though he had other women, he always came to me. Sometimes he only came to me once a month, but I was still happy! Those were good times."

Han tried to follow. "Li Yan? They say he died from a fever. When was this?"

"No, no!" she shouted. "My love is alive! I took care of him for sixteen years. Every day I brought him clean water. I washed him. When the guards dropped off the food, I would feed him. Every night I laid next to him to keep him company. He was my love."

"You stayed here, on this island, to take care of Li Yan?" Han asked. "How did you find him here? How did he end up here?"

"I followed him here of course!" she said with a laugh. "After I did everything he asked me to do, I earned my right to be next to him every night. I did everything he asked. I even brought him the babies' heads."

"You what?"

"His brother's babies. All three were boys. They could all inherit the throne so best to kill them nice and early!" She laughed in a sharp giggle, then a full-hearted bellow.

Han thought about taking Yi Yi now and swimming back out to the boat, leaving behind this demented woman. But Yi Yi was still unconscious and she could drown on the way out.

The older woman stopped for a second, panting for air. "I am the best," she said, patting herself on the chest. "All his great warriors could not kill the Crowned Prince's babies, but I alone killed every single one of them. And I took their heads to show my love and he was happy with me. He really was."

"The Crowned Prince?" Han asked.

"My love's oldest brother was the Crowned Prince. He is dead now. My love's second brother had babies too, and I know where they are. I know where all the babies are."

Then, out of nowhere, she broke down. The old woman hunched her back, and she leaned against the edge of Yi Yi's bed in anguish. "But they cried and cried," she said, her voice high pitched, almost whimpering. "Their babies couldn't stop crying. But my baby, my baby never cried. And my prince didn't care. He didn't care. His own baby never cried. And I…" She broke into sobs, her hands covering her face, her body wracking. "And I held my baby for many days, but still he was so cold. I tried to feed him, but the milk won't come. And he was such a good boy. Such a good boy. He never complained once. He just closed his eyes and waited for me and never cried once. Then my love told me to bury him."

She spun around and glared at Han. "He was such a good baby and he told me to bury him! Why? Tell me why?"

"Your baby was dead," Han said, his own voice weak now.

"His baby," she murmured. "Our baby."

"How did Li Yan end up here?" Han asked.

"His father put him here," she said, staring into the distance. The torchlight was fading, and the ghastly expression on her face eased in and out of the shadows. "My love killed the Crowned Prince's entire family. He almost did the same to his second brother. But you know, my love was superior. He was smarter, better educated, and by far the better prince for the throne. But he was the youngest, and two more brothers had to die before he could be emperor. How unfair. How unfair that the superior man could not be emperor simply because he was simply born later!"

"Who is the Judge?" Han asked, interrupting her. "They say he is the emperor's nephew. Is he Li Yan's son or the late Crowned Prince's? Or not an immediate nephew at all."

The woman shook her head. "I don't know any Judge. But the Crowned Prince no longer had babies. I took their heads in the middle of the night so my love would praise me. I did it for him, even though I still hear them cry at night. I did it for him."

"The Judge came here," Han said. "Didn't he?"

"Some people came," she said, her voice distant. "Four of them. They killed the guards and dumped their bodies in the lake. They took my love. And when my prince left me, he laughed. He said he wouldn't kill me because I took care of him all these years, but I can stay here for the rest of my life."

Her voice trembled. Her eyes widened, flashing fire. "And then they rowed away. But I know his secret too. I know where the babies are."

"Babies?" Han asked. "Whose babies?"

"The babies he wanted dead," she said. "But his useless men never could kill them. Someone slipped a note into my love's monthly supplies to tell him they were not dead. And he was angry! He was so angry!"

She sighed as her tears flowed, her white hair hanging over her face. Her fists clenched and released. "And he said to me, 'Little Sparrow, I want them dead. Go back out there and kill them for me.'"

"Little Sparrow?" Han asked. "Did you say your name is Little Sparrow?"

"But I couldn't," she continued, lost in her painful memories. "But I couldn't. The poor babies. They have already lost their parents. How could I take their heads too? Babies without heads can still cry, you know. I hear them every night. They can still cry. Not like mine. Mine was a good baby and never cried. He never cried."

"Did you send a letter to Master Zuo?" Han asked. "What was in the letter? Did you also send one to General Mu?"

There was movement at the other end of the cavern. Han realized too late, caught up in Little Sparrow's painful memories, that he had never noticed the other entrance to this room. He threw himself toward Yi Yi's bedside to intercept whatever was coming, blocking her body with his, when he heard a thud and a choked gurgle. A knife was embedded in Little Sparrow's belly. Her mouth gaped open in shock, in pain, before she collapsed and lifted her finger. "You came back. Where is my love?"

Whoever came in did not carry a torch, but by then, Han had collected himself. He could hear the footsteps of twelve people, most of them moving in silence, all of them trained in stealth and combat. He shot toward the fastest person moving into the cavern and stood before him. He was face to face with Cut Foot.

Han struck him with a glancing blow before Cut Foot changed direction and retreated. Ten other warriors approached, their metal weapons whistling in the light air. Han never had time to notice their faces. He was unarmed, and every single one of them carried a different weapon. He had never heard of warriors like these, moving together and trained to fight as one yet each attacking with a different style and different display of martial prowess.

A broadsword user approached from the right. At the same time, a spear user advanced from Han's left, probing his spearhead like a snake waiting for an opening to strike. A whip user whirled his silver weapon in front, distracting Han with rapid movement and light and shadows. Han only cared about protecting Yi Yi. He stormed into the blazing whip, enduring a minor cut on his arm while striking a heavy palm against his assailant's chest, sinking him. The attackers behind him were forced to change position, breaking their circle to defend themselves. Han retreated to Yi Yi's bedside.

Little Sparrow was squirming on the cavern floor. She had already ripped the knife from her body, and now she was holding her wound with both hands, groaning in pain.

"What did I tell you, my nephew?" a booming voice called from the far end of the cavern. Han recognized that voice.

Sha Wu emerged in a gray Taoist robe, his hair secured into a topknot by a small dagger. His flowing sleeves dangled by his sides. He was unarmed.

"What did I tell you?" Sha Wu repeated, shaking his head. "Killing out of hate, or killing out of fear, is the wrong reason to kill. And you are afraid, aren't you my nephew? You're afraid the girl will be harmed. And she will be. I will direct my men to attack her from all directions, and we will see whether your movements can still be crisp and clean, or clumsy and burdened by impurities."

Han glanced at Cut Foot, who stood beside the old man, and then he understood. Sha Wu wasn't an unknown after all. "You're the Teacher," Han said. "You're the one who released that fake edict to turn Yi Yi against me."

"A real edict from a real emperor," the Teacher said with a laugh. "No one asked that stupid girl to leave the palace and pick a fight with the Judge."

The nine warriors had taken position around Han, although the whip user was struggling to stand in the background with his ribs broken from Han's palm. They were powerful, but they were no match for the greatest warrior in the world in a fair fight. Yet this time, with Yi Yi unconscious and vulnerable, they had a clear advantage.

Sha Wu pointed to his men. "They're here because the Judge wants you dead. I am here because killing the Commoner would be an interesting experience. It's like raping the queen in her own bed while the emperor watches. So unattainable, but so delicious, and impossible to resist."

"Then leave Yi Yi out of it," Han said. "This is between me and you."

"Did you think for one second," the Teacher continued, "that Cut Foot was sent to steal your map? I'm disappointed, my nephew. You are so naïve. I left the map for you. I instructed that idiot Fu Nandong to always carry it on his body, so you would come to this island. Because here, I can teach you why it's better to fuck a whore, than marry a virgin."

"All this work to get me here," Han said. "And you think it will be easier to kill me?"

Sha Wu laughed. "You were supposed to be unconscious from the poison fog and I wouldn't have to lose any men killing you. Did you think I needed a map to find this place? Cut Foot didn't follow you to burn the map, I sent him to deliver the edict to your lovely archer. The person closest to you was supposed to put a bolt in your head, and if that didn't work, we would deal with you here. But she's a disappointment as well. Everyone kills for the wrong reason, and now people fail to kill for the wrong reasons." Sha Wu stood with his hands on his hips, shaking his head. "You should have killed her instead. The Commoner is already hard enough to kill without an archer protecting him from a distance. But you failed me my nephew. You'd rather sleep with her than slit her throat. In the end, my brother Zuo was a weakling and a fool. He never taught you how it's done."

"Your brother Zuo?" Han asked.

The Teacher pulled up his sleeve and lifted his hand to his face to expose his arm. On the left arm, in the exact same place as Master Zuo, was a blue tattoo of two connected eyes.

"My brother from the Council of Midnight," Sha Wu said with a smile. He glanced at Yi Yi. "She knows. We put our best archers right next to the emperor and he didn't even know it."

A knife whistled by; the same knife thrown at high velocity that injured Little Sparrow. Han flung his hand out to intercept, striking the screaming blade with the back of his hand right before it would have reached Yi Yi's hip. A spear shot for his throat while a warrior leaped into the air, his two heavy cudgels aimed for Yi Yi's face. Han stepped into the spear's path and deflected the warhead, then grabbed the spear user. He tripped his assailant and threw him into the cudgel user, breaking the onslaught just in time. A sword and a saber flashed in front of him. There were ten of them, including Cut Foot, and they had the manpower and weapons to spare.

Han stood in front of Yi Yi with his arms outstretched to cover the length of the bed. On the other side of her bed was the cavern wall. They could only attack her from one direction. Yet, if he remained in the same defensive position, he would be surrounded from three sides, fighting ten heavily armed opponents all at once.

Four men took up position to his left, near the foot of the bed, and another six closed in from the front. No one approached from his right, and with one glance, Han understood why. Sha Wu stood by himself, arms folded, a light smile on his face. The Teacher was enough of a threat all by himself.

Then Han heard it, a stir behind him, a subtle moan and whimper. Yi Yi was waking up. Perhaps she called his name. Once she regained consciousness, they could swim out together. There was hope.

With a roar, Han surged into the six men attacking from the front, his arms a blur. He struck long and deep, then short and quick. He used the martial arts of the Dali kingdom, his mother's, a system unknown in China and completely unpredictable. In a flash he changed direction, ripping across the spear and broad sword users who intercepted him, extending into his enemy's space and using the medium range of the Infinity Palm to pound his assailants' arms and shoulders. He broke two elbows and dislocated another shoulder before returning to guard the side of the bed.

Cut Foot streaked in from behind. Han met his speed, and when Cut Foot hesitated, Han slammed him with his shoulder, sending him flying. The Commoner then turned to assault the spear user. He smacked the warhead off the spear and struck his enemy in the chest with a palm, crushing his breath and sending him gasping in retreat.

The armed warriors had reduced to six men. Almost half had crumbled, some too injured to stand, and none of the fallen men were in fighting condition anymore.

Someone advancing with tremendous power slipped in from Han's right, a destructive force exerting enough pressure to force him into retreat. It was the Teacher, and he was using the Infinity Palm.

Sha Wu's Infinity Palm was even faster and heavier than Han's. He was everywhere at once, wrapping Han in an onslaught both continuous and infinite. Han felt like mountains were collapsing on top of him. The other warriors moved out of the way as Sha Wu advanced. Han was suffocating. He had never fought someone like this before, in all his years wandering the land. He never once imagined that someone so powerful could be virtually unknown. The Teacher encircled him like a hurricane, each palm strike smashing into him. All he could do was evade. Han sensed Sha Wu's men taking precise positions, but he could not move out of the way. The Teacher was pressing him into a corner.

"Now!" Sha Wu shouted.

A throwing knife whipped toward his face. Han slipped away, but the cudgel user entangled him. Han fought him off, only to find Cut Foot wrapped around his leg, keeping him locked in place. Finally, Sha Wu struck Han, and he crumbled.

The sword user was upon him at that point, but Han leaped back to his feet, still choking from the force of Sha Wu's blow, and crushed the sword user's collar bone with a palm.

The Teacher continued his whirlwind palm strikes, pressing Han back. Cut Foot was again sliding across the ground, trying to pin down his leg, hindering his retreat.

The broadsword user slashed from the side. Han had no choice but to divert his attention to fight him off, and with one arm entangled elsewhere, he endured another heavy palm to his chest.

Han stumbled back, unable to breathe, and a thick wad of blood flew out of his mouth.

Then, Cut Foot shot his entire body at Han's waist, pinning him against the cavern wall.

The Teacher coiled back like a snake, his palms drawn back to his side as if holding a ball of fire. This was the final move of the Infinity Palm, the God Slayer, a strike meant to kill on impact.

Han could not move, still struggling to breathe from his new injuries. This was it. The Teacher would kill him here.

Sha Wu roared and shot forward with all his force and power.

Han screamed too late. A figure leaped in front of Han and endured the full impact of the God Slayer.

It was Yi Yi.

Without so much as a grunt, she collapsed in front of him. Han drew power he never knew he had and leaped into the air, kicking Cut Foot all the way across the cavern. He struck someone on the side of the head, killing him, then launched himself at everyone else.

The Teacher stepped back, arms folded, a smile on his face.

Han wanted to kill.

Yi Yi was dead for sure. No one had ever survived a direct hit from the God Slayer. Han felt his vision turn red, the heat on his face burning through his skin. He attacked the scattering men in a flurry of short-range strikes, using his palm, his fists, his backhand, his elbows. All of his movements became convoluted together, random and out of sync. The Teacher laughed from a distance.

Han pulled back, frozen in his step, before releasing two long, unexpected sweeps of his arms that pushed his opponents back.

The outcome of the fight no longer mattered to Han. He was supposed to have died, not Yi Yi. He could still die here with her, but not if he didn't take his enemies with him. Blinded, tormented, wishing his life would end with a long, echoing scream, Han freed himself from all his knowledge of martial arts prowess, abandoned thought and memory alike, and attacked his enemies for the pure joy of fighting. His rhythm was changing but not broken, his movements both fast and slow, himself barren and entangled.

A musician once told him it was the silence between notes that was the loudest. Han suddenly understood. The stillness between his attacks devastated them.

Han paused, and the opponents around him hesitated. Then, Han broke through with a roar and pounded someone, anyone, his Infinity Palm long and streaking, then turned short and explosive like bursts of lightning at close range. This was what Master Zuo saw in him long ago, his ability to create a rhythm that could not be defined.

Somewhere in the background, the Teacher broke into a short

laugh. "The fools hesitated. These men are not of our caliber. Might as well kill them."

Han plowed through someone else. He didn't notice who it was. He spun around, his eyes no longer red, his breaths smooth and easy, and he closed in on the remaining men. This was what Sha Wu talked about a few nights ago. This was the sheer pleasure of the art, the purity of every strike. He didn't know where the Teacher was and why he didn't come in to stop the slaughter. It no longer mattered why. Han had nothing else to live for, with Yi Yi dead, Master Zuo and Lan dead, the world hunting him and all his friends calling him a traitor. A new reality emerged for him.

Han passed by the stone ledge with Little Sparrow's bowl of lake scum, grabbed it and drank everything with one gulp. He didn't care what it did to him. If it worked against the fog, if it did nothing, if it was poisoned and he drowned in the cavern tunnels, it made no difference.

He ran to Yi Yi's body, his mind playing over and over again what happened. Yi Yi awakened somehow and blocked the Teacher's death blow, sacrificing her own life so that he may live. Why would she think he wanted to live if she did not?

His hands trembling, his face stiff, Han lifted her lifeless body and headed for the tunnel. The Teacher's men had not regrouped. Some of them were dead and the rest critically injured.

Sha Wu could've followed the Commoner, but there were no footsteps behind him. Instead, his voice trailed from within the cavern.

"Now, here's an innocent woman I am about to kill," Sha Wu said. Han spun around. Cut Foot had Little Sparrow pinned against the cavern wall, and the Teacher was pulling back, his hands coiling into position to use the God Slayer.

The Teacher turned to him and smiled. "Your beautiful archer is already dead. Want to stay a little longer to save this one?"

Little Sparrow turned to Han, shivering in pain, her face pleading to him.

The Teacher focused his attention on his target. "People like us have a better understanding of how fear and submission work. We should work together."

Han held Yi Yi in a close embrace and backed away. Nothing mattered anymore. He would take her body to a safe place so she could have a proper burial. If he died here, she wouldn't even have that.

The Teacher threw his head back to laugh before launching the God Slayer. Little Sparrow's body didn't even move from the impact, the entire strike penetrating her organs, ripping them apart. She crumbled without a sound.

Han leaped into the tunnel and slid down the slippery rocks that led into the first sharp turn in the passageways. Behind him, he heard the Teacher calling, "Now we're onto something. If more people came down to our level, you wouldn't be alone all the time!"

Han twisted through the bend and dropped into the lower caverns with Yi Yi pressed against him. His mind was numb. He didn't know what to think, what to do next. It wasn't that long ago that she was giggling over another bet with him, so she could stick her tongue out and poke fun out of him when he lost. Where would he go now? Where would he take her body? There was no place in the world for either of them.

He waded into the cold water, crouched down and pushed himself into the flooded tunnels, still clasping Yi Yi against his body. The tunnels narrowed and he swam ahead, dragging her body behind him. Leaving the tunnels felt a lot longer. Of course, there was no reason for him to swim fast.

Maybe he could carry Yi Yi's body back to West Sea and bury her by the bank where he was building his boat. He did promise her she would see his boat when he finished it.

Han emerged into the poison fog, breathing it deep into his lungs, and swam toward their boat. He lifted Yi Yi's body over the hull, cradling her, and rested her on the wooden floor beside her rapid-fire crossbow.

Two other boats were banked against Willow Island. Without a second thought, Han kicked them out into the waters, sending them drifting toward the center of the lake. Someone would have to breathe the poison fog in order to retrieve them.

Han sat back in his own boat and picked up the broken oar leaning against the back wall. Little Sparrow's drink worked—he was not affected at all by the fumes.

He pushed the boat off the shore and, with a weary exhale, rowed away. There was one oar; the other flew away when Han smashed it earlier. A nagging pain emerged when he thought of how Yi Yi threw both oars at him on this same boat. If only she had killed him then. She would be alive now, heading home to her prestigious post as the emperor's bodyguard.

Yi Yi's body slipped, and she fell to her side. Han dropped the oar and rushed to the front of the boat, wrapped both arms around her, and held her close to his heart before moving her back into her seated position.

He couldn't save Little Sparrow. He would never have gotten away if he had allowed the Teacher to draw him back into another fight. He was injured as well. He had no other choice.

The poor woman waited all her life to be with the man she loved, and in the end, the most he would do for her was leave her alive, alone on this poisonous island. What kind of man was this Li Yan? What kind of man was his son?

Then he felt it, so faint he thought he was dreaming. There was a warm breath blowing from her lips onto his neck. By the third time he noticed it, it was unmistakable. Yi Yi was still alive. He reached around her neck and felt for her pulse, carefully, patiently, until he found it. Her heartbeat was faint and weak, but it was there.

He reached behind her back and touched the area behind both lungs. They were clear. Was she conscious enough all this time to hold her breath through the cavern tunnels?

"Yi Yi!" he whispered. He knew she must've heard him. Perhaps she would wake up long enough to smile at him one last time.

"Yi Yi!" he called again. She was lifeless. He felt for the heartbeat. It was still there.

Han pulled her cold body closer and held her in his arms, tears streaming down his face like never before. For a long time, the boat drifted toward the shore where they started. The fog was easing, and the sharp afternoon sun stung Han's wet skin.

He didn't know what to say to her. Nothing he could say would express what he felt. He couldn't tell her he loved her —he should not say something that would keep her here if she was in too much pain and would rather it ended. He couldn't thank her for her sacrifice because what she did deserved so much more than a word of gratitude. She was dying. Nothing he could say or do would make it easier.

"You wanted to hear something else about me," Han said, whispering into her ear. He didn't know what else to say. "I'm not a very interesting person. I'm a statue, remember? I was going to be a hermit, all alone on a big lake."

There was no real current in Willow Lake, but it seemed to drift toward the opposite shore by itself, still propelled by the few attempts Han made earlier to row them forward.

"I never wanted to be around people," Han continued. "I never wanted to build a school like Master Zuo and teach young boys how to fight or settle down somewhere with a house and a garden. I don't like growing vegetables and waiting to harvest them when I can hook a fish out of the water and eat right away.

"I didn't look forward to the path my mother charted out for me, to become a famous master of martial arts so people would come bow before me. I don't even want to be found. I never enjoyed being alone, but it was inevitable. I was ready to live with that. I was even building a boat to live out my destiny.

"But then I met you. I didn't even know who you were until this morning. I thought I would never be alone again. I thought that from now on, I would always have someone to laugh with, someone to share with."

He sighed, a long trembling sigh, almost gasping for air in between. "But now you are leaving me too."

The fog cleared and they drifted through the middle of the lake.

Neither bank was visible and the waters were barren. There was no life on the lake, nor birds in the air. As the carriage driver said, there weren't even fish in there.

There was nothing left for him to say. Yi Yi didn't even open her eyes for one last smile. Han leaned back and faded away as the fatigue from days of fighting drained his energy. He wanted to sleep forever, and maybe dream of better days that could have been.

The dream did come. Suddenly, he was back in Ding Yi, standing in the middle of the carnage. There were bodies everywhere, some of them still twitching, all of them dying from a single sword wound to the throat. He inflicted those wounds. The bloody sword was still in his hand.

Barely clothed girls were running away, screaming. They had been captured by the Three Kills, a rogue gang feared and despised in the martial society. These girls were forced into prostitution. Then they were freed. He freed them.

Everyone in the gang was dead. Han single-handedly killed them all.

Except for one boy, no older than thirteen, who stood with his sword raised and stared down the Commoner. "I just needed something to eat," the boy said. "My mother had nothing to eat!"

"Han."

Han jolted from his nightmare. He was still on the boat, floating down Willow Lake. But he heard it, and it was her voice, a whisper.

"Han," Yi Yi said. Her voice was low, but it was louder than thunder to him. Han peeled away, still holding her, his fingers locked together and pressed against her back. Her lips were parted, the weight of her limp body resting against him. "Han," she said again, trying hard to smile. "I'm so happy."

"Yi Yi…" His mouth was quivering. "I'm so sorry…"

"Why?" she asked. "The emperor will kill me anyway. When I defied his edict, I planned to die so you could live. I am just doing it earlier than I planned."

"Don't say that." Han shook his head. "We can disappear together. It doesn't have to be this way."

Yi Yi smiled a bright, innocent beam of deep happiness, with hints of mischief and playfulness grazing the corners of her lips. "You're the only man who would let me put a bag over his head," she whispered. "You're not a statue. You are… infinitely interesting. I am glad you are the one I will die for."

"No, Yi Yi," Han said. "I've waited for you all these years. I've been wandering the land searching for you. Please don't give up now. I don't want you to die for me. I want you to live for me."

Yi Yi leaned her face against his shoulder. "I wish it was my choice."

"There is a chance," Han said, his voice quick and urgent. His mind churned through countless ideas. With a sharp gasp, he thought of something that Master Zuo mentioned many years ago about an old friend.

"There's a flower," Han said, almost muttering to himself. "An old friend of my Shifu's enjoyed growing exotic orchids and collecting flowers that the world had never seen. They call him the Orchid Farmer. My Shifu said he has a flower from Mount Heaven called the Snow Flower. It can heal any injury, no matter how serious. They say it can even raise the dead."

Yi Yi's breathing slowed but she was still conscious. Han cradled her neck and repositioned her so she would be comfortable in his embrace.

"I know where he lives," Han said. "Valley of the Headless. The Orchid Farmer may be in hiding but I can find him and I will bring back the flower. I will cure you, Yi Yi. Wait for me. Hang onto life and wait for me."

She smiled and reached up with a weak, trembling hand to touch his cheek. Han clasped her hand in his and brought it to his face.

"I don't want you to be lonely," she said. "If I die, who will make bets with you?"

"I love you," Han said, his voice hoarse. "Please hang on. Please let me have a chance."

"I will," she whispered, closing her eyes again. Han held her tighter.

The silence was long and painful. The world was still, motionless, void of life except for the faint heartbeat still beating in her chest. That's how Lan died, in his arms, just yesterday morning.

"I killed her," Han said. Yi Yi did not respond. "I killed my mother. There was a strange bubble coming out of the ginseng in her soup and I didn't say anything. Every night, for all those years I brought the soup to her, there were no bubbles. But that night I saw it and I didn't say a word. I knew something was wrong with the soup but I was afraid she would be angry with me over another problem, maybe even accuse me of trying to poison her. And that's what happened. Before she died, she pointed her finger at me and said I poisoned the soup. Everyone thought I did it. They all wanted to kill me, and I deserved it. I wanted to die."

Yi Yi stirred and whispered a soft murmur.

A familiar voice was shouting in the distance.

Han ignored it and touched Yi Yi's lips with his finger, feeling her weak breath. It was a miracle she was still alive.

She could not live for long, though. Traveling to the Valley of the Headless with her in this state would kill her sooner, but he could not leave her by herself either. Even if he found a nearby inn and the innkeeper promised to care for her while he was away, the Teacher might track their footsteps and find her.

Han woke from his thoughts when the shouting became louder and closer. It was Scrawny Fox's voice. Han almost stood up and jolted Yi Yi's injured body. Scrawny Fox was standing on the hill just above the shoreline, jumping and waving and screaming his name.

"Chen Han! Chen Han!" Scrawny Fox shouted. "You made it! You made it back alive!"

Han exhaled in relief, staring up to the heavens to offer a word of thanks. He was not alone in this.

As the boat drew closer, Scrawny Fox waded into the water to pull the boat into the bank. "What happened? Is the crazy bitch alive?"

Han lifted Yi Yi and stepped onto dry land. Careful not to aggravate her injuries, he carried her to a soft, grassy area and lowered her unconscious body into a comfortable position.

"She's badly injured," Han said to Scrawny Fox. "Can you help me?"

"Anything you say," Scrawny Fox answered. "Just tell me what to do."

"We need a fast horse. And food, supplies."

Scrawny Fox dug his hand into his pocket and pulled out the snuff bottle. "This is worth a lot. More money than anyone has around here."

Han gasped. Scrawny Fox was willing to part with his treasure.

"I will trade it for as much money as I can," Scrawny Fox said, "and I will be able to buy—"

"Hire a doctor!" Han said. "Find a doctor and bring him to me. And buy a carriage with at least four strong horses. I will walk east to the next town and find an inn. Meet me there as soon as you can."

Scrawny Fox pocketed the snuff bottle with a nod. He turned to run off, then stopped. "Is she going to make it?"

"She's running out of time," Han said. "If you don't come back fast with the horses, she won't."

"I will be back," Scrawny Fox said. "When a man loses everything, he still has his honor. When a man who has everything gives up his honor, he has nothing left. You taught me that. I'll fuck someone's grandmother before I forget."

Scrawny Fox spun around and sprinted away, reaching the edge of the forest in a few strides and then disappearing like a gust of wind.

Han picked up Yi Yi and turned once to the sparkling water of Willow Lake, so serene against the afternoon sunlight that at a quick glance, it seemed the image of paradise. He thought about the writings he found on the prison wall, left there by the emperor's brother Li Yan. The Judge's father.

CHAPTER 8

HAN CHECKED INTO the one inn he could find within walking distance from Willow Lake. Located on the outskirts of a small town in the middle of nowhere, the tiny inn had four rooms, all of them empty, and it was managed by an old widow who walked with a cane. If Scrawny Fox didn't return with the carriage soon, the Teacher would find and annihilate them with ease.

It was already dark outside by the time Han lowered Yi Yi into a comfortable bed. Then, he lit an oil lamp and placed it on a small table, closed the only window in the room, and soaked a towel in a bucket of warm water to clean her bare feet.

Yi Yi moaned. "Don't tickle me."

"How do you feel?" he asked. "Can you drink some water?"

She lifted her hand and he helped her into a sitting position, leaning her against the bedpost. He brought a water bottle to her lips and she managed to take a sip.

"As soon as Scrawny Fox comes back with a carriage," Han said, "we will travel to the Valley of the Headless together. I'll ask the Orchid Farmer for the Snow Flower and then you will be alright."

"I want to go with you and finish your boat," Yi Yi said. "And live like fairies on a lake." She lowered her face with a frown. "But we can't. Not yet."

"I understand."

"We still have to stop the Judge," she said. "And if I don't survive you have to do it, Han. You can't let him bully the people."

"I won't. I will finish your mission no matter what." Han reached behind her and touched her right shoulder blade. "Can you tell me about this tattoo?"

"My Shifu gave that to me when I was young," Yi Yi said. "He told me not to tell anyone, so even the emperor doesn't know about it."

"It means you are part of the Council of Midnight, right?" Han asked. "Who are they?"

"I don't know," she said. "He never told me anything, except that my first allegiance is to the council and one day he will call upon me to serve."

"Master Zuo had the same tattoo," Han said. "And so does the Teacher. You all belong to the same secret council."

"That's how I found out from Fu Nandong what happened to the magistrate," she whispered through uneven breaths. "I heard rumors that someone was sent to seduce the magistrate's wife. I showed him my tattoo and pretended I already knew everything. That's why he told me."

"Don't worry about why, Yi Yi," Han said, wrapping his arms tighter around her. "You don't need to explain anything."

"I know my Shifu is among the greats in this Council," Yi Yi said. "He's the most powerful archer in the world."

"What's his name?"

"They call him Lion Beard."

"I've never heard of him," Han said. "It seems the people in this secret council are all great warriors. Master Zuo wrote about a group of elite assassins. They worked for Li Yan. And the Judge must be Li Yan's son. That's the Judge's big secret—Li Yan is still alive and he was a prisoner there. The Judge set him free. But why would that give him so much power all of a sudden?"

Yi Yi leaned back and dozed off. Han wrapped his arm around her and lowered her into the bed, setting her head against the pillow and covering her with a blanket. He then picked up the towel and resumed washing her feet.

She groaned, whether from pain or sorrow he could not tell. When she could speak again, she asked him about Ding Yi.

Han hesitated. She repeated her question. "Why did you kill so many people in Ding Yi?"

Those memories were tucked away, meant to be forgotten forever. Han had wanted to assume the role of a common man since that fateful night, to withdraw from the worldwide fame that this single act brought him. There was a threat to society, a venom that no one dared confront, and he eliminated it all by himself. Everyone called him a hero. Yet, no one even knew what happened.

"I had to," Han said, his face blank. "The Three Kills were dangerous criminals. The inspectors spent years on this case until they were finally routed and brought to justice. But even when they had enough evidence to execute the entire gang, the corrupt magistrate set them free."

"What did the Three Kills do?" Yi Yi asked.

"Everything," Han said. "Murder, rape, kidnapping young girls for their brothels, extorting the common people. The heroes of the Martial Society wanted to deal with them for a long time but the government protected them. Master Song of the White Tiger House was an uncle of the chief inspector, and he brought the evidence against the Three Kills. Even then the chief inspector needed a year to gather enough police. He invited them from distant cities to help with the mass arrest. And it happened. They arrested the entire gang overnight."

"You were the one who wiped out the Three Kills," Yi Yi said.

"I did," Han said, lowering his eyes. "The magistrate came up with an excuse to release them. The chief inspector was jailed and the police were sent home with a warning not to interfere again. So I walked into Ding Yi to serve justice."

"And the magistrate didn't stop you?" Yi Yi asked.

Han heard the pounding of horses rushing toward the inn and leaped to his feet.

"Finally." Han picked up Yi Yi, held her close and ran out the door. A new carriage with iron bolted wheels, drawn by four horses, pulled up to the inn. The cabin boasted light wooden panels, painted in a deep shade of red, the image of a wealthy merchant's vehicle. Scrawny Fox was riding a tall stallion.

An old man with a white beard sat in the driver's seat. He grabbed a wooden box and climbed out of the carriage to greet them.

"You must be the doctor," Han said.

"Bring her inside," the doctor said, pointing back to the inn. "Let me take a look."

Han shook his head. "We need to move right away. Can you examine her in the carriage?"

After a second, the doctor shrugged his shoulders. "If you want. You've paid me for a whole year so I am here for whatever you need."

Han turned to Scrawny Fox. "Go inside and pay the innkeeper." He drew open the double doors on the back of the carriage, jumped in and lowered Yi Yi onto the floor. "Quick, doctor. She needs help."

Once the old doctor climbed into the carriage, Han leaped to the driver's seat and picked up the reins, slapping them on the horses once to urge them forward. They pushed ahead at a steady trot.

The doctor positioned a small pillow under Yi Yi's arm and placed his fingers on her wrist. He read one pulse for a long time, then the other, sighing and shaking his head. Han knew it was not good. She should have been dead already.

Soon, Scrawny Fox pulled up next to them on the stallion.

"We need to go to the Valley of the Headless," Han told him. "How can we lose these tracks so the Teacher can't follow us?"

"The Teacher?" Scrawny Fox asked.

"He's the one who did this to Yi Yi. I need your help."

"You have my word," Scrawny Fox said. "So, crazy bitch is your woman again, isn't she?"

"I am never letting her go."

They turned at a fork in the road. Scrawny Fox watched the back wheel, as well as the hoof tracks on the road. "We need rain," he said. "I don't know when it will rain hard enough to destroy these tracks."

"Then we keep moving until it rains," Han said. "We are at least a day ahead of them. They need to retrieve their boats to leave Willow Island, and then they need to buy horses and find our trail. We have some time."

"I'm sorry," the doctor said from behind. Han allowed the words to sink in, reminding himself that he already knew what the doctor was going to say, that nothing had changed. "I'm sorry," the doctor said again, climbing into the driver's bench next to Han. "She is too badly injured and there is no way to help her. Let's stop and see if she has any last words."

Han shook his head. "Thank you, doctor. Can you find a way to prolong her life?"

"Why?" the doctor asked. "Why let her suffer? Let her go. There is no other way."

"What if I can find the Snow Flower of Mount Heaven?"

The old man froze. Then he laughed a short, uncomfortable laugh. "No one knows where Mount Heaven is. Even if we were on Mount Heaven now, encountering a Snow Flower is so rare, you would never find one in time. I am sorry. I can see that you love her, but if you care about her, you need to let her go in peace."

"What if a Snow Flower is only a day away?" Han asked.

"Impossible," the doctor said. "It hasn't been seen for decades. Besides, anyone who found one would've used it right away. Who wouldn't want a long, healthy life?"

"Maybe there is someone out there who doesn't want to live forever," Han said. "No one knows who lives or dies tomorrow. We have to at least try. That's all we can ask of ourselves. Can you help? Can you keep her alive for as long as possible?"

The doctor nodded, his lips pressed together. His hand rested on the gold ingot Scrawny Fox gave him. "I don't believe you," he said, drawing a deep breath. "But I have been paid already. I will do what I can for her."

"Thank you."

The night was young, and then it was not. Han kept the four horses at a slow trot the entire time. Scrawny Fox had purchased the strongest horses in the area, and none of them were foaming at the mouth when dawn broke through the horizon.

Han pulled on the reins and drew the carriage to a halt. "I need to take your horse and ride east," he said to Scrawny Fox. "Can you hide Yi Yi somewhere? I am going after a medicine that may save her."

Scrawny Fox shook his head. "There's nowhere to hide around here."

"I can't leave knowing the Teacher may find her."

"You said the Teacher is a day behind," Scrawny Fox said. "As long as we keep moving, he won't catch us. We'll go east at a walking pace and you'll have no problem catching up on a single fast horse."

Han smiled. This boy was smarter and more strategic than he could ever be. With a nod, he leaped off the driver's seat and motioned for Scrawny Fox to take his place. The boy dropped from the massive stallion.

"While I am gone," Han said. "I need you to protect Yi Yi at all costs."

"I won't let you down," Scrawny Fox said. "I'll keep the carriage moving but I'll rest the horses often so they're ready to run if needed."

Han patted him on the shoulder and climbed into the cabin. Yi Yi was seated with her back against the side wall. She smiled with a light nod.

Han took her hand. "Yi Yi, I…"

"I know," she said. "Come back soon."

"I will get the flower no matter what."

She shook her head. "Don't do anything wrong, Han. Don't threaten to kill anyone if he doesn't want to give it to you. I am not worth it."

Han disagreed but said nothing. He turned to the doctor. "How much time do I have?"

"One or two days at most," the doctor said.

"Han," Yi Yi whispered. She motioned with her finger for him to come close. Han placed his ear by her lips.

"Don't reveal the Red Crest to anyone," she said. "Promise me."

"I promise," Han said.

"Promise me you won't let anyone know who you are," she said. "And you won't get involved in any more conflicts."

"I promise."

"No fights. Don't kill anyone."

"I won't."

He squeezed her hand once before jumping out of the carriage, backing away with a long, lingering look. Yi Yi managed a weak smile.

Han mounted the tall stallion and squeezed the horse's belly, sending it galloping toward the Valley of the Headless.

The lush valley was quiet, despite numerous footprints and wheel tracks on the lone road. Han knew very little about the Orchid Farmer, other than what his Shifu told him a long time ago, that he was a master at making weapons and that he collected exotic flowers. Like Master Zuo, the Orchid Farmer had been hiding for many years and very few people knew where he lived. But Master Zuo and the Orchid Farmer maintained their friendship and wrote to each other often. More than once, Han was asked to send a letter to the Valley of the Headless, and each time, an armed guard outside the main entrance would receive the letter. He was never invited inside and he never met the Orchid Farmer.

Han stopped his horse at a tree just outside the valley, dropped to the ground and tied the reins to the narrow trunk. He should not be riding into the orchid gardens. Out of respect he should proceed on foot.

The property was as barren inside as it was outside. Han didn't want to call attention to himself, knowing that if he were to secure the flower, it would only be because of Master Zuo's friendship with the weapons maker.

He wandered through the main gate and still did not see a single guard or servant. No one came to greet him. No one came to stop him. The few times he had been there as a boy, Han was always approached by a full staff. Something was wrong.

He picked up pace. What if the Orchid Farmer had died and the mansion was abandoned? Where would he find the flower then?

He crossed the first courtyard, and walked into the main hall, up to the desk where the host of the mansions would receive guests.

There were bloodstains everywhere, drops of blood splattered against the floor and leading out the rear door to the second courtyard. He heard human voices then, not far from where he stood. The voices were aggravated, angry, and filled with hatred. He had no idea what was happening, but he needed to move fast.

Han crossed the second courtyard in three massive steps and stopped in front of a door.

There were shouts within—perhaps an argument. He placed his hand on the doorknob. They were lion-faced doorknobs, just like the banquet hall where he fought his friends a few nights ago. Life had changed so much since.

Life would change a lot more again.

Han offered a half-hearted shove and the heavy doors creaked open, almost reluctantly.

Inside, numerous men held their weapons poised. They occupied most of the room. Han could not see anyone else beyond the soldiers cluttering the room, but he could already tell it was a bad situation.

Yi Yi was waiting for him. He did not have time to waste. He needed to find the Orchid Farmer as soon as possible.

"My apologies for the intrusion," Han said. "I wish to speak to the Orchid Farmer."

"Get out!" someone shouted. It was a high-pitched voice with an arrogant tone. A short man in silk robes, the only person not dressed in military attire, pointed his sword at Han.

These men appeared to be unskilled warriors at best. Han did not need to worry about them. The Snow Flower was everything.

Someone rushed toward him with a sword aimed for his face.

Han snatched the man's weapon and shot to the front of the room where he planted the cheap blade into the floor tiles. Then, with a silent roar that summoned all his strength, he pushed the sword half-way into the ground.

"Orchid Farmer," he whispered. No one heard him.

A slew of dead bodies littered the floor, a woman and two children. They were stabbed, slashed, executed in front of so many. Their bodies lay twisted in the same spots where they were slaughtered. No one bothered to straighten them into a more dignified position.

"Who are you?" the man in the silk robes asked. "What do you want?"

Han stared at the dead bodies, trembling. They were only babies. Yi Yi would have shot these people already. "I don't know what you're fighting over," he said. "I don't care why you're killing each other. But the children are innocent!"

"It's none of your business," the man said. "Interfere and you'll have to answer to the Judge."

Answer to the Judge. That was all he needed to hear.

"Whatever you need from me," someone said. It was a middle-aged man sitting behind a desk. Han had not noticed him earlier. He wore coarse, humble clothing, and his eyes pierced Han with a general's demeanor. His right arm, severed and bloodied, was strapped in a tourniquet.

"I'll give you whatever you want," the one-armed man said to Han. He pointed to a young man standing on the far left side of the room. "But this person cannot be allowed to die."

Han followed the direction of the old man's finger. His eyes landed on someone no older than eighteen with a hawkish gaze, his chin held high despite the fact that half the swords in the room were facing him. There was another man in the room surrounded by guards, a muscular figure dressed as a hunter. He too turned to the young man at the side of the room.

One guard spun around and bolted for the opened door, but the young man by the wall hissed and fired two needles into his back. The guard screamed, drew a bamboo whistle from his belt, and emitted two sharp bursts as he ran, and a few steps outside the door he collapsed into a shaking heap.

So this young man is a poison user, Han thought. A lethal one. He heard voices outside, the shouts of many men. The whistle was meant to call for help.

The big hunter launched himself at the leader in silk robes, bashing through two guards like they were harmless puppies, each murderous swipe with his massive arms more violent than the last.

Han was amazed. He had never seen a fighting system comprised of both prancing and smacking, a tiger devouring its prey coupled with human foresight and calculation of movement and distance. Shouldn't this warrior also be world-famous by now?

Han shook his head. He thought he knew every great fighter in the Martial Society. Yet, in a few days' time, he had encountered Sha Wu, Yi Yi, and now this big hunter whose skills should have propelled him to the forefront of fame and fortune. For a second, Han could not imagine how he would fight against a man with the power of a raging bull, the agility of a cat, and the combat intelligence of a human being who had seen it all.

Four guards closed in on Han. He yanked the sword from the tiles and glanced at the bloodied corpses on the floor. These people murdered defenseless children. He spun around and stabbed every single one of them in the eye, maiming them for life, ensuring they would forever remember this day. He wanted them dead, but he had promised Yi Yi not to get involved. He came for the flower and nothing else.

The one-armed man picked up a sword from behind the desk and charged into the thick of battle. "Blacksmiths!" he shouted. "Shut the gates! Shut the gates!"

This was the man who offered to give Han whatever he wanted as long as the poison user was protected from harm. He must be the Orchid Farmer. There was no one else in a position to demand something like that.

The Orchid Farmer was still bleeding, despite the tourniquet, his face ashen white and his left arm trembling from weakness. Yet, he was continuing to fight. If Han didn't protect the Orchid Farmer, he would never get the flower and Yi Yi would die. If he did not protect the poison user, then it might not matter whether the Orchid Farmer lived or not.

Han launched himself into two guards approaching the young man. The greatest warrior in the world had to be able to fight more than one front in any battle. He wove in and out of the crowd like a ghost, slashing and stabbing his enemies' elbows and wrists, disarming them in a flurry before slipping back to fight alongside the Orchid Farmer.

The battle raged. The hunter was pounding his way across the room, destroying any guards who closed in to protect their commander. Han disabled two guards approaching the Orchid Farmer from behind, when he heard the young man shout, "Colonel Ko Sun!"

The leader in silk robes froze.

"Your men will testify that you're running from your post," the poison user shouted. "Can you lose the Red Crest and still face the Judge?"

Ko Sun turned around.

Han was mesmerized. The young man launched a deceptive handful of needles, all decoys, while he kept the actual weapon hidden in his other hand. Ko Sun was leaping back into the room when a single needle struck him in the arm.

What tactics, Han thought. This young man is a genius. The poison user was more than one step ahead of his opponents at all times. He would not be easy to kill.

Then, a scream of pain. Han felt his heart sink to his stomach when he saw the guard standing over the Orchid Farmer.

Han shot forward and slashed the guard's neck open, then turned to two other approaching men and slaughtered them with two rapid jabs of his sword.

The Orchid Farmer was curled up on the floor, clutching the deep wound in his stomach.

Han was distracted and failed to protect him.

Then, men poured in from the front door, swinging their heavy weapons, and two of them rushed to the Orchid Farmer's side. One took his hand while the other worked to hold down the bleeding with a cloth.

Han needed to focus. He needed that flower. Why entangle himself in the web of other people's politics when the woman he loved was dying?

Then it dawned on him, and a cold chill crept up his back. The Orchid Farmer was dying. He would need the flower to save himself.

There was no other way. Maybe the old man had more than one, or maybe he would only need half. Han did not know but he had to ask. Yi Yi was dying.

The men who rushed in were the Orchid Farmer's blacksmiths, some of them carrying unfinished weapons. With the help of the unarmed hunter, who was smashing the guards with a wooden bench, they turned the tide of the slaughter. There was nothing Han could do but wait. The Orchid Farmer was gravely injured but he wouldn't die right away, and the battle had to subside before Han could talk to him.

Han drew back and lowered his sword. The hunter was nowhere to be seen. Han didn't know whether Ko Sun survived the poison needle but there was no corpse with silk robes on the floor. He must have escaped.

"Sir," the poison user said, approaching the Orchid Farmer. The dying man reached for his hand.

"Why?" the younger man asked.

"I left the Judge's father to die," the Orchid Farmer said. "The Judge would never spare my family. He will use me, and then he will kill us all."

Li Yan didn't die, Han wanted to say. The Judge's father was alive and escaped imprisonment. But again he refrained. He promised Yi Yi not to get involved.

"I'm not worth it," the young man said, a tear streaming down his face. "How could you? How could you watch them die like that?"

"I will see them soon," the Orchid Farmer said. Han listened to every movement to ensure that no more threats emerged. He had to wait for his turn to speak. After all, the Orchid Farmer defended this person with his life.

The urgency of the Snow Flower rattled Han's core, but he suppressed it. Other people were worried about loved ones too. Others had lost everything today.

"I don't have magical powers, sir," the young man said.

The Orchid Farmer was fading, and a stream of blood gushed from his mouth. Han needed to ask him for the flower soon or it would be too late. Still, he held his posture. He had learned, over the years, that waiting was not a defeated circumstance robbed of victory and glory. Waiting was about forgetting that he was waiting.

"Sir," the young poison user said. "Tell me what to do. Tell me how to stop him."

"Go to the City of a Thousand Heroes," the Orchid Farmer said. "Go and show General Yang what you showed me."

"General Yang? Why?"

"He will protect you. He will know what to do."

"Why protect me?" the poison user asked. "Why does it matter if I live or die?"

"Master!" someone shouted. It was a blacksmith carrying a damaged weapon. "Master, we've killed all forty soldiers in the second unit. We sealed the doors and our men are tending to the wounded."

"How?" the Orchid Farmer asked. "How did you defeat forty professional soldiers?"

"The big hunter killed most of them all by himself," the blacksmith said. "We've never seen anyone like that. He fights like an animal . . . And their archers were all dead."

The Orchid Farmer lifted his left hand and pointed out the door. His large sleeve rolled back, and Han could not believe what he saw. He froze, staring at the sight, no longer aware of what the young man was saying. Tattooed on the Orchid Farmer's left arm were two eyes in the exact same position as Master Zuo and the Teacher. The symbol of the Council of Midnight.

Someone stood beside him then. It was the big hunter, his hands stained with blood—other people's blood. He had a smile on his face. Then his expression changed with one look at the Orchid Farmer.

"Is he going to make it?" the hunter asked.

Han shook his head. "He has very little time."

"Zhuge Nu," the Orchid Farmer said between gasps. "The cylinder at the head of the bolt is heavy. They may fly far, but they have to rain from above. They cannot shoot anything close."

"So we need to charge them as soon as they release the arrows," the poison user said.

"Yes! You've got it."

"You made the cylinders whistle so everyone can hear them coming," the young man continued. "Your weapons are flawed. Then their other weapons must also be flawed."

So, the famous Orchid Farmer, a member of the Council of Midnight, made the Zhuge Nu arrows for the Judge, Han realized. How could that be, if the Judge killed off his entire family?

Wait—the Snow Flower!

"I know time is precious now," Han said. "Please, if you can spare just one minute for me. It's urgent."

The Orchid Farmer nodded. "I will speak to this master alone."

"Yes, sir." A teenage boy with a group of blacksmiths stepped back. The poison user withdrew as well.

"Is the boy your son?" Han asked.

The Orchid Farmer nodded. "The last in my family." He struggled to lift his hand and motioned for Han to come closer. Han knelt down, took his hand and leaned his ear closer to the Orchid Farmer's trembling lips.

"You came here to ask me for something. Is it a weapon?"

"A flower," Han said. "Someone I love is dying and I need the Snow Flower from Mount Heaven."

"It is yours," the Orchid Farmer said. "In exchange for a favor."

"Really?"

"Escort the young poison user to the City of a Thousand Heroes. Protect him at all costs. Once you hand him over to General Yang, your obligations for the flower are complete. I will trust you to your honor."

"Who is he?" Han asked. "Why don't you want the flower for yourself? Don't you want me to protect your son instead?"

The Orchid Farmer shook his head. "My life is nothing. The poison user can unite the people and stop the Judge. Make this promise to a dying man."

Han squeezed his hand. "I promise. In exchange for the Snow Flower, I will bring this young man to safety."

The Orchid Farmer smiled. "Is there anything else?"

"The Council of Midnight," Han whispered, pointing to the tattoo on the Orchid Farmer's arm. "Who are they? Do you work for the Judge or oppose him?"

"I have not been a part of the council for fifteen years," the Orchid Farmer said. "They support the Judge. I heard they are planning something, and they are targeting the Tiger Generals. I don't know anything else."

There was little time left, and the Orchid Farmer still needed to speak to the poison user. "Thank you," Han said, then withdrew.

The Orchid Farmer motioned for his son. The young man, who had been standing a short distance away, ran over and held his ear to his father's lips. Han stepped back and waited.

The Orchid Farmer whispered lengthy instructions and sent the boy away. He then supported himself on one elbow and motioned for the poison user to approach. The big hunter followed right behind him.

The Orchid Farmer noticed the hunter, and motioned for him first. "You have something to ask me?"

"Yes, but I need to ask you in private," the hunter said, crouching down.

"You will," the Orchid Farmer said. "I will tell you whatever I know. That's a promise."

"Thank you."

"But first, I have a favor I must ask."

"Say it," the hunter said.

"Promise me," the Orchid Farmer said, pointing to the young poison user. "Promise to escort this young man to the City of a Thousand Heroes. Make sure he arrives safely."

"Why?" the poison user asked. "Why am I so important?"

"It's best that you don't know," the Orchid Farmer said. "You'll be safer."

The hunter clasped the Orchid Farmer's hand. "It'll be my honor to fight beside the poison user. He's a great warrior."

Han stepped forward to introduce himself. "My name is Chen Han. I also promised the same. The three of us will travel together."

"And your son?" the poison user asked. "Who will protect him?"

"I can protect myself," the boy said. The Orchid Farmer's son emerged from behind them with a silk embroidered box tucked under his arm. He handed it to Han.

Han bowed his head and received it with both hands, then stepped aside and unhooked the locks. Inside was another wooden box, and when he slid the cover off, he found a dried flower, meaty and thick and browned with age, sitting on a bed of charcoal.

Han had never seen a Snow Flower before. Very few people had. But he trusted the Orchid Farmer, and he knew, from the care and details in how it was preserved, that at least the Orchid Farmer believed it was a real Snow Flower. Han whispered a word of thanks, his throat tight.

"My name is Ah Go," the hunter said, who walked over to stand in front of Han. "I have never seen a warrior like you."

"The respect is mutual," Han said.

"We should fight one day. I want to see how fast you really are."

Han smiled and said nothing. He had never seen a man fight like a predator before. To fight Ah Go one day would mean experiencing combat like he had never before seen in China.

The Orchid Farmer's son ran back into the room panting, followed by two other men. He was carrying a long box wrapped in cloth.

"I have great inventions," the Orchid Farmer said. "They are all here."

The teenage boy opened the heavy box in front of his father, revealing a massive saber inside. It was thick and wide, the steel blackened and the curved edge razor sharp.

"This is for you," the Orchid Farmer said to Ah Go. "It can break other weapons. Other weapons cannot break it. It looks big and heavy but it can dance in the air with ease. I named it the Butterfly."

"I'll treasure it always," Ah Go said, picking up the weapon. "It's not heavy. How can it be so light?"

The Orchid Farmer smiled. "*That* is my secret."

The next box contained a double-edged sword—narrow, thin, and blackened, but the surface dull and uninteresting. The Orchid Farmer motioned to Han.

"I recognize you," the Orchid Farmer said. "There can be no one else. With your help, this young man can be safe. I offer you this gift. It's the greatest sword I have ever created."

"I can't accept this gift," Han said. "I don't deserve it. But I have given you my word that I'll escort . . . " He stopped. "You don't even know his name," Han whispered.

"Mu Feng," the young man said, stepping forward. "My name is Mu Feng."

The Orchid Farmer smiled. "Of course. The Tiger General's son." He turned back to Han. "This sword may look flimsy, but it can't be broken. It has no glimmer and it makes no sound. With your speed, your opponent won't be able to see it and won't be able to hear it. This weapon will make you so much more powerful. I've named it the Dart."

"I . . . " Han could not accept. He didn't know what to say, nor what was appropriate behavior in a situation like this.

"You must," the Orchid Farmer said. "You must, so I can die knowing that I've thanked you for the favor."

Han continued to stutter in response. "I thank you."

The Orchid Farmer was fading. He pointed to the last box, a smaller, square container made of dark wood. "For the general's son," he said.

"How can I accept another gift from you?" Feng asked.

The Orchid Farmer's son pulled a thick leather belt and a pair of long silver gloves out of the box. The gloves were thin as silk but reflected a cold metallic blue.

"If you don't . . ." the Orchid Farmer mumbled. ". . . If you don't take care of yourself . . . Then none of this will be worth it."

He planted a shaky elbow, his eyes dimmed, and turned to Ah Go. "Your question . . . in private."

Han bowed and took one last glance at the Orchid Farmer. He would not see this man alive again. What kind of person would give up everything he had, including the lives of his family, in exchange for the safety of someone he had never met? What could be so important about this Tiger General's son?

Han turned around and withdrew. Feng and the Orchid Farmer's son followed him out the door, leaving Ah Go alone with the dying man.

Feng caught up with him as soon as he got outside. "My name is Mu Feng," he said with a bow. "I'm not sure who I am, and . . . and I'm ashamed that you have to protect me."

This young man trapped Ko Sun with a few words and a diversion, almost killing him with a poison needle. Very humble for a man with such a powerful mind.

Han returned the bow. He wanted to say that he didn't know who he was either. But he remembered his promise to Yi Yi.

"How about this?" Han said. "One day, when you have to protect me, I promise not to feel ashamed either."

"I can barely see you when you move," Feng replied. "Who can harm you?"

Han rubbed the silk embroidered box. He had little time to lose, but he also had a promise to keep, an agreement with a dying man. This young poison user seemed to know nothing about the world, yet he carried foresight in battle few had ever possessed.

Feng turned to ask the Orchid Farmer's son for something, and Han walked toward the entrance of the property, eager to reach his tall stallion and ride toward Yi Yi's carriage. If Scrawny Fox kept his word—and Han had no choice but to trust the little thief—the carriage would be traveling east at a steady pace. Han's fast stallion would catch up to them in half a day.

He needed to leave now. Yi Yi's life depended on it.

For a long time, the road leading out of the valley was quiet. Han was alone, waiting for Feng and Ah Go while pondering his own thoughts. Four Tiger Generals each protected a critical city along the Great Wall, facing aggressive barbarian nations outside the northern border. Barbarian kings like the Silencer posed a horrific threat to the country, and it was the four Tiger Generals, the most talented and experienced commanders in the world, who prevented men like him from invading.

General Mu, Feng's father, guarded the mouth of the Silk Road via the City of Stones, a fortress that bordered the Uyghur nation. He was known as the shrewdest among the generals. His battle strategies were devious and unorthodox, and his son showed the same qualities.

East of General Mu was General Wu in the City of Eternal Peace. He faced the Mongol kingdoms, now almost all united under the Silencer. General Yang in the City of a Thousand Heroes also faced the Mongols. Han recalled his long friendship with General Yang, a great martial artist and the most experienced and formidable of the Tiger Generals.

General Lo guarded the eastern part of the Chinese empire against the Khitan border. Han heard that he was killed by the Silencer. His prodigy Zeng Xi, almost as capable, took over Lo's army.

If the Tiger Generals were killed, the nation could fall. Without them guarding the borders, any of the barbarian nations would march through the Great Wall and burn their way to the capital. The Imperial Army would be no match for the Silencer.

Han clenched his fingers around the hilt of his new sword until they trembled. This Judge, this Council of Midnight, had been hunting him and killing the people he loved. And now, they were threatening the survival of the people. For what reason he did not know, but it was time to fight back. How could the greatest warrior in the world build a boat and go into hiding while the world burned?

Feng and Ah Go emerged from a bend behind him.

"One day I want to learn your fighting style," Ah Go said to Feng.

"My fighting style? I don't . . . "

"You can predict what your enemy will do next," Ah Go said. He pointed at Han. "That makes you faster than him."

Even the hunter noticed it. The general's son could see the future.

"Stop making fun of me," Feng said. "Before today, I didn't even know such skill existed out there. Where did the two of you learn how to fight like that?"

"I learned from my family," Ah Go said. "From my brothers Shiny, Silly, and Sulk."

"What?"

Ah Go laughed. "They're mountain leopards. They taught me everything I know about killing people."

Feng turned to Han.

"I was fortunate to be raised by a great master," Han said, trying to say something generic. Both men seemed genuine enough, but Han did not want to call attention to himself. The Commoner was not a popular person right now. "He taught me well. And you?"

"My father is General Mu. He guards the Uyghur border in the northwest."

"You're really a Tiger General's son?" Han asked.

Feng nodded. He paused for a moment before saying, "I have a favor to ask."

"Say it," Ah Go said.

"I promised the Orchid Farmer that I would go to General Yang's fortress right away. But, on our way there, if the enemy attacks me, would you fight by my side?"

"Of course," Ah Go said. "That's what we promised the weapons maker."

"Even if I invited the enemy to hunt me down?"

"I see," Han said. "You want Ko Sun."

"Ko Sun has fled," Ah Go said with a laugh. "You can get him to follow us? I really want to learn your fighting style."

"Help me," Feng pleaded. "I won't be able to sleep at night until the child killer dies a horrible death."

"We have to kill whomever attacks you," Han said. "That's why we're traveling together. You know that. You're using our promise against your enemies."

"Ko Sun can choose to go home and retire," Feng said. "He doesn't have to come after me. I won't need to be protected if he makes the right choice."

"Your approach is not exactly noble," Han said. "But it would be good to rid the world of this scum. I will help."

"It's my honor to fight beside you," Ah Go said. "And I would love to see how you plan to find him."

Feng drew a map from his belt, unrolled it on the ground, and knelt in front of it. "Here's my plan," he said. "We need to travel north. There are three towns and sixteen villages around this valley. Most of them are a single day away."

Han and Ah Go stepped closer.

"We can go due north and wait for Han in the village farthest from here," Feng said. He pointed to a spot on the map labeled Zhun Yang. "I've already paid the blacksmiths to travel to all sixteen villages and three towns. They will visit every village doctor for their injuries and then spread rumors of someone badly injured carrying the Red Crest."

"Red Crest?" Han asked. How did Feng know about it? He

wished he had never promised Yi Yi to keep the symbol on his body a secret.

"I've already described to them what it looks like," Feng said.

Han sucked in his breath. Perhaps the same symbol was on the general's son as well.

"That's what Ko Sun is after," Feng continued. "He's lost his arm and he would need a doctor to change his bandages at least for the next two days. Every doctor will be paid to spread the rumors. Ko Sun will hear the rumors and he won't be able to resist."

"What are the rumors going to say?" Ah Go asked.

"That the injured person carrying the Red Crest is traveling north and he needed help finding a small village named Zhun Yang."

"And we're going to wait for him in Zhun Yang?" Ah Go asked, laughing. "This is going to be fun."

"Ko Sun is crafty and careful," Feng said. "He would suspect a trap. But he lost the Red Crest and now his life depends on finding it again. Chasing after this trap would be his only hope."

Feng pointed to Zhun Yang village on the map. "We'll wait for him here. He can't assemble a large army in a short time without risking his leads disappearing, so at best, he would summon a small regiment. Big or small, we can't have any surprises. Han, I need you to stay behind and wait for them to pass you. Have a good look at how many men they have and what kind of weapons and training they bring. Afterwards, join us in Zhun Yang village and we'll prepare for them together."

Han barely followed the plan, but he understood. He placed a hand on the brilliant poison user's shoulder. "One day, when you have to protect me, I promise not to feel ashamed."

"Maybe he'll follow in disguise?" Ah Go asked.

"Ko Sun is very careful," Feng said. "I noticed it when he surrounded the valley with archers even though he was in complete control of the Orchid Farmer's mansion. But now he's missing an arm and he's afraid we'll recognize him. He'll come after me with plenty of men and we'll spot him easily."

They reached the mouth of the valley where Han's horse was waiting outside, tied to a tree. Han needed to chase down Scrawny Fox's carriage and get the flower to Yi Yi right away. "I apologize for leaving," he said. "I'll be there as soon as I can." He spun around and ran off.

CHAPTER 9

It DIDN'T TAKE long for Han to find the trail left behind by Scrawny Fox's carriage. He drove his horse to a gallop, its hoofs pounding the soft road and leaving a cloud of soil and dust behind them. With the embroidered box clutched in one hand and the reins in the other, Han stood on his stirrups and rode with his head down. In a moment, he pulled up behind the carriage, which was traveling due east at a comfortable walk.

Yi Yi was conscious and smiling, and the doctor was grinding herbs in a stone mortar in anticipation of the Snow Flower arriving. He had already started preparing the life-saving medicine.

Han instructed Scrawny Fox to change course and head toward Zhun Yang. He then sat next to Yi Yi and explained to her what happened in the Valley of the Headless, the promise he made and the sacrifice he witnessed.

"Are your new friends fun to be around?" Yi Yi asked. The doctor had finished grinding the Snow Flower and mixing it with his other herbs. He spooned the medicine into her mouth. Yi Yi made a face. "It's nasty."

"I don't know if they are fun," Han said. "But both are extraordinary and formidable. I have never been afraid of anyone before, but I would be afraid of Feng if he ever became my enemy."

"I'm so glad," Yi Yi said.

"Why?"

"Then he can protect you until I'm fully recovered," she said.

The doctor continued spooning the bitter paste into her mouth. Han sat back and watched her chew. Her complexion was improving.

"It's coming! It's coming!" Scrawny Fox shouted from the driver's seat.

"What is?" Han asked. Then, an unmistakable flash of lightning streaked across the sky, followed by a distant rumble of thunder. Rain was approaching, and it would arrive with a vengeance. Their trail would be impossible to find once the roads flooded.

"Go!" Yi Yi said, her voice stronger already. "You have a promise to keep."

Han leaned forward and took her hands. "I have something to tell you before I go. The Orchid Farmer told me the Council of Midnight is plotting something big. They may try to kill the Tiger Generals. If we are to stop the Judge, we need to stop him from harming the Tiger Generals first."

"I've heard of this too," Yi Yi said. "I don't know what they are plotting but I know my Shifu Lion Beard is involved. I heard they plan on killing tens of thousands of people."

"After I escort Feng to General Yang's fortress," Han said. "I will stay to protect him. Maybe the council is planning to send assassins."

"You're one person Han," Yi Yi said. "And there are three Tiger Generals, plus Zeng Xi."

Han sighed. "You're right. Who do I defend first?"

"I'm always right." She broke into a wide grin.

"Where can we find help?"

"After I recover," Yi Yi said, "I will try to convince the heroes of the Martial Society to help. No assassin will confront hundreds of martial arts masters, even if he can sneak past the Tiger General's guards."

The first heavy drops of rain struck the roof of the carriage, and in a moment, the storm swept in above them, pounding the earth with a heavy downpour. Scrawny Fox drew the carriage to a halt in the middle of the road. Then, he climbed off the exposed driver's seat and crawled into the cabin to avoid the rain.

"You need to go," Yi Yi said, lifting a weak hand to touch Han's face. "We're safe now. The wheel tracks are gone."

Han clasped her hand against his cheek, mesmerized by her gaze and her voice. She was everything to him, the one who would pull him out of his lonely existence, the girl who would be his home and forever change his destiny as a wanderer.

Yet, he was distracted by thoughts of the Orchid Farmer. The weapons maker also had a home and a beautiful family. He gave it all up, watched his children die in front of him, sacrificed everything because he believed that Feng could stop the Judge.

"I have to go," Han whispered. He never thought he would be able to say it with resolve. "But it's not because of my promise to the Orchid Farmer. It's because, maybe, Feng really could stop the Judge."

After a long, lingering goodbye, Han leaped onto his stallion and galloped away. The heavy rain drenched him, and he couldn't see through the downpour. But his horse was strong and he was determined to reach Feng and Ah Go before nightfall.

The cold rain and rhythmic trot allowed Han a quiet moment to think about what was happening. The past few days, he had faced one threat after another, from the warriors of the martial society to the Zhuge Nu, then the Teacher, and then Yi Yi's close brush with death. The Judge was too far ahead. He had too many people, weapons, money. He was too well established for Han to have a chance to fight back. He still did not know why the Judge was hunting him. He didn't even know who the Judge was.

Ever since meeting Feng and Ah Go, it felt possible. They would travel together to the City of a Thousand Heroes and convince General Yang to deal with the emperor's rogue nephew.

If the Judge wanted the Red Crest so much, Han should be able to lure him out into the open.

A blast of thunder sent his horse lurching back, pawing the air with its front legs, and Han almost fell out of the saddle. Three more flashes of lightning ignited the dark heavens. Han pulled the reins, struggling to calm his horse. The storm was too intense. He needed to stop somewhere and wait for it to pass.

In the distance waved a large cloth sign with the word "liquor" on it. It was an outdoor liquor stand with a cloth canopy, and several people stood underneath, taking cover from the rain while sipping on bowls of hard alcohol. Han rode across a short field, splashing through deep puddles of water, and pulled up next to a row of wooden stakes planted into the ground. This was where patrons tied their horses. The water troughs next to the stakes were overflowing with rainwater and Han's stallion had no interest in drinking.

There was one person running the liquor stand, a thin bearded man with a short saber, sitting at the far end of the canopy. There were a few casks of liquor behind him on the ground, and beside him was a table with a stack of clean bowls.

"A bowl of liquor?" he asked Han with a smile.

Han's pockets were flushed with the coins Scrawny Fox handed him when he departed. The sale of the snuff bottle yielded a lot more money than the boy knew what to do with.

"I'll take the whole cask," Han said. He threw down a gold piece and picked up the clay vessel from the ground, shredded the paper seal covering the spout, and poured the liquor into his mouth.

It was cheap liquor, but after a few gulps, he felt better. The alcohol took effect right away and he felt a stinging heat in his stomach, warming his cold body.

"Get out of here!" someone shouted. They drew forth a weapon, which sharply reverberated.

It was a group of soldiers, about twenty of them, armed and wearing plate armor. One other soldier showed his saber to the civilians sitting around the table, and they all grabbed their bowls and retreated. Some ventured back into the rain.

"Bring all your liquor!" a soldier shouted to the owner. "Please, general," he said, his voice suddenly taking on a much more courteous tone. "Come sit here."

Han could not believe his luck. The general was Fu Nandong. It was just the person he needed at this time.

Without a word, Han shot into the nearest soldier, striking his shoulder and dislocating it. He stomped out the knee of another soldier, then broke the elbow of a third man's sword arm before reaching Fu Nandong. He grabbed the category three general and threw him into the rain and mud. Then, he drew the Dart, spun around and ran diagonally across the row of soldiers.

They never had time to draw their weapons. The plate armor didn't protect their legs below the knees, so he stabbed the soldiers in the ankle, every single one of them. The Dart was so light and effortless to use that even Han was surprised. They started to fall over sideways like wooden chopsticks. Han sheathed his weapon without a word and in two steps, he was hovering over Fu Nandong.

Fu Nandong had not recovered from the fall. It took him a while before he recognized the Commoner. By the time he did, Han had grabbed him by the belt and lifted him over his shoulders. He headed to his horse, unhooked the reins, and threw Fu Nandong onto the saddle. Then, after swinging himself onto the general's back, Han urged the horse into a rapid trot.

The soldiers behind him shouted, but none of them could walk. Han rode into the blinding rain unhindered.

Fu Nandong was whimpering, then screaming, then muttering a winded tirade of profanities. Han ignored him and drew his horse around a hill, out of sight from the injured soldiers, and pushed deep into the muddy fields flooded by rain.

Once they reached a clearing, Han jumped off the horse, grabbed Fu Nandong by the belt and dragged him down to the ground. He was gripping the Dart in his hand, and his heavy footsteps kicked up wide splashes of water. Fu Nandong scrambled to his knees after a hard landing and had just turned around to orient himself when Han drew his black sword and slashed him vertically, splitting his plate armor in half. He did not cut through skin, but the broken armor sliding off his body sent Fu Nandong into a new frenzy.

"What do you want! Get away from me!"

Han kicked him in the chest and leaped forward. He stabbed the general through the arm, driving the lean blade deep into the earth and pinning Fu Nandong to the ground.

Fu Nandong arched his back and screamed while reaching for the hilt of the sword with his other hand. Han grabbed Fu Nandong's hand and twisted his thumb backwards, breaking the ligaments. Fu Nandong squealed in pain, then broke into short, heaving sobs. "What do you want from me?"

This was the coward who seduced Lan, then the magistrate's wife. Both were killed, and he never experienced a moment of remorse. Han's eyes flashed fire. The anger and frustration of what had happened to him, happened to the world, burned through his clenched fists.

He promised Yi Yi not to kill this scum.

Han grabbed the sleeve of Fu Nandong's shattered hand and shredded it.

There was the symbol of the Council of Midnight, right where Han thought it would be, tattooed under his left forearm. Han locked the wrist and twisted his arm, triggering more pain. Fu Nandong had lost his voice. Though he arched his neck back with his mouth open, there was no scream.

"What is the council planning to do?" Han shouted.

"What are you talking about?" Fu Nandong wailed. "Which plan are you talking about?"

Han twisted his wrist again and Fu Nandong squirmed and shrieked. "The plan against the Tiger Generals!" Han said. "What is it?"

"The Manifestation," Fu Nandong tried to say through choked whimpers.

Han relaxed his grip to allow him time to recover and talk.

"The Manifestation," Fu Nandong said again. "It's happening in three weeks and the Grand Chancellor is leading it himself."

"Who is the Grand Chancellor?"

"I don't know." A wave of fear swept across the general's face. "No! No! Don't hurt me. I don't know. My rank is not high enough in the council to meet him. That's the truth."

"What is the Manifestation?"

"It's the plan to destroy the Tiger Generals so the Judge can install his own in their place."

"I see," Han whispered. "Who are these people? How can members of this Council be everywhere, yet no one knows anything about them?"

"Maybe they don't want people like you to know, you piece of…"

Han pulled the sword halfway out of Fu Nandong's arm, inciting another round of choked screams. Han never knew he had it in him, torturing a man for information, inflicting so much injury and suffering upon a person. But sometimes, when the world was about to burn, honor and nobility became second priority.

"No one can hear you," Han said. "I will hurt you over and over again until I am satisfied with what you tell me."

Fu Nandong collapsed into pitiful whimpers, shivering and shuddering. It was only two days ago that the same man was broken the same way.

"The Council," Fu Nandong said. "They are a secret group of some very powerful people. You're no match for them, Commoner. There's too many of them so all you can do is run. They will have you for breakfast and spit out your bones for the dogs."

"What do these people do?"

"They formed the council to bring Li Yan to power," Fu Nandong said.

"The emperor's younger brother Li Yan?" Han asked. "He has not been around for many years. Why is this Council still active?"

"Li Yan is not dead," Fu Nandong said. "They can still get what they were promised if he becomes emperor, or if his son becomes emperor. His son made the same offer as his father."

"What? A lot of money?"

"Ha! So naïve," Fu Nandong said with a laugh. "You think

the Council would settle for a few gold coins? They will get land! Enough land to each declare themselves kings in their own piece of the empire."

Han frowned. "How much of the country can be given away to so many kings?"

"Just five," Fu Nandong said. "The Chancellor and the other four founders."

"What's in it for you?"

"My father sent me here," Fu Nandong said. "We have a partnership with the Judge. Besides, I get all the beautiful Chinese women…"

Han shoved the Dart deep into his arm again. Fu Nandong screamed.

"Partnership with the Turkic kingdoms?" Han shouted. "Is he selling our country? Is the Judge a traitor?"

Fu Nandong could not speak. Han wanted to kill him but he knew this was not the time. "What is the deal between the Judge and the Turkic kingdoms?" Han asked again. "If you don't tell me I will kill you."

"I don't know," Fu Nandong said, sobbing. "I don't know what my father plans to do. He ordered me to come here and report to the Teacher. The Teacher gave me a category three rank so I could lead their secret army. I don't even have experience leading an army—I was given all this power, and I don't know why. All I know how to do is get into a woman's bed."

Fu Nandong broke into long wails, weeping like a child.

"How did he know about Willow Island?" Han continued in a harsh voice, one he did not recognize. He had no patience for this pathetic pretty face. "How did he know his father was still alive and locked up in there?"

"I don't know," Fu Nandong whimpered.

Han crouched low and hovered over his face. "How did he know there was a map? How did he know who had this map?"

Fu Nandong, trembling in fear and begging for mercy, shook his head.

"How did you know to seduce the magistrate's wife?" Han shouted in his face.

"The Teacher told me to."

"When? Why?"

"I…" Fu Nandong gasped. "The Judge met with the emperor's mother. He… he's her grandson too. And shortly afterwards he knew about the map and where to find it."

"I see," Han said, sitting down and leaning away. "After you stole the map, the Judge found his father on the island. Since then, he gained control over the Zhuge Nu and all the spies in the country, and now he is trying to wipe out the Tiger Generals and take the throne. No one knows how he attained so much power. But what does the Red Crest have to do with it? Why am I being hunted?"

"I don't know," Fu Nandong whispered. "You asked me before, but I don't know. After Zuo Lan told me you have the Red Crest, I went back to instruct the magistrate's wife to blame you for her husband's death. No one knew where you were. The Teacher forged the secret letter between you and the Silencer so the Martial Society would hunt you down. That's all I know. I swear."

"All this to kill a common wanderer?"

Fu Nandong turned his head into the mud. He was shivering from the pain, from the cold, wet ground. He was losing too much blood from the wound in his arm, and he would lose consciousness soon. Han yanked the Dart free and sheathed it. Fu Nandong grimaced once and closed his eyes.

Han turned to leave. He wanted to kill Fu Nandong, but a nagging thought resurfaced in his mind, one that had bothered him ever since he rode off in the rain. The tracks behind Yi Yi's carriage were washed away by the downpour, but what if the Teacher somehow found her anyway? Scrawny Fox could not hold off the Teacher, even with four fast horses drawing the carriage. Han needed to do something and this was the opportunity he had been waiting for.

"I'm on my way to Zhun Yang," Han said. "If the Council of Midnight wants me, they know where to find me."

Han backed away toward his horse. Fu Nandong should be able to bandage himself with what was left of his other hand, and find his way back to his men. Han knew he would encounter this low-life again. Fu Nandong, clearly not his real name, was sent by his father from the Turkic kingdoms to become a category three general in the Chinese empire, in a deal with the Judge. Maybe foreign invasion was imminent, and not by the Silencer.

With a sigh, Han mounted his horse and rode off. The rain was slowing and the path in front of him was clear. Feng and Ah Go would be waiting for him in a town on the way to Zhun Yang, and he would need to find a way to convince them to help. Both were among the most powerful men he had ever encountered, but he had just met them. He knew nothing about them, and it was not time to discuss this yet. However, Feng's father was a Tiger General, so surely Feng would go to any lengths to stop the Judge if he knew his father was under threat.

Han thought about Yi Yi then and wondered whether the doctor had given her the entire flower yet, whether she could recover in ten days like he said she would. If the Teacher followed Han and not Yi Yi, then she had time. Scrawny Fox was a pleasant surprise at a time when the rest of the world was hunting him.

A short distance away, he found the town that Feng pointed out on the map, a mid-point to the village of Zhun Yang. They would meet there before proceeding.

Han pushed his horse forward with renewed vigor. In a town this size, there would be one street with businesses and maybe one inn.

He slowed to a walk. The main road leading into town was well paved and wide enough for four carriages to travel side-by-side. It had to be a wealthy town to have a paved road the width of those in the capital.

At the end of the road a covered porch protruding into the street. It was a large inn with a second floor, a curious construct for a town this small. Only in large cities did people have the wealth and man-power to build a second floor.

Han dismounted, tied his horse near a water trough and stepped into the inn. The innkeeper came forward to greet him with a big smile.

Feng and Ah Go had not arrived yet and there was no one inside. Han pointed to the porch. "We will sit outside." He drew a gold coin from his pocket. "Your best liquor please."

"Certainly!" the innkeeper said. "How much liquor?"

"Everything you have."

The innkeeper held the coin in his hand. "This is a lot. Would you like me to feed your horse too?"

"Yes," Han said. "We will need food later as well."

Ah Go and Feng approached from the far end of the road. Han lifted a ceramic liquor jug from the floor, one of many lined up behind him, and placed it on the table for them to see. He leaned back to sip.

Ah Go was the first to leap over the waist-high banisters. Han laughed and handed him a bowl of liquor, then poured one for Feng. The general's son hesitated outside the porch.

"What are you waiting for?" Ah Go asked after taking a sip from his bowl. "The wine is very good."

Han pushed the bowl toward the seat next to him and motioned for Feng to sit. "This bowl has been empty for half a day now."

Feng leaped onto the porch. Han grimaced at how the poison user landed, like he was never taught how to jump or how to land. Feng sat down and grabbed the bowl, and with a nervous smile he tilted his head back to drink.

"Do you like it?" Ah Go asked. He poured himself another bowl. "I don't drink wine like this back home."

"Neither do I," Feng said.

Han watched Ah Go's expression of contentment, then Feng's controlled gestures of gratitude and fine manners, and almost laughed. The liquor was disgusting to the general's son, adequate for the Commoner, and somehow, a riveting experience for the big hunter.

The innkeeper stepped in with a slab of roast pork on a platter. Its pungent aroma permeated the air.

Ah Go brought his heavy saber around like it was a fruit knife and slashed off a piece of meat. Han watched. This big hunter had control of his weapon to the most minute precision, where he could use a saber meant for killing a person to carve out a thin slice of pork.

Han turned back to Feng and noticed how weak he was. His energy was poor, and he had limited command of his body—a normal civilian, as they were often called in the Martial Society. Someone not enhanced by powerful martial arts.

Yet, Feng's quiet, hawkish gaze resembled that of a great general observing the battlefield. If he trained in martial arts, he would never need to be protected again.

"There will come a time, Feng," Han said, "when you're caught by surprise and you have no weapon nearby, and there's no one around to help you. You'll have to defend yourself. Let me teach you a set of empty hand techniques. It'll help you when you need it."

Feng jumped to his feet. "Really? You'll… you'll teach me your martial arts?"

Han stood up. "Of course."

The rain slowed to a light drizzle before stopping altogether. Locals emerged one by one, hanging lanterns outside their doors to illuminate the streets. There were no other travelers who braved the storm like Han, Feng, and Ah Go did. There were no other guests in the inn that night.

Han thought about what he had told Fu Nandong. With the storm over, the Council of Midnight could already be on their way to find him. He should not have put Feng at risk, but he couldn't tell him either. Feng would know, or at least question why the Council was after Han, and it would bring up the topic of the Red Crest.

"You can't stay here too much longer," Han said. "We don't know how far away Ko Sun was when he encountered the first rumor. You shouldn't run into him until we're ready."

"Ko Sun wouldn't charge through the villages on a speeding horse," Feng said. "He's too careful for that. We should still get to

Zhun Yang village as soon as possible. We'll start rallying the villagers to help us."

Ah Go stood up and flexed his muscles. "What I don't understand is why you're doing all this to kill Ko Sun. We should wait for him here and kill him when he passes by."

"We can't kill him right away," Feng said. "We need to question him first."

"Question him?" Han asked.

"He's a colonel," Feng said. "He's high enough in the army to know things. Who is this Judge? Why is he so powerful? What does he really want? Why did he raise a secret army?"

Fu Nandong was higher in rank than a colonel, Han thought. But he was a puppet and knew very little.

"We'll help you capture him alive," Han said. "But you may not get the answers you're looking for."

There were two jugs of liquor left when Feng and Ah Go departed. Ah Go took one for the road. Han's stallion was well-rested, fed, and ready to carry the two men on its saddle. Ah Go was muscular and heavy while Feng was thin, so their weight balanced out. Han's horse pulled away, moving at a comfortable trot.

Han rented a room upstairs with a window facing the street. He brought the last jug of alcohol up to his room and sat by the window. It was late, but he was expecting his pursuers to have arrived already.

It wasn't a long wait. Out of nowhere, a deep puddle in the middle of the main road caught fire. A streak of flames sprouted on top of the water in the shape of two adjacent eyes before dying with a whiff of smoke. Someone had poured oil on the water without Han noticing.

The Council of Midnight was here. Han tilted his head back to finish his bowl of liquor. Then, he leaped out of the window and landed on a puddle with a resounding splash.

Han stepped into the middle of the road and waited in silence. Raindrops falling off the tiled roofs continued to tap the pavement rhythmically, but otherwise, there was not a stir in town.

An arrow whistled through the air, then another, and another. Han dodged, slipping left and right to avoid them but never once charging the archer. He knew this was Lion Beard, the greatest archer in the world, firing his Zhuge Nu with deadly speed and precision. So far, Lion Beard had not revealed himself. Han needed to remain far away if he were to evade the arrows. Any closer and he would not have enough time to react.

In a flash, Han had dodged all sixteen shots and somewhere in the darkness, Lion Beard paused to reload. Someone leaped off a roof from across the street, sword in hand and charged the Commoner. Han drew the Dart and rushed at him, stabbing, cutting, enclosing his opponent in a whirlwind with his fluttering blade. The enemy swordsman held his ground, fighting back with equal vigor.

More arrows approached. Han slipped around his opponent to force Lion Beard to change angles, else he would be striking the swordsman.

A high-pitched chuckle sounded from the darkness. Han recognized it. The Teacher was watching and waiting to join.

Han changed angles again to press the swordsman toward the hidden archer. He knew that he wouldn't beat all three of them with ease, with an archer attacking from afar, a swordsman fighting medium distance, and a martial artist hidden from view, ready to ambush when the opportunity arose.

An arrow whistled past Han's ear. Lion Beard had changed location and this time, he was in full view on the street. Han pressed the swordsman, forcing him to back toward the archer. Spinning past him, in a flash he reached Lion Beard and pressed the tip of the Dart against his throat.

The sword user paused. Sha Wu clapped his hands, emerging from the shadows with a proud smile on his face.

Han lowered his sword, shaking his head. "What happened to killing for the pure joy of the art? If you're not serious about fighting, then stop the nonsense and have a drink instead."

The Teacher laughed. "Exactly what I was thinking, my nephew. And I brought the most exquisite liquor with me. Let's have a drink."

Han motioned for them to sit on the covered porch. "You must be Lion Beard," Han said to the archer. He turned to the swordsman. "We haven't met."

"Han, his name is Liu San," Sha Wu said. "We use our real names among good friends."

"Good friends," Han repeated with a laugh. He swung over the banister and seated himself under the covered porch. The stack of bowls was still on the table.

The Teacher pulled a porcelain flask from his bag. "Of course, good friends can still kill each other. Anyone can kill anyone." He uncorked the liquor and a powerful aroma wandered into the air. "A man cannot drink with an infant," Sha Wu continued, "would not die for his enemy, would not urinate with his daughter or sleep with his sister. But anyone can always kill anyone. That's what makes it so universal—there are no inhibitions. Killing is the only path to absolute freedom."

Han laughed. "I am glad we are good friends then. I was worried for a moment about what I would tell the world after I killed every single one of you." He passed the bowls around the table. Lion Beard struck a match and ignited a small candle in the middle of the table. Sha Wu poured the liquor, filling all four bowls and almost emptying his flask.

Han took a sip of the liquor, remembering Sha Wu's words on why he would never poison someone. It was a drink for the elite, with complex notes of different florals dominating the aftertaste. "Why are you here?" Han asked.

"We want to offer you a very special opportunity," Sha Wu said. "Very few people ever receive this offer."

"As special as smelling the fear of death in a man's sweat?"

"Almost as special," Sha Wu said. "Let me explain who we are first. Liu San, Lion Beard, your Master Zuo, and I were the original four elders in the Council of Midnight. Of course, Zuo retired early and his seat has been vacant for many years."

At the mention of Master Zuo, Han shuddered and turned away from Sha Wu to steady himself. His Shifu was among the founders of this secret organization. He was one of them.

"We are a society of martial arts elites," Sha Wu continued. "Li Yan brought us together to help him attain the throne many years ago. Unfortunately, treachery and misfortune allowed Li Gao to take the empire, but our mission remains the same. Now, if we help Li Yan's son become emperor, we will reap our rewards."

"And what's the reward?" Han asked. "A piece of land large enough for you to declare yourself a king?"

"Very good, my nephew. So you already know." The Teacher sipped his liquor and sighed. "A man of your talents should be a king, not a poet. Writing poetry is for those who can't get paid to kill people. You know there is an empty seat in the council, and who better to fill it than Zuo's best student?"

"Come and join us, Han," Lion Beard said. "With your help, Li Yan's son will be emperor of China, and you will have an army and a kingdom all your own."

"And what can I do," Han asked, "that men of your talent can't already accomplish?"

Sha Wu threw his head back to laugh. "We are assassins. We kill people."

"Let me repeat the question," Han said. "Who do you want me to kill that the three of you cannot?"

"Even we cannot fight an army," the Teacher said.

"I see," Han said, reaching for the liquor. "So you are after the Tiger Generals."

"You're right again, my nephew."

"I'm always right," Han said, mimicking Yi Yi's line. He poured himself another drink and offered the flask to Lion Beard, who held up his hand to decline.

"And why would I help you kill those who defend our borders?" Han asked.

"They are not the only ones who can defend the border," Liu San said. "There will be new Tiger Generals of equal talent. Great men who support the Judge. If you join us, you are guaranteed Zuo's seat in the Council, and you will be a king within a year."

"What exactly do you want me to do?"

"General Yang is an accomplished martial arts master," Lion Beard said. "He's very difficult to kill. We need you."

"Because I am friends with him," Han said. "I can get close."

"I witnessed what you did in that cavern," Sha Wu said. "In a fair fight, only you could defeat him. An unfair fight would be even better."

Han's face burned but he maintained his composure. "Is that what the Manifestation is? The plan to kill the Tiger Generals?"

"You do know a lot for a poet," Liu San said with a smirk. "Join us, and you will be on the winning side when the Manifestation happens."

"It's a big request," Han said, "coming from the very people who have been trying to kill me. Why should I trust you? How do I know I will receive my reward? How do I know you won't kill me after I kill General Yang for you?"

"Once you join us, you will be our brother," the Teacher said.

"Anyone can kill anyone," Han said with a smile.

The Teacher broke out laughing. "You learn fast, my nephew. One day you could be a teacher too."

"I need to hear it from the Grand Chancellor himself," Han said. "I need assurance from the supreme leader of the council that this offer is real and that promises will be kept. I need to know what it means to be an elder of the Council of Midnight."

"Certainly," the Teacher said. "Come to our next conference and meet the Grand Chancellor. We will all have a drink together and he will answer any questions you have. Once you are satisfied, we will proceed with the induction ceremony, and you will experience power and influence like you have never seen."

"And you will be a king within a year," Lion Beard echoed.

Liu San handed a small folded note to Han. "This is the time and place where we are meeting. Make sure you show up or you will regret it."

Han smiled at the veiled threat and pocketed the note. He then stood up and clasped his hands together. Sha Wu bowed once to him, and without another word, the elders of the council departed.

Han couldn't remember when he last slept☐it must have been four nights ago☐and the fatigue overwhelmed him.

Back in his room, Han drew a wicker chair to the window, leaned back and watched the street again. He had to wait for Ko Sun. Feng depended on it.

Han thought about the colonel with the arrogant, raspy voice, the woman and children he murdered, the soldiers who killed the Orchid Farmer. Here was a man who deserved to die, and Han could kill him if he passed by on the street below. Ah Go suggested doing the same. But they promised Feng to capture him alive for questioning. This was Feng's battle. Han was only there to help.

He wouldn't remember dozing off, but once again, he was in Ding Yi, standing in front of a teenage boy. Dead bodies littered the ground, and young prostitutes were crying and running away.

"I just wanted something to eat!" the boy shouted.

Han jumped to his feet. The sun was already high in the heavens and he was still waiting at the window. Merchants, farmers, and blacksmiths from the area had gathered in the road to sell and barter. An old man was pushing a small wheelbarrow full of sweet potatoes under Han's window, while another was hanging cured meats on a roadside stand across the street. The arrows fired from Lion Beard's Zhuge Nu crossbow were nowhere to be seen.

Han walked around the crowded market all morning, looking for something interesting to buy for Yi Yi. There were no jewelry merchants in this remote town. Most of the vendors were selling produce and household items. There was not even a picture of him as a wanted criminal in this part of the country.

Han wandered back and forth, lost in thought. Who was he? The Teacher told him last night that his Shifu was among the original founders of the council, and it made perfect sense that Master Zuo knew the Infinity Palm if he lived among the martial arts elite. Zuo was sent to assassinate a young boy and the boy was Han. If the Council of Midnight was formed by Li Yan to make him emperor, then Han's parents must be Li Yan's enemy.

There would be no way of finding Li Yan to ask him questions, and it must have something to do with his birthmark. Li Yan and his son wanted Han dead when he was a boy, and they still wanted him dead now.

A commotion arose at the end of the road. A large group of armed men, some with sabers drawn, were pushing people to the edges of the street. Han stepped to the side of the road with everyone else and lowered his head to avoid attracting attention.

It was a very large group coming down the road. Han counted at least sixty armed men with Ko Sun in front, scanning left and right at every face. His severed arm was bandaged but no longer bleeding. The crowd of civilians was significant, but Han was taller than most and Ko Sun would spot him. He dropped into a squat and waited.

Trailing behind the armed men were almost forty women and children. Their hands were tied and they were all connected by a thick web of rope. None of them could run off alone.

Han clenched his fists. So this was Ko Sun's new weapon. Women and children. They were ordinary villagers, some of them bruised and bloodied, many of them weeping. There were mothers with nursing babies, toddlers clinging onto the rope around their little arms, teenage girls with blood on their faces. How much more despicable could this Ko Sun get, all to hunt down the general's son?

He could kill Ko Sun now. The meager sixty men surrounding the colonel were not the Commoner's match, and the women and children would be free. Who knows what other torment they would endure in the next two days, just so Feng could question this colonel in the Judge's army. Killing Ko Sun now would enable Feng to go to General Yang's city right away.

Han could not do it. It was Feng's battle, not his. He agreed to only collect information.

As they breezed by, the armed men shouted profanities at those who did not step aside in time, waving their naked blades and kicking over any vendor stands that were still on the road. Han waited. As Feng predicted, Ko Sun walked into the inn with the protruding porch. The innkeeper was already paid to point Ko Sun in the wrong direction, and Feng would have an extra day to prepare his ambush.

Han stood up and backed away, slipped into a narrow alley and headed toward Zhun Yang. Ko Sun had to travel with women and children, and he would be at least a day behind, if not more. Feng had plenty of time.

CHAPTER 10

HAN REACHED THE little village of Zhun Yang under a clear sky and a full moon the following night. There was a pond in front of the village, not large enough for farming fish but still a valuable source of fresh water. People slept with their doors open in these remote areas. Everyone knew each other and no one had much to steal.

One door was closed and a candle flickered inside. Han pulled the door and found Ah Go in front of him, saber in hand.

"It's me," Han said.

Ah Go laughed. "I didn't hear your footsteps until you almost reached the door. I should've known it was you."

Inside, Feng was seated in front of a Wei Chi set on the table. "You're here. So Ko Sun already passed our last meeting point?"

"Exactly as you planned it," Han said, stepping through the doors. He unhooked his sword from his belt, took a bowl of liquor from the square table and drank all of it with one gulp. "It'll be another two days before they find us."

"They're two days behind you?" Ah Go asked. "How?"

"They brought a different weapon," Han said. "Hostages. Forty women and children."

"Only women and children?" Ah Go asked. "That means the men are already dead."

"We'll change our approach and target the civilians first," Feng said. "It'll send him a clear message that we don't care, and his weapon will be neutralized."

Han turned to him. "Did I hear you correctly, Feng?"

"I have a powerful poison," Feng said. "It doesn't kill when it's diluted, but it will still cause a lot of pain. After the pain passes, it's harmless. We'll strike the hostages first, then some of the soldiers in front. When Ko Sun sees that we're indiscriminate, he'll cast the hostages aside to make himself mobile."

"You're sure of how the poison works?"

"I'll have an antidote ready," Feng said. "Once we capture Ko Sun, we'll treat the civilians."

Han knew Feng was a masterful poison user. But the thought of poisoning women and children, the same babies and toddlers who passed by him on the road, crying and bound and helpless, was too much of a risk. "I'll test the poison on myself before we use it on women and children," he said. He felt Yi Yi talking through him then. "We're going to avoid any unnecessary loss of life. Soldiers are honorable men who happen to serve the enemy. Let's not kill anyone we don't have to."

"We need more arrows," Ah Go said. "I'll shoot the civilians for you."

That night, Han punctured his arm with a poisoned arrow and then sat down to meditate. The effects of the poison struck at once, shooting streaks of pain from his arm all the way to the back of his head. For a long time, he trembled through hot flashes, debilitated, dripping in sweat and hallucinating.

The poison was superficial as Feng claimed. When it faded, Han drank the antidote already in his hand and washed away the pain.

Again, Han could not sleep, despite the fatigue. He leaned back and thought about what was happening to him, to the world, and then thought about Yi Yi and finally dozed off. It was fourth watch by the time he woke up.

Ah Go was standing outside, breathing in the cool air and stretching his oversized muscles.

"A lot on your mind?" Han asked, standing next to him. "I couldn't sleep much either."

"Are you world famous, Han?" Ah Go asked.

"I am. And I bet you are too."

Ah Go laughed. "Then is Chen Han your real name?"

"What makes a name real or not real?"

"If your parents gave you the name at birth, it's real."

Han sighed. "I guess Chen Han is not my real name then."

"I see," Ah Go whispered. "I'm sorry. I hope you find your name one day."

Both were silent for a moment, watching the first hints of dawn appear on the horizon. "Let's take a walk before the sun comes out to ruin this perfect air," Ah Go said.

"Great idea."

They trod down the wide road that served as the main passageway for Zhun Yang, and shortly after, they ascended a hill outside the village. The cool wind weaved through the surrounding trees, swaying the branches side to side and rustling the leaves.

"Do you believe Feng can stop this Judge?" Ah Go asked.

"Without a doubt," Han said. "I wonder why he's not world famous."

"Like the two of us are?" Ah Go asked with a laugh.

"Not exactly," Han said. "Feng is the Tiger General's son, but General Mu's son is not famous for anything. Yet, Ko Sun and the others are determined to capture him."

"Good luck capturing the poison user," Ah Go said. "But I agree, we need to keep him safe. That is what we promised the Orchid Farmer. We can't let him take on the Judge until he is ready."

"The Judge is out to kill the Tiger Generals," Han said.

"I know."

"If Feng knows about this, he will not hide for his own safety," Han said. "Especially since his own father is a target."

"That's why I haven't told him about it," Ah Go said. "Although, I don't see why this Judge is so hard to kill. If you know where he is, I will help you kill him."

"Maybe he's surrounded by an army of two hundred thousand."

"I'm going to need more arrows then."

They approached a barren rock hanging over a sharp decline. "Let's sit here," Ah Go said. "I have liquor."

They settled down next to each other and Ah Go drew a bulging leather flask from his belt. He uncorked it, poured a couple of big gulps down his throat and passed it to Han.

The thunder of galloping horses emerged a short distance away, approaching them. Both men stopped and turned to listen.

"Someone is in a hurry at this time of night," Ah Go whispered. "He's a messenger for the Judge."

"How do you know that?"

"This is his vast communications network," Ah Go said. "The messengers change horses throughout the night to keep them fresh and running strong. This horse coming at us is a fresh horse."

"Let's take him then."

They stood up, in the darkness and waited. The thundering of hooves pounding the hard ground grew louder, and in a moment, a tall stallion charged into sight, carrying a messenger with two small satchels slung across his chest. Ah Go pounced onto the rider and dragged him off his mount, tossing him onto the dusty ground. The horse continued running and disappeared.

"Who are you?" Han asked the messenger.

"The hell with you." The messenger spat on the ground, climbed to his feet and drew a saber from his belt. In a flash, Han snatched the weapon and tossed it away.

"Are you a messenger for the Judge?" Han asked.

The messenger spat again, crossed his arms, and lifted his chin. "You dare assault a messenger for the Judge! You will be gutted and hung upside down before sunset."

Ah Go placed a firm hand on the messenger's shoulder and whispered something into his ear.

It didn't take long for the messenger to start trembling. "W-w-what? Are you… Are you for real?"

Ah Go laughed and ripped the two cloth sacks off his chest with a single jerk, almost yanking the messenger back to the ground.

"Let's see what the Judge is not about to receive," Ah Go said. He pulled open the drawstrings of one satchel and emptied its contents into his big hand, a single folded note with a few lines of writing on it. He handed it to Han.

Perhaps Ah Go is illiterate, Han thought. The note was addressed to the Judge from Ko Sun. In two sentences, he updated the Judge on where Mu Feng was and when he could expect to kill him. The information was wrong of course. Feng's false rumors and diversions were working.

"Are… are you going to kill me?" the messenger asked, his voice still trembling.

"Where is this one going?" Ah Go asked, holding up a cloth scroll. With his other hand, he tossed away the empty satchel and unrolled the scroll.

"I… I don't know who he is," the messenger stammered. "Someone named Tan Hei. I have never heard of him."

"And where is this Tan Hei?" Han asked.

"I don't know," he said. "Maybe the next messenger knows. You can ask him when I change horses at dawn."

"Maybe I should follow him," Ah Go whispered. He unrolled the scroll in front of Han.

Han shuddered. It was a detailed map of the City of Eternal Peace, General Wu's fortress, and there were red circles drawn everywhere throughout the city. "What do those circles mean?"

"Something important," Ah Go said. "But he won't know."

"Please, I'm simply a messenger. I was handed these satchels from a previous messenger."

"Exactly," Ah Go said. He smacked the messenger across the face, cracking his neck and killing him. The body fell without a groan. Ah Go scrolled the map and tucked it into his pocket.

"Why did you do that?" Han asked.

Ah Go thought for a second. "You're right." He pulled out the map and handed it to Han. "You should keep this."

"I meant why you killed the messenger," Han said. He stuffed the map into his pocket.

"I had no other choice," Ah Go said with a shrug. "He wouldn't have stayed quiet. Tomorrow we wait for Ko Sun, and Feng doesn't need to be surrounded by an army coming for the map at the same time."

Han sighed, a deep frown settling on his brows. Ah Go was right. It was kill or be killed at this point.

"There's a traitor in General Wu's army," Han said. "Someone drew this map and offered it to the Judge. Whatever he circled in red must be important to the enemy."

"Let's get Feng to a safe place," Ah Go said. "Then you can show this map to General Wu. He may recognize these circled areas."

"I'll keep it safe."

They started to walk toward Zhun Yang again. The pitch-black heavens had yielded to a deep gray, and the first crows of many roosters flooded the air with a sloppy chorus. The light wind that had danced around them faded along with the coolness of the night. The people of Zhun Yang began to stir.

"I need a nap," Ah Go said. "I should go back to bed."

"Can I ask something first?" Han said. "What did you say to the messenger earlier that made him so afraid of you?"

"Nothing much," Ah Go said. "I just told him I'm the Silencer."

They both broke out laughing. In another few steps, they reached the house where they were staying, a small structure with a big door that belonged to an aging farmer.

"I won't be able to sleep," Han said. "I'll stay out here and wait for Feng to get up. His Infinity Palm needs work."

"I'll be snoring."

Before the sun emerged, Feng stepped out of the door, dressed and ready. Han was watching the village with his back turned. "I heard you like to practice before sunrise," Han said. "Let's see your progress."

Without a word, Feng attacked him from behind.

"Good!" Han said. He slipped away with equal speed, watching Feng's every movement. They sparred for a long time and Feng showed remarkable improvement. It was late morning by the time he collapsed with exhaustion.

Han trained him until noon, then spent the rest of the day rehearsing with those who would participate in the ambush. The villagers were in fine spirits, confident that they needed to do very little for a lot of money, hopeful that they would be able to build new houses and buy more animals.

By nightfall, Feng purchased a small pig and roasted it over a large outdoor fire. Jugs of liquor formed a line behind Ah Go, and they ate and drank deep into the night.

"So, why did your father go to Mongolia?" Ah Go asked Feng, chewing through a huge pig leg while gulping down a bowl of liquor.

Han sat cross legged and leaned forward to listen. Having finished eating, he threw his pork bones deep into the heart of the village so the dogs could feast. The bowl of liquor in his hand was never empty—Ah Go made sure of that, and he was beginning to feel the alcohol.

"He received an imperial edict the night before," Feng said. "He also learned that his daughter was abducted. But he chose to leave instead."

"Do you know what was on the edict?" Han asked.

"I can only guess," Feng said, shaking his head. "General Lo—he's another Tiger General—received an imperial edict ordering him to go to Mongolia and attack the Silencer. My father must have gotten the same."

"He didn't attack the Silencer," Ah Go said, still tearing large chunks of pork off the leg in his hand. "If he moved his army the day after the edict, he was not prepared for war."

"But to move away the army when my sister was in danger," Feng said, "and then not even try to rescue her? Is that even human?"

"What happened to your sister?" Han asked.

There was a long pause. Han and Ah Go both turned to their liquor, gulping down the strong drink to avoid speaking.

"My sister was murdered in front of me," Feng said. Han lowered his bowl and exhaled in relief. The young poison user trusted them enough to talk about his painful past.

"And I did nothing about it," Feng continued. "She was so close to where I was standing. I could've saved her. I stood there frozen, like an idiot, while they slit her throat. They didn't have to do it. They got what they came for. There was no reason to kill her. But if my father hadn't run away and instead sent his entire army of fifty thousand after her, she wouldn't have died either. He didn't send anyone. He left her to die."

Han sighed and held out his bowl so Ah Go could fill it. Nothing he could say would ease Feng's guilt and anger. Maybe it was Han's turn to share.

"I was raised by my martial arts master and his wife," Han began. "They were among the greatest in the world."

Han told them how he trained in their separate martial arts systems while no one in the world had the same privilege. He told them about the night he brought the ginseng soup to the woman he called mother. Ah Go and Feng listened without a word.

Han released a long, lingering sigh, as if trying to let go of a past that clung to his every waking moment. When Master Zuo and Lan died a few days ago, what happened to him at age sixteen became old wounds of a past life.

"I wandered the world on my own," Han said. "I enjoyed it. To this day I enjoy traveling the land by myself. There's something special about being a common man. Much later, I found the man who poisoned my mother. I killed him. I'm ashamed of it, but I killed him, and in front of his daughters too. And I regret doing it."

"Why?" Feng asked. "He murdered the woman who raised you. Why would you regret killing him?"

"I never found out why he did it," Han said. "Everyone deserves to tell their story, but I killed him and dumped him into a waterfall without asking questions, so I will never know. And now, I no longer want to know."

"So much better for you," Ah Go said. Up until now he had been more engaged with his drink than the conversation. "Like Feng, I also watched my sister die. She was raped in front of her fiancé, in front of everyone! And then they shoved a dagger into her hands and forced her to stab her fiancé before they killed her."

Ah Go clutched the pork bone in his hand so hard his fingers trembled, and with his lips pressed together he fixated on the fire. After a moment, he threw the bone into the flames. "If there was a warrior like you protecting us, my sister would be alive today. I was twelve at the time. We were farmers and we raised chickens and I helped my parents sell eggs at the market every morning. I never got to go to school, I never drank wine as good as this. But we were happy. My sister was already sixteen and she was about to be married.

"Then they came. The barbarians. They crossed the Chinese border—just a handful of them—no more than fifty. What were we to do against armed barbarians? They razed our village, they killed the old and the sick and the infants, and then they captured everyone else. Our homes were burned. We were taken into Mongolia and we were sold as slaves. The clan who bought us—they beat us every day, they didn't give us any food, and they worked us to death. Then that clan was invaded and most of them were killed. The invaders were worse. They entertained themselves by torturing their captives. They stood in a circle, clapping and laughing while my sister was violated by one thug after another. And I watched. Her fiancé watched."

"Some people enjoy seeing others afraid," Ah Go said in a cold, dark voice that was not his own. "They love to watch others beg for mercy. It makes them feel powerful. Some people kill for money. Some do it for revenge, and some do it out of fear. We don't concern ourselves with those people. But what about those who kill for fun? What about those who take pleasure in seeing other people's houses and lifelong savings burn to the ground, those who are entertained when others weep?"

Ah Go swallowed the entire bowl of liquor in three gulps, then swung his saber around to slash off a piece of pork for himself.

"You're right," Feng said. "We can't allow the people to suffer for no reason. Those with an extra ounce of strength should step forward and protect the weak. We're not animals. We don't leave the old and sick behind so the predators can capture them first."

Han sighed. "People killing each other. Will it ever end?"

"Not with us it won't," Feng said. "I lost my sister and I did nothing about it. You lost the woman who raised you and you could do nothing except seek revenge. Ah Go lost his entire family because he was too young to do anything. What about those who are still alive, who can still be happy, who have not lost anyone yet?"

Han gazed into the glowing cinders supporting the dying campfire. All he ever wanted was to wander the world as a commoner, so he told everyone. So he told himself. But perhaps that was not what he really wanted. Maybe it was all he could have. Perhaps when he was chased away from Zuo Mansions, all he wanted was a home, and when Master Zuo, his wife, and his daughter died, all Han wanted was a family.

Maybe he would have a family one day with Yi Yi, but the Teacher almost killed her. Maybe all of these villagers in Zhun Yang could have a safe home if the Judge didn't burn it to the ground first.

"The Orchid Farmer also lost his entire family," Feng said, finally. "So at least I have to try, whatever it is I'm meant to do, at least I have to try. Those who are capable do have a responsibility. I just wish I am more capable."

"You're the most capable among the three of us," Han said. "You just don't see it yet."

That night, Han fell asleep right away. He no longer carried the burden of what happened to him all by himself. His new friends shared some of his memories now, some of his pain, and in return he shared some of theirs.

Han awakened to the sound of grinding and hammering in the middle of the night. It came from the kitchen. He strolled in to find Feng grinding something in a stone bowl and simmering a dark liquid in a clay pot.

"What are you making so late?" Han asked.

Feng brushed the sweat off his brow. "It's for you," Feng said, stirring the pot. "And Ah Go of course."

"Is it a medicine?"

Feng peeled open a cloth book that lay next to the stove. "Ming gave me this book," Feng said.

"Ming?"

"She's…" Feng stopped for a long, awkward moment. "Ming is the leader of the Venom Sect. There's a formula in here to make these pills. When you take one, you become immune to poison for one day."

"Venom Sect," Han said. This Ming must be the daughter of the man who killed Lady Zuo, the same Venom Sect leader he threw into a waterfall. How did Feng become acquainted with them?

"You have given me so much," Feng said. "Both of you, and I have no way to repay. What could I give back? Your skills are so advanced, I can't even see you when you move. But you are still vulnerable, Han. You can be poisoned. This pill will keep you safe. If you take it in the morning, you will be immune until the next morning."

"I don't want to say anything," Han began, "but isn't it a low-handed approach to battle, using tools from the Venom Sect?"

"There is no high or low in war," Feng said. "There is only victory or defeat."

"Is there honor in waging war like this?"

"After you become immune to poison," Feng said. "You will still be vulnerable to honor."

"My honor?"

"When you live by a code of honor," Feng said. "When you live by a set of rules, you become predictable. Then the enemy is always one step ahead of you. They can see the future but you can't."

"I don't understand," Han said. "No one can see the future."

"That's true," Feng said. "But you can manufacture the future."

"How?"

"With deceit. With preparation. By enticing the enemy to do what you want him to do while your trap is waiting."

"How do you entice him?" Han asked.

Feng stirred the pot again and then poured the crushed ingredients into the mixture. He crouched down to blow into the fire, fanning the smoke with his palm. "Anything can be used to entice the enemy," he said. "Use his anger if he's an angry person, or false rumors if he is a suspicious person. Show weakness if he is an arrogant person. Anything. But right now, the enemy knows you are honorable so they always know how you will react."

"I see," Han said. "Since when has honor become a flaw?"

"Anything can be a flaw," Feng said. "And anything can be used to your advantage. It depends on whether the enemy expects it or not."

Han sighed. All his life he was taught to protect the innocent, save the old and the weak, fight the aggressors. It was the life of a hero, of a knight of the Martial Society. Now this general's son, a young man so much more powerful than himself, was teaching him the truth of how to always win.

Did he want to win if it involved deceit and ambushes?

Feng read his mind. "You can't blame the sword for killing someone. It's a man's intent that kills. The sword is merely a tool, just as strategy is a tool. You can use deceit to stay ahead of the enemy, to protect the innocent and defeat the oppressors, or you can use honor and fairness to exploit the weak. You know you have the advantage in a fair fight, Han. That's why no one would ever fight fair with you."

Han sighed. "I see."

"We don't know anything about the enemy," Feng said. "This

Judge has been ahead of us from the beginning. I've been caught by surprise every step of the way."

Han stood back and leaned against the mud wall, his body weak all of a sudden. "I've been caught by surprise every step as well. In the end, I always managed to get through it. But was it because I was prepared for the surprises, or did I simply live through them? There is a difference. I wish I understood what it means to live through my destiny with a smile and enjoy every moment, no matter what it is."

At dawn, Han stood in the same place as the morning before, facing the looming sunrise.

"Wouldn't it be wonderful," Han said, when he sensed Feng approaching from behind. "If today we didn't have to ambush Ko Sun and tomorrow we didn't have to pursue the Judge? Wouldn't it be wonderful if this morning, all we needed to do were to water the vegetables and clear the weeds and feed the chickens?"

"The common people don't have it so easy either," Feng said, standing next to him. "It'll be worse for them if we hide here and plant vegetables and feed livestock."

Han nodded. "Let's continue working on our devastating palm techniques then."

They trained until noon, and Feng stopped to rest just as Ah Go appeared, his saber strapped to his back, a hunting bow and a quiver of arrows in either hand. "They're here," he said.

"Ko Sun is early," Feng said. "Are the villagers ready?"

"All morning," Ah Go said.

The villagers were mobilizing. Some picked up shovels and ran off, some moved into position behind hay carts near the mouth of the village, while others ran into their houses and closed their doors.

"Be careful with the loss of lives," Han said, wary that they were using untrained civilians to rig this ambush. Losing any civilian life would be a disaster.

"I understand," Feng said. "Ko Sun deserves to die. Everyone else goes home unharmed." He sorted through his weapons, the belt, the poison needles, and the gloves that the Orchid Farmer gave him. The Dart was already hooked to Han's belt.

"No need for you to carry weapons," Han said. "They have a mere sixty men. If everything goes well, I won't be drawing my sword either."

"Mere sixty," Feng mumbled. He headed toward the dry hill outside the village and Han followed. Ah Go flipped his bow and walked into a small farmhouse close to the hill. He drew the door shut.

They were stationed behind a group of farmers carrying shovels, circling the hill and ascending from the back. The front of the hill, which faced the road into the mouth of the village, was dried and full of pebbles, while tall trees and small bushes covered the back. Feng directed the farmers to lower themselves behind piles of sand and rocks to remain invisible to anyone from the road.

Han noticed that the sun was behind them. Feng planned this so Ko Sun would be staring into the stinging light as he ascended the hill.

"Nothing will go wrong," Feng said. "We'll free the hostages before going after Ko Sun." He signaled to the peasants waiting by the hay. One villager waved back, picked up a blazing torch and shoved it into the straws. The other peasants followed, each igniting their bundles stacked around the road. Stinging black smoke swept across the front of the village.

"What did you put in the hay?" Han asked.

"Just water."

The smoke reached as high as the top of the hill, dispersing and lightening to a dull gray as it groped for the heavens. Ko Sun and his armed men arrived in a moment, pushing the train of women and children ahead. The civilians were still bound by rope, their wrists strapped and connected. They walked with their heads down, no longer weeping, though many were stumbling from fatigue or injuries.

Then, an arrow floated into the scene from a tremendous distance. Ah Go had initiated the battle. The blunt arrow glanced a soldier in the arm before falling to the ground. The poison took effect right away. The soldier screamed and collapsed to his knees, shaking in agony.

Ko Sun reacted, shouting orders and pointing with his only hand, and in response the armed men shoved the hostages together, forming a wall in front of themselves. Some held their bare swords against the women's throats.

Another arrow floated through the air and struck a woman in the thigh. She screamed, falling the instant the blunt arrow embedded itself. Ko Sun was shouting something when another arrow struck a hostage in the shoulder, this time a teenage girl.

Ah Go was hitting his targets from afar, through black smoke, even as they were moving. He struck another soldier before Ko Sun ordered his men to abandon the hostages and take higher ground.

The soldiers shoved aside the women and children and ran up the hill. Feng held out his hand to steady the farmers, waiting for the soldiers to come closer.

Han also waited for Feng's signal, eager to see how a genius conducted warfare. The general's son was patient, calm, calculating every movement and expression.

Ko Sun was holding back half his men, presumably waiting to see if there would be an ambush on the hill before sending the second half. Feng read his mind. He held back the farmers and allowed the first wave of soldiers to come dangerously close.

Ko Sun made his decision when another arrow struck a nearby soldier. He ordered his men to abandon the remaining hostages.

Teenage boys emerged from behind the smoke to help the hostages on the ground. Feng grabbed a heavy rock and leaped out from behind the hill. "Now!" he shouted, throwing the rock into a soldier's knee.

The farmers jumped from their crouching positions, shovels in hand, and flung sand and pebbles into the soldiers' faces.

Han was amazed. Feng managed to stage his attack with what the farmers were good at—shoveling soil and rocks. The soldiers were screaming, collapsing against the heavy onslaught of dirt and pebbles, blinded and disarrayed.

Han stepped aside, and wondered if he would need to draw his sword today. Sixty armed men with flashing blades were being pummeled by a small handful of peasants with dirt shovels, and they were falling back, scrambling for safety, some even rolling back down the hill.

Meanwhile, the teenage boys were cutting the ropes with wheat sickles and moving the hostages into the village. Then, an arrow struck Ko Sun in the shoulder of his good arm, the one he used to communicate signals. Ko Sun arched his back and shrieked in pain, his high-pitched, raspy voice standing out from the sea of bellows.

Despite the chaos, some soldiers were regrouping in the middle of the hill where the soil and rocks could not reach them.

"Nets!" Feng shouted.

The farmers dropped their shovels at Feng's command, charged down the hill and reached a predetermined position. Han had not noticed the markers on the hill until the farmers dug into the soil and pulled. Thick rope leaped out of the ground. They were attached to large fishing nets hidden under the surface, and as these nets came to life, they climbed over the soldiers' heads before collapsing onto them. The farmers yanked harder, turning around with the ropes stretched over their shoulders and pushed their way back up the slope.

Then Han noticed it. Behind the chaos, behind the men scrambling to untangle themselves, a cloud of black smoke rose in the air. It was far away and reaching much higher into the heavens than the scattered smoke the villagers created.

Han dashed to Feng's side, just as the shrieks of a thousand Zhuge Nu bolts ripped through the air.

Feng turned to Han in alarm. Han grabbed Feng's slender shoulder and together, they leaped to the large trees at the top of the hill and crouched low, pinning their backs against a tree trunk. The farmers, the soldiers, the women and children, the teenage boys, the villagers blowing black smoke by the haystacks, would all be dead in the blink of an eye.

The Zhuge Nu bolts dropped in from above and pummeled soldier and civilian alike. The horrid screams of pain and suffering reached the heavens.

The second round was a hailstorm of arrows, sinking into the already bloody corpses, bodies of so many that were already dead, to ensure that the one they wanted to kill did not escape.

"It's my fault," Feng shouted. "Why did I involve civilians when I knew they were after me? They would murder a colonel in their army just to ensure that I die."

Han placed a hand on his arm. "Stay calm. We're counting on you to lead."

There was silence. Not a whimper or a twitch from anyone on the hill, on the road below, or at the mouth of the village.

Then, the screams of a third volley approached. Han gritted his teeth. Did they want him dead, or were they after Feng? It didn't matter. They weren't taking any chances.

Han released Feng's arm. "I'm going to see where the Zhuge Nu is positioned. Wait for me here."

"By yourself?"

"They can't shoot me if they don't know I'm coming."

Han spun around and charged through the dense foliage, slipping and weaving through the thick trees. The third round pummeled an area deeper within the village, laying waste to dogs and livestock, children who emerged from their houses to watch, the elderly who could not withdraw in time. Han's face burned. He knew Feng and Ah Go were safely hiding, but the civilians who died would never even know what happened.

Han ran as fast as he could, moving like a cat along uneven terrain, prancing and skirting around dense foliage and slippery inclines. In a moment, he spotted the smoke operator, a tall, lanky man on a horse. After the third volley, he began preparing to leave and rejoin his battalion.

Han leaped off a tall stone structure from high above, grabbed the smoke operator by the back of his collar, and dragged him off his horse. Han stood over his squirming body with his arms folded, waiting for the man to come to his senses.

"Who did you signal your battalion to target?" Han asked. His voice was menacing, carrying with it every bit of the anger and hate that coursed through him when he watched the villagers mowed down. "Who are you trying to kill?"

"Who are you?" the scout asked, his voice loud and defiant. "How dare you attack…"

"A smoke operator?" Han asked, drawing Lai's second smoke tube from his pocket. "Do you think the Judge will miss you if you never return to your battalion? Any fool can ride up to a target without showing his face and point a smoke tube into the air."

"How… How did you know? Why do you have one of our…"

"Tell me what I want to know or I will kill you."

"I… I don't know who he is," the scout stammered. "Target Two. I only know he is Target Two."

Feng must be Target Two, Han thought. He reached down and grabbed the scout by the collar, dragged him halfway to his feet with one hand and drew his face closer. The scout was trembling.

"And where is your battalion going next?" Han asked. "To kill Target One?"

"N-no, sir. We are preparing for the Manifestation. It's happening anytime now."

Han released the man's collar and the scout crashed to the ground with a hoarse choke. "Where?" Han shouted. His clenched fists were shaking by his side. "Where are you going next?"

"The City of Eternal Peace."

"General Wu's city," Han whispered.

The scout tried to climb to his feet again, but Han grabbed his shoulder and threw him back to the ground. "Why? What is this manifestation? What are you supposed to do outside General Wu's city?"

The scout curled into a ball, choking and coughing. While gasping for air and clutching his chest, he outstretched his hand, palm facing outward, as if that could stop the Commoner from throwing him again. "I don't know. I'm just a smoke operator. I do as I'm told."

Han wanted to kill him. The code of honor he was taught to live by, the integrity that he took pride in, all dissipated when the civilians in Zhun Yang were mowed down after one stream of smoke left this man's tube. Han stepped closer, hungry to see blood, with the crazed eyes of an animal closing in on its prey.

The scout shook, whimpering, scrambling backward on the dry ground. "No, please. Please don't kill me."

Han froze. What was happening to him? This man was no longer a threat. Han had already reduced him to a whimpering child begging for his life. How could he kill him?

"Who ordered your battalion to come here?" Han asked. "Who directed you to fire the smoke over Zhun Yang?"

"Our general."

"Who is the general?"

"General Fu Nandong."

Han sucked in his breath. He could have killed Fu Nandong three days ago. He could have stopped all of this.

Honor is my obstacle.

Han drew the Dart like a streak of lightning and severed the scout's neck, lopping off his head with one clean stroke. Blood spewed from his neck onto the dry earth.

If he hadn't killed this man, tomorrow he would fire his tube over another group of civilians while hunting for Target One or Target Two. He would report back to his battalion that someone survived the Zhuge Nu onslaught, and they would pursue him and attack again and again. Han could not protect Feng if every day the Zhuge Nu fired upon them.

Without another glance, Han turned and walked away. It was not the first time he had killed someone, but this was a man already defeated and begging for mercy. Strange, how he did not feel any remorse. Perhaps, in these violent times, killing was the norm and those who lived with honor were the fools.

Han picked up pace. He should not have left Feng for that long. Yet, all of Ko Sun's men were slaughtered and Ah Go was with him. Besides, as Ah Go would say, the poison user was impossible to kill. Nevertheless, he broke into a sprint to hurry back.

Feng and Ah Go were sitting near the top of the hill, taking in the devastation. Wisps of gray smoke continued to float out of the collapsed stacks of hay, shrouding the dead bodies littered across the land. Han approached them from behind, and Ah Go turned to acknowledge his presence.

"The Judge commands an undeclared army on Chinese soil," Feng was saying to Ah Go. "No one knows how he came up with the money to train and arm so many. No one knows how the nephew of the emperor can possess so much power and yet the emperor does nothing about it. Does it mean the emperor is permitting him to attack the Tiger Generals?"

Han stood behind them, staring at the death and destruction, unable to shed a single tear for the loss of innocent life. They needed to be avenged, not mourned. Anyone who survived needed to be protected before they met the same fate. The Judge must be stopped and his minions eliminated.

"I can no longer stand by and let this Judge do whatever he wants," Feng said. "He's after these banners that the Tiger Generals are guarding, and he will kill tens of thousands to get them. I have to try to stop him. I have to."

"*We* have to," Han said, placing a hand on Feng's shoulder and sitting down next to him.

Feng looked up. "You'll help me? Even after you've fulfilled your promise to the Orchid Farmer?"

"Yes," Han said. "We have to work together to be powerful. Innocent civilians are being mowed down for no reason. We have to put an end to this." He turned to Ah Go. "We need you."

"It'll be my honor," Ah Go said. "You two are the greatest warriors I've ever seen. Count on me."

"I… I don't know what to say," Feng said. "I've lived my life with my eyes closed. I thought I was important—I'm a Tiger General's son—of course I thought I was important. But the world is so much bigger, and meeting the two of you… I've never had a real brother and all my friends are dead. You two have been like brothers to me. You taught me about the road ahead—that there is a road ahead for me. I would feel so honored if…"

"Yes!" Ah Go said, grinning. "Let's become sworn brothers. I don't have brothers either and I would celebrate for a year if you two became my brothers. Then I can go home and tell my woman she's now second place in the family."

Han chuckled. "Then let's do it now. We'll swear our oath in front of the people who gave their lives today. We'll always remember this oath."

"The three of us can make the world tremble," Ah Go said.

Han climbed to his feet and motioned for both of them to stand. "Do we have wine?"

Ah Go unhooked from his belt a sheepskin flask filled with liquor and passed it to Han. Accepting the flask with one hand, Han drew his sword with the other, knelt to the ground, and planted the Dart into dry soil. Feng pushed three throwing needles halfway into the ground while Ah Go stabbed the dirt with the Butterfly.

One after the other, they swore their oaths in front of the dead. That day, they became sworn brothers, vowing to die on the same day and same year, even if they could not be born on the same day and year. They poured the liquor into the soil and exchanged their most precious possessions as gifts to each other. Han gave the Dart to Feng. Feng gave his needles and gloves to Ah Go. Ah Go gave the Butterfly to Han.

Han laughed, receiving the big saber with both hands. "How do you know I can use it?"

"Is there any weapon you don't know how to use?" Feng asked.

"I don't know how to use a bow and arrow," Han said. "But Ah Go is so good at it that I'll never need to learn."

Soon, the surviving villagers of Zhun Yang hesitantly opened their doors to peek outside, eager to find their loved ones, hoping that someone may have survived.

A rock dropped in Han's heart. What would he say to them? He could give them whatever money he had, but beyond that, there was nothing else he could do. He rose to his feet. "The villagers are coming out of their houses. We need to talk to them."

For the rest of the day, anguished cries tore through Zhun Yang village. They first recovered the bodies of their loved ones for proper burial. Then the few remaining able-bodied men dug a pit for the mass burial of Ko Sun and his soldiers. The elders made it clear that Han, Feng, and Ah Go were not welcome there, and although they could not chase them away, the villagers cursed and threw manure until they left. Han and Feng pooled together all the money they had and left it in the village. The apologies, the remorse, the commitment to justice for the murdered civilians fell upon deaf ears. The common people did not care who was right or wrong, who ruled the empire or who had power over whom. They simply wanted to live.

The three sworn brothers traveled in silence, each pondering their own memories and emotions. Han thought about Fu Nandong. If he had killed him a few days ago, then he would never have ordered the strike against Zhun Yang. But then, another general would be sent in his place. Ah Go killed the messenger with the map of General Wu's city because he thought that would prevent the Judge from finding Feng, but the Judge found out anyway and sent a Zhuge Nu battalion. Maybe Han should have killed Ko Sun when he had the chance.

"Ko Sun told me the Judge is after these banners," Feng said, reading Han's thoughts. "Each Tiger General guards a banner. The Judge is the emperor's nephew, and the emperor doesn't have sons, which means he's already next in line to take the throne. Yet, for some reason, he wants to eliminate the Tiger Generals for these banners. What are they for? Why would the Judge kill the generals for them?"

Han said nothing. Ah Go walked with his head down.

"Ko Sun said the Judge has a secret army of twenty-thousand foot soldiers," Feng continued. "Plus one thousand light cavalry. It doesn't make sense. I thought he would have much more. And now, he is inciting civil war and attacking the Tiger Generals for a throne that would soon be his anyway. None of this makes sense."

By nightfall, they stopped to rest and build a fire. There was nothing to eat and they had no money for liquor. But they had filled their water flasks at a nearby stream during the day and no one was hungry. Ah Go fed the crackling fire until it grew to a huge blaze.

"Do we know who the Judge plans to attack first?" Han asked.

"General Yang," Feng said. "The secret army is already positioned near the City of a Thousand Heroes, and they're waiting for Zeng Xi to mobilize. We have to help him. At least tell him where the enemy weapons are vulnerable."

"We don't know what his plan is," Han said. "But war is upon them. If the Judge is out to kill the Tiger Generals, he won't be using honorable tactics."

"He may try to send assassins," Ah Go said.

Han glanced at Ah Go. Feng's father would be at risk, which would further complicate their mission to hide Feng in the City of a Thousand Heroes. Assassins operate in the dark, unlike armies that scouts can watch weeks ahead of time. General Mu was revered as a great strategist but not as a master of martial arts. He could not out-maneuver assassins if he didn't know he was a target.

"The assassin wouldn't know where the banners are," Feng said. "The only way to take the banners is to take over the city and search the vaults over the course of many days."

"It would be much easier to invade the cities and capture the banners if the Tiger Generals are dead," Han said. "General Yang is known for his martial arts skills and he's very difficult to assassinate.

This may be why the Judge is concentrating his attack on the City of a Thousand Heroes."

Feng stood up. "We need to protect the Tiger Generals. I have to go home."

Han and Ah Go glanced at each other again. It was as they expected. Feng would not hide somewhere to protect himself while his family was under threat.

"If there are assassins out there," Han said. "They would be some of the best fighters across the land. Your Infinity Palm is improving every day but you're not the best person to defend your father."

"I will go to your city," Ah Go said. "I will stay close to your father and wait for the assassin."

Feng turned to him in disbelief. "You will?"

"And I should go protect General Wu," Han said. "I heard he's also a brilliant martial artist but if the Judge is out to assassinate the Tiger Generals, he's just as vulnerable."

"I'm going to the City of a Thousand Heroes," Feng said, "like I promised the Orchid Farmer I would. General Yang needs the information I carry. The enemy helmets puncturing the soldiers, the shields cracking, the swords breaking near the handle. I have to tell General Yang."

"And the Zhuge Nu," Ah Go said. "The Orchid Farmer told us how to defeat them."

"We need fast horses— and we need a lot of them," Ah Go said. "We can charge the archers and they will have no way to take aim."

"That's right," Feng said with a crafty smile. "They can be defeated that way. But the Tiger Generals are there to defend the Great Wall and their heavy cavalry are not meant for speed."

"I know where to get them," Ah Go said. "Thousands of them. I'll borrow them from some friends."

"Friends with many horses?" Han asked. "Where?"

Ah Go laughed. "I have friends everywhere."

"When can you borrow these horses?" Feng asked.

"I can be back in two weeks. Strong, fast horses."

"But my father…"

"Didn't you say your father is not in the City of Stones?" Ah Go asked.

"I… I don't know. He left when he declared martial law in the city and I don't know when he'll be back. I don't know *if* he'll be back."

"I'll bring the horses to the City of Stones then," Ah Go said, "I'll wait for him there, and when he returns, I'll make sure I stay with him."

"He'll return before the Judge invades the City of Stones," Feng said. "And if General Yang falls, the Judge will move on to the next Tiger General, and then the next."

"Then we'll proceed as planned," Han said. "Ah Go will borrow the horses and wait for your father in the City of Stones. I will protect General Wu. We'll escort you to the City of a Thousand Heroes and then we'll part ways from there."

"Going all the way to the City of a Thousand Heroes would take you out of your way," Feng said. He opened the map and showed his brothers, pointing to a spot in the middle of the map. "We need to be quick. We can part ways here, about two days from now, and I'll go to General Yang myself. It'll save you at least a week of travel."

"It's not safe—"

"I know," Feng said. "The secret army is scouring the land and every thug and whore is out there looking for me. But when is anyone safe from death, or disease, or being murdered by bandits in the woods? When is anyone guaranteed to survive and prosper? If a man is born with talent and he hides in a cave because he's afraid to die, then he was never born with talent. If we don't step forward when the people are suffering, then we're already dead."

"The Orchid Farmer sacrificed everything so you can live," Ah Go said.

"The Orchid Farmer sacrificed everything so the people can have a chance," Feng said. "And we need to move fast so the people can have a chance. If the Judge wipes out the Tiger Generals, we'll never be able to stop him."

Feng was right. The spirit of the Orchid Farmer's sacrifice was for the people, not for Feng. But Han promised to bring Feng safely to General Yang in exchange for the Snow Flower, and promises cannot be reinterpreted on a whim.

Han hesitated. General Wu was in imminent danger, and if Feng's information was correct, General Yang would soon face the Judge's secret army, Zhuge Nu battalions, even troops from another Tiger General led by Zeng Xi. Feng's father would be threatened afterwards, if not already. The world was falling into chaos and they could not waste time traveling together to one Tiger General's city.

Ah Go was quiet, hanging back and watching Han, then Feng.

"Your Infinity Palm is taking form," Han said. "But empty-hand martial arts are forever inferior to well-armed opponents. You have to learn how to use the sword. Let's travel together for the next two days, up to the point where we should part. If you can learn four sword sets by then I will not follow you to the City of a Thousand Heroes."

"Four of your sword sets in two days?" Ah Go asked. "Has it ever been done before?"

"Half the Infinity Palm set in five days was never done before either," Han said, gesturing to Feng.

For the rest of the night, Han passed on the advanced sword skills he learned from Master Zuo. Feng learned fast and trained hard, staying up well after Han fell asleep beside the campfire. By morning, Feng had already mastered two sets.

The following night, while Ah Go sat by the campfire roasting a wild boar, Feng completed the remaining two sets. Han could not believe what he saw. Even he didn't learn the first part of Zuo's sword system with such speed. The next day, they approached the town where they agreed to part ways.

"I want to tell you to be careful," Han said to Feng. "I want you to protect yourself at all times, but I know you won't listen to me. You'll do whatever you want when the time comes."

"I will," Feng said. "I'll be careful."

"Don't worry Han," Ah Go said. "Feng will be fine. The enemy should be afraid he's coming."

They laughed, bowed to each other, and split into different directions.

CHAPTER 11

SOMEONE WAS FOLLOWING him. Han trudged forward with head down, pretending to be lost in thought, the soft grass under his feet absorbing his footsteps. Someone with two horses was watching from afar, fast and quiet but not trained for tracking. Han smiled. He knew who it was.

Han lurched to the side, slipping behind a tree. Then, he circled around his target in silence, reemerged and pranced onto the second horse, sending it rearing onto its hind legs.

It was Scrawny Fox on the other horse. He shrieked and almost fell off. Han threw his head back to laugh, squeezed his own horse's belly and rode forward, waving for the boy to follow.

Scrawny Fox pulled up next to him, nostrils flaring. "You tub of dog shit. Why did you scare me like that?"

"Why did you let me detect you like that?" Han asked.

"I saw those other two men with you," Scrawny Fox said. "I didn't want to get too close. One of them looks really dangerous."

"The skinny one," Han said. "He's dangerous."

"How..."

Han laughed. "Both of them are impossible to kill."

They rode side by side down a small slope, the soil underneath them still soft from recent rain. Han pulled out a bottle hooked against his saddle. "Is this water?"

"No."

"Thank you," Han said. He unplugged it, brought it to his lips, and smiled. "That's a nice liquor."

"I have plenty of money left," Scrawny Fox said. "Do you want some for gambling and whoring?" He drew a handful of gold coins. "I sold the fourth horse and carriage."

"Where is Yi Yi?" Han asked, weighing the coins in his hand. It was a substantial amount, but he was certain the little thief pocketed most of the money for himself. He deserved it. "Why did you sell the carriage?"

"She doesn't need it anymore," Scrawny Fox said. "She took one of the horses and rode off."

"She's fully recovered?"

"Like magic," Scrawny Fox said with a bright smile. "She slept for three days, and then one morning I woke up and she was already outside strapping one of the horses. She was still weak but she said she didn't need strength to fire her crossbow. She told me to send the doctor away and to come find you. She said she was leaving to look for the other Houses in the Martial Society."

"Does she expect them to join her?" Han asked, almost to himself. "They don't know who she is."

Scrawny Fox rubbed his nose, his chin raised. "I advised her…"

"You? Advised her?"

"I advised her," Scrawny Fox began again, "to say that the people need them right now, because the Tiger Generals are in danger and there is no way to stop the Silencer from invading if we lose the Tiger Generals."

Han paused. That was a smart thing to say. "Where are we meeting her?"

"I've left markers everywhere," Scrawny Fox said. "She knows how to find us."

Han drew the folded slip of paper Liu San gave him. "Yan An. This is where the next Council of Midnight meeting is taking place."

Scrawny Fox stretched his neck to see. "That's five days from now," he said, his thick eyebrows knit together. "But we are more than five days away from Yan An."

"I know," Han said. "I am late."

"It's close to the City of Eternal Peace."

"Zhuge Nu battalions are positioning outside General Wu's city," Han said. "They are trying to invade and the Council of Midnight knows what the plot is. I need to attend that meeting and find out."

"Why were you invited?" Scrawny Fox asked. "You didn't plan on joining them did you, you piece of dogshit. I thought…"

"Quiet Scrawny Fox!" Han said, his voice thundering. "I will explain everything later. We are two people and we cannot confront an army. But we can help General Wu by finding out what is behind this Manifestation. Are you going to help me or not?"

Scrawny Fox swallowed. "Yes, I will," he said in a quiet voice. "How can I help?"

"Take both horses," Han said. "I will buy another in the next town. Change horses often and try to get there one night ahead of the meeting. I need you to sneak into the mansion where this is taking place and find the banquet hall. Can you get in and out without being detected?"

"Of course I can. Bet your shit-eating mother that I'm good at this."

"The Council of Midnight is full of great warriors," Han said, ignoring him. "I can't fight all of them by myself. I need you to plan firetraps inside the main banquet hall. After I get the information I need, we'll set an ambush and burn them into confusion."

"Really?"

"My new brother taught me that," Han said. "Deceit and preparation. Confuse them and drive them into chaos."

"Let me guess," Scrawny Fox said. "That's the thin one you said is most dangerous."

"The one who can manipulate the future in battle."

"I knew it!" Scrawny Fox snatched the bottle from Han's hand, still full of strong liquor, and took a long, satisfying gulp. "He's dangerous because he is smart. I am smart too."

Han smiled. "Yes. Now, when I attend the meeting the following night, I need you to come back and lock the doors outside the banquet hall. Can you do that?"

"Wait! But you will be inside."

"I know," Han said. "And I will find my way out. Secure the backdoor with something you know I can break. I will set the place on fire. I need you to hide the alcohol high up where no one would notice. Maybe in the upper beams supporting the roof."

"I know what to do," Scrawny Fox said.

Han took the bottle back from Scrawny Fox, drew the Butterfly from his saddle and handed it to the boy. "Hide my weapon as well. I will need to go in unarmed."

Scrawny Fox nodded. "You can count on me."

"I know I can." Han pointed to the road in front of them and the boy understood. They drew their horses close together, both animals still moving at a rapid trot, and Han handed him the reins before leaping off. He smacked both horses' buttocks at the same time, and they lurched forward. Scrawny Fox rode with his head down, shouting obscenities about someone's mother, and disappeared.

It was a short walk to the next town, and from there, Han bought a fresh horse and continued onward, riding at a consistent trot with sporadic rests. He changed horses once a day, and by the third day, he was far enough north to once again see posters of himself.

Han bought new clothing, gray and coarse. Dressed as a woodsman, his hair was untied and partially covered his face so he no longer resembled the drawings posted in every town and village. With a large straw hat covering his eyes, he rode north unhindered.

The meeting would take place at midnight on the fifth day, and Han arrived by late evening. It was a bustling town, not large enough to be a city but still densely populated. The streets were paved with white bricks. The wooden houses, though not large, were well decorated with intricate motifs.

Yan An was alive. Shops and inns, with their wood panel doors pulled apart, welcomed travelers and local residents to spend their surplus coins. Wealthy merchants flooded the inns to eat and drink; aristocrats held noisy parties behind white concrete walls. Thousands of torches and lanterns illuminated the world around them. The wide streets, paved and clean, were full of people, full of music, singing, dancing, and laughter.

Han had left his horse behind and walked with his head bowed such that the straw hat cast deep shadows over his face. He kept a cheap sword that he bought from a hunting store tucked inside his belt. He never realized that such wealth and abundance could be found this far north in the empire, that people up here lived to enjoy themselves rather than to survive, that good liquor and meats were available to anyone who could afford it, and everyone could.

This was why the barbarian nations north of the Great Wall were waiting for a chance to invade—waiting for centuries. This civilization, built over thousands of years, could be taken with a single invasion. All they needed was for one Tiger General to fall, and the Silencer would find the opening he needed to breach the walls.

Han listened to the laughter and watched the dancing on the streets, the children playing. Perhaps Li Gao was a good emperor after all. Perhaps, if the Judge assumed power, the empire would never be the same again.

The address given to Han was located in the northernmost part of town, in a quiet area where the roads were smooth and polished. A few stray peasants were pushing wheelbarrows of unsold goods back to the villages outside. Han turned into a path that winded through a small forest—a cluster of trees that hovered over the stone road, separating the center of town from the mansions along the northern edge of Yan An.

The road straightened and the banquet hall loomed, a mammoth of a structure with a front door spanning the height of two stories. Thick concrete walls surrounded the main entrance and fired porcelain tiles painted in an elegant green ran along the top. Behind the doors stretched a large courtyard before the main buildings inside. It was an unabashed display of wealth and power.

The Teacher, who was standing outside greeting the council members, turned his back to his guests when Han arrived and approached with his hands clasped. He bowed low and said, "Good to see you, my nephew."

Han returned the bow. "I've been looking forward to this."

When a guard came forward, Han unhooked the sword from his belt and handed it over.

"A cheap weapon for a great hero," the Teacher said.

Without a word, the guard dropped the sword into a tall basket by the entrance.

"Not at all," Han said. "The true weapons—great heroes—are already inside."

The Teacher laughed, placed a hand on his shoulder and ushered him forward. "I hope you join us tonight."

Han stepped into the main hall. Many more members were arriving for the meeting, and he followed them to the largest structure on the property, a banquet hall with a ceiling that reached the height of two stories.

Han strolled in and glanced up at the thick wooden beams above that held the tiled roof together. He could not reach them with a single jump, and if his weapon, and the alcohol caskets were hidden up there, then he would need to find another way up to those supporting beams.

Han smiled. He was confident that Scrawny Fox planned this well. No one would search the beams. The true weapons were up there, intact.

He passed a chair shoved against a tall cabinet on the wall. Above the cabinet, a beam extended close to the front door. This would be his entry point to the place where Scrawny Fox likely hid the alcohol. He had a plan.

The hall was deep but not wide. Long narrow tables lined either side of the red carpet leading in from the front door, covered with porcelain cups, bowls of fruits and rice pastries. Behind each table stood two heavy armchairs. On either side of the room were more layers of tables and seats, a total of three rows deep on each side of the room, and at the far end, a luxurious seat was raised on a small platform. The Grand Chancellor would sit there, no doubt.

Many members of the council were already seated. Han took a quick glance—with five tables per row, there should be no more than sixty warriors locked in here. He lowered his head and wandered toward the front, and as he passed by, he felt the eyes fall on him, heard men who were talking amongst themselves become silent. Sixty seasoned warriors would still be a struggle. These could very well be sixty masters of martial arts, all having achieved greatness in their own right. Han needed to start a fire strong enough to escape alive.

Liu San approached with his hands clasped together and bowed. Han bowed back.

"Welcome," Liu San said. He took Han's sleeve and guided him to the front. "Sit here, right in front of the Grand Chancellor. You are our special guest."

"It's my honor," Han said. He stepped around the table and seated himself, leaned against the back of the chair and yawned. No one else shared the table with him.

More council members trickled in, all unarmed. Not even Liu San had his sword with him. Perhaps the Chancellor alone would carry a weapon in here.

Numerous lanterns hung from the pillars, and dozens of oil lamps covered the narrow tables. Fire. Han's only concerns were the two windows opposite from where he sat, covered by fine cotton tapestries. They were large enough to leap through—he would need to burn that area first and prevent the warriors from fleeing.

Young girls in fine silk walked around with delicate porcelain bottles. One placed a bottle in front of Han, who nodded politely. He poured himself a cup and breathed in the refined liquor, the deep florals, the complex aromas that reminded him of agitation and tranquility mingling. He allowed the smooth liquid to glide down his tongue. This was a drink for the gods.

The room fell silent, and everyone sat up straight and faced the door. The girls serving liquor hurried out the side and disappeared. Then, two guards stepped in, armed with broadswords. One of them announced, "Welcome the Grand Chancellor!"

Everyone stood up, folded their hands and bowed. Han remained seated and tilted his head back to drink more of the heavenly liquor, waiting for the main villain to show himself. The minute they shut those doors, Scrawny Fox would lock them in and Han would have to face some of the most powerful warriors in the country all by himself.

The Grand Chancellor was a robust man with a short beard, and he wore long green robes made of fine fabric that fluttered behind him. A gold-plated sword, which bore an intricate motif of an eagle on the scabbard, hung from his belt.

Han had seen this sword before. He had seen this person before, but he struggled to remember where.

The Grand Chancellor seated himself at the very front. He leaned back in his heavy armchair, and when he began to scan the faces, he noticed Han right away.

"Commoner," he said. "It's good to see you again."

Han sucked in his breath. The voice, the demeanor. This man came to visit the City of a Thousand Heroes once, when Han was General Yang's guest there. They had met before.

The Grand Chancellor was Tiger General Wu.

Han felt his heart pounding, his palms sweaty, his nostrils flaring out of control, but he maintained his composure. "You still drink the most exquisite liquor, General," he said with a smile.

General Wu laughed, motioning for someone to bring more. The Teacher approached Han with a small jade bottle and poured the liquor into his cup with both hands. "Now this is a worthy drink," he said.

"Let's have a toast!" Wu said.

The Teacher stepped onto the platform and offered the same

liquor to the Grand Chancellor in a little gold cup. Wu grabbed the cup and lifted it above his head. "A toast! Welcome, Commoner!"

Han threw his head back to laugh and swallowed everything in his cup at once. He threw the cup aside, leaned back in his chair with fingertips together, and watched the Grand Chancellor with a steady gaze. For a second, General Wu seemed uncomfortable, but eventually he too sat back and relaxed.

"I am honored to have a hero like you here," Wu began. "It has been a long time since the greatest warrior in the world graced this council with his presence."

Han smiled. "We all have different roles now, general. Let's just talk business."

"I like that!" Wu said with a deep chuckle. "A man of few words and many actions. How would you like to begin?"

Han leaned forward. Sixty great fighters were waiting for him to say or do something wrong, and all it would take was a signal from General Wu for the slaughter to begin.

"Let's be direct, shall we?" Han said.

"Of course," Wu said. "Direct and transparent is the only way we communicate here."

Han held back a smirk. The Judge had done nothing but try to kill him for the past week, and now his council suddenly wanted to work with him. That was not the transparency he had in mind.

"Let's start with the land," Han said. "How much land? Where is it?"

"Fair question," Wu said. "The land that was set apart for Zuo is located in the south. A hundred million *mu* of land against the ocean, with fertile soil and ample rainwater..."

"Is there a human population there?" Han interrupted. He chuckled to himself, and Wu laughed half-heartedly. A few others in the hall snickered.

"There is an army already trained to defend the walls of the capital there," Wu said. "Ten thousand men strong. You will inherit the existing infrastructure and bureaucracy, plus gold—plenty of gold to help you build your kingdom. The new emperor will summon the governor to the capital to be executed, and the land will be yours."

"To be a new governor?" Han asked, his voice excited. He could sense the smirks behind him.

"You will be a king," the Teacher said with a mischievous twinkle in his eyes. Despite the Commoner's obvious insincerity, Sha Wu played along—enjoyed himself, even.

"Your land will no longer be a province of the Middle Kingdom," Wu said. "You will be a loyal ally to the new Chinese emperor, but you won't be taking orders from him. You will be king of your own land."

"Very tempting," Han said under his breath. "What do you want me to do in exchange for so much?"

"Once you join us," Wu said, "and you are sworn in as an Elder of the Council of Midnight, we will share our plans with you. We'll discuss what each of our responsibilities are."

Silence filled the room. Han sat back with one foot on the chair and an elbow on his raised knee, all while holding a full cup of liquor. Everyone waited, watching him. Sha Wu had a brilliant smile on his face.

Han tilted his head back and gulped the drink. "It sounds like my task will be a risky one—dangerous even—in exchange for an entire province. There is no guarantee I would receive my reward after shedding my blood and sweat and tears for the council."

The silence became more uncomfortable. A few men fidgeted in their seats, watching and waiting for General Wu to respond.

"I know what you want, Han," Lion Beard said, drifting to the front of the room. "And I will give it to you upfront as a gesture of good will."

"And what may that be?" General Wu asked.

"I have a student who is an orphan," Red Beard began, "and as her Shifu, I would be the one to decide her hand in marriage. She is beautiful, and she is as accomplished an archer as I am. You see what I am getting to, Han?"

"I don't," Han said. "Especially since she would marry me with or without your approval."

Red Beard shook his head and clucked his tongue, wagging his finger. "Little Yi Yi defied the Council when she picked a fight with the Judge. She needs to die—there's no way around it. Do you want to marry a corpse?"

Han swallowed the threat and forced a smile, raising his cup to his lips. He took a sip and sighed. "It looks like the only way to save your star student is for me to marry her. Then she will be one of us, another subject loyal to the Judge."

"One of us!" the Teacher proclaimed, turning to the relieved audience in the hall. "Why didn't you say so earlier?"

General Wu threw his head back to laugh. "Then it is settled. You marry the lovely Yi Yi, and you may consider your promised kingdom as our wedding gift to you. Let's begin the inception ceremony!"

A young man dressed in a light blue robe ran down the red carpet with a golden platter in his hands. There were several bamboo needles on the plate and bowls of black and blue ink. He bowed before General Wu and presented his tattoo equipment.

"Excellent," Wu said. He waved his hand over the gold platter to bless it and motioned for the young man to begin.

"I still have more questions," Han said, rolling up his sleeve and extending his arm onto the table.

General Wu shifted uncomfortably again, but he forced a smile. "Certainly."

The young man lined up the needles on the table, situated his ink, and picked up a small brush to etch the two eyes into Han's forearm.

"When the tattoo is completed," the Teacher said, "you will be our brother, an elder of the Council of Midnight. It represents our unity and our undying loyalty to each other. No one in the Council would ever harm another member of the Council. This, you swear to in a blood oath."

Han nodded with a smile. He could almost hear the Teacher

saying, *anyone can always kill anyone. Because there are no inhibitions, killing is the only path to absolute freedom.*

"The Manifestation," Han said. "What is my role?"

"What do you know about the Manifestation?" Wu asked in return.

"I know you need me to kill someone." Han glanced at Red Beard, then the Teacher. "Someone none of you are qualified to kill."

The Teacher stepped forward to pour him another drink. "You are so right about that, my nephew."

"The great Commoner is qualified to kill anyone," Red Beard said. "And we've already told you, Yang Xin needs to go."

"Just one man?" Han asked. "In exchange for an entire kingdom? Even General Yang cannot be that hard to kill."

"He's harder to kill than you." The Teacher's smile never wavered. "He has an army surrounding him, and he doesn't waste his time writing poetry."

Han ignored the Teacher's jab at poets. "And how do you expect me to get through his fifty thousand professional soldiers?"

"You don't need to worry about his fifty thousand men," Wu said. "We will wipe them out for you. As his friend, you will be able to get close to him. Then, while we destroy his army with one ambush after another, he will be distracted. That will be your chance."

The tattoo artist had finished drawing the symbol of the council on Han's arm. When he reached for the first bamboo needle, Han tapped the young man's wrist and pushed it away. "Where are the pupils going to be?" Han asked. "I need to see the blue ink painted on my arm first. It's my big day. The symbol has to be right."

"Yes, sir," the young man said.

"You are to address him as Elder," General Wu said, lifting the cup to his lips for a casual sip. "From now on, you take orders from him."

"The City of a Thousand Heroes has never been breached," Han said, turning back to Wu. "No offense to you, General, but how do you plan on destroying the most powerful army in the world from behind fortified walls?"

"Yang's army won't be inside his walls," Wu said with a solemn expression. "They will be inside mine."

A chill ran up Han's back. "Your walls? The City of Eternal Peace?"

"That's where the ambush will be," Wu said. "That's the Manifestation."

"Somehow Yang will bring his entire army to your city?" Han asked, almost whispering. "And that's where I will kill him?"

"Exactly, my nephew," the Teacher said.

The artist had finished drawing the entire tattoo on Han's arm. Han waved his other palm over the wet ink, fanning it to dry, and then turned back to Wu with a smile. "Even then, you have fifty thousand men and he has fifty thousand. A surprise attack inside the city would be an ugly pit fight. You will lose most of your men killing his. Do you want that?"

"Who ever said we will be inside my city?" Wu said. "The traps are inside, and my men will surround the gates so they can't leave. Once you kill Yang, his men will surrender."

"And then you will absorb Yang's troops," Han said.

"The most powerful army in the world, as you called it." Wu sat back and sipped on his liquor. When he finished, he broke into a brief chuckle. "Zeng Xi will arrive with General Lo's siege weapons, and we will invade the City of Stones with a hundred fifty thousand men. Do you think old Mu can handle us?"

"He certainly cannot," Han said, mustering what little enthusiasm he could. He clasped his shaking hands together and flexed his arms as if waiting for the ink to dry, attempting to hide the deep fear creeping through his skin.

"Allow me to let you in on a little secret," Liu San shouted from across the room. "Tiger General Mu is famous for his mastery of the Art of War. But he is nothing. It's his son that everyone is worried about."

"Mu Feng?" Han asked.

"That son of his is dangerous. He doesn't use military classics; he just makes it up as he goes along."

"Then we need to kill him too," Han said with a smirk. "When will Yang be in your city? When do I kill him?"

"In two days," Wu said. "We've sent multiple distress messages, and he has already mobilized his entire army. He should arrive in two days."

"Then who is guarding his city?"

"Our spies are securing that information now," Wu said. "We will know when our messengers arrive tomorrow."

The tattoo artist dipped his first bamboo needle into the black paint, but Han whipped his arm away to pick up a full cup of liquor. He leaned back to sip his drink, allowing it to swirl and move on his tongue, absorbing the deep violet florals and subtle hints of charcoal fire, before the liquid glided down his throat. It was a smooth velvety texture that left a glistening aftertaste of morning dew.

Han slapped the tattoo artist's forearm, crushing the bones, and sent the young man scampering to the floor. Han threw his head back to laugh while the tattoo artist screamed in pain. "I've changed my mind," Han said. "I'm not going to kill General Yang. I'll kill General Wu instead."

Wu stood up, his nostrils flaring, and squeezed the handle of his gold-plated sword. The warriors of the council looked at each other in disbelief.

The Teacher maintained his bright smile. "That's unfortunate," Sha Wu said. "I am worried for you, my nephew. You are truly naïve. Do you think the Grand Chancellor would tell you his plans without securing something in return?"

"Your drink," Red Beard said, his booming voice overriding the Teacher's soft, whispery tone. "You've drank our poison. If you don't beg us for an antidote every month for the rest of your life, you will die a most horrible death."

Han launched himself at Red Beard like a spear, who shouted in alarm and slipped away just in time to avoid a direct kick to his neck. Han was out to kill. The sixty warriors in the Council of Midnight stood up, but they were unarmed.

"You are truly naive," Han said without turning around. "I'm immune to poison." He grabbed a lantern and leaped onto the chair against the wall, then the cabinet, moving faster than anyone could react. He built up his momentum and jumped all the way up to the beams under the roof.

"And which Venom Sect member gave you a supreme antidote to all poisons?" the Teacher asked with his hands behind his back, strolling across the red carpet.

Han grabbed the first porcelain bottle he could find and threw it underneath the row of windows on the right side of the hall. Strong alcohol splashed across the floor tiles below the row of chairs. Then, he twisted the lantern with his other hand, pushed the paper into the candleflame, and tossed it across the room toward the splattered alcohol.

The fire ignited with a roar, and hungry flames clawed at the cotton tapestries. Han didn't bother to look. He had already spotted the Butterfly on a higher beam across the room and at least four porcelain jars hidden close by.

"You would stoop so low and use something from the Venom Sect?" Liu San asked.

Han laughed. "In war, there is no high or low, only victory or defeat."

"I see," the Teacher said. "It was Mu Feng."

Below Han, the sixty warriors gathered around their Grand Chancellor and awaited their orders. General Wu's face burned red, his lips quivering in pure rage, yet he could not decide. In that moment of indecision, Han threw another two jars of alcohol at the ripping flames and sent the fire shrieking upwards. Two men caught fire, and as the flames engulfed their robes, they flailed and clawed the air, shrieking the most horrible cries.

The tables and chairs on one side of the room burst into flames, and black smoke funneled toward the ceiling. Han had little time to remain on the upper beams.

The men below him were shouting and pushing and shoving each other, scrambling to avoid the flames. They rushed for the front door all at once.

There was one last jar that Han could see through the thickening smoke. He grabbed the Butterfly and leaped to the far end of the room, close to the front door, and kicked the remaining jar of alcohol onto the middle of the floor. The red carpet caught fire, and so did a number of warriors.

The dreadful cries of men burning alive filled the room. Those already at the heavy doors realized it would not budge, and some of them kicked the hinges while others ran toward the back. All the while, the flames were spreading.

"Chancellor, we are locked in," one of them shouted.

· Han jumped, soaring over them with his weapon drawn, and spun around to slash someone, anyone. None of them should get out of there alive.

"Find a way out!" General Wu screamed. He pointed to the row of windows, now covered in flames. The cotton tapestry was burning well.

Liu San broke off the leg of a table for a makeshift sword and rushed at Han.

Han slipped away. "You are not my match." He hurled himself at Wu with a wide, heavy slash. Wu parried and drew his sword to stab back, but Han had already changed directions to attack the others first.

The men were not armed and they were crashing into each other to avoid the growing flames—but even then, they were not easy to kill. All of them being accomplished martial artists, every single warrior found an object to use as a weapon.

But Han's weapon was a legacy of the Orchid Farmer's. It slashed through the wooden tables and chairs like he was cutting through bean curd, slicing through human joints and ligaments with every swipe.

Red Beard threw a table at Han. He plowed right through it, cutting the table in half, and flipped his saber around to slash Red Beard across the chest. The Commoner briefly twisted away to kill someone who came too close, then returned to his attack on Red Beard.

Suddenly General Wu was upon him, his powerful sword swinging at incredible speeds. Han knew this was coming. Among the Tiger Generals, Wu would only lose to General Yang in a sword fight. Han slipped away, slashing through a couple more men, and all of them scrambled away in the chaos. He charged directly at Red Beard with full speed, then past him, spun around and slashed Red Beard in the back of the neck, decapitating him. The greatest archer in the world was nothing without his crossbow.

General Wu screamed. "Kill him!"

The powerful warriors of the Council assembled. Han knew he could not fight all of them; even killing General Wu alone would be difficult. Yet, there was no other way to stop the Manifestation. Even with Red Beard dead, this council of martial arts elites would still go after Yi Yi. They had to be eliminated.

The thought of Yi Yi brought a burning sensation to his face. With a roar, he slashed to kill. His saber lashed into full flight, and he quickly lost his signature finesse and precision.

Maybe he left West Sea to stop the Manifestation. Maybe he desperately needed to keep Yi Yi safe. Maybe he just wanted to kill them. It didn't matter anymore. The greatest warrior in the world pummeled the line of men in front of him, cutting and stabbing and kicking all at once. Blood flew in short spurts, and the screams of dying men, warriors who never thought they could be killed, enveloped the air. Han didn't know what had possessed him, but he moved like a demon. Soon, the dead and maimed were piled across the floor.

Han spun around and attacked again, his Butterfly dancing in the air, his strokes hungry and formless. He found himself entangled in a brief exchange with Liu San, but Han easily tore through him, slashing his throat and chest and belly. Liu San died with a light whimper.

The Teacher stood in a corner, his arms crossed, his rosy smile unabated. Han ignored him and rushed into the remaining men, still avoiding Wu, hoping to kill off as many as possible to isolate the general.

General Wu charged from behind, his sword generating hot wind with its rapid movement, but Han changed course and killed another man before turning around to fight Wu.

The stinging heat in the room suddenly ripped away from Han's face, as if it were sucked out of a tunnel. Someone had punched his way through the back door. Han had little time left. He attacked General Wu, the swipes of his saber silent and controlled, yet rapid and unpredictable. Wu stumbled back, blocking but never retaliating.

"There is a way out!" someone shouted.

"Protect the Chancellor!" another person screamed. He was right behind Han.

The Teacher laughed, folded his hands together, and walked out the back door.

Han killed another man, slashing and pummeling like an enraged fiend. Once again, he was killing for the pure love of the art. Wasn't this how his brother Feng commanded his battles? Classical strategy was too restrictive. Feng innovated every war. And now, Han also found freedom in battle.

Wu closed in with a vicious sword strike, and Han could not evade a deep cut to his ribcage. He didn't have time to see how bad his wound was. Without a second thought, he launched into an unsuspecting man and killed him with one stroke of his saber, kicked a flaming chair into General Wu and continued to attack the remaining warriors.

Most of the men had escaped through the back door, but there were a few who remained, standing in a single line in front of their Grand Chancellor.

Wu grunted, glared once at Han and turned around to leave. The back door was swinging wide open and the cool breeze was sucking the energy out of the fire trap. Han assessed his position. There was a group of eighteen men in front of him, unarmed but ready to die for their cause. General Wu was escaping. The Teacher was the last remaining elder of the Council of Midnight but he had already fled.

There was no point killing these men, Han realized, if the Grand Chancellor could still realize the Manifestation with fifty thousand men. He had one goal.

The cotton tapestry had collapsed and the windows had shattered from the heat. Han sprang toward the men in front of him, slashing and cutting. They screamed and retreated from the sudden, brutal onslaught. Han killed three men in the same breath, and as they retreated to regroup, he leaped through the windows and into the nighttime air.

Han ran as fast as he could. The back door could not lead to that many roads. General Wu would not be far.

In a moment, Han spotted him. Wu had tossed aside his long robes, revealing his disheveled hair, and he was walking away with at least twenty warriors by his side. Somehow, a few of them found weapons outside the mansion.

There was no time to plan his attack, nor did he know how. He was not Mu Feng anyway.

Han shot in from behind, like an arrow without a hiss, and slashed the closest warrior in the back. His victim died with a horrid scream.

Those with weapons turned to confront their enemy while General Wu continued to run with his men by his side, pushing into the main road and toward the center of town.

Han needed to dispatch of them right away. If he waited too long, General Wu would disappear and he would lose this chance to slay the Grand Chancellor. Yet, his opponents were no longer easy kills.

Han rushed in with a roar, taking the gamble with his own life, and penetrated the forest of dancing blades. He could not avoid them all. Every one of the men was an accomplished warrior, and killing them all would take too long.

Han screamed as they cut deep gashes into multiple points on his body, but he managed to tear through a thicket of men, killing several and wounding even more. He pierced through them, past them, into a wide-open road behind General Wu. He was faster, despite the injuries, and he never stopped running. The men behind him, whoever was left, shouted their profanities and their commitment to protect the Grand Chancellor, but they didn't give chase.

Han pulled closer to his target. General Wu and a handful of men, most of them armed, pushed to gain distance between themselves and the Commoner. But Han was world famous for his speed. Despite the trickling blood that left a dotted trail behind him, Han surged forward and slashed the closest assailant in the back, killing him instantly.

General Wu had no choice but to turn and face his enemy. He barked at his men to deal with the Commoner, and that's when Han saw his chance and took a big step in retreat.

Wu's men charged at Han, but they were confused by the sudden distance between them. In that split second of confusion, Han shot forward while their weapons were raised high above their heads, timed to strike a second later. The Butterfly slashed at waist level, delivering death and murder in a flurry of sidearm strikes. Han endured another deep wound in his shoulder, grunted against the pain, and passed his victims with one deep lunge. He now stood face to face with General Wu.

The few that did not succumb to his mad rush, who didn't fall with grave injuries, stood behind him to shout their profanities. They urged each other to kill the traitor, cursed Han's mother and many generations of his ancestors, but no one moved.

General Wu faced the Commoner alone. His jeweled sword was drawn, his feet planted, his eyes narrowed and focused.

"You fool!" General Wu said. "You dared to defy the Council of Midnight. You dared to attack the Judge!"

Han's clothes were soaked in blood, a lot of it his own. He was tired, and each sharp breath was painful to him. But if the men behind him were not attacking, then his window to kill General Wu was now. He stepped around his target, circling to Wu's left so his own back wouldn't face the remaining warriors.

"Did you believe for one second," Han said, "that I would kill General Yang for a piece of land?"

"Yang will die either way," General Wu said. "Never in his wildest dreams would he guess that I would ambush him. I will rain fire on him so dense his entire army cannot save him."

"After I kill you," Han said. "I will be there to warn him about your ambush."

"Look around you, Commoner. Do you think you can kill me? And sixteen accomplished warriors?"

General Wu's men continued to hang back.

"Your accomplished warriors are afraid of me," Han said. "And you are unable to fight outside of your own rhythm."

Wu tilted his head back to laugh and twirled his sword, slow and deliberate at first, then shifting to high speed. "I can fight at any rhythm, Commoner. It's not that easy to beat me."

"There's an attack speed that changes at will," Han said. "A rhythm that doesn't follow any rules. It's called, the Common Rhythm."

Han moved, barely, then all at once.

Wu charged him with a roar, twirling his sword like a cluster of angry wasps defending their nest. Han slipped around him silently, parrying with his saber. The blades collided with a whisper, as Han's weapon yielded, swayed and maintained contact with his opponent's. Wu fought to withdraw his blade but Han leaned harder. Then with a flick of his wrist and an inch forward, Han pushed away the jeweled sword and slashed Wu across the thigh. The Tiger General stumbled back, gasping in disbelief.

Han was upon him then, angry and vicious, every stroke decisive and clean. Wu struck out in a flurry of swipes before realizing he was swinging at thin air. Han had stopped and was standing as motionless as before.

Wu's nostrils flared. "Kill him!"

His men shuffled in place and did nothing.

Han shot forward with his saber high above his head, this time moving at lightning speed. There was freedom in the wind ripping through his hair, pure joy in the fear and shock on his opponent's face.

Wu struck out to intercept and again swiped at empty air. Han stopped inches away from Wu's sweeping sword, dropped his arm, and stepped in to slash Wu in the armpit. Wu shrieked as his weapon flew away, but it was too late. His sword arm had endured a heavy cut, and he stumbled further back with one hoarse shout after another.

The time was now for Han. His trump card was ready.

"What are you going to rain fire with, General Wu?" Han stepped forward, glaring deep into his opponent's eyes. He slashed a shallow cut across Wu's chest, and Wu crumbled.

General Wu clambered to his feet. "Attack!" he shouted to his men. "I order you to attack!"

No one moved. Han struck again, cutting Wu across the waist. A cough muffled Wu's scream.

"I will find your ambush either way," Han said. "You can't hide that many soldiers around the city without me detecting them."

Wu laughed, a weak but taunting chuckle. "You wish! Do you think I'm stupid?"

"I see," Han said. "You're not raining fire with men. You have machines."

Wu's smile faded. He gasped for air and lifted his trembling finger to point at Han.

"Siege equipment modified for use inside the city?" Han stepped forward and slashed the extended arm. "Where are these machines?"

A good distance behind Wu, half hidden within deep shadows, two people stood on a nearby hill. It was Yi Yi and Scrawny Fox, and they were intently focused on Han. Han saw Yi Yi's crossbow raised, and that's when he realized she was protecting him from the warriors behind him, keeping them at bay.

Then, Han gasped in horror. The Teacher was standing behind her with his hands folded and a gleeful expression spread across his face. Yi Yi did not notice him at all. Why wasn't Scrawny Fox watching her back?

Sha Wu was daring Han to decide, and he was enjoying himself. Han grew frantic then. His hands began to shake, his mind still focusing on General Wu, but he was no longer in control. Yi Yi was a mouse under the Teacher's paw. Han had to attack now if there was a single chance to save her.

His gut wrenched in his belly, and every nerve in his body streaked waves of icy heat. If he didn't find out where the ambush was, General Yang would fall, and three out of four Tiger Generals' armies would be absorbed by the Judge. Feng's father alone would remain to defy the Judge's massive war machine.

Han tore his eyes away and slashed Wu's chest again. He waited, then slashed the general again and again, never deep enough to end his life, but enough to inflict pain.

Then, Yi Yi screamed. Her voice grew more and more distraught, shrieking at a high pitch, until her cries faded into the darkness. The Teacher took his position. It was time for Han's move.

Han drew the map from his pockets, the one that Ah Go took from the messenger in the middle of the night. He held the map open in front of General Wu. "I already know where they are," Han said. "The red circles."

Wu gasped in bewilderment, and Han closed the scroll. There was no doubt anymore. The red circles pinpointed every ambush.

With a roar, Han swiped General Wu across the neck, decapitating him, and then rushed after Yi Yi. His own injuries continued to bleed, but he could not stop, even though he knew there was a trap ahead. The Teacher didn't kill her because he couldn't. He was hurting her so she would scream, so Han would follow.

The skies were dark and the terrain rugged with jagged rocks protruding along the steep uphill climb. Han entered an enclosure of stone walls, but it was too dark to see where the ambush would be, or how many attackers were lurking in the shadows. There was not so much as a rustle anywhere.

Yi Yi's screams had stopped. Han knew the Teacher hadn't killed her yet, though. He still needed a hostage for now.

"The Council of Midnight has been decapitated," Han said. "All the leaders are dead. There's no future for you here. If you walk away from this, I will too. Let's part ways as friends instead of enemies."

"Have I failed to teach you my nephew?" the Teacher asked. His faceless voice echoed against the stone walls.

"No one should trust their friends in this world," the Teacher continued. "If you want to be friends, I will have to kill you."

Han felt a gust of wind behind him. The Teacher charged in, the glimmering weapon in his hand blazing. Han jumped with a roar, and with one swipe, he dislodged his opponent's weapon and slashed him across the face, killing him.

Then, he felt a heavy palm strike the side of his neck. The real Sha Wu was behind him, but Han was too weary to look back. The one he killed was a decoy. Darkness swooped in before his eyes.

"Tell me about Ding Yi, my nephew."

CHAPTER 12

ONCE AGAIN, HAN was standing in front of the magistrate's mansion in Ding Yi. Archers stood in front of the door on the top step, all of them aiming their drawn bows at him. A row of soldiers formed the front line, and two more rows of men with long spears stood behind them.

Han was alone. He held a damaged sword in his hand, and blood was trickling down his wrist. His blood. The slaughtering of the Three Kills was brutal, and he had sustained multiple injuries. But he had wiped them off the face of the earth. The young girls they enslaved were free, and he was the hero he always yearned to be. There was one last job to finish, and then he could rest.

The crooked magistrate who released the Three Kills stood behind his archers with his flaring nostrils raised high. He lifted his hand, then dropped it with a single word. "Fire!"

Arrows whipped through the air, but Han spun to the side and evaded the onslaught. He charged into the soldiers, burst through them, and pummeled the archers before they could draw their bows again. The magistrate screamed and stumbled back into the mansion. "Close the door! Close the door!"

No one lived long enough to touch the heavy red doors.

A woman and her child came running in to find the magistrate stabbed in the belly. "Father! Father!" the child cried.

The structure of the front hall was devastated in the battle. Somehow, Han had slammed a nearby pillar, and the roof started to cave in. Both Han and the magistrate cried out too late. The magistrate scrambled for his child, holding his guts with one hand, but the ceiling beam had already collapsed onto the woman and her toddler.

The magistrate screamed in agony, grabbed a chunk of wood from the floor and charged at the Commoner. Han turned his face and ran his sword through the magistrate's throat.

Han woke up heaving his chest. He was in a dark, empty room with no windows. There was a single fire bowl next to him, and the uneven floor tiles jabbed his back. His wounds were aching, and every part of his body was stiff. By the time he realized his hands were strapped behind his back with rope, his vision had adjusted. Yi Yi was a short distance away, panting for air. Multiple wounds marked her body. Her hands were also tied, and a gag stretched across her mouth. Two men stood against the far wall, watching. When the sting of the light faded, he realized who they were.

Scrawny Fox stood next to the Teacher. He was smiling.

Han jolted. Scrawny Fox had turned? How did the Teacher entice Scrawny Fox to betray them?

A wave of cold air brought dripping sweat to Han's back. His head felt numb, swollen, and the multiple inflamed cuts on his body seared with pain.

At least Yi Yi was still alive. Barely.

"I hope you had a good sleep, my nephew. We have a long night ahead of us."

"Let her go," Han shouted, twisting within the ropes. They were extra thick and he was too weak to break them. His eyes started tearing from the fire bowl's smoke. His hands were sweating, and his breathing grew more rapid. If Scrawny Fox could betray them and work for the Teacher, for the Judge, then who else could Han trust in this world?

I trust my brothers. And Yi Yi.

"Let's make a deal," the Teacher said softly. "I tell you what you want to know after you tell me what I want to know. And then I let you go."

"I have nothing to say to you," Han said. He wouldn't get out of this alive, but if there was a way to free Yi Yi, to give her the map of the City of Eternal Peace, then his death wouldn't be worthless.

The Teacher stepped closer and crouched down in front of him.

"Just kill me," Han said. "I don't know anything that you don't already know."

"But I know something that you don't," the Teacher said. "About you."

"What are you talking about?"

"You don't have a plan, is that right my nephew?" the Teacher asked. "You have never been in a position like this before. Injured, tied down. It's a sad place to be."

Han jolted the ropes again. He could not break them, but he had no words anymore. "What do you want?"

"Tell me what happened in Ding Yi."

"Ding Yi?" Han asked, his brows knit together. "There's nothing to say about Ding Yi."

"Burn her," the Teacher said with a casual smile on his face.

"Yes, Grandfather," Scrawny Fox said.

Han jerked away with a gasp. "Grandfather?" he whispered.

"I'm glad you see it now, my nephew. My grandson was never a stray thief. I've been raising him since he was born."

Han struggled to kick the fire bowl but he was too far away. Scrawny Fox strolled over and shoved a metal rod into the flames.

Han screamed, squirming on the floor. "Get away from her! Get away from her!"

Scrawny Fox laughed. The Teacher clucked his tongue and shook his head, wagging his finger at the Commoner. "Did you want to be the father figure for my boy here? You didn't notice his stealth skills? I taught him myself."

Scrawny Fox pulled the hot iron from the flame and turned to Yi Yi.

"No!" Han shouted. "Stop it or I will kill you!"

Scrawny Fox ignored him, tore apart Yi Yi's robe, exposing her shoulder, and planted the searing hot iron into her skin. As soon as the rod made contact, she arched her back and screamed through the gag. Dark smoke rose from her burnt flesh when the boy pulled it away.

"I swear I will kill you," Han said. "I'm going to kill you!"

"Now we are starting to understand each other," the Teacher said, waving his hand. Scrawny Fox shrugged and pushed the hot iron back into the flames.

Han wrenched his wrists again, but the rope wouldn't budge. "You better kill me now. Once I break these ropes I will slit your throat."

"You would enjoy that, wouldn't you my nephew?"

"I am not you."

"Is that true now? Then what about Ding Yi?"

"What about Ding Yi?"

"What did you really do there?"

Han tried to climb to his feet but the ropes strapped around his wrists were taut against a ring in the floor. He fell back. "You know what I did. I killed a criminal gang because they were a threat to the people. I killed the magistrate because he was corrupt."

"You are a hero then."

Han glared, his eyes so wide they bulged out of their sockets.

"Burn her!" The Teacher flung his sleeve and Scrawny Fox grabbed the hot iron.

"What do you want from me?" Han shouted, yanking at the ropes again and again.

Scrawny Fox spun around and planted the hot iron into Han's chest instead. As he screamed, the searing heat and the smell of burnt flesh tore through his drained body all at once.

Once again he was in Ding Yi, standing alone inside the mansion of the Three Kills. His trembling hand clutched a damaged sword, dripping with blood. He had slaughtered so many that he could barely remember where he was or when he started killing. There were a few more, and they were running away. The cowards! He chased them like a gust of wind, cutting and stabbing with his bent sword, delivering cruel cuts that were hardly clean, that failed to end his victims' lives. One man, already slashed across the neck, was still begging for his life. Han hacked him across the throat, but the sword was too bent and dull to decapitate him. The man's throat spewed more blood and yet he was still alive. "Why won't you die!" Han screamed. He hacked him a third time, then a fourth.

"Why did you leave West Sea?" the Teacher shouted into Han's face, jolting him from his memories.

Han choked on a wad of blood in his mouth before coughing it out.

"Why did you leave West Sea?"

"To find out who was hunting me!" Han screamed back, deranged. The sweat and blood dripping from his body hit the floor in resounding thumps.

"Why do you need to know?" the Teacher asked. "You wanted to live on a boat like a fairy."

"To clear my name."

"You don't care about your name. You're a commoner! Why did you come here?"

"To kill them!" Han screamed. "So I can bring justice to the world."

"Was Ding Yi justice?" the Teacher asked. "What about the teenage boy who wanted something to eat? Or the magistrate's son who had just learned how to walk?"

"I did what I did at Ding Yi to rid the world of predators."

"The women and children who died? Were they predators? Burn her!"

Scrawny Fox spun around and shoved the hot iron into Yi Yi's thigh. The heat scorched her robe, burning through fabric and into her flesh. She screamed and writhed away from the iron.

The boy laughed.

Han squirmed within the ropes but they weren't about to break. With a hoarse roar he collapsed to his knees.

Once again he was in the banquet hall, surrounded by the heroes of the Martial Society. They were his friends, people he used to call brothers. But he was faster than them, more brutal, more precise. He struck every one of them. Even the ones he didn't need to injure he spun around and destroyed. He didn't want to hurt his friends. But in that moment, when they all seemed to move too slow for him, nothing felt better than his palm crushing their ribs, plowing through tendons and tearing apart muscles.

"You wanted glory didn't you?" the Teacher asked. His voice was tense, taut. "You wanted to be a hero."

"I am a hero!"

"If you're such a hero then why didn't you come back to save Little Sparrow?"

"She killed little babies!"

"And you came out from West Sea to kill bad people, did you? Did you want to kill them?"

"Yes!"

"Why?"

"They deserved it!"

"Even your friends in that banquet hall? Were they bad people?"

"No!"

"Was the leader of the Venom Sect a bad person? The one you dumped into a waterfall?"

"Yes!" Han shouted.

"Did you kill him for revenge? Or did you do it because you're a hero?"

The vision passed before Han again. He was striking Rustam, leader of the Venom Sect, over and over again with the Infinity Palm. Rustam spat blood and threw a wave of poison smoke, but Han easily dodged it. Holding his breath, Han struck him again, pressing him toward the waterfall. Rustam's daughters were firing poison darts from behind, but Han evaded all of them and continued to push his victim. He could have killed the Venom Sect scum with one strike, maybe two. But he didn't want to finish it so quickly. He didn't want to stop. Finally he pressed Rustam over the edge of the cliff and into the waterfall. The girls shrieked.

"So you're the hero!" the Teacher shouted. "Were all your heroics just an excuse?"

"Excuse for what?"

"You tell me!"

"I'm not a hero!"

"Then why did you kill all those people?"

"I don't know!"

"Yes you do! Burn her!"

Scrawny Fox planted the hot iron into Yi Yi's arm. She screamed, but her voice caught in her throat. She couldn't even move from the excruciating pain.

"Stop it!" Han shouted. Yi Yi screamed again.

"Why did you kill all those people?" the Teacher barked.

"Because they were criminals."

"That's not why. Why did you kill them?"

"Because they deserved it!"

"Don't lie to yourself!"

"Because I enjoyed it!"

The wind outside died, and both men were silent, leaving an eerie state of calm.

The only sounds were the crackling fire and Yi Yi gasping under her breath.

Han remembered decapitating the smoke operator outside Zhun Yang. He remembered feeling a smile on his face when he tortured Fu Nandong.

"I enjoyed it!" Han shouted again. His chest heaved in painful spasms, and he began to sob. "I enjoyed killing the scum of the earth!"

The Teacher sat back with a fulfilled smile. "You and I are the same, except you are a hypocrite. Why do you enjoy being a hero, my nephew?"

"Because no one can kill me," Han said, panting for air, blurting out his choked words between heaving sobs. "Because I don't like myself! Is that good enough for you? Because Han was too afraid to save his own mother but the Commoner is not afraid of anything!"

Han collapsed to his side and closed his eyes, shivering, drained.

"Burn her again?" Scrawny Fox asked.

The Teacher shook his head, the light smile fading from his face. "He's broken."

"You planted that boy next to me," Han said, his voice trembling, his breathing more and more labored.

"Like how I planted the map to Willow Island in Fu Nandong's clothes," the Teacher responded. "He was instructed to carry it always. I was expecting you."

"Why?" Han asked. "Then why have Cut Foot burn it?"

"How else would we get our lovely archer alone to hand her the emperor's edict?" the Teacher asked. "My grandson here was assigned to take you to Willow Lake. The map was fake, completely useless. Its only purpose was to lead you to the place where Scrawny Fox was waiting."

Han released a deep, defeated sigh. He could not find the right words. Everything that had happened to him since he left West Sea— the deaths, the losses, the hope—all culminated in this.

"You were supposed to find out from Little Sparrow what the Red Crest meant," the Teacher said. "But you didn't. And then we were supposed to kill you and show her your symbol, but we couldn't. No archer, no poison fog, not even my God Slayer could do it. You even managed to evade the Council's poison last night.

"After that morning on Willow Island, though, I had a different idea. I didn't need to kill you. In fact, I realized I would enjoy it a lot more if someone else was killed. And my grandson would be right there to help you get it done."

"Kill General Wu," Han said in a hoarse whisper. "Why?"

The Teacher wagged his finger at Han again, shaking his head. "Don't be so shortsighted my nephew. What good is killing the Grand Chancellor alone? I needed them all dead. Now that they are, it's my Council of Midnight, and the Judge relies on me if he wants the throne. Now I negotiate."

"How could you know I wouldn't have burned you alive in there?"

"My own grandson locked the doors," the Teacher said. "Do you think I didn't know the way out? The problem with you is that you don't think, my nephew. How could a boy lure away all those men standing guard outside? Unless they recognized him as my grandson."

Scrawny Fox laughed again.

Han coughed up another swath of blood. His lips trembling, he pointed a crooked finger at Scrawny Fox. "Why? Why did you help me save Yi Yi's life?"

"Can't have her dead yet, can we?" the Teacher answered. "Why would you kill General Wu unless your lovely archer's life was in danger?"

"You could have done it yourself."

"Then I would be blamed, instead of you," the Teacher said. "You see, my nephew, someone needs to take the fall for all these wars. Someone needs to pay for all these Tiger Generals falling one by one. Why not the greatest warrior in the world who turned traitor and colluded with the Silencer?"

Han exhaled and faded. He had no more strength to think. Maybe he shouldn't be alive at all.

"You didn't disappoint me, my nephew. You killed them all. The council's entire body of leadership. I didn't think you could operate at my caliber, but you did. You and I, we are very much alike."

Han was in too much pain, too weak, his mind gripped by fear and self-pity. He didn't deserve to live anymore. How he wished his two sworn brothers were by his side.

"Cut his ropes," the Teacher said. "A man must keep his word. I promised to release you after you told the truth."

"Release me, only to bear the blame for your crimes," Han muttered.

"Of course," the Teacher said with a laugh. "And for future crimes that you have already set in motion. Not all the Tiger Generals are dead. Yet."

"Do you think General Yang is that easy to kill?"

"We have many ways to kill him," the Teacher said. "General Wu may be dead but he wasn't crucial."

Scrawny Fox laughed again and severed Yi Yi's ropes first, pulled the gag out of her mouth, and planted a goodbye kick against her ribcage. He then slashed Han's ropes, leaned closer and whispered, "I like beautiful girls, too, just like General Yang. If my grandfather had let me, I would've had my fun with your Yi Yi."

"Let's go," the Teacher said. "They're coming after him."

"Shouldn't we…" Scrawny Fox stopped, crouched over Han's curled body, and cocked his head to listen. For a long time there was silence, except for Han and Yi Yi's uneven, shallow breaths. Then Han heard it as well. Hundreds of footsteps approaching.

"They're coming," Scrawny Fox said.

"Let's go," the Teacher repeated.

The Teacher and his grandson, masters of stealth and speed, disappeared without a trace. Suddenly, all Han could hear was Yi Yi's short, painful gasps for air. Han didn't want to look at her. He could never face her again. He was not the hero she thought he was. He was not even a decent man.

Yi Yi crawled over, her body weak and shaking. Her injuries were shallow, but she was in pain and had lost a lot of blood. She groped her way across the floor and pulled herself next to him. Han ignored her. What could he still say to redeem himself?

Yi Yi lifted Han's head and cradled it in her arms. "Han?"

Han squeezed his eyes together to prevent the tears from seeping through. There were so many things he wanted to say to her, but now, under these circumstances, the quiet sobs that escaped his lips choked any words he had.

Yi Yi stroked his hair, caked in blood and sweat, and brushed the tears from his cheeks. "Don't say anything," she whispered. "You're a good man. And a hero. No one can ever take that from you."

Han melted into her embrace. "I don't want to live but I don't know how to die."

"Han?" Yi Yi asked. "Can you live out your destiny with a smile on your face and without worrying at every turn?"

The footsteps outside grew louder. There had to be over four hundred people approaching. They were not marching in unison like military, but the slight clangs of steel striking against belts and ornaments said it all. Seasoned warriors were rushing toward their little hut.

"How did you end up here?" Han asked, regaining his senses. "How did you find me?"

"I followed clues that Scrawny Fox left," Yi Yi said. "I was gathering the Martial Society for help and somehow he found me. He said you were fighting difficult enemies and I needed to come and help."

She stopped. Her crossbow was lying next to the Butterfly in a corner, still intact. The Teacher never bothered to destroy them. "The heroes of the Martial Society are coming," she whispered, "but now I think Scrawny Fox reached them first—I don't think they're coming to help. I'm sorry, Han."

"It's fine," Han whispered. "It's as it should be." He pulled the map of the City of Eternal Peace from his robes and unrolled it. "Take this map to General Yang before he enters the city. Tell him these red circles show where General Wu's ambushes are waiting for him."

Yi Yi took the map with trembling hands. "General Wu? He wants to kill General Yang?"

"He was the Grand Chancellor of the Council of Midnight."

"Is that why you killed him?"

Han nodded. "I killed your Shifu too."

"But… General Wu, a traitor? Are you sure?"

Han nodded silently.

Yi Yi's eyes glazed over. "What is happening? How can a Tiger General murder another Tiger General?"

"The Manifestation," Han said. "It involves ambushing General Yang, and the machines that will annihilate his men are hidden inside Wu's city. The circles show where they are. Now, you have to go warn General Yang."

"Let's go." She took his hand and pulled. Han would not budge.

Yi Yi sucked in her breath. "No, Han. Don't do this. Please come with me."

"I don't deserve to go with you," Han said. "Go, before they get here. I will face them myself."

"No, please don't."

"Go."

"I'm not leaving you."

The first gray light of dawn was upon them. The footsteps grew louder, approaching like thunder, and stopped a short distance from the front door. The warriors of the Martial Society knew the Commoner was inside, and they would proceed carefully.

Yi Yi scrambled for her crossbow, and when she pulled off the top load cartridge, she noticed four bolts inside. Her supply had run out.

"Han," she said. "Get up."

Han sat upright and rested his chin against his knees. "They're here to kill me, not you. They were my friends once—I'm glad they will be the ones to take my life."

"Han!" Yi Yi said, raising her voice. "Get up! We need to go."

"I think I will sit here awhile," Han said. "After what I did to them in the banquet hall, they deserve to hear the truth."

Yi Yi grabbed his wrist and pulled, but Han lowered his head and curled into a tight ball.

"Chen Han!" someone called from outside the door. It sounded like Master Kwan. "You are surrounded. There's over four hundred of us and one of you. We are here to seek justice for Tiger General Wu, to protect our country. If you have a shred of goodness left in you, I beg you to put down your weapon and surrender."

Yi Yi sucked in her breath and tried to pull Han to his feet again but he wouldn't budge. "I'm sorry, Yi Yi," he whispered. "I'm not worth your time."

"None of us are afraid to die protecting our country," Master Kwan continued. "You may kill many of us, but you cannot fight us all. Now, let's not waste any more human life. Come out and surrender."

"You may come in," Han said, tucking his chin between his knees. His voice was low, but it carried into the open air outside. For a long time, no one moved.

Han flexed his ligaments and felt the stinging pain in every injury on his body. The injuries were deep and there were many, but none of his organs were damaged. He could still run away with Yi Yi if he wanted.

Scum like me should resign to their fate.

The flimsy front door creaked open and Master Kwan stood alone at the entrance. A small distance behind him stood an army of warriors. Han lowered his face with a sigh. "Come on in."

Kwan stepped inside alone, followed by a surge of men rushing to his side. All at once they poured through the small doorframe and lined up against the wall behind him, and before Kwan reached the center of the room, over fifty men had joined. Some carried torches, others held weapons at their sides.

"Chen Han," Kwan began as the shuffling footsteps behind him came to a pause. "Last time you fought your way out of the banquet hall, you injured many of our brothers. We couldn't kill you then, but that doesn't mean we won't now. You've denied your victims' accusations against you, but this time, there is no hiding from the truth. Everyone on the street saw you murder a Tiger General in cold blood. You taunted him, tortured him with multiple superficial cuts, and then executed him when he was unarmed and helpless. Do you admit it?"

"I do," Han said.

"No, that's not what happened." Yi Yi stepped in front of Han with her crossbow raised. Everyone in the room drew their weapons.

"Don't be so blind!" Yi Yi said. "General Wu was a traitor. He served the Judge and he was the leader of the Council of Midnight. Han killed him to save General Yang."

"What nonsense are you spewing Yi Yi?" someone shouted from the back. It was Master Zhou. "You told us you were the emperor's personal guard. How can you side with a traitor?"

"He is not the traitor," Yi Yi said. "Let me have a chance to explain."

"Enough!" Kwan said, holding up his palm. "Neither of you will talk your way out of this. If you want to live, Yi Yi, step away from the Commoner and stand behind me."

Yi Yi lifted her crossbow and leveled it point-blank at Kwan's forehead. The warriors behind him approached with weapons raised. Master Kwan gnashed his teeth, but he held up his hand to halt them. "Wait."

"Let them kill me," Han whispered. "I don't want this."

Yi Yi clenched the handle of her weapon so hard her knuckles turned pale. "Please don't do this, Han."

"Master Kwan," Han said. "I've never been the hero you thought I was. I'm a murderer and a criminal. It's time to end it for me."

Kwan frowned. He turned to the warrior next to him, then to the faces behind him. "What are you trying to do, Commoner? You are not getting out of here alive."

"I don't want to."

Kwan stepped forward. "Confess, Commoner. How did you plan to kill General Yang? Who else is working with you? The Teacher? The Silencer?"

"Who said he planned on killing General Yang?" Yi Yi asked, raising her voice. "General Yang is his friend."

"The traitor cannot hide the truth," Master Zhou said from behind. "Eventually, someone did the right thing and told us his plans."

"Scrawny Fox," Han whispered.

"Yes," Kwan said. "He told us everything."

"That boy is the Teacher's grandson!" Yi Yi shouted.

"That boy told us what you are about to do to our country!" Kwan screamed at Han. "You've hidden machines in General Wu's city. Modified siege machines that can firebomb the streets when General Yang arrives. You want to kill all the Tiger Generals so the Silencer can invade. Admit it, Commoner!"

Han shook his head. "That, I didn't do."

"Where are those machines?" Master Zhou demanded. His voice was strained and heated. "Where are they hidden?"

Han couldn't decide whether to tell them about the map or not. No one was supposed to know he had it, no one except Ah Go and now Yi Yi. Knowing the secret locations of the machines was the one advantage Yi Yi had over the Teacher. If four hundred people knew about the map, then it would be a matter of time before the Teacher also knew.

"We don't know what you're talking about," Yi Yi said.

Kwan glared down at the Commoner, tapping the handle of his sword with his fingers. "Chen Han, do you admit that you instructed the boy to lock the doors so you could burn General Wu alive?"

"Of course I did."

"Why?"

"To destroy the Council of Midnight," Han muttered. Images of him destroying an entire clan of people, memories of him butchering the Three Kills in Ding Yi, flashed through his mind again. "Because I enjoyed it very much."

"General Wu worked for the Judge," Yi Yi interjected, lifting her crossbow to Kwan's forehead again. "If you ignore what I say one more time I will put a bolt in your head. I told you, General Wu was the traitor. Pay attention, and don't try me."

The men of the Martial Society looked at each other again in bewilderment.

Han gently touched Yi Yi's arm. "They won't believe a Tiger General could betray his country," he said. "When they joined the Martial

Society, they swore to uphold justice and protect the innocent. They must kill me, Yi Yi."

"I'm glad you remember that, Commoner," said a voice behind Kwan. "What happened to *your* vows?"

"I've spat in the face of justice," Han said. "I didn't even try to save Little Sparrow. I've killed the innocent…"

"Who is Little Sparrow?" Master Zhou asked.

"The woman who cared for Li Yan on Willow Island," Han said. His voice was calm, almost distant.

"Li Yan?" Kwan asked. "What are you talking about? The emperor's brother has been dead for many years."

"There's more than meets the eye," Yi Yi said. "Just listen, dammit!"

"We are not going to listen while the Commoner talks his way out of his crimes," Zhou said. "We will listen to his confession and then we will deliver justice. That's it."

"What else are you going to confess, Commoner?" someone else shouted.

Han sighed. "Everything." A wave of murmurs passed through the room. The warriors outside were talking amongst themselves again.

Kwan flung a hand in the air. "Quiet!"

Yi Yi's crossbow remained level but Kwan brushed it aside. "You're not going to shoot me." He turned back to Han. "What nonsense are you blurting? We don't have patience for your games, Commoner. If you are ready to die for your crimes, then get up and face your death like a man."

Han sighed. "I am ready." He climbed to his feet.

"No!" Yi Yi said. "I can't fight them all alone."

"Come clean, Commoner!" Master Zhou shouted. "What crimes are we executing you for?"

"For killing the innocent in Ding Yi," Han said.

"Ding Yi?" Kwan asked. "That was your finest moment. They were all criminals." He held up his hand again to quiet the men. "Something is wrong," he whispered.

"For the innocent who died in Zhun Yang," Han continued in a trance. "For letting my mother die. For every death I've caused that wasn't for justice."

"Not for justice?" someone asked.

"What are you talking about?" another voice interjected.

"Who? And why did you kill them?" Kwan asked.

"That's who I am," Han said through clenched teeth. "I am a monster made for killing. I can take any life I want. That's why I enjoy it so much."

"So you confess to killing Magistrate Li?" another voice shouted over everyone else.

Han shook his head. "The Teacher killed him with the Infinity Palm."

"Liar," someone said. "You are famous for the Infinity Palm. No one else."

"And Lady Li! You killed her too," another warrior added.

Han shook his head again. "The Council of Midnight killed her. She stole the map to Willow Island and gave it to the Judge."

Uproar broke out in the room. "How dare you accuse Lady Li!" someone screamed.

"You traitor! Still blaming others!"

"Kill him! Kill the Judge's dog!"

"Wait, my brothers!" Kwan shouted, facing the men behind him. "Something doesn't add up. Let me do the questioning."

He turned back to Han. "What is Willow Island? What is the Council of Midnight?"

"General Wu was the leader of the Council of Midnight," Yi Yi said. "They exist to put the Judge on the throne. General Wu positioned the ambush in his city to kill General Yang. He was the one plotting with the Judge to kill off the Tiger Generals."

The room started to fill with heated murmurs and agitated voices again, but Yi Yi shouted over them. "We can't stop General Yang from entering the City of Eternal Peace, even if we tell him about the ambush—he has sworn an oath to defend another Tiger General's city under siege. But someone can slip into the fortress before he arrives, find the machines and neutralize the ambush. Does anyone here want to do that?"

The angry voices faded like a candle deprived of air. Yi Yi waited before she asked again. "You all said you would die for your country. Who will sneak into Wu's fortress and destroy the weapons he installed?"

The men stiffened, waiting for Kwan to say something. They shuffled in their positions, some staring at the floor, others lowering their weapons. No one could respond.

"None of you can," Yi Yi said, her voice more defiant than ever. "Because there's no way for all of you to breach those walls undetected, and none of you have the skills to do it alone. That's why you need a man made for killing. That's why Chen Han is the only one who can stop the Manifestation."

"Don't try to distract us with fancy rhetoric," Zhou said. "You are accusing a Tiger General of betraying his country and attempting to kill another Tiger General. You expect us to believe you? What proof do you have?"

"I have proof!" a booming voice said. The roof caved in on the side of the hut. Shingled tiles and splintered wood came crashing down, scattering across the floor in an explosion of gray dust. The warriors in the room lifted their weapons to face the new threat.

Standing under a hole in the roof, a layer of dust still settling around him, was a muscular man dressed as a hunter. He wore thin silver gloves that reached his elbows and he did not carry a weapon.

Yi Yi fired twice, but the big man swerved in time and the bolts struck the wall behind him.

"Wait!" Han called. "It's Ah Go."

"Who are you?" Kwan asked.

"Chen Han's brother." Ah Go strolled toward them, casual and menacing at the same time. One man flashed his saber and swung for his throat. Ah Go shot forward, grabbed the man's armpit and tossed him out the door. He sent two more men flying out the hut before the rest of the warriors had time to react.

"Wait!" Han shouted again. "Don't fight them, Ah Go."

Another warrior slashed at Ah Go with a heavy saber. Ah Go lifted his gloved arm and blocked it, sending the warrior stumbling back with a damaged blade. The remaining men paused.

"I'm not here to kill you," Ah Go said. "Even though I should. You are all blind and deaf and stupid as camels."

"So the Commoner hid reinforcements," Zhou said. "Is this all? One man?"

Ah Go lunged at him, plowed through two men in his way, grabbed Zhou and flung him out the door. Then, he swiped at the warriors in front of him and grabbed their naked blades, twisting them apart before throwing them aside as well.

"A worm thinks harder than you," Ah Go said. He crossed his arms over his broad chest and pointed his nose at the men with contempt. "Who told you to come here and find my brother? That boy you met outside Yan An? Did none of you wonder how he knew Chen Han would be imprisoned here tonight?"

The men turned to each other again. Those who had raised their weapons started to lower their arms.

"Do you think there are one or two machines that can rain fire on an army of fifty-thousand?" Ah Go asked. "Or would there be hundreds? Can Chen Han operate them all by himself? In a city still controlled by General Wu's son?"

"Chen Han doesn't have a brother," Master Kwan said. "Who are you?"

Ah Go ignored him. "Who can install big firebomb machines inside Wu's city? My brother, or Wu's son?"

"But…" Master Kwan paused with his mouth hanging open and his eyebrows knit together.

"Stupid as a toad," Ah Go said. "None of you left a trailing scout to watch for anyone who might be following you. None of you sent runners to scope out the terrain before you marched here. If an army were coming up behind you, where would you run?"

"Why would an army be following…"

"You tell me!" Ah Go's voice was a deafening boom, so much so that two men standing close by stumbled back. "Ten regiments coming this way," Ah Go said. "That's ten thousand men due here before sunrise."

Han touched Yi Yi's hand. "They need to run. Take the men and disperse across the land. I will delay the troops."

Yi Yi shook her head. "Stop it, Han. I'm not letting you die here."

Kwan spun around and pointed at two of his men. "Verify this information and report back. Now!"

The two men, both lanky and young, bowed and ran off. Meanwhile, the rest of the warriors gathered outside the hut were fidgeting, uncomfortable with themselves.

"If there's an army coming," Master Kwan said. "It will be General Wu's men coming for the Commoner's corpse."

"You're not thinking!" Ah Go shouted. "Who could mobilize Wu's army within the few hours after he died? How would he know he could follow you to find Chen Han?"

The men stepped back, frightened and confused at the same time. Ah Go's voice carried deep into the night, and the four hundred men outside all heard every word. Their debates and discussions blended into a single drone.

Kwan stood at the doorway outside the hut. "Jing! Come here."

A young man ran up to him—he couldn't have been older than seventeen. "Yes, Master Kwan. How can I help?"

"Didn't you serve as a scribe under General Wu before?"

Jing nodded. "Yes, Master Kwan. One year in the imperial palace, two years as General Wu's scribe."

"Do you know who is second in command for General Wu?"

"That would be his son, sir."

Kwan frowned and glanced at Ah Go, then turned back to Jing. "His son is inside the City of Eternal Peace. If General Wu dies, can a third in command mobilize ten regiments without permission from Wu's son?"

"He cannot, Master Kwan. The chain of command is clear."

Ah Go drew a letter from his pocket and unfolded the bottom of the paper to reveal the signature and the stamp. "Come look at this, Jing."

Jing hesitated, his hands trembling, and turned to Master Kwan for guidance. Ah Go laughed. "If I wanted to kill you, you would already be dead. Come on, step a bit closer. I need you to read this."

Jing gulped, resting one hand on the hilt of his sword, and inched forward. He leaned closer to the bottom of the paper. "That's... That's General Wu's signature and stamp! Why do you have one of his official communications?"

"I stole it," Ah Go said. He flipped the rest of the paper open and handed it to Jing. "Read this nice and loud for everyone."

Jing took the paper with shaky hands and glanced around for support, but everyone was quiet. The men standing closer to the hut leaned in to see the letter. Jing lowered his head to read.

"To the great hero known as the Silencer." He froze, gaping at every bewildered face surrounding him. His trembling hands almost dropped the paper.

Han drew a sharp breath—for a second he was unsure that he heard correctly. He knew General Wu worked for the Judge and headed the Council of Midnight. But to conspire with the Silencer was a new low.

All the men had turned to face Jing outside the hut. Han took Yi Yi's hand and inched closer so they could hear.

Jing was frozen, holding the letter as far away from his body as possible as if it were infected with disease. Master Kwan snatched the paper and stood at the doorway facing the crowd. He read in a slow, solemn voice.

"To the great hero known as the Silencer," Kwan repeated. "I hope this letter finds you well. Our country and yours have never been in conflict, and I understand that you are not interested in our affairs. Allow me to offer you a small gift of one thousand taels of gold with this message, and a promise of something much more substantial if you agree to my proposal. I have prepared for you a caravan of riches, ready to depart from the City of Eternal Peace immediately. It consists of ten thousand taels of gold, twenty thousand taels of silver, one thousand heads of oxen, ten thousand Chinese engineered shields and broadswords, and three hundred beautiful women. It is a full year's supply of virgins that you are free to dispose of each night, however you see fit."

Master Kwan paused to take a deep breath. For a moment, his quivering lips could not shape the words. Every warrior of the Martial Society stood with his mouth wide open and his hands frozen at his sides. No one uttered a word.

Kwan continued after a long pause. "In return, I ask for a simple favor, something that I am certain you would enjoy. Tiger General Mu will be leading his men into Mongolia shortly. He may pretend to search for his daughter but he is actually seeking an opportunity to invade. To defend your honor and your sovereignty, I ask that you annihilate Mu's entire army and execute him in public for the world to see. As a gesture of good will to you and to your empire, I am offering the above gifts in exchange for General Mu's head. I look forward to your response."

Han shuddered. Feng knew nothing about this.

With a roar, Kwan shot his arm out and clenched Jing by the throat, choking him and almost lifting him off his feet. Jing struggled, eyes wide with terror, his arms flaying and feet jerking in short steps. "Read carefully!" Kwan shouted into his face. "Is this signature real? Was his stamp stolen?"

Jing gasped for air, lifted a quivering finger and pointed at the signature. He managed to nod his head.

Kwan released him and stumbled back two steps, his troubled face more wrinkled than ever. Jing fell in a heap on the ground, coughing and gagging and scrambling to his feet.

"Why?" Kwan whispered. He spun around and pointed a crooked finger at Ah Go. "Where did you get this? Are you in on this?"

Ah Go shrugged. "I took it from his messenger."

"Where is the messenger?"

"I killed him."

"And you took the gold that the messenger was carrying, no doubt."

"Of course," Ah Go said with another shrug. "I spent it already."

Kwan laughed. "And where would a ruffian like you spend a thousand taels of gold?"

Ah Go glanced at Han with a smile. "I bought some fast horses."

Two men pushed their way through the crowd. "Sir!" they shouted. "Sir! Urgent!"

The two young men from earlier had returned. They were struggling to catch their breath, and their faces had flushed pink. "Master Kwan," the taller one said. "There's an army of ten thousand approaching us. They are armed with…"

"Archers?" Kwan asked.

"No archers," Ah Go said.

"Then we'll outrun them," Master Zhou said. "Did you see how many are on horses?"

"Just a few commanders in front," the shorter scout said. "Four at most."

Kwan sighed in relief. Ah Go spun around and grabbed two people from the room and tossed them both out the door with a roar. They landed hard, bruised, scraped, scrambling for footing. The men around him drew their weapons again.

"You idiots!" Ah Go shouted. "Why do you think they are after Chen Han? You know these men did not mobilize on a whim, so they must have been assigned to hunt him much earlier. Maybe on General's Wu's orders."

"What are you talking about?" Master Zhou asked. His voice was shaky and timid. "No one uses the military to hunt civilian criminals."

The hut was empty now as all the warriors from the Martial Society had gathered out front to watch the events unfold.

"I came to tell my brother about a different army coming this way," Ah Go said, turning to Han. "A much bigger one."

"How big?" Kwan asked.

"I couldn't even count," Ah Go said. "But you don't need an army that size to kill the Commoner. They are after General Yang."

Han stepped closer, his stiff fingers closing into a fist. "That's what the Teacher meant when he said Wu's firebombs aren't crucial. They will try to kill General Yang by other means."

"Our brother is with General Yang," Ah Go whispered back, stepping outside of the door to face the rest of the men. "Feng was supposed to be safe there."

Yi Yi followed him outside. "I told you," she said. "Han is the only one who can slip into Wu's fortress unnoticed and destroy the ambush. They are afraid of him—that's why they are sending an army. Are you all going to run like cowards so he can stand here and face them alone, or are you going to do something about it?"

Ah Go slammed the door shut, leaving Han alone in the dark room. "There's another reason," Ah Go said, his voice booming from the other side.

Han sat down beside the fire bowl and wrapped his torn robe tighter around his body. The injuries began to sting again but he hardly noticed. Whatever Ah Go was trying to do for him, whatever Yi Yi was arguing for outside, didn't make sense. What were they trying to accomplish? He didn't deserve to live, and he certainly should not die with so many warriors fighting by his side. He would face the army himself and give them a chance. Perhaps, if they stopped haggling with words and rhetoric, there would still be plenty of time for everyone to flee.

Yet, one thought continued to nag him. General Yang was his friend. Feng might or might not be with General Yang, but either way, Han could not die here while they were in danger.

But the men outside were also his friends. How could he leave them to hold off an army?

Han climbed to his feet. The monster created for killing should do it one last time.

Then, there was a roar outside, a commotion so loud that Han thought a new enemy had emerged. Before he had time to throw himself out of the hut, the commotion died, and the door creaked open. Ah Go and Yi Yi stood outside, waiting for him.

"We need to leave," Yi Yi said, stepping closer to take his hand. "General Wu's troops are already here. We need to get to those machines and help General Yang defend that city."

"Go," Han said. "I will hold them off."

"No," Yi Yi said. "You are the only one who can get into that fortress, and only the greatest warrior in the world stands a chance if they are detected. It has to be you."

"Ah Go can do it," Han said. "He's not injured, but I am."

"Ah Go has other promises to keep," the big hunter said. "Fast horses to borrow, bad people to scare off." He moved closer to Han and placed an arm around his shoulder. "You can't die, my brother," Ah Go whispered. "The world still needs you. The country still needs killers before all this can end."

"Listen to me, Chen Han," Master Kwan said from the doorway. "I don't know if we were wrong about you, or if you are wrong about yourself. Whether you're a killing monster or not no longer matters. Ten thousand troops are coming for you. We will hold them back and we will fight to the death until you are out of their range."

Han leaned forward to interrupt, but Master Zhou rushed in with his palm outstretched to stop Han from talking. "You have to go, Han. You have to! We will hold them at the bridge so they can't surround us. That should buy you enough time to escape."

"What is going on here?" Han asked.

Yi Yi shook her head. Ah Go's big hand was still resting on his shoulder.

Master Kwan spun around and stormed out the door. "Brothers of the Martial Society!" he called. "Are you ready to die for your country?"

The men outside responded with passionate shouts, some beating their weapons against their chests, others pumping their swords in the air.

"I need ten people who wield throwing weapons to kill the enemy's horses from the side of the road. The rest of us will hold the bridge!" He then pointed toward the water. "Ten people can cross shoulder to shoulder. We will surround them at the mouth of the bridge and fight them two to one!"

The men roared with approval.

"What just happened?" Han asked, feeling more delirious than ever. He was having a bad dream. This could not be reality.

Han turned to Yi Yi. "What did you say to them?"

Suddenly, Ah Go moved. The big man was too close, and much too fast. The heel of Ah Go's palm struck Han against the side of his neck, and darkness blurred before his eyes.

CHAPTER 13

BY THE TIME Han woke up, the heavens were bright and the sounds of battle droned in the distance. He had found himself on a soft patch of grass on a lush hill, the morning sun behind him. He had been asleep on a soft patch of grass. His wounds were bandaged, the scent of strong herbs rose from every injury on his body. Someone with knowledge of medicine had treated him.

Ah Go and Yi Yi were standing beside two horses at the edge of the hill, their backs turned as they watched the battle unfold.

Han climbed to his feet, and the energy he so depended on all these years started to course through him once again. Yi Yi turned and rushed to him. "You're awake," she said. She pushed a pill into his mouth. "Swallow this."

Han gulped down the medicine. Below the hill, past a stretch of swamp land, a bridge hovered over a rushing river. The men surrounding the mouth of the bridge were but tiny specks from his vantage point. It was clear they weren't well organized. The men attempting to punch past the bridge stood in perfect lines, marching forward and backwards in unison, obeying every beat of the drum. These were General Wu's crack troops, ten thousand in all, preparing to fight past the four hundred warriors of the Martial Society.

"Why?" Han shouted, his voice hoarse. "Why are they sacrificing themselves so I can escape?"

Ah Go turned to him. "An old man who calls himself the Coroner told us to give you this. It's medicine." He shoved a pouch into Han's hand. "He also asked for you to contact him when you need him to examine the Judge's body. Before that, heal yourself and occupy the City of Eternal Peace before General Yang arrives."

The battle at the bridge was devastating. Many had fallen, most of them soldiers, but his friends could not possibly escape the onslaught. The nature of the terrain had allowed the battle to continue for a while, but eventually, the four hundred men would falter from fatigue and wave after wave of seasoned troops would tear through them.

"My friends are dying down there," Han said.

"That's what they want," Ah Go said. "Don't rob them of a glorious death. Make it worthwhile."

"Why?" Han asked again. "Why would they do this?"

"They are doing it for their country," Yi Yi said. "We're running out of time. We have to take over the fortress before this army catches up to us. Our friends cannot hold them much longer."

"No," Han said, shaking his head. "They wanted me dead. Why would they do this for me?"

"Han," Yi Yi whispered next to his ear. "If we are to survive this, you need to embrace who you are."

Han crumbled to his knees, his head bowed. "I am a monster," he whispered. "I am not worth it."

Then, the troops broke through the bridge, their long spears advancing into the blockade like a wall of spikes. The Martial Society never had a chance. The soldiers plowed through them, their trained formations and meticulous rhythms of war rapidly destroying the scattered lines.

Master Kwan shouted something and the men retreated to the far end of the road and formed a new line for one last stand. They were getting slaughtered. Four hundred men, no matter how well trained, no matter how advantageous their terrain, could not hold back ten thousand. Six rapid beats of the drum and the soldiers assembled, their lines compact and organized. They were ready for the next advance.

Han buried his face in his hands. He ought to be down there dying with them. Why did they sacrifice themselves? Why should he live?

"We need to go," Yi Yi said. "They can't hold the army. They will die for nothing if you don't take over that fortress."

Han shook his head, his trembling hands still holding his face. He could not bear to watch, could not bring himself to understand what was happening. He was a monster. All he knew was how to kill people. Nothing else. Now, all his friends were giving their lives for him.

"Big brother," Ah Go said. The muscular warrior crouched down before him and placed both hands on Han's shoulders, peering into his broken face. "I heard the Commoner likes to kill bad people. If that's the only way for you to get it done, please go ahead and enjoy yourself. We're up against too many enemies. The Tiger Generals are getting killed one by one, and General Yang is next. This country can't withstand foreign invasion without them. You need to set yourself free, Han. The world needs the Commoner."

Han shook his head. He would block it all out. He would wake up from this nightmare.

No, that wasn't an option. He had the map and he was capable. His friends were dying down there, so he could do something. The world needed the Commoner. The Commoner knew how to kill the enemy.

What Yi Yi said to him finally sank in. General Yang was walking into more than one lethal ambush. The Commoner must not stop killing the enemy.

Then, it dawned on him that he could still save his friends. Killing many, or saving many, took a lot more than a monster or a hero. It required the right medicine for the right illness. Who was he to believe he mattered?

Han climbed to his feet. He did not bother to wipe the long rows of tears streaming down his cheeks. "Let me kill off that army down there."

"How?" Yi Yi asked.

Han drew the second smoke pipe from his robes. "Ah Go, can you help me kill everyone down there?"

Ah Go took the tube with a smile. "What is this?"

Han charged toward the City of Eternal Peace on his stallion, the Butterfly hooked against his saddle, Yi Yi seated behind him with her crossbow in one hand. Before he parted from his brother, they made one final agreement on when they would meet again. Ah Go would bring his fast horses to the City of Stones so he could protect Feng's father as promised, and Han would meet him there. When Ah Go's eagle—a rare bird with a purple neck—descended on the city, that would mean he was close by.

Han turned back once to a streak of black smoke shooting into the morning sky, hovering above the bridge where the ten-thousand-man army held their formation. Ah Go had launched the signal to invite any nearby Zhuge Nu regiments to fire. Soon, the grounds near the bridge would be covered in a carpet of arrows. Most of the warriors of the martial society would evade the onslaught, since the barrage would be aimed at the bridge. The soldiers would either run when they saw the smoke or they would succumb. Either way, most of Han's friends would make it.

The horse slowed to a brisk walk. For a long time, neither Han nor Yi Yi said anything. The pacing of the horse hooves maintained a steady background rhythm, and up above, thick clouds were forming.

Yi Yi leaned her head against his back. "What are you thinking about?"

Han sighed. "I thought I did the things I did to rid the world of villains and do right for the people."

"You did, Han."

"I didn't do it to protect the old and the weak. I did it because I had fun killing the scum of the earth."

The horse settled into a rhythmic trot. It was soothing, steady like his own heartbeat. Han pulled the reins to slow the horse some more.

"Would you enjoy killing a civilian?" Yi Yi asked.

"Of course not."

"What if the civilian were an old woman stabbing a younger, stronger man so she could rob him?"

Han paused. He urged the horse to move faster again. "I don't know. I would stop her."

"What about a well-trained warrior," Yi Yi said, "killing an old woman because she poisoned forty people? Would you stop him?"

"I wouldn't," Han said. He had no idea where she was going with this, but he trusted her.

"I heard what the Teacher said to you," Yi Yi said. "He twisted the idea of being a hero with finding joy in killing people. You are a hero and you should be proud of it."

"I wish that were true," Han said. "I wish it were that easy to determine whether the old woman who poisoned forty people did it to people who deserved it. Or a way to know for sure the old woman stabbed the younger man to rob him. How can anyone know what the truth is? How can anyone be a hero, or a villain, if they can't tell what justice is?"

For a long time, they rode in silence. Dark clouds converged above them, but not enough to be a threat. Soon they dispersed, and the sun pierced through for a brief moment before the heavens darkened.

"What if one day," Yi Yi said, "you had to do something disgraceful to protect the weak? What would you do?"

"I would do something disgraceful," Han said without thinking. "I would be the villain."

"That's why you are not." She reached around and placed the heavy crossbow on his lap.

"Anyone can be labeled a criminal," Han said. "And then people like me would be out there eliminating them without knowing the difference between a label, and an actual villain."

Yi Yi didn't respond. Han lowered his head. "Who am I to decide who is evil and who is not? What arrogance."

Yi Yi dozed off, but Han continued to think about what the

Teacher said to him, and then what his friends in the Martial Society did for him.

Yi Yi sat up. "What did Scrawny Fox whisper into your ear when he released your ropes?"

Han tried to recall. It was something insulting. "He said something about how General Yang likes beautiful women."

Yi Yi lifted her head to laugh, a deep, full belly laugh. "Why would he say that? Unless he said something about me that you don't want to repeat. I know how he looked at me. I bet you that's what it was."

"It was."

Yi Yi fell silent, her brows knit together. "Perhaps the next assassin will be a beautiful woman. The Teacher said there would be many ways to kill General Yang."

Han tensed and slapped the reins. "We need to get there as soon as possible."

"We can't search for every beautiful woman in the city."

Han kicked the horse to push it harder, sending it into a gallop again. "General Yang is very hard to assassinate. Beautiful women may be his one weakness and the Teacher knows it."

For a long time, they said nothing as they each cycled through the scenarios where a beautiful woman could kill a powerful Tiger General.

"But how?" Yi Yi asked. "She won't be fast enough to stab him. He won't fall asleep with her around."

Han sucked in his breath. "It must be with poison."

"He gets his wine and tea directly from his servants," Yi Yi said. "Where else could she slip the poison?"

The heavens darkened as deep, heavy clouds rolled in, stretching across the sky for as far as they could see. The oncoming rain might last for days.

"Remember when Scrawny Fox talked about Demon Face?" Yi Yi asked. "He said Demon Face was delivering a letter to General Wu."

"General Wu and Scrawny Fox were both working for the Judge," Han said. "Which means—"

"Scrawny Fox wanted us to find Demon Face," Yi Yi said. "But why? If they have him already, why would they need us to find him?"

Han answered by shrugging his shoulders.

"I bet you Demon Face is in Wu's city," Yi Yi said.

"I'm not betting with you anymore."

"You have to," Yi Yi said. "If you don't, then you'll never find out whether he is or not."

"Wouldn't Wu have killed him already? Unless they didn't find the letter."

"That must be it," she said with a gasp. "Maybe they still need something from him."

"The letter... My Shifu burned it right away. What was on that letter?"

The first drops of rain struck their clothes. The downpour was near.

"The city," Han said, lifting a pointing finger. "Maybe we can take shelter there."

Yi Yi smacked the butt of the horse with her crossbow and sent it into a gallop.

The City of Eternal Peace loomed before them, a massive fortress with fortified walls that stretched for as far as Han could see. The front gates towered several stories tall, and the walls were so thick that the lookout towers on top were the size of multi-level houses.

Han slowed the horse to a walk and pulled up to the front gates. A few sentries stood outside.

"Identification," the guard at the gate said in a booming voice.

Han reached into his pocket but hesitated, considering whether he should kill this guard and alarm the entire city so soon. But his identification book would have the Commoner's name on it, and General Wu's son was hunting him.

"Show him your book, Master Kwan," Yi Yi said. She laughed and produced her official pass. "I am his superior," she said.

"But..."

Han drew the identification book from his pocket, glanced

inside and realized that he did have Master Kwan's book all along. He showed the soldier, and without another glance, the soldier let them proceed through the gates.

There was another document in his pocket, which Han drew out once he passed the gates. It was the letter from General Wu to the Silencer.

"Your brother thinks of everything," Yi Yi whispered into his ear. "This letter is more useful to you than him, after all."

"Do you know where the general's mansion is?" Han asked in a low voice.

"Let's follow the good food."

"Good food? Like an expensive inn?"

Yi Yi giggled. "Like a whole pig slaughtered for roasting."

It didn't take long for them to spot two men carrying a small pig strapped to a bamboo pole. The pig was fresh, recently butchered, and they were rushing toward the north end of the city.

"How did you know that?" Han asked.

"All generals' sons are fat from eating too much fatty pork."

Not my brother Feng.

The two men carrying the pig veered into a larger road toward a majestic structure in the distance, a mansion that was as glamorous as it was fortified. This could not be a mere aristocrat's home. It had to belong to Tiger General Wu.

Han and Yi Yi leaped off the horse together and hid on the side of the road to watch the mansion. Two guards stood by the heavy metal doors in front, both sleepy and distracted. It was too obvious.

"They're expecting us," Han said. "With only two guards, there has to be an ambush inside."

"Let's lure them out." Yi Yi pulled the map from inside her pockets, traced the large avenues of the city with her fingers, and pointed to the mansion drawn in dark ink and unlabeled. There were two red circles close to it.

Han nodded, and Yi Yi pointed to a taller structure with a second floor to the left of the mansion, then another building—similar but shorter—to the right.

Han nodded again. "That's where the firebombs are."

"You take one and I take one," Yi Yi said. "When Wu's son shows his face, you go down there and kill him. I will cover you from a distance."

"You have two shots left."

"I will have more by then. Even if I have to throw a spear, I will protect you from above. Don't worry."

"I never did." Han slipped away and headed toward the shorter structure. The rain tapped the pavement with light, persistent droplets. As Han leaped off a wheelbarrow and landed on a narrow balcony, he felt a rush of energy—the thought of the approaching battle, the focus he would need to eliminate the enemy, brought a warm tingle to his face. He almost forgot what had happened to him that morning. He was about to do what he did best.

Two people were waiting inside, both clumsy soldiers in heavy armor. Han pushed through the flimsy doors and jumped in.

The room was small and empty, except for two large machines stationed in front of a row of windows. The soldiers were standing guard next to them. Han drew his saber and killed one before he could react, then held his blade against the other soldier's throat.

"What are these?" Han asked.

"Who are you?"

Han slashed him across the head, splitting his helmet, and a long stream of blood trickled over his eye. "What are these machines?" Han asked again.

"Mounted crossbows! Triple... triple bed crossbows with gunpowder warheads."

"How do you use them?"

"You draw the pin on the side to ignite the warheads and then you release the trigger."

"Are they aimed at the street?"

"Y-yes, sir."

Han grabbed his shoulder and tossed him out the window, sending him screaming to the pavement. Then, he sat down in front of the massive crossbow, found the flint ball on the side, and waited. Han noted large, multi-level structures behind the wall around the general's mansion—too large to be residential houses. Perhaps the general's mansion served as a lookout tower as well.

Two guards rushed to the squirming soldier on the street—he was still alive. Then, someone whistled. Han clenched the plate with the flint ball. By now the rain was pouring outside. He was running out of time to use the gunpowder weapons.

Before long, troops were swarming through the main courtyard. The first group pushed through the heavy doors and lined up in front, four layers deep, their sabers already drawn. Inside the courtyard, the soldiers stood in blocks of ten men per line, ten layers deep, with a rear group of archers assembled into an arc.

Han waited while the thousand men positioned themselves for battle. Inside the perimeter wall, four older men in plate armor watched from their position near the main hall. Those had to be the commanders.

Yi Yi struck first. A flaming ball rose into the air, and Han smiled. She must have found a modified trebuchet that could catapult flaming balls packed with gunpowder, instead of boulders. The Judge had advanced weapons, after all.

The ball was as large as a man's torso. The soldiers screamed and crashed into each other, but they were packed together with nowhere to run. The firebomb landed directly into their formations, and when it exploded, a wave of flaming bodies surged upward, screaming and flailing in agony as chaos and fear ripped through the dense lines.

Han pulled the trigger next. Three long bolts with explosive warheads caught fire on their way out, screeching over the walls and pounding the fleeing soldiers in the courtyard. When the gunpowder weapons burst into a ring of flames, more men caught fire. Their horrid screams were muted only by the shouts of those trying to stay alive. This was what Wu had planned for General Yang's army.

Han jumped to the second machine and pulled the trigger, launching another three bolts into the courtyard. Yi Yi fired another volley, a flaming ball that soared high into the air before dropping into the courtyard. By then, most of the men were charging through the front gates, rushing for the buildings where Han and Yi Yi were. It was time to move.

Grabbing his saber, Han leaped from the back of his second-floor structure to the tiled roof of an adjacent house and rolled onto the dusty ground. Then, using a small tree as a springboard, he threw himself against the perimeter wall and began to scale his way up. For a moment he worried about Yi Yi, but somehow he had no doubt she would find a way to evade the enemy as well.

The distraction was complete. Wu's troops were ordered to charge the enemy, frantic, unplanned, the leadership not understanding how their own firebomb machines could be used against them.

Finally, Han flipped over the wall and into the courtyard. It was utter chaos inside. The flames, the smoke, the dying men burning alive and screaming to the heavens muffled any sign of his presence. He charged the generals unnoticed.

Han didn't know which man in plate armor was General Wu's son, but it didn't matter. One of them had to be, and he would kill them all. In that moment, the balance of the world depended on whether he was willing to kill them or not—whether he wanted to kill.

He wanted to. He enjoyed it.

Han held his breath before plowing through the smoke. When he appeared in front of the commanders, they didn't see him—much less recognize him—before he cut down three men with one surge forward. The fourth man didn't even have time to draw his sword before Han pressed the Butterfly to his throat.

The man opened his mouth, speechless, and stared at one of the bodies that Han had plowed through. It was a short, bearded man in silver plate armor. His neck was severed, and he was twitching on the ground as spurts of blood shot out from his wound.

Han pushed his blade harder against the man's throat. "That's

Wu's son. He's dead, which means you are in command now. I want the flags to the city."

The man in armor spat at him. Han dodged the spittle and slashed the man's throat.

A few soldiers recognized the new threat and roared back into the courtyard. Han had little time to lose. He grabbed the shorter man in silver armor and decapitated him. When he held the head high in the air, the men froze.

"I am here on behalf of General Yang Xin!" Han shouted. "The traitor has been killed. Who is next in command?"

Shouts echoed across the courtyard, drawing many more soldiers back toward the mansion. Han stood firm, waiting. The soldiers were without a leader until the next person in the chain of command came forward. It was only a matter of time.

One gruff warrior stepped forward. A red flag protruded from the back of his armor. "Who are you! How dare you…"

Out of nowhere, a bolt lodged itself in his neck, and he fell where he stood. Yi Yi took him out from somewhere up above.

"Who is next?" Han shouted. "Who else is a traitor planning to ambush a Tiger General?"

"Kill him!" someone shouted. It was a tall man emerging from the mansion behind Han, gripping a heavy spear at his side. Han slipped past the man and decapitated him with one stroke.

The army in the courtyard shouted, some of them charged—when multiple bolts whistled through the air and toppled them.

Han stepped back in front of the crowd of soldiers and shouted again. "Your leaders are all guilty of plotting to kill a Tiger General! But they have now been executed. I am Tiger General Yang's deputy and I have come to take the city. Who else wants to fight?"

"How dare you kill General Wu's son," someone shouted. "The Judge will…" Han leaped forward and decapitated him, sending his head flying into the crowd. Two more arrows, both of them flaming, took down the soldiers who came too close. The crowd retreated.

Han knew Yi Yi was already on the ground, perhaps even among them. The angle of the arrows made it clear.

Han stepped back and held up the head of Wu's son again. "Is there anyone else? General Wu is dead and so is his son. Anyone else want a fight with General Yang?"

The murmurs in the courtyard grew louder. Hundreds of men, all caught off guard, debated what to do next.

"General Yang demands the flags to the city," Han shouted. "Who has them?"

"I do!" An old man emerged unarmed from the mansion, his hands folded behind his back, his head held high. "I am Magistrate Guo."

He glanced at the dead generals strewn across the tiles. "I am next in command. And who are you to demand the flags to the city?"

"I am claiming this city on behalf of General Yang. General Wu is dead and so is his son. Another Tiger General will occupy this city from now on."

"Why should I believe you?" Magistrate Guo asked.

"You are all guilty of treason," Han said. "Look around you. What do you think these gunpowder weapons are for?"

"They are for the Silencer when he invades," Guo said. He stood firm and tilted his nose upward, displaying his nostrils. "If he breaches our walls, we will fight him inside the city."

Han reached into his robes for the map, but he stalled before pulling it out. He hadn't thought through what would happen if so many soldiers saw what he had. Word would reach the Judge right away, and he would no longer have the element of surprise.

Han pushed the map deeper into his robes.

"I don't know who you are," the magistrate said, "but you have killed a Tiger General's son. For that, you will be executed for treason." He turned to the soldiers in the courtyard. "Arrest him!"

"No you won't!" Yi Yi shouted from behind them. Two bolts ripped through the air. One dislodged Guo's scholar hat, and the second bolt cut through his cloth headpiece. His hair scattered around him.

"I am your superior officer." Yi Yi appeared magically with her imperial pass in hand. "Category three. I'm the emperor's personal guard and I am in charge of his safety."

Guo turned to her. "You?"

Yi Yi lifted a crossbow, this one different from what she normally carried, and pointed it at the magistrate. "This is how I protect the emperor." She pulled the lever, and her hand blurred, shooting multiple arrows almost all at once. None of them struck Guo. They each grazed his robe and pierced the wall behind him.

The soldiers in the courtyard surged forward but Guo held his hand up. "Wait!"

The magistrate looked to his left and right, then at the shreds in his robe. He held up his hand again. "Stand down!"

Yi Yi held her pass up to Guo's face. "I protect the emperor," she said. "Wu's son is a traitor and he has been executed. No one else needs to die. When General Yang arrives, I will hand him the flags. I give you my word."

Guo took a few deep breaths, his hands shaking, and inched forward to inspect Yi Yi's identification. It was a gold-plated tablet, the size of her palm, with an engraved dragon and the emperor's stamp on the bottom. Every official was taught to recognize the emperor's stamp. There was no mistake.

Magistrate Guo dropped to his knees. "General, I was not expecting you."

Yi Yi giggled when he called her General. "Step inside. We will talk with you alone."

She walked past him, stepping through two big doors into the mansion. The soldiers tried to follow.

"No," Guo said. "If either of them wanted to kill me, I would already be dead. All of you wait out here."

"But Magistrate," someone said.

"It's an order."

The men mumbled to each other, then drew their weapons and stood firm, ready to charge with a single command.

Han followed the magistrate into the mansion and closed the doors behind him. Yi Yi was waiting with her back turned.

"How did you know where to find the firebomb machines?" Guo asked.

"You don't need to know that," Han said. "What you should be worried about is why they are concentrated near the southern gates. Is the Silencer expected to attack the Great Wall from the north, or from inside China down south?"

Guo did not respond. His hands were tucked behind him still, and he was fidgeting with his fingers.

"It doesn't matter why," Yi Yi said, turning around. "General Yang is taking over this city. Your military leadership are all dead. You are a civilian officer and you are not to give military orders. No one is to firebomb the streets when Yang arrives. Hand over the flags and dismantle those machines, and then a Tiger General will occupy this city."

"Can I legally do that?" Guo asked.

"You are the magistrate," Yi Yi said. "You should know the laws. And you should know where the ambushes are. Are you going to order your men to attack General Yang when he comes through the southern gate?"

"I don't have orders to attack anyone," Guo said. "Why do you think I would attack a Tiger General? But you are asking me to dismantle the city's defenses, weapons that are meant to protect our country against the Silencer. You should kill me now—otherwise, it's not going to happen."

"Fine," Yi Yi said. "Don't dismantle them yet. But you can't use them against General Yang when he arrives. On behalf of the emperor, I order you to summon every soldier trained to operate those machines. I want them here, in front of me, and nowhere near the machines."

"Yes, general," the magistrate said, his head bowed. "That I can do for you before General Yang arrives."

Yi Yi giggled again when he called her general. She turned to Han with a big smile. "I'm about to win another bet."

CHAPTER 14

"Where did you get that crossbow?" Han asked, taking Yi Yi's weapon into his hand. It was a shiny new Zhuge Nu bow, made of metal like her original weapon, but it had an extra mount underneath the main shaft.

"It can fire flaming arrows," she said, pointing toward the building where she launched the trebuchet. "There are hundreds more up there and a room full of bolts."

The rain pounded the stone pavement and flooded the streets. Yi Yi sat in the general's seat inside the mansion, and the magistrate arrived shortly after and presented her with the flags to the city. "How are the injured being cared for?" she asked in a stately tone.

"The doctors in the city have been summoned," Magistrate Guo said. "Some soldiers have stopped their wounds from bleeding, but the ones who were burned…"

"Now you know what General Wu planned to do to another Tiger General," she said. "Now you understand how deeply the Judge has penetrated our empire."

"But why?" Guo asked. "I don't understand anything you are telling me."

"The Judge wants to kill the Tiger Generals," Han said. "They are the biggest threat to his plan to take the throne. This was the plot to kill General Yang. You know he's arriving soon."

"Yes," Guo whispered. He hung his head and gazed at the floor. "He will enter through the South Gate and most of the weapons are positioned there. I never thought to ask."

"It's not your fault," Yi Yi said. "But from now on we will do the right thing. Defend our country, protect our sovereignty, and never, ever harm our civilians."

"Yes, general," the magistrate said with a deep bow.

Yi Yi held herself together this time and contained her giggle, lifted her head and waved him away. "You may go. Come back when you've gathered all the assault machine operators. I will speak to them myself."

"Yes, general."

"Wait," Han said. "I need to know where the dungeons are."

"The dungeons?" Guo asked.

"Where you keep your prisoners."

"Follow me." Guo bowed and gestured toward the door.

Han turned to Yi Yi in amusement. "You're about to win another bet."

Yi Yi stuck her tongue out. Han smiled and pulled the magistrate by the sleeve. "Do you have a map of the Tiger General's mansion? General Yang needs it as soon as he arrives. He will also need a map of the city that includes the grain storage, the soldiers' barracks, and the weapons storage. Do you have anything like that?"

"I do," Magistrate Guo said. "You will have them right away." He turned to a guard standing outside the door and gave him instructions. The guard bowed and took off.

"Are you also a military general?" Guo asked.

"I'm a common man," Han said. "But I have a brother who is in the military and he taught me to think ahead like that."

The rain continued striking the flooded pavement with drops determined to penetrate the floor tiles. Han stepped out of the corridor to cross the courtyard when two servants rushed forward with umbrellas. "Sir!" one of them said. "Let me cover you."

"Why?" Han asked. "It's just water."

Guo laughed. "Either you are a tough soldier, or you really are a mere common man." He took the umbrella from the other servant and sent him away.

A horse-drawn carriage was waiting outside. Han and Guo boarded from the front and sat down behind a cloth curtain that somehow held back the heavy wind and rain.

As the carriage trekked through the storm, the thunder startled the horses more than once but the driver was experienced and kept them steady on the road. The flooded streets were empty, and all the shop windows were shuttered.

"You are really friends with General Yang?" Guo asked.

"Better than friends," Han said. "We were competitors. His thunder spear system still cannot beat my sword. It took over thirty rounds to beat him but he lost, and he had to drink ten bowls of liquor as a penalty. He was hungover for two days and his deputy had to run his city for him."

"I heard about that," the magistrate said. "So that was you who made him drink so much."

"He lost the fight."

Guo laughed, shaking his head. "You talk about treason. Did you know it is illegal to inflict illness or injury on a Tiger General to the point that he can't defend his country?"

"Magistrates know the laws," Han said. "Not the common people. We just drink good liquor and make bets on sword skills. Besides, his honor was at stake if he didn't drink."

Guo continued to laugh, shaking his head. The carriage veered to the east toward the far end of the city. A brief streak of lightning ignited the sky with a beautiful pink shade. The sun was far from ready to set, but the dense clouds, filling every corner of the horizon, brought an early dusk to the land.

"All the shops are closed?" Han asked.

"This rain will last at least two more days," Guo said. "When people come out again, the shops will open."

"Strange," Han said. "People don't need food or supplies when it rains?"

"Everyone here keeps supplies at home. If the barbarians invade, they won't need to leave their homes while the siege is ongoing."

"I see."

Guo reached into his pocket and pulled out a thick bronze platelet. "You don't have military rank," Guo said, handing him the pass. "But if you carry this you can give orders to my men as if you are the magistrate. Give it back to me when General Yang arrives, and he can bestow a military title on you."

Han took the pass. "Why do you trust me? I killed General Wu's son."

"Yes, but I'm also wondering why the machines are concentrated by South Gate," the magistrate said. "Given how quickly you were able to kill Wu's generals, I believe you are who you say you are. Also... Very few people know about General Yang being hungover for two days. He was pretty embarrassed."

Han chuckled. "So, you never trusted them either?" he asked. "When did you notice something suspicious?"

Guo sighed and changed the subject. "Why do you want to see the dungeons?"

"I am looking for someone."

"What's his name?"

"I don't know. But he is missing his nose and his hair is all white."

"He's here," the magistrate said, his voice tense. "Why are you looking for him?"

"Do you know him?"

"No. I've judged and sentenced every prisoner in those dungeons, except this one. General Wu locked him up, even though he did not commit any crimes."

The carriage slowed to a halt. "We are here," the driver shouted from the front. More thunder and lightning pounded the earth.

"Did they torture him?" Han asked.

"I don't know," Guo said. "I sentence the criminals. I don't visit the dungeons."

They had stopped in front of a stone fortress with multiple guards under an awning with spears at their sides, waiting by the door. The structure was not tall, but steel gates blocked the entrance. Past the gates was a steep descent, presumably one that led underground.

The magistrate hustled out of the carriage with his umbrella open. The guards in front of the prison bowed to him.

"Open the gates," Guo said. "We have an honored visitor today."

One guard bowed deeply, turned and cranked the chain to open the metal gate. Han stood in the rain and watched. The walls around the fortress would be easy for any martial artist to jump over, and these guards, though strong and armed, seemed poorly trained. Anyone with the skill to break out of the dungeons would have no trouble leaving the fortress. How could General Wu, leader of the Council of Midnight, overlook this if there were important prisoners in here?

Two men in straw raincoats rushed toward them. "Sir! Your maps!"

Guo waved them to the awning, then through the gates. "Show me."

The men bowed, pulled scrolls from inside their straw coats and presented them to Guo, who then pointed to Han. "Explain the maps to this master."

"Yes, magistrate," one man replied. He turned to Han, presenting the scrolls with both hands. "Sir, this is the map to the military positions and stockpiles in the city. Our weapons are distributed throughout the city."

Han drew one scroll open and smiled. None of the modified gunpowder weapons were on the official map. "Give me the other map."

The other scroll detailed the general's mansion, as requested. The general's bedroom, dining area, and meeting halls, were all secluded far away from ambush. Why did the Teacher believe he could assassinate General Yang so easily? Perhaps, a beautiful woman would infiltrate his bedroom?

"Dismissed," Guo said to his scribes, to which they bowed and ventured back into the rain. The magistrate turned to the guards. "Take me to the prisoner with no nose."

One of the guards stammered. "But General Wu has ordered…"

"General Wu is dead," Han said. "A category three official is holding the city until General Yang gets here."

"That's true," Guo said. "General Yang is expected anytime. Meanwhile, General Yi has ordered that we cooperate with all plans for the incoming Tiger General."

The soldier bowed. "Yes, sir." He pulled on a nearby chain, and the barred metal door leading into the underground dungeons cracked open. Han leaped through the opened gates and into the darkness.

"Wait!" Guo shouted behind him.

The dungeons were simple, barren, dim, but Han's eyes adjusted. The structure was basic: caged prisoners lined both sides of the corridor. In his haste, he scarcely noticed a rough group of filthy criminals locked in their cages, barely mobile. He charged swiftly through the corridor and turned a bend into a darker, more foreboding part of the dungeon.

He waited for the screams of the caged prisoners behind him to calm and listened to what was in front of him.

The whimpers of women, the frightened gasps of little girls, the debilitating moans of those who were waiting to become victims— Han processed it all, but he did not understand. Why were there so many women locked in a dark dungeon in General Wu's fortress?

Han pressed his face into his hands. Every movement these women made were distressed. If they were not attached to a chain, they were disabled altogether. Han heard everything. There were hundreds of women around him. Some were moaning in discomfort, some were crying, but none of them were walking.

Then, Han remembered Wu's letter to the Silencer, the one Ah Go stole from the messenger, which contained an offer of riches and women, three hundred virgins for him to dispose of after every night. There were at least three hundred women packed in the row of cells, some who couldn't be older than thirteen.

Fire burned behind his eyes. He bit his lip, fingers taut, and projected his deep voice across the dark caverns. "Did Wu mean to send you all to the Silencer?"

For a long time, no one responded.

"That's what we heard," someone finally said in a weak voice. "They've put nails into our ankles, so we can never run again."

Footsteps pattered behind him. Han lurched back and clenched someone's throat with one hand, then shoved another two men down to the prison floor.

"Wait!"

In his fury, Han hadn't bothered to check whose throat he was crippling. It was Magistrate Guo.

Han pulled his face closer. "Why!"

Several soldiers rushed in with sabers drawn. Han pushed Guo across the dungeon, and pranced on the incoming guards, seizing their weapons with one swipe of his palm. He struck each of them in the shoulder. All four men collapsed at once.

"Give me the keys!" Han shouted.

"Sir, what is going on?" the magistrate asked, still sprawled on the floor.

The Commoner stood towering over him. "I thought you were a decent man. How could you permit this?" He pointed to the row of cells packed with young women.

Once the magistrate's eyes adjusted, his face fell. "Who? Where did these girls come from?"

"You tell me!" Han roared into his face. Guo wrapped his arms against his body and backed away. The soldiers scrambled to their feet, but none dared to approach.

"You said you've judged and sentenced every prisoner in here," Han said. "Tell me what their crimes are."

"I... I've never seen them before," Guo said. He covered his face with one hand.

Han spun around to the soldiers. "The keys!"

"Bring him the keys," Guo shouted.

A short guard limped over with a chain of keys in his hands. Han snatched it from him. "Remove the nails from their ankles."

"I... We don't know how," the soldier said. "We need the doctor."

"There's a special doctor who inserted these nails?" Han asked.

"Every prisoner here gets one. It prevents them from escaping."

Magistrate Guo stood up. "Since when did I authorize this kind of torture?"

One soldier stepped back and bowed. "I'm sorry, sir. General Wu came here and gave the instructions. We were not supposed to tell anyone."

"Wu is dead." Han's voice was cold. "Go get that doctor, and tell him that if the nails are not removed from every girl in here by nightfall, I will personally kill his entire family."

The soldier shuddered; Han stepped closer. "I am the notorious Commoner. I may not be a hero, but I love killing lowlifes like you who take advantage of women and children. Now, before I enjoy myself too much, go get that doctor."

"Yes, sir!" the soldier hobbled away.

"What is going on here?" Guo asked. "How can all these women be locked in here and I don't even know their crimes?"

A young girl banged on the metal bars in front of her. "We didn't do anything, you old fool! We were abducted from our homes."

"What kind of magistrate are you?" another girl shouted.

"How did all of you get down here?" Guo asked, wringing his hands. "This didn't go through my court."

"They are gifts for the Silencer," Han said.

Guo gasped. "What?"

"You old fool!" another girl shouted at Guo. "Is there no law in this empire? Did the emperor approve of us being locked up and tortured?"

Han wandered deeper into the dungeons. More cells and more prisoners, most of them filthy and huddled on the piles of hay meant to be their beds. They smelled horrible—human urine and feces overflowed from small wooden buckets, and rats circled the prisoners, waiting for them to die.

Han turned away from the cells. He didn't come down here for this—he had to find Demon Face.

A little further down the passageway, Han pulled a torch off the wall and waved it back and forth, searching for a man with white hair and no nose. Some of the prisoners stared back at him, but most of them were unconscious.

Then he saw him, a prisoner who lay straight on his back with his hands folded over his chest and his long white hair twisted into a bun above his head. Han stepped closer. This man's nose had been cut off.

Han fumbled with the keys and tried several before the lock clicked open. He ran in and knelt beside Demon Face. The man was still alive, though his breath was weak and his heartbeat rapid and unsteady.

"Sir," Han whispered. "Are you awake?"

Demon Face stared at the ceiling blankly. Han waited, and eventually he came to, glanced at the open cell door, and nodded.

"There is a letter," Han said. "You were delivering a letter to General—"

"Mu," Demon Face finished the sentence in a light whisper.

"General Mu?" Han asked. "Not Wu?"

Demon Face nodded.

"Then why are you here?"

"Wu captured me…"

"Who wrote the letter?"

Demon Face was struggling to breathe, and his hands and feet were immobilized. There was not much life left in him. "My sister. Little Sparrow."

"Little Sparrow?" Han knitted his brows. "Where is the letter?"

Demon Face shook his head with a grimace. "I can only give it to General Mu, or to the man with the Red Crest."

Han sucked in his breath. Demon Face's breath was shuddering and strained. He did not have much time. Han spun around and drew back his trousers halfway, exposing the symbol on his buttocks. Demon Face gasped.

"You," he whispered.

"Do you recognize it?"

Demon Face nodded. "It's the Red Crest. My sister drew it for me to see."

"Where is the letter?"

"Behind the big Buddha," Demon Face said, gasping for air. "The city's main temple."

A sudden draft of air rushed through the dungeon. Han sucked in his breath. Someone was there, waiting and listening all along. Han failed to detect him. That person heard what Demon Face said.

Han leaped out of the cell and bolted for the surface. He shot past Guo, who was still questioning the women, and threw the chain of keys at him. The speed master had already reached the mouth of the dungeon, and he was flying past the guards. Han recognized him. It was Cut Foot, the same man who stole the map to Willow Island.

The Commoner surged forward. His injuries weren't healed but he could not lose Cut Foot, or he would lose the letter—then he would never know what this Red Crest meant.

The rain had not subsided. The raging wind and the streaks of water running down his face made it even harder to see the speed master ahead of him. He did not know where the main temple in the city was, and there was no time to stop and ask. He had to follow closer.

The streets were broad and well paved. The main thoroughfare leading into the center of the city was wide enough to march an army through, and most of the buildings on either side had a second floor. This would be where General Wu stationed most of his firebombs, hidden high above to kill another Tiger General as he processed through the streets.

A grand Buddhist temple loomed before Han. Cut Foot was nowhere in sight but Han knew he was there, and it might be too late. He would have to kill this man to take the letter.

Han leaped in and attacked the one person in the temple. Cut Foot, who was standing by the Buddha, shot away before shoving a piece of paper into his mouth and swallowing.

Han froze, horrified. Cut Foot ate the letter.

Han summoned his energy, despite his injuries. He was out to kill, out to destroy this person who swallowed the one clue that would explain why the world was hunting him. He rushed forward with his fingers shooting out for Cut Foot's throat. The speed master gasped in alarm and slipped away, out into the wet streets, where pure speed, and not dexterity would determine survival. Han chased. He knew he was not as fast, but any mistake or collision would be in his favor. Cut Foot was nimble, and he could change directions and leap onto slanting surfaces like he could run on walls, but he could not fight the Commoner.

The rain continued to pound the City of Eternal Peace. Every rapid step on the paved road was an explosion of water. Han ignored his injuries—accepted the aching of his body, of his mind—and lurched forward. The letter was gone. He didn't know why he was still chasing Cut Foot. Maybe, that was what it meant to be the Commoner. Maybe, taking down the person who interfered with truth and justice was all that mattered.

Cut Foot twisted into an alley, a narrow road covered by bamboo and wooden awnings, where breakfast porridge with tea eggs was sold each morning. Dumpling steamers and scallion pancake pans were everywhere.

Han continued to chase. He was losing ground to Cut Foot's superior speed, but the speed master was still within reach. He passed a person standing by a doorway, a familiar face, but there was no time to stop and ponder. He had to make Cut Foot answer for his crimes.

What were his crimes?

Cut Foot struck a bamboo pole that supported a thatched awning, collapsing it. Han veered onto the cement wall, running three steps against the wall before resuming his chase on the ground. Cut Foot slammed another awning, hurling it into the Commoner's path. Han leaped over the crashing debris.

For a long time, Han chased. Cut Foot would throw things to stop him, collapsing roofs and awnings to block his path. But Han never slowed, despite losing distance with the faster man he was pursuing.

Then, Cut Foot barreled through a thick wooden support, destroying an awning built with heavy shingled tiles. Han screamed in alarm. A toddler was standing underneath it, watching with wide eyes.

Han cried out and burst forward, but he was too far away.

Cut Foot heard and responded. He twisted his body, changing direction with incredible speed, and leaped into the collapsing roof. The heavy porcelain tiles pummeled into him, burying him, and crashed into the earth with a resounding blast of dust.

Once the dust settled, Han scrambled into the mess, the broken tiles, the ripped cement that held up the roof of an outdoor breakfast area that was now a pile of debris. As Han tore away the thin rubble, Cut Foot blew apart the shingles and climbed to his feet with the child in his arms. The toddler was bruised and too scared to make a sound, but he was not harmed. Cut Foot, however, was bleeding in multiple places.

Armed guards hurried into the disaster. Han reached Cut Foot in one step, his steeled fingers clenched around the speed master's throat. He controlled the man who ate Demon Face's letter. And then what?

The toddler was safe in Cut Foot's arms. "Return the child to his parents," Han said to the soldiers who were gathering. "Arrest this man. Put him in the dungeons, but no nails in his ankle."

When the patrol guards paused, Han displayed the plate that the magistrate offered him earlier. The guards took a step back, hands folded, and bowed deeply.

"Yes, sir!" they said in unison. Then, they took Cut Foot under custody and hauled the limping speed master away.

Han stood where he was, head lowered, thinking about the person he passed earlier when he was chasing Cut Foot. The face was familiar—foreign, even.

Fu Nandong!

Han spun around and retraced his path. Why would Fu Nandong be here? He should have heard by now that both General Wu and his son had been killed. Why would the Judge send a different category three general to infiltrate Wu's city?

Han stood a good distance from the doorway where he last saw Fu Nandong. It was early evening, and the waning sunlight, hidden behind dark clouds, would retreat for the night in a few short hours. The door belonged to a very ordinary civilian home, the brown paint old, chipped and lifeless.

Han pummeled through the door, almost blasting off the hinges as he forced his way into the humble room. Fu Nandong was alone, his mouth gaped open in shock, teeth missing from his pretty face. Han almost laughed. He pushed away the square table and clutched the frightened man by the throat before tossing him into the opposite wall. Han kicked the door behind him to close it, grabbed his victim's face and hauled him to a brick stove at the far end of the room. The ashes inside the stove were still hot.

Han thought about the villagers in Zhun Yang. This man gave the order to annihilate civilians at will. He pushed Fu Nandong's face toward the small opening of the stove.

"No! No!" Fu Nandong shrieked.

"Why not?" Han asked. "I'll enjoy it very much."

"No! Not my face!"

"Maybe I should castrate you so you won't need the pretty face."

"What do you want from me? Why are you doing this?"

Han pushed him within inches of the hot cinders until the searing smoke scorched his facial hair. He wanted to burn that pretty face right then and there. He promised the villagers in Zhun Yang.

But Fu Nandong was a mere pawn. There would be no justice for the villagers who died, or for those who would be slaughtered in the future, if he didn't stop the Judge.

Han yanked him back and threw him across the room. Fu Nandong crashed into a wooden chair and squirmed against the hard floor, cradling his hip.

"Why are you here?" Han asked.

Fu Nandong didn't answer, so Han lifted him by his collar and dragged him back toward the hot stove.

"Wait!"

"Why are you here?" Han asked again.

"Please. Why are you doing this to me?"

"Because I don't like you," Han said. "And I can't wait to see your head on a stake outside the city walls."

Fu Nandong gulped.

"I'll let you live," Han continued, "if you tell me exactly what I want to know."

"And then you'll let me go?"

"I did let you go every time, didn't I?"

Fu Nandong nodded, gasping for air. Han released him and waited for the general to pick himself up, before motioning for him to sit on a wooden stool next to the stove.

Fu Nandong lowered himself onto his seat. Han stood towering over him, his arms crossed. "Once again, why are you here?"

"This city ... My father's army will be received in this city," Fu Nandong said. "The Judge is running out of time to kill the Tiger Generals so my father is coming to help him."

Han sucked in his breath. Feng's father was in trouble. He had not heard of any attacks on the City of Stones, so the Judge must have dispatched assassins to kill General Mu. "How is he running out of time to kill the Tiger Generals? Doesn't he plan on killing General Yang in this city when he arrives?"

"See, General Lo's body was never found," Fu Nandong said. "And no one knows where he is. Any one of these Tiger Generals could still show up at the capital for the emperor's annual conference."

"When is that conference?"

"In a month."

"And why is the Judge so scared of the Tiger Generals meeting with the emperor?"

Fu Nandong shook his head. "I don't know. I've told you everything. Can I leave now?"

"Not yet. You said your father has an army. Who is your father?"

"A Turkic king," Fu Nandong said. "That's why you will be hunted for the rest of your life if you do anything to me."

"I'm used to it," Han said. "A Turkic army is coming here? The Judge is opening the gates to China for a foreign army?"

Fu Nandong nodded.

Han's eyes burned, and his mouth ran dry. He could barely muster his next question. "How big is his army?"

"Over eight hundred thousand."

Cold beads of sweat formed on Han's back. General Yang could not possibly defend this city with his fifty thousand men, even without the Judge closing in on the rear. These were times of peace. Who would maintain an army that size, unless it was raised for an invasion?

General Mu faced the beginning of the Silk Road, also the immediate entry point for the Turkic Khaganate. If they assassinated Feng's father, the Turkic army would march through the City of Stones without resistance.

Han smacked Fu Nandong, sending him flying off the stool and sprawling onto the floor.

"What the hell?" Fu Nandong squealed, clutching his face. "I answered all your questions, you scum."

"The truth?" Han asked, stomping onto Fu Nandong's hand.

Fu Nandong arched his back and screamed. "Stop it! Stop! I told you the truth."

"The Turkic Khaganate doesn't have an army that size. Don't lie to me!"

"I didn't lie! My father has been raising it for years!"

"Why?" Han asked, pressing harder with his foot. "Does he plan on invading China?"

Fu Nandong choked. "Let me go! I told you everything I

know. Everything else is between him and the Judge. He doesn't tell me anything."

Han lifted his foot slightly. "When's the first time you saw this Judge? Don't lie to me. If your father is moving his entire army for this Judge, then you must have seen him before."

"W-when I was a child," Fu Nandong said. "He came to my father's palace."

Han drew a sharp breath. "When you were a child? Then the Judge was also a child. He has been communicating with a Turkic king for that long?"

Fu Nandong nodded.

Han's mind churned. There was so much more he needed to know, but the more answers he obtained, the more confusing the world seemed. He had to tell General Yang, and he needed to rush to the City of Stones to tell Feng's father. But he didn't know where Ah Go was or when he would return, and he also didn't know if Feng would be under General Yang's protection yet.

Han needed both his brothers right now.

"Wu is dead," Han said.

"I know, you've killed him."

"Then why do you think your father can still come here? Don't you know that General Yang will be occupying this city with his army?"

Fu Nandong laughed. "The Judge will take it over by then. I will still be opening the gates when my father arrives."

"How?"

"He could've taken it with or without Wu's army," Fu Nandong said. "Zeng Xi will be here with siege weapons. They can't defend these walls with the Zhuge Nu firing nonstop. And once the rain stops, they will send in blankets of flaming arrows and burn the entire back of the city. None of Yang's men will be able to come anywhere close to the walls to defend them."

"I see," Han said.

"I don't mind telling you, either. Just because you know about it doesn't mean you can stop it. There is no way for the Commoner to stop an army."

Han's mind raced. Was there no way out? If he could persuade Yang to abandon this city, then the Turkic army wouldn't bother fighting Feng's father. They could stroll into China through the City of Eternal Peace. If Yang stayed, though, then he would have to defend the city from the inside, losing the advantage of the Great Wall.

If Yang lost the city, the Judge would open the gates for the foreign army. There was no way to prevent this.

What would Feng do?

Feng would understand where he had an advantage. He would figure out how to subvert the enemy.

Han jumped with surprise. Of course Yang could defend the city from the inside. He had the modified gunpowder weapons aimed at the streets. That was Han's greatest edge. No one else, except Ah Go, knew the locations of the ambush. Few knew they existed. Yet, the Judge might suspect Yang of finding the machines within days of occupying the city. Han needed to move fast.

He would entice the enemy to march into the city. To do that, he would need to open the gates. He would need to become a traitor.

Han stood in a daze. No one would believe the ruse if he opened the gates while General Yang was protecting the city. He would need to show the world that he killed General Yang.

Han sighed and took a step back, then another. He plopped himself down on a stool and pressed his lips together.

I have to. Even if it makes me a villain. Even if I don't enjoy it.

Fu Nandong, his brows knitted together, climbed to his feet. "What are you doing?" Han didn't hear him.

He came out of hiding to clear his name. He walked into this chaos because honor came first.

"I've already killed a Tiger General," Han said. "They will hunt me forever. I wanted to kill you too, but I won't. You may be my ticket to freedom."

"How?"

"Your father is a Turkic king," Han said. "He can welcome me into his kingdom and protect me from the Chinese."

Fu Nandong laughed. "After how many times you've beaten me and tortured me, why would he do anything for you?"

"Because I will give him General Yang's head."

Fu Nandong took a step back, startled. "What... What did you say?"

"I will deliver Yang's head tomorrow when the rain stops," Han said. "But I must have an agreement signed by the Judge that I will have safe passage through the Silk Road, and an agreement signed by your father that I will have money and safety in his country. Can you get me that?"

"Is this real? Or another one of your tricks?"

"What do you have to lose?" Han asked. "After I dump Yang's head over the wall and open the gates, the agreement will stand."

Fu Nandong hesitated.

"I've been hunted long enough," Han said. "I'm tired. I tried to do the right thing and I am still cast as a traitor. My country betrayed me, even though I've never betrayed my country. I want out, and you can help me. I promise you, if you help me, we will be brothers from now on. I will never hurt you again."

"You—you will stop?"

"Haven't I always honored my word?"

"You have, the scum that you are," Fu Nandong said. "And I certainly don't want to help you, but I can't accept or reject an offer like this by myself. We have the fastest messenger pigeons in the world. Write the letter, and you will have your answer tomorrow."

That meant the Turkic army was already close to the Chinese border.

"If this city surrenders before the Zhuge Nu starts burning it down," Han said, holding himself together, "we can spare many lives. Let's do this. How will you contact me when the agreement arrives?"

CHAPTER 15

HAN STOOD ON the top of the wall at sunset to watch General Yang's enormous army approach the southern gates. Under the magistrate's orders, the troops at the southern wall answered to him—although, he was only going to give one order that evening. He would open the entrance when his old friend, Tiger General Yang Xin, arrived.

The flags for General Yang's army whipped violently in the wind. Once the army came within a few steps of the gate, the mounted units in vanguard shifted aside to make room for their general to approach on his massive charger. Yang Xin wore shiny, gold-plated armor and gripped a long spear in one hand. Many had fallen to that famous spear.

"Brother Yang!" Han shouted from the top of the wall. He turned to the soldier next to him. "It's General Yang. Open the gates."

"Open the gates!" the soldier called to the men below. Han rushed to the side stairs and descended the wall, stepping onto the stone tiles just as General Yang dismounted and strolled in. Yang stood firm in front of the Commoner, his spear still in hand.

"Brother Yang," Han called again, thrilled to see his friend. Yang held up his hand. His face was expressionless.

"Hold it," he said. "You have a lot to explain, Han."

Han paused. He almost forgot he had killed a Tiger General just the night before. It seemed like so long ago.

"Let's sit down somewhere dry and talk over a drink," Han said. "I have a lot to tell you."

By the time the sun had set, Han and General Yang were already on their fifth gourd of liquor. They were drinking in the main hall of the Tiger General's mansion. Yi Yi had vacated the general's seat, and after greeting General Yang, she retired to a bedroom to rest.

"Are you worried?" Han asked.

"About the eight hundred thousand men?" Yang asked.

"Yes, the Turkic army coming down the Silk Road," Han said, shaking his head. "Do you think General Mu can hold them off?"

"Mu is a crafty old snake," Yang said. "He should be able to trick them into thinking the Silencer is right behind them."

"The Silencer?"

Yang Xin looked up. "They hate each other—the Turks and the Mongols. Maybe the Silencer will kill them all before they get to China."

Yang turned back to the map in his hands. He had already memorized the locations of all the firebomb machines in the city, and now he was drawing his own circles with black ink.

"What if the Silencer wanted to sit back and watch the Turks and the Chinese kill each other?" Han asked. "Why do we have so few troops to defend our borders?"

"These are the numbers we have during peacetime," Yang said. "If there was a real threat from the north, the emperor could raise a million-man army within months. Now we are caught by surprise— the person in charge of our spy network is committing treason and the emperor will do nothing about it."

Yang finished drawing on the map and pushed it to the side so the ink could dry. "I've sent numerous reports to the emperor and my messengers never return. The land is in complete chaos. I need to go to the capital to ask his majesty myself, but I cannot. War is looming."

"What can I do to help?" Han asked.

"Tell me what else you know."

Han began to talk about his past two weeks—how the Council of Midnight was decapitated of nearly all their leadership, how the Teacher continued to taunt him, how he met his two sworn brothers when the Orchid Farmer sacrificed himself for Feng. Yang stopped him there. "Mu Feng is your sworn brother?"

"Yes, is he in the City of a Thousand Heroes?"

"Of course not," Yang said. "I heard he beat back twenty thousand men with his two thousand to save my city, and now he is heading to the Glimpse of Sky to wait for Zeng Xi's army."

"What!" Han jumped to his feet. "Zeng Xi's army is fifty thousand strong. And Feng has only two thousand? You were supposed to keep him safe, Brother Yang!"

General Yang took a sip of liquor and laughed. "Sit down and drink. He's safer than you. Safer than all of us."

Han seated himself. He knew there was nothing he could do about it, but still it nagged him, the thought of his brother fighting a battle against impossible odds. He grabbed the gourd and chugged the rest of the liquor.

Yang slid the map across the table and leaned forward. "Can I count on the man who just killed a Tiger General to live as a hero? For the people?"

"You can count on me to die as a villain," Han said. "For the people."

Yang nodded. "I've known you for a long time. Are you really on my side?"

"I'm on the people's side," Han said. "If you are too, then we're on the same side."

"Good. I have a plan, but I'll need your help."

Yang pointed to several major arteries of the city and explained in detail. Han listened. He didn't always understand the reasons behind each maneuver, every repositioning of troops, but Yang was the most formidable of the Tiger Generals. Han had no doubt that every move was well calculated.

"In the end," Yang said. "We're not going to destroy them with the firebomb machines. Their fear of the firebombs will."

"I understand."

"Your ruse is superb," Yang said. "It almost sounds like something Mu Feng would cook up. Tomorrow you dump my head over the wall and the fight begins. Are you ready?"

"The agreement with the Turkic king should arrive tomorrow," Han said. "I am always ready."

"And then the Commoner will be a traitor again. It may be a long time before the truth can clear your name, so you're going to have to watch your back."

"I'm used to it."

Yang stood up, folded the map and stuffed it into his pockets. "The rain is expected to stop tonight, which means the flaming arrows will bombard the southern part of the city soon. Shall we meet again for morning tea?"

"Sure," Han said. "And where are you sleeping?"

"I will take Old Wu's bedroom then. It should be nice enough to invite a beautiful young lady."

Han wagged his finger at the general. "Be careful of assassins. The Teacher said they have many ways to kill you."

"Where is she going to hide the knife when I take her clothes off?"

They both laughed.

"I promise you I won't eat or drink anything else tonight. How's that?"

Han shook his head with an uneasy grin. He wanted to see Yi Yi again but she was probably asleep. He bowed and departed.

Late that night, with the rain already easing into a drizzle, Han sat on the roof of his bedroom, which overlooked the rear courtyard. The large room across from him was the general's bedroom, and a small candle was still burning inside.

Someone leaped onto the roof and sat down next to him. It was Yi Yi, her crossbow in one hand and a gourd in another.

"Want a drink?"

Han took her gourd and unplugged it. The floral fragrance of a five-grain blend rose to his face. "Exquisite."

"What are you watching?" Yi Yi asked.

Han pointed across the courtyard. "That's where Yang is sleeping. A beautiful young woman just went in there."

"Do you think she's an assassin?"

"It has to be a woman," Han said. "Only I could kill General Yang in a sword fight, and it would not be easy."

"Then why are we still watching from the roof?" Yi Yi asked, standing up. "She's going to poison him."

Han took her hand and pulled her back down, then leaned back to rest on the slanted tiles with his hands folded behind his head. "I slipped one of Feng's pills into his drink earlier. He's immune to poison for the night."

Yi Yi giggled. "So you're letting him have fun. But now, how will we know if she is the assassin or not?"

"I'm going to follow her when she leaves."

A shrill scream escaped from inside General Yang's room. Han leaped off the roof, saber in hand, and charged across the courtyard with Yi Yi close behind. The light inside the room brightened.

Han pushed through the door to find Yang putting on his robe, his spear already at hand. A nude woman was curled on the floor, shaking, blood streaming out of her mouth. There was no wound on her perfect skin. Han reached down to feel her pulse, but it was already too late. In a moment, she became limp.

"She was poisoned," Han said. "But how?"

Yang pointed at her lips. "Her lipstick was poisoned. It must have become active once my saliva touched it, but I don't feel anything yet."

"You're immune for a day," Han said. "I slipped an antidote into your drink earlier."

"You did?"

"Feng gave it to me. His woman is the leader of the Venom Sect."

Yang stalled for a moment, then threw his head back laughing.

"You've saved my life again, Commoner. What would I do without you?"

A group of soldiers rushed into the room, saw the dead woman on the floor, and dropped to their knees. "General! We heard the noise and—"

"Forget it," Yang said. He waved them away. "Bring me the head servant and Magistrate Guo."

"Yes, sir!"

The soldiers rushed out of the room, and Yi Yi closed the door behind them. "She's beautiful. Even General Yang doesn't have those kinds of seduction skills. How did you find her so quickly?"

"The head servant hired her from the brothels," Yang said. "He told me she's worked there for many years and she's very popular."

"Then someone gave her the lip balm," Yi Yi said, reaching down to touch the girl's cold forehead. She lowered a candle closer to her lips. "The color was just applied before she came in, probably because she didn't know it was poisoned and would've eventually licked her lips. Someone who came with her applied the color right before they left the carriage outside."

"That makes a lot of sense," Yang said. "We know where to start looking."

"You're so smart, Yi Yi," Han said.

"The Judge has spies all over the city," Yi Yi said. "General, you need to impose martial law. That way, anyone watching on the street will be arrested. I will shoot them myself to make sure they can't run."

"Another bolt through the ankle?" Han asked. He never had the chance to tell her about the young women he found in the dungeons, a memory that refused to fade. "Just shoot them in the buttocks please."

Yi Yi giggled but nodded.

"That's a good idea," Yang said. "Who are you, Yi Yi? I see that rapid-fire crossbow in your hand. Were you once part of the Judge's Zhuge Nu?"

Yi Yi pulled out her category three official pass and showed Yang. "I am the emperor's personal guard."

Yang picked up a lantern and held it close to the pass. "What are you doing here?"

"I'm Han's woman. Han is my man."

When the door opened, the headservant and Guo tumbled inside at the hands of several armed soldiers.

The headservant stumbled in front of the nude body on the floor and dropped to his knees. "General! I don't understand. I did exactly what you ordered."

"Get up," Yang said. "You're not being charged."

"Thank you, general. Thank you!"

"Which brothel did she come from?" Yang asked.

The servant kept his head bowed. "The Flying Phoenix Palace, sir."

"Who else came with her?"

"A servant girl, sir. She already went back."

"Did you see her apply lip balm on this girl?"

The servant thought for a second. "Yes, I did. How would you know something like that?"

"The brothel should still be open," Yang said. "You are to go back there and tell them that this woman tried to assassinate me and has been executed. Bring the servant girl before the magistrate for questioning. I suppose she was given the balm for a little money. Magistrate Guo, surround the brothel with watchers and follow anyone that leaves. I want to know who went where and said what."

Magistrate Guo bowed. "Yes, general. Will that be all?"

"The Judge has an extensive spy network in the country," Yi Yi said. "It's time we find out how they operate."

Guo turned to Yi Yi with a bow. "Yes, general."

Yi Yi couldn't contain her giggle.

After the head servant and the magistrate departed, Yang threw his head back to laugh, and said to Yi Yi. "You really are something. Maybe you should lead an army." He turned to Han. "Brother, you have good taste. When the emperor hosts your wedding, make sure I am not busy fighting any wars so I can show up and drink all night."

"Message!" someone shouted from outside.

"Come in," Yang called.

A soldier pushed through the door and dropped to one knee. "General! The Zhuge Nu outside South Gate have started to fire. Our men have retreated from the top of the walls."

"Is it still raining outside?" Yang asked.

"Barely, sir," the soldier said. "They haven't used the flaming bolts yet."

"The city is too wet," Yang said. "We have at least until tomorrow morning. Meanwhile, I am announcing martial law for the next two days. Every citizen must remain in their homes. Anyone who steps foot onto the streets will be arrested, even shot."

"In the buttocks," Yi Yi added.

The soldier bowed his head, noticed the general's stern expression, and bowed deeper. "Yes, sir!" He backed out the door.

Yang threw on a thicker robe for outdoors, and turned to Yi Yi. "I've heard of you before. You can shoot a fly that comes too close to the emperor."

"That's an exaggeration."

"What would you say is the most important weapon in an archer's arsenal?" Yang asked, tying his hair and setting his headpiece. "Distance? Numbers?"

"Fear."

Yang studied her. "Interesting."

"There will be panic if they don't know where the enemy is," Yi Yi said, "and if the enemy is panicking, then we have plenty of time to shoot them."

"I see." Yang picked up a sword that hung on the wall next to his bed and sat down to put on his boots. "Will you command my archery unit during tomorrow's assault?"

"Me?"

"You are a category three military official. My archery battalion is led by a category five commander."

Yi Yi glanced at Han with an impish smile, then turned back to

Yang with a bow. "I don't know how to lead an army, sir. But I will do what I can to help."

"Do exactly what you told me," Yang said. "Remain hidden. Use fear. You're good at it, general."

Yi Yi bowed deeper; her face flushed with excitement. "Yes, sir!"

"My archers are used to firing into open plains from the top of a wall," Yang said. He reached into a box on the desk beside him, drew forth a jade plate and handed it to her. "But this is an urban battle, and they've never fought in a crowded city before. They need training. You have one morning to train and position them."

Yi Yi kneeled and received the plate with both hands. "Yes, sir! I will start preparing right away."

"Wait," Han said. "Yi Yi has never commanded a unit before. She's always worked solo—"

"My current commander will oversee the battle details," Yang said. "But this time it's city warfare with civilians close by, and Yi Yi knows how to find good hiding spots. Trust me on this one."

"You've killed Red Beard," Yi Yi said. "I am the greatest archer in the world now."

"Follow me," Yang said to her. "I will introduce you to my battalion." He turned to Han. "Get some rest. You are the main character in tomorrow's show."

Han nodded, smiled at Yi Yi and stepped outside.

Yi Yi pointed her crossbow at his forehead. "I'm a general now, so if I catch you near Flying Phoenix Palace, I will shoot you in the buttocks." She stuck her tongue out and made a face. Yang laughed.

CHAPTER 16

CHEN HAN WANDERED the city streets in the dead of night, carrying the signed agreement from the Turkic king in one hand and a small lantern in another. It was official. The Commoner was a traitor many times over.

So many thoughts crowded his mind. Tomorrow he would lure the Judge's army into the city where the ambush would be waiting. Once he closed the gates, he would join the battle, and do what he did best. He would kill everyone on the street.

Who would lead General Wu's army to attack the City of Eternal Peace? Would the generals and unit commanders be willing to fight another Tiger General's army? Would Yang's men be willing to bomb and annihilate fellow countrymen? He never had the chance to discuss these concerns with Yang Xin—and he struggled to believe General Yang could kill so many Chinese in this ambush.

Then came the most difficult question, one he did not want to face. Once it became clear that Yang was alive, would the eight hundred thousand Turks assault these front gates, or those guarded by Feng's father instead?

Han paused in the middle of the quiet street, unable to wrap his mind around his questions. All his life, he killed bad people to protect the weak and the innocent. Perhaps he was a monster hiding behind honor and chivalry. But the thought of killing so many soldiers tomorrow made no sense to him. Yes, soldiers died in war. That was a given. But he would be killing men who joined a Tiger General's army to protect their country. They were no different from General Yang's soldiers.

Han found himself in front of the dungeons again. He had wandered the streets most of the night and dawn would be upon him in a couple of hours. It was time to check on an honorable man, a person he wouldn't mind befriending in another life.

Han flashed the magistrate's pass and one of the guards promptly opened the gates for him.

"Where is the man I arrested today?" Han asked.

"Sir, he's detained downstairs and awaits trial with the magistrate," the guard said.

"I want to see him."

"This way, sir. Follow me."

The guard picked up a large torch and started down the stairs. He stopped in front of the second cell closest to the entrance, a clean space with a window. A tray of uneaten rice and yam and a bowl of water lay on the floor. Cut Foot sat alone inside, his eyes closed, as if meditating.

"Bring us some liquor," Han said, "and then leave me alone with the prisoner."

"Yes, sir."

The guard opened the gate before running up the stairs. Soon he came back with a gourd and two cups.

"Thank you," Han said. The guard bowed and left.

Cut Foot inhaled deeply. "Cheap alcohol," he said with a smirk.

Han sat down next to him, filled both cups and handed one to the prisoner. Cut Foot took the liquor and chugged it in one gulp. "I'm not telling you anything."

"You don't have to," Han said. "I'm here to drink."

"Don't you have someone better to drink with?"

"Everyone is busy."

Cut Foot released a short laugh. "Don't disgrace me with your presence."

"The child you saved was returned to his parents," Han said, ignoring the comment.

"Good."

Han sipped on his liquor, then reached over to pour more into Cut Foot's cup. "Why do you think people like us get involved in all these wars?"

"I have no idea."

"We train all our lives to fight one person at a time," Han said, clasping his hands together. "Or maybe even twenty, thirty opponents at a time. We're martial arts masters. We compete with other masters for fame and fortune and attract hundreds of students to our schools. Since when do people like us face off with thousands of professional soldiers?"

"I am not a master like you," Cut Foot said. "I am also not a traitor like you."

"Why do you think I am a traitor?"

"Don't lie, Commoner," Cut Foot said. "You're going to open the gates to China for the Silencer. You and that fool Yang Xin."

"Is that why you work for the Teacher?" Han asked. The name alone forced a chill down his back, but he tightened his muscles. "He convinced you that a Tiger General is colluding with the Silencer?"

"Don't deny it," Cut Foot said. "I've seen the evidence. How could you? You of all people."

Han reached into his pocket and drew out the letter that General Wu wrote to the Silencer, that Ah Go somehow obtained and used to convince the heroes of the martial society.

Where is Master Kwan? What happened to all his friends?

He poured himself another drink and refilled Cut Foot's cup before handing the letter to him. "You're right. A Tiger General tried. Just not Yang Xin."

As Cut Foot read through the letter, his eyes widened for a

moment, but then he tossed it aside. "Why would I believe you? You're the one who killed General Wu. The letter is fake."

"How long were you hiding here watching the man without his nose?"

Cut Foot gulped the liquor. "A long time."

"You were waiting for me."

"Absolutely."

"Did you notice the young women by the middle of the dungeon?"

Cut Foot's haughty expression faded. He reached across the hay on the floor and picked up the letter again. "Three hundred virgins," he whispered under his breath.

"I had them released," Han said. "But they can no longer walk. They had nails drilled into their ankles so they could never run away."

"So they couldn't run from here?"

"So they couldn't run from the Silencer."

"I see," Cut Foot said. For a moment his voice was distant. "But that doesn't mean you're not a traitor. Plenty of people saw you with the Silencer."

Han sighed. There was no way he could cleanse his reputation. The more rumors floating out there, the harder it would be to make friends. Besides, the Judge would still hunt him for the symbol on his body. Just like Feng, the man with the Red Crest was targeted by every whore and thug out there. "How can a man have a new beginning?" he asked.

"You want a new beginning?" Cut Foot asked. "You start by being a better man."

"I'm not the great hero I wanted to be," Han said. "Whatever that means."

"It's not who you've defeated, it's who you've saved," Cut Foot said. "Who are you going to save when you open the gates for the Silencer? How much gold did he offer you?"

"I don't know how I can restore my name," Han said. "But I give you my word, I have never contacted the Silencer."

"Your word is worth the feces I left under that bucket over there."

"The rain has stopped," Han said. "Tomorrow the flaming arrows will burn the south side of the city and the gates will fall. You and I should finish this liquor, and then tomorrow, we will face each other as friends instead of enemies."

"Face each other?" Cut Foot asked, his brows knit together. "What are you talking about? I'll be here, and you will be fighting the Teacher out there."

Han could not contain the shudder this time. "The Teacher?"

"He will be here." Cut Foot laughed. "And he will break you again. Your life ends tomorrow, Commoner. I'm looking forward to it."

Han lowered his eyes. "I do too…"

"Do you want to die, Commoner?" Cut Foot asked, raising his voice. "Then why live like this? Why not join the emperor's nephew and fight foreign invasion? Keep our country safe. Die for something."

Han winced. Everyone believed they were on the right side of justice. No one considered otherwise.

Which side is the right side of justice?

"I have," Han said. "That's why I am here to let you go." He dug into his pockets and produced the agreement between the Judge and the Turkic Khaganate. "Tomorrow I will deliver Yang Xin's head. And then I will have safe passage out of this country. You have all deemed me a traitor, so it's time for me to find a new life elsewhere."

Cut Foot stared at the signed agreement, reading it over and over again. "You're… You've switched sides? You're letting me go?"

"I didn't switch sides but I am letting you go," Han said. "Once this city is secured, I am leaving. I was never paid by the Silencer and I will not open the gates for him. I promise you."

Cut Foot studied him for a long time, his arms wrapped around his knees. Then, he lifted the gourd, leaned his head back and swallowed the liquor in deep gulps.

"Why should I believe you?" Cut Foot asked finally, putting down the gourd. "How do I know you are doing the right thing for once?"

"Because I am not big enough to be a hero," Han said, "which means I am not big enough to be a villain, either. I'm a commoner, and I will do what a common man always does. Survive and keep myself safe."

"You will deliver Yang's head?"

"So the Judge can hold this city against the Silencer. That's the plan." Han poured the last of the liquor into Cut Foot's cup and his own, just enough for one final drink. "You said you were waiting for me here. How did you know I would come for the man without a nose?"

"It was going to be either you or Mu Feng," Cut Foot said.

"General Mu's son?" Han asked. "Why?"

"This noseless messenger hid the letter and wouldn't break under torture," Cut Foot said. "He would only tell the man with the Red Crest. Mu Feng's uncle was supposed to bring him here but he never arrived."

"I see."

"Too late, Commoner. The secret of the Red Crest died when I shat the letter out of my ass."

"So the letter is about the symbol on my body," Han said.

"I don't know. You didn't give me time to read it."

Han climbed to his feet, drew open the gates of the cell and stepped out.

"They say a hero must make the ultimate sacrifice for what he believes in," Cut Foot said. "If you want to do the right thing, why don't you stay and fight the Silencer? Show the world you are not a traitor. Defend this country like you are destined to do."

Han lifted his face and sighed. "What is my destiny? Do you know?"

"Do you want to know?" Cut Foot asked. "Do you have the courage to be bigger than a commoner?"

Han shook his head and leaned his hand against the bars of the cell. "Who is bigger? Who is smaller? Is a man who sacrifices himself as a villain any smaller than a man who sacrifices himself as a hero?"

"I thought you wanted to live," Cut Foot whispered.

"I have already lived many lifetimes."

"But not as a real hero."

"I never was—never will be." Han stepped through the gate and away from Cut Foot's cell.

"So the beautiful woman wasn't able to kill General Yang," Cut Foot said.

Han paused without turning. The stealth master had something interesting to say.

"Don't worry," Cut Foot said. "The Teacher has many ways to kill him. Can't count on some whore to do a man's job."

"Apparently not," Han said. He walked out of the cell with his head lowered and his arms dangling beside him, venturing into the depths of the dungeon.

"Don't forget I shat under the bucket, not in it," Cut Foot called behind him. "When I leave, make sure you clean up after me!"

It was already dawn by the time Han emerged from the dungeons. The trap had been set—Cut Foot would return to the Teacher and reveal that the Commoner had switched sides with the intention of taking Yang Xin's head. Fu Nandong would have notified them the same, and the second confirmation should offer the enemy enough confidence to rush the gates when opened. Han would open them personally. He was really beginning to think like Mu Feng.

The Teacher was coming. The old man would be here to assassinate General Yang and Han had to be there to intercept. He had to keep General Yang alive.

Han knew he would die here before sunset. The Teacher was ready for him but he was not ready to face the Teacher. He didn't know how to beat this old man who called him nephew. He dreaded seeing him, knowing that this time, Sha Wu had no reason to let him live. Han already volunteered to take the blame for Yang's death.

What was the last thing he wanted to do before dying? Maybe eat something he enjoyed or drink a raging good liquor. Maybe discuss the battle plan with General Yang again to ensure that after he died, Yang could finish the battle without losing too many lives.

Han stood facing the first light of dawn. He just wanted to see Yi Yi. Nothing else.

She was with the archery battalion, so she would be easy enough to find. Han stopped a few patrol guards along the way, flashed the pass that Magistrate Guo gave him, and asked for directions to General Yi. He soon found her positioning her archers in the most populated area of the city.

"Is this where thousands will die?" Han asked her.

Yi Yi waved away her men. She then spun around and pointed her crossbow at his head. "Where are the other three brothels in this city?"

"I don't know," Han said, "but if I have special orders from the general, I can go and find out."

"You wouldn't dare," Yi Yi said.

The archer battalion withdrew to the far end of the street, and they were alone, beyond earshot. She lowered the crossbow and ran forward to hug him, then froze. He wasn't excited at all.

"What's wrong?" she asked him.

Han took her hand and pulled her toward the other end of the street. "Let's take a walk."

The archers under Yi Yi's command continued to mobilize and settle into their hiding spots—their squad leaders had followed her strict orders to place the troops in the most secretive positions.

"What's wrong?" Yi Yi asked again.

For a long time, Han held her hand but said nothing. Yi Yi waited.

"The Teacher will be part of the invasion today," he said, finally.

Yi Yi clenched his hand and drew him closer. "How do you know that?"

"Cut Foot told me. He also said they have many ways to kill General Yang and that the Teacher will personally come in to do it."

"You can't be afraid of him," Yi Yi said. "You can defeat him."

Han knit his brows and shook his head. "I can't beat him. I'm not smart enough. I need my brother Feng."

"How can the greatest warrior in the world admit defeat before the battle has even begun?"

Han shook his head, scrunching his face until deep lines formed on his forehead. Yi Yi placed a hand on his cheek. "All you have to do is stay one step ahead of him."

"I can't. He's already several steps ahead of me."

"Maybe not the same step," she said. "Let's talk about this. Where will he enter the city?"

"I don't know," Han said. "He would arrive among the tens of thousands of soldiers. There's no way to know."

Yi Yi took both his hands in hers. "Han?"

Han turned his face, unable to meet her gaze.

"Han, you can't say there's no way to do it when you haven't tried. That's not you. You found a way to bring me back even after he struck me with the God Slayer."

"I know," Han said. "But… He knows everything about me. I know nothing about him."

Yi Yi reached into her robes, paused, and then pulled out the map with the red and black circles where the old and new ambushes were located. "How did you get this map?" she asked.

"Ah Go and I intercepted a messenger in the middle of the night," Han said. "He was sending it to the Judge. That's why I think the Judge doesn't know it exists."

"But have we thought about why the Judge needs this map?"

"I don't understand."

"The firebomb machines were meant to ambush General Yang's men last night," Yi Yi said. "Yang Xin is the most powerful among the Tiger Generals. The Judge has to believe General Yang is expecting an ambush and that he may not succumb to the firebombs."

"What does that mean, Yi Yi?"

"It means that if General Yang wins, then the Judge's invading force needs to know where the machines are when they retake the city. And that's what's happening now. As soon as the city dries, they will use the Zhuge Nu fire bolts."

Han grabbed the map and tilted it toward the early sunlight. Then he saw it. A major road ran down the side of the City of Eternal Peace, bending into the center of the city toward the general's mansion at the gates of the Great Wall. Not a single ambush was planned there. General Yang had moved the machines overnight, but no one knew that. Meanwhile, he had also declared martial law across the city—anyone caught in the streets was supposed to be arrested, or shot if they tried to run.

"Here," Han said, pressing his finger against the map. "This road is not marked to be firebombed."

Yi Yi leaned closer. "That must be where the Teacher is coming through."

"If I've already dumped General Yang's head over the southern wall, why would the Teacher still come here?"

"They won't believe you, Han. The Judge will still send the Teacher just in case." She folded the map and tucked it back into her pockets. "Now you know where to find the Teacher. You're one step ahead of him. What other advantages do we have?"

"HHe's coming," Han said, his voice distant. "I released Cut Foot to tell him I am a traitor. He's coming."

"What's your biggest weakness in battle?" Yi Yi asked.

Han shook his head. "I don't know."

Yi Yi grabbed him by his shoulders. "You can't let him break you, Han."

"Maybe I'm already broken."

"Then kill him so you can put it behind you."

"How?"

"What else do you know that he doesn't?"

Han sighed. "Maybe nothing. I've never tried to hide my talents. I used to use a sword but now I use a saber to honor my brothers. I am famous for the Infinity Palm but I've taught that to Feng, and—"

"Then what are you not good at?" she asked.

Han shook his head. "Too many things. There's no way to name them all."

Yi Yi sucked in her breath. "I know how to beat the Teacher!"

"What?"

"You said your brother Ah Go is so good with the bow and arrow that you will never needed to learn. You hate archery! Everyone knows the Commoner doesn't know how to shoot."

"Why is that important?"

CHAPTER 17

"WHY WON'T YOU dress as regular infantry?" Han asked. He was sitting against the inside of the southern wall on a bamboo rack less than a man's height, just below the top of the wall where guards and patrols moved in clusters five men wide and twenty deep. The sun was beginning its descent and it was a dry, beautiful evening.

General Yang was sitting next to him. "A warrior has to fight in his own armor and use his own weapon," he said. "Otherwise the enemy will think we are cowards."

"Dead people don't think," Han said. "But if the enemy can tell you are General Yang, then they will know it's a ruse and everyone will attack you all at once."

The Zhuge Nu had been hammering the buildings by South Gate with flaming arrows all afternoon. The rain had stopped overnight and the thousands upon thousands of fire bolts took hold of the wooden houses in the southern neighborhoods. When the flames grew too hot for troops to stay in position there, the Judge's army would charge the undefended gate and breach the city walls. Then the fight would begin.

"The Teacher is after you," Han said. "Just in case he finds you before I find him, can you please just change into a foot soldier's armor?"

"You like it when everyone becomes a commoner," Yang said with a laugh. "Yes, I plan to be an ordinary soldier today. Listen brother, not only are we going to annihilate the enemy, we are going to win this war."

"Are my men ready?" Han asked.

"Of course they are. But why did Yi Yi ask for only two hundred men to help you? Why not more?"

"Maybe she knows I won't be able to lead more."

Another wave of flaming bolts screeched in the air. Han was all too familiar with it, the screech of slaughtered animals. The structures by the southern gate were burning to the ground, but this time, the arrows flew deeper into the city, perhaps the furthest they could reach. They struck an unscorched row of streets farther north, and wave after wave of flaming bolts rained on the residential homes in a systematic assault to disintegrate them.

The storm of arrows died after ten rounds. Rapid drumbeats emerged in the distance and tens of thousands of footsteps approached the City of Eternal Peace.

"Are you ready?" Han asked.

General Yang placed both hands on the Commoner's shoulders. "Are you ready, my brother? Are you ready to become a traitor again?"

"I already am," Han said.

"Then let's fight," Yang said, leaping over the inner wall. "I wish I were allowed to beat you this time so you could get a hangover tomorrow."

Han jumped onto the top of the wall, and with a shout, he drew the Butterfly from his back and launched himself at General Yang. The Tiger General's spear swept at him in hungry strokes. The glistening spearhead would dart back and forth, then hammer down on him wave after wave. Han remembered this opponent. Before he met the Teacher, General Yang was the most dangerous man he had ever fought.

The thought of the Teacher distracted him, and Han almost failed to evade a lightning-fast spear thrust. Yang hesitated, surprised, but

Han focused again and fought back. Yang smiled and withdrew. Han chased, swiping like he was possessed.

"Don't make me tired," Yang said. He stumbled, backing away, exhibiting fatigue. Han laughed—a dark, cold laugh that could be heard well below the gates. Then, he launched himself at Yang and enclosed the general in a flurry of overhand strikes, pushing him further along the surface.

The footsteps drew closer, as did the shouts below from the approaching army. Horses galloped back and forth from the front of the lines to the back. They could easily see the fight happening on the top of the wall, and scouts on fast horses were rushing back to report.

"Are they close enough yet?" Han asked.

"Just a little longer."

Han surged forward, struck General Yang's spear and slipped behind him. He then pounded him with rapid sidearm strikes, moving too close for Yang's long-range weapon to be effective. The distant drumbeat hastened, and the army picked up speed as they pushed toward the gate.

"Let's do it," General Yang said.

"Give me a good angle."

Yang held up his long weapon in a horizontal block against Han's sudden overhand strike. "I loved this spear," he said. The Butterfly slashed right through the heavy wood, and Yang's famous spear split in half. Han swept the front half of the weapon over the wall where a mounted soldier rushed forward to retrieve it.

Han grabbed General Yang by the throat and spun him around to face the advancing army.

"Struggle," Han whispered.

Yang pushed Han away, but the Commoner was stronger and pressed him back against the front of the wall. Yang Xin grabbed Han's wrist and twisted it, forcing him to drop the Butterfly. Han grabbed Yang's topknot amid the struggle and released his hair. Yang became a wild man fighting for his life. Han shoved him left—Yang fought back. Han shoved him further left. They were in position.

The army below, still a short distance away, stopped advancing to watch.

"Let's do it," Han said. He forced Yang into a chokehold, swept him off his feet and dropped him onto the cold stone surface. Yang rolled away. Then, Han picked up the Butterfly, raised it high above his head for all to see, and swept it across the neck of a corpse lying at his feet.

The dead man's hair was already as disheveled as Yang Xin's. Han held it high in the air for a second before throwing it over the edge, then spun around and walked away. General Yang rolled to the edge of the inner staircase to descend the wall unnoticed.

Han sheathed the Butterfly behind his back. "Did you notice they all carried large metal shields and long spears? Not a single small shield saberman in their infantry."

"I saw," Yang said. "But your smart woman anticipated it."

"You're ready for this?"

"Go open the gates like a good traitor," Yang said with a laugh. "I need to change into a commoner's armor."

"See you on the battlefield, brother." Han leaped down the stairs.

The footsteps of approaching soldiers started again along with a set of rapid horse hooves. The soldiers were advancing, and someone was bringing the fake general's head back to the commanders. There was no time to lose.

Han reached the massive metal doors and nodded to the four soldiers standing by. They bowed and removed the heavy bar holding the doors together. Han took a deep breath—he was ready. Maybe even ready for the Teacher.

The Commoner heaved the doors open and stood with his arms folded. The enemy army was less than a hundred steps away. Han threw his head back to laugh, then strolled back into the City of Eternal Peace.

The drum beats in the distance began to tremble. Someone in the front shouted, "Charge!"

The Judge's army roared and rushed for the opening.

Han turned a corner, out of sight, and covered his face with a piece of wet cloth to shield his lungs from the stinging smoke. His men were waiting for him: two hundred of the strongest, biggest men in Yang's army, each armed with a single sledgehammer. Han's role in the battle was Yi Yi's idea. She wanted him fighting, not standing around thinking about the Teacher until it was time to confront him.

They were all on horses, but they dismounted to bow. "Commander!"

Han held up a hand. "I'm not a military commander. I am a warrior. And today, I need all of you to be warriors and not soldiers. Soldiers follow orders. I don't know what that means. Warriors strike the enemy whenever they see fit. Can you do that for me?"

"Yes, sir!" they shouted in unison.

"You have your gourds?"

"Yes, sir!"

"Let's have one drink together," Han said. "And then we fight together as wild animals and not as disciplined soldiers." He pulled a gourd from his waist, uncorked it and tilted his head back for one massive gulp of strong liquor. His men followed suit. They each tossed away their gourds, picked up their sledgehammers, and mounted their horses. Han leaped onto his. "Let's go!"

The Judge's men were already inside the city walls, spilling into the streets in large clusters with their heavy spears in hand and their massive rectangular shields outstretched. They marched with slow, heavy footsteps, each soldier already carrying too much weight. They encountered no resistance.

Han and his men circled around them through the small roads, snaking through almost half of the city before hiding in a number of small alleys. Yi Yi and a group of her archers were close by—hidden within the shadows of second-floor windows, crouched on rooftops or waiting inside civilian homes.

Han wanted to see her, if only a glimpse. The Teacher was coming, and this might be the last time he would see her beautiful face and her beaming smile.

But then, he may beat the Teacher yet.

Yi Yi was certain he could win. The third big advantage they had, she said earlier that morning, was that the Teacher didn't know her. She was among the smartest guards in the imperial palace. The emperor told her so.

There was complete silence then, a little too silent for Han's comfort. Shouldn't the enemy expect to see civilians screaming and running away? Shouldn't General Yang's army be scrambling for a way out after they heard their Tiger General was decapitated on the city wall?

Perhaps other military generals, caught in the heat of battle and looming victory, were not much smarter than he. Maybe the enemy general, once inside the city, had merely executed their orders as planned.

Han could hear the heavy footsteps then, a large regiment of enemy troops approaching. They were already deep inside the city, so deep that most of the Judge's army, if not all of it, was within the city walls.

Han leaped onto a window ledge, then bounded across the alley and onto another ledge before jumping to the opposite roof. This was the area, more than halfway to the Tiger General's mansion, where every building along the street had a second level. This was where the ambush would take place.

Not far down one of the main avenues of the city, Han glimpsed a spectacle that he had never seen before. Tens of thousands were marching in lockstep. They held their heavy shields in front of themselves, each shield almost as tall as the man holding it.

The enemy soldiers, dressed in deep red with shiny armor, trudged through the main thoroughfare unopposed. Each had a spear in his right hand, but none of them carried broadswords. Perhaps the oversized shields were already too heavy.

Strange, Han thought. Every man's spearhead was pointed at the ground behind them. Wouldn't they direct it toward the enemy in front?

Han dropped back to the ground. "They're not using them as spears," he said to his men. "No one is carrying a broadsword and their formation is too dense. That means we can get close to them. This will be easier than I thought."

Han spun around and leaped onto his horse. "Positions!" he shouted before grabbing the reins and kicking his stallion into a full gallop. He had memorized every alleyway near the zones he was assigned to attack, and he made a direct charge around the marching enemy to begin the bombardment. Twenty-five men trailed behind him, and the rest took their positions elsewhere.

Han waited. The enemy soldiers were still moving in perfect unison from right to left—these must be General Wu's men. Perhaps they were told that the traitors had taken their city, that they needed to come home to reclaim it.

Then, the bombardment began out of nowhere. Flaming balls of fire sailed into the streets from the fire bomb machines, which were hidden immediately below the roofs where Han stood. Streaking metal missiles burst into flames and rained on the enemy. These were the gunpowder weapons rumored to exist.

The enemy lifted their shields over their heads. Then, each soldier secured the butt of his spear in a hole on the underside of his shield and planted the spearhead into the ground. The canopy of shields, supported by the strength of a hard wooden spear, was so dense that there was not a single gap among them. The spears withstood the pressure from the burning rocks collapsing on them, and the flaming missiles could not a way through their metal roof.

There was a shout, followed by the enemy shuffling forward one small step, coordinating the movement of their spears to advance in unison.

Han reached for the handle of the Butterfly behind his back. His special saber might not carve through the enemy's metal shields, but their thin plate armor wouldn't stand a chance. It was almost time to break into their lines and foment chaos.

Then, another round of bombardment from above. Han heard

a few screams from down in the street, but they weren't many—the battle had not begun yet. For a long time, showers of flaming stones pelted the invaders. When it finally stopped, Han drew his saber and leapt off his horse.

"Now!" he shouted, rushing into the unsuspecting troops from the side alleyway. The enemy spears were planted against the ground, their shields above their heads, their bodies exposed from the sides. Han tore through them, cutting down six soldiers before the big men with sledgehammers barged in.

Han slashed his way across the road to the mouth of the opposite alleyway, killing over twenty defenseless men. They never even had time to turn their spears around.

The densely packed enemy troops lowered their shields and raised their spears to confront the new threat. Most of Han's men ignored them, swinging their sledgehammers at the troops who passed. They were the ones with room to continue advancing. They were the ones who couldn't turn around in time. Within seconds, twenty-five sledgehammers swept away shields and spears alike, sending the enemy soldiers scrambling away.

"Out!" someone shouted. Han and his men leaped onto their horses and retreated into the alleys.

As soon as they escaped, something collapsed onto the street from above. Multiple wheelbarrows full of wood, branches, and coal coated in oil tumbled into the street from the second-floor windows, crashing into the gap that Han and his men had created. A number of flaming arrows screeched in from above, sparking an instant inferno, and the same happened at the other end of the block shortly after. Over a thousand men were trapped on a single street between the two raging fires.

Then, doors and windows on both sides of the street flew open, and General Yang's men rushed out onto ground level, slashing and stabbing the frantic enemy who tried to lower their shields.

"Fire!" It was Yi Yi's voice. The men who lowered their shields and turned their spears around were shot from above. Those who raised their shields to protect themselves from the descending onslaught were cut down in horrible numbers. Screams of pain and suffering filled the streets.

The street behind them met the same fate. Han's second group of twenty-five men had plowed another rift through the invading army, and they too were enclosed within raging fire. Yang's soldiers were waiting inside the civilian homes and storefronts, and they were ready to kill.

"Next position!" Han shouted. He kicked his horse into full gallop and winded through the narrow alleyways of the city to circle toward another opening.

The sounds of slaughter, the screams of death and dying were deep in the city. Han's eight groups of twenty-five men with sledge-hammers separated the long rows of invading troops at every dark alley, trapping them with pyres of coal and wood that could burn for hours. All the while, soldiers slaughtered them from all angles.

"Next position!" Han shouted to his men before they turned into the next alley. "I will do this one by myself."

His bloodlust was back. His eyes red, his feet light, his strength coursing through his meridians, Han forgot about the Teacher coming into the city. He chose to be a warrior, not a martial arts master. He would kill his enemy in battle.

The Butterfly shredded the enemy's armor like paper. Channeling his immense strength, Han delivered lightning strokes that nearly cut them in half. He tore through them with such speed that the advancing men didn't even have time to lower their shields. Meanwhile, the coal was falling into the street before the retreating men could evade it. Han leaped over the pile of flammables and onto the street full of enemy soldiers. Then, the flaming arrows ripped through the air. The wall of coal and wood exploded, the flames groping like thousands of men clawing out of a live burial. Han was trapped inside with over a thousand enemy soldiers. He threw his head back to laugh.

The enemy tried to turn and lower their shields but they were too late. Han was among them, inside their metal canopy and cutting through their lines. There were too many people, their lines too dense. No one could see what was killing them.

Yang's men poured out of the first-floor storefronts and windows, joining Han in the slaughter. Arrows ripped from above, aimed at any soldier who lowered his shield to protect his body.

Han roared and charged forward unopposed, slashing left and right. Each horizontal stroke he made deeply severed an enemy soldier's neck. No soldier in red survived if Han passed them. He had never been in a war before, yet he had never been so certain that he stood on the right side of justice. The Judge was killing the Tiger Generals and was trying to kill his friend General Yang. The Judge killed his Shifu, killed Lan, and had turned the world against him. These men in red uniforms served the Judge. Today they had to die.

Blood flew in random spurts all around him. He was no longer running, but rather leaping from one layer of dead bodies to another. The soft carpet of corpses slowed him, but it gave him more time to kill the soldiers to his left, to his right, or anyone behind him that he missed. The soldiers in blue uniforms, General Yang's men, ravaged the ones he could not get to.

In a moment, he was standing in front of a wall of flames again. He had reached the other end of the street.

The Commoner turned around and stared at the devastation behind him. Every single enemy soldier was dead. The archers hiding in the upper levels had already withdrawn to reinforce other units elsewhere. Within the time it would take to drink a bowl of wine, over a thousand men were slaughtered.

Han wanted to vomit. He felt dizzy, nauseous, not because he had never seen death and destruction before, but because these men had also joined a Tiger General's army to protect their country. He had killed his own countrymen. Wasn't this what it meant to be a real traitor?

Fire tingled the skin on Han's face. The Judge used men in the Chinese empire to kill each other. Men who signed up to fight foreign invasion, not a power-hungry nephew who wanted the throne.

"Message!" someone shouted. He ran into the street from an open door. "Commander Chen," the messenger said with a bow. "Just as you expected, three civilians have violated curfew. They are walking down the outer perimeter."

Han's eyes widened. That had to be the Teacher. The time had come.

"We're coming," one soldier said. "Let's go support Commander Chen!"

Hundreds gathered, but Han held up a hand and shook his head. If he could not overcome his fear of the Teacher, he would always be a frightened little rabbit in a world full of Sha Wu's. There would be no point in living then.

"I need to do this alone," he said.

He sheathed his bloody saber and ran into a storefront. Moments later, he leaped out a rear window and into a narrow alley. The Teacher was coming in from the western perimeter, as expected. If he still expected to find the Tiger General alive, he would not seek out General Yang in a raging war where the Tiger General, already hard to kill, was surrounded by his army. Sha Wu would head for the general's mansion and position himself somewhere in disguise.

Han took to the roofs so he could cut across the city without getting tangled in another battle. He ran across rooftops, leaping over the wide streets where the carnage never relented. The four vertical avenues of the city that ran from south to north were packed with piles of dead bodies, thousands of them. But Yang Xin promised to block their retreat out of south gate and force their surrender. Then there would be no more bloodshed. The Judge's men—General Wu's men—would be absorbed into General Yang's army, and then they would once again be housed in the City of Eternal Peace.

Han stopped one more time. The devastation was disgusting. Those fortunate enough to be dead were strewn on top of each other, their faces frozen in that final expression of horror as they realized their lives were ending. Those who were still alive—some whose limbs were nowhere in sight, others bleeding and crying out in pain—

waited for a soldier in blue to come by and put them out of their misery. Many scrambled over their dead brothers, hoping to find a weapon for one last kill, before one of General Yang's men stabbed them from behind. All around him was death in numbers that he could never comprehend.

There were no heroes in war. Only victims. The men who won, who survived, had to go home and tell their parents they had killed fellow countrymen. Perhaps their elderly fathers would beat them with a cane and tell them to live in shame for the rest of their lives. They were victims too.

Han turned and leaped onto the next roof, then the next, before dropping to the ground. He had already reached the Western Perimeter.

CHAPTER 18

AN OLD BEGGAR trudged down the road with his son and grandson. They were dressed in tatters, carried very little, and the old man was leaning on a shaky walking stick.

The City of Eternal Peace guarded the border against the Silencer, so everyone knew to hide when there was war. These three were stealth masters.

Han stepped into the road with the massive black saber in his hand. The sight of the Teacher brought a creeping dread, a sense that he would die here today no matter what he did. He felt a shiver in his spine and a wash of cold sweat on his back.

I have the element of surprise today. I am not afraid.

Han thought of what the Teacher brought back from his memory. How he killed a child in Ding Yi, how he enjoyed hurting his friends in the banquet hall, how he tortured the Venom Sect leader before killing him. Then, just moments ago, how he carved his blade into human flesh, looking back to see only whom he had failed to kill.

He had failed his Shifu in the most miserable way. Master Zuo wanted him to become a great hero, a prestigious martial arts master who would carry on the Zuo lineage. He had failed the friends who sacrificed their lives for him on the bridge, who held back an army so he could come here to help. To kill more and more.

But this time, he didn't enjoy it.

"If it isn't my nephew Chen Han," the Teacher said. "How is your day going, great hero?"

"There are no heroes in war," Han said, stepping forward. "Only victims."

Sha Wu smiled. "You're wrong, my nephew. There are no victims either. There are those who've killed, and those who've failed to kill."

"Is that your world, Sha Wu?" Han asked. "Kill or be killed?"

"Not true at all, my nephew," the Teacher said. "It's believe or not believe. You see, in war, all you have to do is believe. Believe with confidence that you are on the right side of justice. Believe that the label you've assigned to your enemy is real, and then you can kill anyone you want. Simply change the label from man to demon, or from father of his babies to killer of our babies, or from hardworking farmer to barbaric invader, and then you are free to kill him. With that conviction, anyone is free to kill anyone. It doesn't matter who he is or what he did. You think you're good and you say he's evil and then you can do whatever you want. If everyone understands that, how can there be victims in this world? The art, my nephew, is in how to get yourself to believe every time."

The two men next to the Teacher were poorly disguised. One was Cut Foot and the other was Scrawny Fox. A surge of heat crept into Han's chest at the sight of the boy. He trusted this little scum. He placed a vulnerable Yi Yi into his hands.

"I see you are waiting for me here," the Teacher said. "Someone must have told you I was coming." He glanced once at Cut Foot. Then, without a word the Teacher surged behind him and struck him in the back with his palm. Cut Foot stumbled forward, spinning around. Then, the Teacher lunged forward and palmed him in the heart, a blast with enough energy to kill. Cut Foot collapsed.

No! Han crouched down next to Cut Foot and placed a finger over his nostrils, hoping for breath, but he knew there was no way the stealth master could survive this.

"Don't... don't forget," Cut Foot whispered. "Clean my shit under the bucket."

He released a weak breath and died.

Han rose to his feet. Scrawny Fox was jeering, wagging back and forth in amusement. A compassionate smile spread across the Teacher's face.

The sun was setting, and a light wind caressed Han's face and weaved through his disheveled hair. The West Perimeter road was not wide. On his right stood the fortress wall, and on the left were shops and tea stands and some residential homes. All shops were closed and the residents had locked their doors. There was no one else on the street.

"How is your lovely archer, my nephew?" the Teacher asked. "I hope my grandson didn't burn her too badly."

Han's heart pounded at the thought of the Teacher in the dark little hut torturing Yi Yi resurfaced in his mind. He would never be able to shake those memories. His survival today depended on whether he could avoid reliving that night or whether he could embrace it.

"She enjoyed herself," Han said with a smile. "Without pain, she would never understand pleasure. She wants to thank you for it."

"Would it be pleasure that you gave her?" the Teacher asked. "Because after today, she will be finding pleasure from a corpse."

Han's eyes caught fire, and with a roar he lifted the Butterfly and charged. His face was red, his ghastly expression twisted and frozen in rage. The Teacher laughed, pulling apart his walking stick to reveal a long sword. Scrawny Fox also drew out a short sword from behind him.

Han threw the Butterfly and sent it spinning at the Teacher, but Sha Wu stepped aside to avoid it. Then, Han smashed an urn on the side of the road and grabbed the Zhuge Nu crossbow hidden inside.

"Run!" the Teacher screamed. Han pumped the lever and charged forward with all his speed, closing the distance while firing. Two arrows struck Scrawny Fox in the abdomen and the thigh at the same time. He collapsed. The Teacher retreated, shimmering left and right to dodge the rapid-fire bolts. But he never gained enough distance to regroup, and he was never able to pull close enough to fight back.

Then, Han threw the Zhuge Nu crossbow at the Teacher, darted into a small bush on the side of the road and extracted a fully loaded one. He continued to chase, firing as fast as he could. He was not precise, nor was he fully in control of his new weapon, but he didn't need to be. The Commoner possessed outrageous speed. The Teacher swiped away whatever arrows he could while evading the ones he couldn't. But Han was too close to him. Always too close. Sha Wu could hardly see each approaching bolt before it had already arrived.

Then, the Teacher stumbled on a crack in the road and Han surged forward to strike him with the metal crossbow. The Teacher blocked with his sword, pressing the crossbow down, and Han fired. The arrow struck the Teacher's thigh from arm's length—Sha Wu screamed and stumbled back. Han threw the crossbow at him and grabbed another hidden under a pile of dirt. He resumed the chase, this time against a foe who had lost his speed.

The Teacher swiped his blade in front of him frantically, but it was not enough to redirect so many rapidly fired bolts from close range. He had slowed from his thigh injury, and in a minute, two more bolts buried themselves in his body. He froze.

Then, Han shot him two more times in the chest before casting his weapon aside. He launched at the Teacher empty-handed, grabbed his enemy's sword and stabbed him in the stomach.

Streams of blood trickled from the Teacher's mouth, and he gasped for air in short, heaving breaths. "Are you... Are you enjoying this, my nephew?"

"Of course I am," Han said. "I enjoy smelling the fear of death in your sweat."

The Teacher smiled, then broke out into a strained laugh. "I'm so glad. I'm so glad you listened to my teachings. Soon you will be the same as me. Soon, you can be a teacher too."

"Thank you," Han said. "Now listen to my teachings before you die." He pushed the sword deeper into the Teacher's body. Sha Wu grunted as his frozen face trembled in agony.

"You can always label someone evil," Han said. "It doesn't mean you get to kill him. The more labels you slap on others, the more you become a label yourself. I don't enjoy killing people, not even the ones everyone deems evil. I enjoy saving them. Sometimes, I had to kill people to stop them from hurting the innocent. But I didn't relish in the lives I took—I relish in the ones I've saved. Everyone deserves a chance at life, except those who believe they can kill anyone they want."

The Teacher was gasping for air, and his gruesome face was pale and lifeless, already fading. Han yanked the sword out, and the Teacher crumbled to his knees. Han inserted the blade straight down Sha Wu's neck behind the collarbone, planting it deep into his heart, and held it there for a second before pushing the entire length of the sword into his body. The Teacher died without a twitch.

Han then turned around and approached Scrawny Fox. The boy was whimpering in pain, clutching his abdominal wound while crawling on the ground. The arrow was still protruding from his thigh. Han towered over the pathetic figure. He picked up the Butterfly.

"What…" Scrawny Fox said between pants. "What do you want?"

Han swung his saber and severed the tendon behind the boy's ankle. Scrawny Fox arched his back and screamed.

"You won't be running again," Han said. "But I won't kill a child if I don't have to. Wait here for the magistrate to arrest you and put you on trial, and if he has enough evidence to behead you, then that's your fate. I don't want anything more to do with you."

Han sheathed the Butterfly and walked away. Perhaps he should join the battle with General Yang. But General Yang had never summoned his help once the beheading ruse was done, and without General Wu, the Judge's army had no chance against the greatest Tiger General.

Maybe Yi Yi needed him. But she was hiding somewhere, directing her archers to fire from the shadows. He only learned how to shoot that morning. Why would she need him?

He walked by Cut Foot's body and paused to whisper a word to a decent man. Cut Foot believed he was doing the right thing, protecting his country and his people. This was what the Teacher taught him mere moments ago. All you had to do was believe, and then you could do whatever you wanted.

Cut Foot's dying words, just like his parting words before Han left the dungeons, were about something under the toilet bucket in his cell. Maybe it really was important. The bucket was freshly emptied when Han was there, so no one would have moved it if Cut Foot left without using it.

Han picked up pace and headed for the dungeons. It was not far.

The sounds of war had faded, but Han took to the roofs again to avoid another battle. Below him, most of the Judge's army had surrendered, and they were being marched away without their weapons and pushed into the town square. They would huddle there as prisoners until General Yang decided their fate.

The battle remained heated near South Gate as Yang blocked the enemy from leaving the city, but it wouldn't be long before the Judge's men on that front also surrendered. There was no reason to fight to the death. They were all Chinese.

Han leaped across an alleyway and onto another roof, keeping himself above the chaos until he could drop to the street in front of the dungeons.

Once he arrived, Han flashed his pass before stepping into the cold underground. The three hundred women were already freed and gone. The most serious criminals remained, but they were silent.

Cut Foot's cell was wide open. Han stepped in, and for a second he remembered his conversation with Cut Foot. The speed master only wanted to defend the country against foreign invasion. They didn't deserve to be enemies. Somehow, Cut Foot recognized that too.

Han kicked over the toilet bucket and crouched down to brush away the layer of hay underneath. A faded brown envelope, smaller than the size of his palm, rested on the cold stone floor.

The envelope was opened. Han drew a letter from it, held it against the fading sunlight from the small window above, and read in a whisper.

"Dear General Mu. The bearer of the Red Crest is a son of emperor Li Gao. Sincerely, Little Sparrow."

Han read the same words over and over again. Little Sparrow knew where the babies were. Han was one of them. Li Gao's babies that Li Yan's men failed to kill.

Han was dazed. He thought he had stopped breathing, and his hands shook so violently that he couldn't see the words. When he came to his senses, he could only whisper one thing. "Feng, my blood brother."

"He's down there by himself, General," one of the guards said above. Then, rapid light footsteps descended the dungeon steps. Han recognized them. Why was Yi Yi looking for him at a time like this?

"Han!" Yi Yi called. "Where are you?"

Han stepped outside the cell just as she emerged. He handed her the letter in his hands. She ignored it.

"Han," Yi Yi said. "They've released an assassin against General Mu that he couldn't defend against—your brother's father, Han. We have to do something."

"He really is my brother," Han said. Then the words sunk in. Tiger General Mu could be assassinated soon. "How do you know?"

"I don't have time to explain," Yi Yi said, stomping her foot. "You need to go! If General Mu dies, the massive Turkic army will breach the City of Stones in one day."

Han gasped, breaking out of his trance. Prince or not, inheritor to the throne or not, the one thing that mattered was saving General Mu. Han leaped to his feet and charged out of the dungeon.

"I will come for you when things settle down here," Yi Yi called from behind.

There was a horse outside—it didn't matter whose. Han leaped onto the mount and sent it into a hard gallop. The city around him was still in chaos, and dark black smoke still groped the air from the firetraps that bombarded the streets.

Han veered toward the west gate, taking the smaller alleys of the city to avoid the nearly hundred thousand men. The guards at west gate recognized him and opened the doors, but Han halted his horse. It was a long ride to the City of Stones. He had no food or water on him.

"I need your water bottle," Han said, holding out a coin on his palm. One guard unstrapped a bottle from his belt and handed it to him.

"Are there stables along Major Pass?" Han asked.

"There are several," the guard said. "They are all along the road for people to change horses. You can't miss them."

Han kicked his horse and charged out of west gate without a word. The air was cooler outside the city. Han lowered his head and rode on.

Everything started to make sense. Li Yan was trying to kill his older brother's babies, and Han was one of them. Li Gao must've branded the babies with a crest and sent them to safety while he fought with his brother, hoping to find them again when the turmoil was over. Li Yan sent the Council of Midnight to kill the babies, and Master Zuo was assigned to kill Han.

Please, please tell them your name is Chen Han and never tell the truth…

If Feng was sent to General Mu, then maybe Han was being sent to General Yang when Zuo attacked the caravan. Emperor Li Gao never found his babies—which must've meant Mu Feng was not named Feng at birth either.

If the emperor still had sons, then the Judge was no longer next in line to the throne. He realized this when he freed his father in Willow Island. Li Yan knew his brother's babies were still alive, and the Judge needed to hunt down the princes and eliminate them before anyone else found out they existed.

Han grimaced at the thought. He didn't want to be a prince; he wanted to be a commoner. And the Judge was not about to kill him either way.

The horse started to foam at the mouth, so Han slowed it to a rapid trot. The sun had set by the time he came across the first stable.

Han paid his fee, changed to a fresh horse and charged forward again. He had enough money on him to get to the City of Stones at a light gallop.

He would change his horse three more times before the City of Stones came within sight.

Han didn't want to explain the blood on his clothes or the massive black saber strapped to his back. Keeping his face hidden, he rode up to South Gate and flashed the military pass from Magistrate Guo. "Message for General Mu!" he shouted to the guard.

The guard hardly glanced at the pass before waving him in. It was too easy.

Han guessed that the governor's mansion, like Wu's in the City of Eternal Peace, would be close to the Great Wall. He rode due north, pushing through a bustling city and winding through crowded markets and town squares until he spotted it. The Tiger General's mansion in this city was no less grand than General Yang's, or Wu's.

There were too many guards at the mansion gates and he didn't have time to haggle with them. The most strategic of the four Tiger Generals was about to face an assassin that even he would not expect.

Han leaped off his horse and ran to the side walls of the mansion. Then, he scaled a nearby tree, crept onto a trunk that extended toward the mansion, and jumped onto the top of the wall. He crouched there for a moment to watch for guards.

Strange. There was no one patrolling the mansion grounds. Why would General Mu be so relaxed at a time like this?

Han sucked in his breath in horror. The person in charge of security patrols must be working with the assassin. General Mu was in imminent danger.

He dropped to the ground and halted. Where would he go? He didn't know where the general was, nor did he know his way around. There was nothing left to do but expose himself and hope for the best.

"General Mu!" he shouted at the top of his voice. "General Mu!" His voice carried across the grounds. Then, he stopped to listen— there were no guards rushing to surround him, no servants hurrying to greet their guest. There was one set of footsteps to his left, a single person running away.

Han rushed after the footsteps and came upon the general's study. He pushed the door open.

On the floor lay the Tiger General in a pool of blood, his own blood. There was a dagger inserted deep into his back, but his eyes were open. His chest heaved unevenly.

"Uncle Mu," Han said, rushing to the dying man's side.

"Who are you?" General Mu whispered. Han drew acupuncture needles from his robes to seal the bleeding, but the blade was deep inside the old general's organs. There was no time left.

"I am Feng's brother," Han said. "I am also General Yang's close friend."

"You are the Commoner," Mu said. "I recognize you. A great hero. A great, unfortunate hero."

"Father! Father!"

General Mu lifted himself just as Feng barged in. The poison user took two steps forward and stood frozen, staring, trembling.

"My brother," Han whispered. "Feng, come help me. I can't stop the bleeding."

Feng didn't respond. General Mu lifted a trembling hand, reaching for his son.

"I'm sorry," Han said. "I couldn't get here in time."

"Come here Feng," General Mu called. He turned to Han. "I need to talk to Feng alone."

"Of course, General," Han said.

Feng stumbled to his father's side. He crumbled to his knees and took the hand of the man who raised him. Han headed to the door. He would leave Feng alone to hear General Mu's final words.

"Han!" Feng called after him. "Are you the Commoner?"

Han released a deep sigh. "That's what they call me. We have a lot to talk about, Feng." He walked out of the door without turning.

Outside the mansion gates, the original guards posted by the entrance remained where they stood, ignoring Han as he left. He didn't know where else to go. He would find a tavern and have a drink while he waited for Feng.

Han rounded a corner of the mansion and stepped into a wide road. This perhaps was the major avenue running from North Gate to South Gate. The heavily fortified North Gate, built against the Great Wall, was guarded by a long row of troops standing on the top of the wall. There weren't enough men standing by for a Turkic invasion of eight hundred thousand. He needed to warn Feng as soon as possible.

North Gate Tavern was close to the wall and had a first-floor balcony that extended into the road. Han stepped inside and seated himself, threw down some coins and ordered a flask of strong liquor.

There was a lot he needed to tell Feng. They were blood brothers. They were the emperor's sons. And with General Mu dying, Feng would need to defend this city against the Turkic Khaganate. Even with General Wu's army surrendering to Yang Xin, the Judge still had plenty of men.

If Feng had already come home, he either defeated Zeng Xi, or he lost and fled. Either way, the Judge still had Zeng Xi's fifty thousand.

A screaming eagle soared over the Great Wall and dove into the city. It hovered for a moment, turned around and then headed back over the wall.

Han noticed the eagle's neck—it was purple, a very rare color for such a bird. It was Ah Go's eagle. He was coming back with the fast horses.

Six strikes of the war drums echoed from the top of the wall, followed by six more. Again the drums throbbed. Then, a round of clacking horse hooves approached.

"Open the gates!" someone shouted.

Han stepped outside and into the road. Ah Go was coming in with the fast horses. He needed to notify Feng so they could plan this together.

"Wait!" someone on top of the wall shouted. "They don't look Chinese!"

"It's the signal of the Tiger General," someone else shouted. "Can someone notify General Mu?"

The eagle floated over the walls again. Han stared at the purple feathers. It had to be Ah Go's eagle. Why weren't they opening the doors?

"It's a Tiger General!" someone else shouted from above. "Open the gates!"

The men on the ground hesitated, looking at each other for guidance. "Where's the order from the general?" one of them asked.

Han shook his head. The general is dead, he wanted to say. There was no time to waste. The Turkic Khaganate was close, and they were also approaching the North Gate. Ah Go would be trapped if they didn't let him enter the city.

Han ran forward, picking up speed like the wind. Catching the soldiers by surprise, he lifted the heavy bar that held the metal doors together, tossed it aside, and drew open the gates.

Han stumbled back with a gasp. He expected a few men and tens of thousands of fast horses. Instead, trickling through the gates was a massive army, all cavalry. Their light armor and curved sabers matched the standard attire of the Mongol kingdoms. Han stepped aside.

"What have I done," he whispered.

The soldiers next to him scrambled away. One picked up a bullhorn and emitted two long blasts, then two more.

The city awakened, and men rushed out of nowhere to assemble. But it was already too late. The massive Mongol army had penetrated the city.

Then, a chariot drawn by six horses entered the gates, waving the flag of the Silencer. The Mongol King, dressed in golden armor and seated with a bow and arrow at his side, held up a hand to halt the driver.

Han's face was hot, and he felt like he was swooning. This couldn't be happening. He opened the gates to China for the Silencer. He thought he would faint.

The Silencer stepped off the chariot and approached him. "My brother!"

Han gasped. He recognized that voice. He shook his head clear, and then the Silencer took off his helmet to reveal his face.

"Ah Go!" Han whispered, shuddering. "Ah Go is the Silencer."